Cat Lumb is a writer and Writing Coach who lives in Stalybridge, Manchester, with her fiancé and a rather mischievous Westie. Her debut novel, In Lies we Trust, reached #16 in the Bestseller charts for Espionage Thrillers on Amazon in March 2021. She writes from her Plotting Shed in the garden.

You can get in touch with the author via:
Website: www.catlumb.com
Twitter: @Cat_Lumb
Instagram: The Write Catalyst

You can also sign up for her Enewsletter via her website to receive exclusive updates about where and when any of her writing might be published.

Also by Cat Lumb
In Lies We Trust

Short Story Collections
The Memorial Tree and Other Short Stories

THAT WHICH IS LEFT IS LOST

CAT LUMB

Two Foxes Publishing

Two Foxes Publishing

ISBN: 978 1 7396465 0 9

For Mac;
the best writing companion I didn't know I needed.

PART I

THAT WHICH IS

Chris arrives home readying himself for an argument. He is parked outside the poky, end of terraced house in Sheffield where he and Holly live. Even after twenty years it still stings that Holly's parents loaned them the money for the deposit. Their dreams of a bigger house disappeared years ago, along with the money they'd saved to buy it. When he steps into the hallway the jangle of his keys in the porcelain bowl announce him. He doesn't like the chipped, cream ornament but it was crafted by Holly the first time she took maternity leave. Hanging on the wall above it is a collage of photos of the two of them she made after their second loss. Once he might have smiled at the pictures of them both but now he only sees what is missing.

In the kitchen the scent of food, deep and rich, wafts into his nose. Holly sits at the fold-down table with an empty plate. He glances up at the clock as he removes his tie and stuffs it into his pocket, already knowing what it will show.

"Am I late?" He leans in to kiss her forehead but she remains stiff, her dark brown hair falling in soft curls down her back. "I take it mine's in the oven then?"

She nods, her lips a tight thin line. He can feel her stare boring into his back as retrieves a sad-looking dinner from a warm oven. She holds his gaze as he sits opposite her. Her chair creaks as she leans back into it but his wife remains silent. Chris lifts a forkful of cauliflower up to his mouth and tastes the slightly browned edges as it falls apart on his tongue. After a few moments of unnecessary chewing, he swallows and offers a conversational opener.

"How was your day?"

This is when he recognises the fury written in the lines of Holly's narrowed eyes and the pinched creases on either side of her hard-set mouth. He lowers his fork.

"What's wrong?"

She averts her gaze, shifting it to look over his shoulder. He discards his cutlery and reaches out for her hand. "Still nothing?" The chill of her skin grazes his palm as she deftly slips it out of his grasp.

"They all want a reference."

"You just need something to take your mind off things for a while."

"Well, sitting around here all day with nothing to do isn't helping."

Chris returns to his dinner. "You could always help—"

"Don't you dare."

"You don't even know what I was going to say."

"I don't want to help you and your patients."

"Fine, I won't mention my work again, okay?"

They listen to the rhythmic whirr of the fan oven as it cools. Chris pushes his plate away, his stomach knotted and empty.

"I know why you want to help them, Christopher, but look what happened with Tony Porter."

"His wife shouldn't have contested the will. It was what Tony wanted."

Holly gives a dismissive laugh. "Tony didn't know what he wanted, he was dying and delirious. His daughter had already swindled him once. If I'd known that I wouldn't have thrown my job away to track her down in the first place."

"Tony was willing to forgive her."

Holly folds her arms. "So you think his wife was just meant to stand back and live with his bad choices?"

"Let's not go over this again." He is tired, the day's weight heavy on his shoulders.

"No, I want you to answer the question."

"In that case, I think his wife should have trusted his judgement."

"Well, we know how that turned out for the wife."

Chris is confused. "What do you mean by that?"

Holly sighs. "I lost my job because of it. Now all I do is sit at home on my own."

Chris stands and piles his plate on top of Holly's. "I can't keep having this conversation. I'm sorry you lost your job, but you were the one who suggested looking for the girl through the Probate company database."

"Well, it's fortunate for our mortgage that you got to keep your job, isn't it?"

"We're fine, Holly. Don't worry about the money." Chris scrapes the remnants of his dinner into the bin and puts the plates in the sink. He runs the tap, the feint aroma of washing up liquid melding with the steam from the hot water. As he begins to wash he thinks of all the homemade paraphernalia scattered about their house. "You just need a project, something to do instead of applying for jobs all day."

After a moment Holly stands and retrieves the tea-towel.

"Maybe you're right."

They work together with only the occasional chink of a pot or clatter of knives punctuating the silence. When they are finished Holly lowers her head and asks: "Do you still love me?"

Chris covers the space between them in a step and wraps his arms around her. "Of course." It is an immediate reaction: Holly is his wife. They've been through too much together for it not to be true. She remains in his embrace just long enough for him to feel her shoulders tense and then she steps free.

"We have to stop putting other people first and start focusing on what we want."

He hesitates. "I don't know if that's a good idea. We're not as young as we were before, I don't even know if—"

"No, you don't understand." She hurries over to pull a sheaf of papers out of the drawer behind him. "This. I want to try this."

He examines the debris of information she spreads in front of him. Adoption leaflets, application forms, printed success stories. His mouth dries up and when he tries to speak his lips feel numb.

"How long have you been collecting this?"

"Not long. It's the only thing I've had to stop me going crazy."

"I thought we talked about this, after the last..." his gaze rests on Holly's flat, toned stomach and he recalls how many times it has swollen up, only to reject what is within.

"That was two years ago Christopher. And we can't go through that again. Something has to change."

Chris' legs weakens and he sits down. "But, we agreed. An adoption wouldn't be our child. We wouldn't really be parents."

"We would. We could get a baby. No one would know."

"We'd know. And eventually so would the child."

Holly shakes her head. "Not necessarily."

"We couldn't lie, Holly. They'd find out sooner or later and hate us for it. Or we'd tell them and they'd use it against us one day." The subtle reference to Tony Porter lingers in the air. He gathers the papers back into a pile. "I don't know how it could work. Not for us."

"It doesn't always end badly. We'd make sure we loved them right. You're not your step-father Christopher." Holly reaches out to place a hand on his arm. Chris shrugs it off.

"I'm sorry, Holly. We both agreed—"

"I don't want us to grow old and end up lonely patients on your ward. No family or friends, because everyone we know already has children and they're too afraid to invite us over out of guilt."

The shrill sound of a telephone cuts through Holly's impassioned spiel. Her brown eyes lock on him, large and wide. She shakes her head, making no attempt to move.

"We need this. I need this."

The ringing is insidious. Chris runs his fingers across his forehead trying to rub away the tension gathered there. "I need to answer that. I'm on call."

Still, Holly remains statuesque, framed by the doorway. He considered pushing past her, but sees her jaw stiffen even as he considers it.

"Please?" she whispers

"Let me think about it, okay?"

She smiles and steps out of the way, and then leans in to kiss him on the cheek as he passes. Like she's already won.

~~~

The phone call is from the Palliative Care Unit, as Chris knew it would be. No one else would try and reach them on the landline. He slips on a jacket and escapes, Holly already retreating upstairs wordlessly to take a bath.

When he reaches Dove Break, Nurse Betsy waits for him at the entrance. She is illuminated by the low sun as it sets between the Pennines and it gives her a renaissance glow. As he retrieves his tie from his pocket, he concentrates on the act of fastening it, allowing it to draw his attention away from the stony-silence of his home life. Yet, it's not much different here at the Unit.

"Records and admission form," Betsy says as she steps out of the golden light with a thick folder. "Patient is in room four."

She focuses not on him, but on a spot just above his left shoulder. As soon as he has the file in his grasp, she hurries away, no further pleasantries offered. When he follows, towards room four, his feet settle into a rhythm and his shoulders relax. He reads through the file of one Madeline Tailor - a thirty-eight year
~~~

old woman with advanced single cell lung carcinoma whose condition has not improved with chemotherapy. She is younger than many of the patients that come into Dove Break – younger than Chris himself, at forty-two – and so she may be unprepared for the difficult weeks ahead. The support and care of family and friends will be crucial to accepting the inevitability of her condition.

He taps on the door and is surprised when it is opened by a diminutive woman with cobalt blue eyes and short, pixie-red hair. Very few patients are mobile when they are admitted. They pause to take one another in before speaking. Chris runs a hand through the dark, unruly crop that he has neglected to comb. He clears his throat.

"Miss Tailor?"

She smiles: a sharp grin that lights up her pale face. "I am," she says, stepping back to welcome him into the room.

"You really should be in bed."

"I reckon I'll be spending far too much time there once I'm in it, so forgive me for being reluctant." She narrows her eyes. "You're Doctor Wright?"

"Yes."

"I imagined you'd be shorter." She is barely five foot two and Chris towers over her at six foot. A slight hunch in her shoulders betrays that she is in pain.

He chuckles politely and offers his hand. Miss Tailor squeezes it with vigour. Her hands are cold with blue veins visible beneath the skin and Chris does not tighten his own grip for fear of hurting her.

"I need to do a quick examination if you don't mind." He gestures to the bed, where a blanket has already been spread across the pale pink sheets. It's clear Miss Tailor has been unpacking. Most patients bring photographs, ornaments or magazines as scattered reminders of home. So far, she has unpacked several small canvases decorated with playing cards, keys, safety pins and combs; the backdrops of which all show maps with locations circled. The only other things he can see are a few notebooks and a selection of boxes of various sizes and patterns.

"Well, first things first," she says as she pulls herself up onto the bed and tucks her gown around her. "I'll have no one calling me Miss Tailor. Please, just Madeline. I think sticking to polite etiquette when you're going to watch me die is far too macabre."

Beneath the eloquence of her words Chris detects the Yorkshire cadence to her voice. Her attitude is just as telling - forthright and simple, no messing about. She leans back into the bed and Chris notes that her translucent skin is clear of any marks or wrinkles, excepting the dark circles under her eyes. The cheekbones that jut out from her face would once have been the sculpted features of a beautiful woman, but the ravages of the disease, along with the effects of the poison used to treat it, has left her looking scrawny with limbs more bone than muscle.

Madeline settles into a half-sitting, half-laying position propped up by pillows on the adjustable bed and he steps forward to do the examination.

"And no sugar coating the truth," she adds. "I'm under no illusion why I'm here."

Chris places a hand on her shoulder as he listens to the wheezing in her lungs. "May I ask why you chose to forgo further radiation therapy?"

Madeline diverts her gaze but keeps her chin up. "No point in fighting if your heart's not in it, is there?" She refolds the edge of the blanket as she speaks. "Besides, it's nothing I don't deserve."

Chris' stethoscope falls from her chest. "I can't imagine anyone deserves this."

"I'll have none of that," Madeline snaps, a finger in the air. "No sympathy. You do what you can to make this transition bearable, but that's it."

Chris breathes in through his nostrils – a long deep breath that allows him to swallow his immediate response. He's worked in palliative care for fifteen years and never heard any patient suggest they deserve to die in such a matter of fact tone.

He clears his throat, refers back to the file. "I notice that you don't have anyone recorded for next of kin."

Madeline stares at him with dazzling blue eyes. "No," she replies. "And no one will be coming either."

He doesn't expect this. She is relatively young, where are her family? Her friends? He opens his mouth to ask, but Madeline shakes her head.

"There's no next of kin, no visitors and no one to mourn my loss."

"I hardly believe that."

But she is already rolling her eyes at his words as he says them. "I heard what you did, you know." A vague smile crosses her cracked lips.

Chris places the stethoscope back to her chest and returns to his inspection of her lungs to avoid the potential accusation. Madeline simply raises her voice.

"An adopted daughter, wasn't it? From a previous marriage; one his second wife never approved of?"

He marks an imaginary note down in her chart. "I'm afraid I'm not permitted to speak about it."

"I bet. Is it true your wife got fired?"

Chris snaps the file shut. Her records are recent and up to date: a full examination isn't necessary. He can bring up the issue of next of kin another time, or ask Betsy to do it. "I'll leave you to get settled in."

"No, no." She flaps a hand out toward him. "I didn't mean anything by it. It sounds to me like you did what was necessary."

This stops him. There is a short silence, interrupted by a hacking cough from Madeline. Chris snatches a tissue from the box on the bedside table and hands it to her. She holds it up to her mouth and a deep rust-coloured stain soaks into the thin sheet. He waits for her to regain even breaths.

"We find that patients who have a support system do better, under the circumstances."

Madeline screws up the tissue and scoffs at him. "Better? You mean they don't die?" She plucks another tissue from the box and wipes her lips.

"That isn't what I meant."

"I know." She looks up at him with a frown. "But even if I asked, no one would come. The world will be a better place without me in it. My art will speak for me, after…" She trails off and then changes tack. "Was it Christopher, your first name? I can't quite remember from the newspaper."

He winces. The incident was reported to the local press by a member of the board – Chris has his suspicions who – and the article included a quote from him trying to explain the situation. The hospital board had been angry, angrier still when they discovered his wife's part in it. After three months he had been hoping his patients wouldn't remember it.

"Chris," he corrects.

"Right then, Madeline and Chris it is. No formalities. Okay?"

He finds it strange that Madeline is intent on facing her death alone. As a child Chris had imagined the terror of spending the last few weeks of his life with strangers. It is a recurring fear, one that he certainly hopes he would never have to face.

"Madeline and Chris it is," he agrees.

"And that nurse – the pretty one with the blonde hair and Irish accent – what's she called?"

"I believe her friends call her Betsy."

There is a missed beat before she replies. "Do you need anything else, Chris? If not, I'd like to sort out my things, though I suspect however you dress it this place still looks like a hospital room."

He glances around the private room, one of their better ones but still marred by hospital essentials. "What are these?" he asks, pointing to one of the canvases she has propped up on the soap dispenser.

Madeline sighs and reaches out for the nearest one. "My art, made from all the lost things I've found. I'm a collector of found objects. It earned me quite a decent sum, once upon a time." She offers him the canvas; on it is a medical wristband and a radiology dosimeter, used by x-ray staff for monitoring radiation levels. They are set over a map of the main hospital in Sheffield. Blue circles highlight particular locations. "Haven't been out much," she says with a shrug. "Restricted in what I can find these days."

Chris nods and hands the artwork back. He wonders what items she used when her work was popular and if he has seen it before: they look familiar in some way, yet it is their uniqueness he admires. Madeline is peering down at her work, lost in her own thoughts.

"I'll get out of your way. Try and get some rest too."

He isn't sure she even notices him leave.

As he makes his way across to the Nurses' Station to return the file he glimpses Betsy with a young girl he recognises. The nurse has a protective arm wrapped around the girl's shoulders as they travel down the corridor. Without Betsy, the elderly woman who died earlier today wouldn't have had any relatives with her when she passed. But Betsy had called every number in their patient's address book and discovered a granddaughter two counties away. The grandmother had slipped away only an hour after the girl had arrived, as if that's what she had been waiting for all along. Chris' gaze follow the nurse and girl until they turn into another corridor and they are out of sight. There won't be any mourning relatives left to comfort once Madeline Tailor has gone. It makes him wonder, who might she have left behind to come and die here alone?

~~~

The next day, after sneaking into bed whilst Holly slept the night before and leaving before she awoke, he spends time catching up on paperwork and checking in with other patients, but between each task his thoughts flicker between Madeline and Holly. One of them he can help. But he knows it's the wrong one.

He has seen patients come into Dove Break alone before; typically the old and infirm who outlive their peers and have no family remaining. Yet Madeline is only thirty-eight, she should at least have friends, colleagues, a husband or boyfriend perhaps? A support system can be a positive thing, even at a late stage it provides solace, not just for patients, but for those that care for them too. Madeline must have someone, somewhere that wants to say goodbye. He will have to talk to her again. His certainty of this grows as he eats his lunch at his desk with his office door closed, as he has for the last few weeks.

The weather has taken a turn and raindrops patter against the window. Chris' view is of the inner quad; a dark, dull place that he is glad his patients do not have to endure. A lone willow stands at the centre with its branches already stripped of leaves and knuckled roots visible underneath. He visualises what Madeline might look out at in room four: a vista of the hills spoilt by the tarmac of the car park. It is better than the opposite side of the building where the Pennines flatten out into houses that mark the area as residential.

When Chris started working here, ten years ago, there was only a scattering of detached homes hidden by thick hedges. Dove Break had been tranquil and he'd thought it a peaceful place to support those who were admitted. Chris has slowly risen in the ranks, despite opposition from his predecessor who criticises his rapport with patients and their families. For Chris it is about making patients comfortable as a whole, not just prescribing drugs. He wants to make the process bearable: mostly he doesn't
~~~

want his patients to have regrets. He knows what it is to realise too late a mistake that was made.

So, after his lunch, he goes straight to Madeline's room and knocks on the door. With no response he peers inside. Around the room, there are more decorated boxes, a pile of notebooks and a stack of papers to accompany the artworks. Madeline is lying on the bed, snoring gently. The unfamiliar surroundings, a strange bed and distant noise of people creating distractions, not to mention the terror of the inevitable, often make it difficult for new patients to sleep. Therefore it surprises him to find so at ease in her surroundings already.

He resolves to come back later, however, he catches sight of an envelope on the speckled blue linoleum floor, perhaps dropped in the fervour of unpacking. It is only a footstep away and Chris goes to retrieve it with the intention of placing it on the bedside cabinet, yet when he raises himself back up he pauses. Might the letter be from someone who can help Madeline, who could be there when she needs some support? He turns the envelope over in his hands, searching for a name, an address or any clue as to who the letter is from, but Madeline shifts and a sharp snort escapes her nose. Backing away, he tucks the envelope in his pocket for safekeeping. He will return it later, when there is no fear of waking her.

Chris pulls the door shut with a soft click. Betsy is seated at the Nurses' Station examining a patient chart. She glances up.

"How's Miss Tailor?" she asks.

"Sleeping, for now." He moves off in the direction of his office.

"Do you think she has long?"

He stops. A few weeks ago he would stay to talk over Betsy's astute observations about their patients. But it would be best not to get drawn back into that.

"It's a difficult one to call. Could be a few days, could be weeks."

Betsy taps the file she has with a clean, clipped nail. "There's no next of kin."

Chris expects this. "Apparently there are none. And if there were, they wouldn't come anyway."

Betsy leans back in the chair and folds her hands over her stomach. "She told me the same thing." Her eyes maintain a steady, even gaze on Chris.

He thinks of the letter in his pocket. He should never have picked it up. "It's not our concern."

"Since when?" Her accent makes the question seem soft but the tone is accusatory.

He checks the corridor for any other staff. "Betsy, please, you know the board would fire either one of us if they thought we were interfering."

"Are you saying what I did was wrong?"

It takes Chris a moment to realise she is referring to the granddaughter he saw her with yesterday evening. Had Betsy not thought to search that faded address book and track down the girl based on an out-dated address the old woman would have died alone. "No, you did what was in our patient's best interests."

Betsy nods. "So you'll speak to Miss Tailor again?"

Chris curls a hand into a fist and takes a deep breath before answering. "I've already suggested her situation would be easier were she not alone, but the decision is hers to make and we should respect that." He hears the hypocrisy in his tone. Is that not what he should be telling himself?

"Based on what I've seen, she won't change her mind."

"We're here to care for their physical symptoms, not interfere in their personal circumstances."

Betsy stands and the chair careens backwards on the wheels. She leans in closer to him. "You sound like Doctor Gregory."

A vivid heat rises into Chris' cheeks. He's repeated the exact words his predecessor used to convince the board to suspend him.

"Don't you want to prove that we can do more than just give them the medicine?" Betsy asks.

He isn't sure if it is a test. Either way it means trouble. He folds his arms. "We should only intervene if it affects patient care. And right now, Madeline would prefer to be alone." At this moment, he thinks, so would he.

Betsy copies his stance. "You and I both know that will change. Don't you feel we have a duty to protect our patients' interests in the long run?"

Chris can't answer that without making Betsy's point for her. Thankfully, he is saved by the screech of trainers on flooring as another nurse hurries towards them. Chris takes the opportunity to escape Betsy's expectant glare.

~~~

When he reaches his office he closes the door and leans against it. Is he a coward for abandoning the conversation with Betsy? Of course, he is. He knows where it would lead, and he can't have that discussion again, not with the well-meaning nurse or his wife.

As he moves to his chair, Madeline's letter rustles in his pocket. He pulls it out and places it on his desk. The long, cream envelope looks similar to one he received in his final year of medical school. That one contained a bill from a hospice he'd never heard of for the care of his mother. It was a shock because he believed his mother was in Spain with her husband. His step-father suggested the foreign sea air would revive her from the sluggish, tired and often confused state she was in when Chris visited at Christmas. As it turned out, her husband went without her. According to the nursing staff Chris' mother deteriorated rapidly and, unable to cope, her husband absconded, leaving her in the care of people she didn't recognise on the premise she no longer recognised the man she'd married either.
~~~

By the time Chris got to the hospice it was almost too late. He tumbled into the room and she was barely conscious. He liked to believe that when her eyes fluttered open she knew who he was, but he couldn't be certain. She died on the day of his graduation. Instead of shaking the hand of the chancellor on stage, Chris held the hand of his mother who was no longer present. If it wasn't for that letter, Chris would have missed the opportunity to be there for her, all thanks to the lies of a man whom he'd refused to call father.

Chris' jaw clenches even though the thought of his real father is only a fleeting one. The familiar weight of guilt spreads over his shoulders and his fingers twitch. He stares at the envelope sitting on the dark wood of his desk. The sloping characters of the address have faded over time and the handwriting is wide and looping - nothing like his father's scrawl. A water stain spreads out and obscures Madeline's name. Chris recalls a single sheet of cheap paper clasped between his fingers and the smudge of ink before he threw it in the fire.

He shakes his head to dislodge the grief. That letter is gone. His gaze naturally rises to the notice board across from his desk. Pinned up, sometimes one on top of another, are photographs of all the patients he's helped at Dove Break. They number close to a hundred and only a handful have died without friends or family. Chris lingers over a few of the luckier ones

The Berts family gathered around their matriarch; a grandmother for whom Chris had tracked down a brother. The brother was in the photograph, clasping the hand of a sister he had not seen in twelve years, both of them smiling. Mrs Berts died the day after, and Chris had been invited to the funeral – an acknowledgement of the fact he had brought a family together, even in mourning.

Then there is Jonathon Devon who was checked in alone. At the time they didn't know his real name. His Alzheimer's robbed him of who he really was and other than the repetition of stories about 'George and Diane' there was little else to identify him. It was Holly who suggested they try and track down some family using the techniques she had learned at the inheritance company where she worked. They discovered a son and daughter searching for a father who had been missing a year. Although Jonathan couldn't recognise them, the relief and appreciation George and Diane felt for being able to say goodbye to their father was reward enough.

Chris fixes his eyes on Tony Porter's photograph, impossible to avoid. It is pinned right in the centre of the board. He told Betsy it was in such a prominent position because he needs reminding of the mistakes he's made. Both he and Betsy know this isn't true.

Looking at the photograph, Chris still can't see any tell-tale signs of the devastation that followed. Tony lays in bed, pale and weak, with his smiling wife on one side and adopted daughter on the other. For the first time since his arrival, two weeks before, Tony seems happy and at peace with his situation. Chris has examined those static faces in great detail, searching for disapproval on Mrs Porter's face or impending betrayal in the young woman's eyes. But nothing appears out of place. Chris believed—like Tony— that the adopted daughter had turned her life around and the second Mrs Porter accepted she was wrong to judge her step-daughter. All that changed when Tony Porter died and the new will was revealed. Chris was apologetic in the face of Mrs Porter's wrath, but that photograph is the only evidence Chris needs to prove that Tony Porter died a happier man for having reconciled with his daughter.

Yet, Chris has never come across a patient like Madeline. He recalls her words from their initial meeting: 'The world will be a better place without me in it.' It wouldn't be unusual for her to be depressed given the young age at which she is facing mortality. Still, the flat, matter-of-fact tone and other comments about no one mourning her loss are disturbing. Knowing that Madeline's disease is not a kind one he would not wish for her to suffer it alone.

He stares back down at the rectangle of paper. It would be a risk to read it. Madeline has made it clear she wants no friends or family. Might she regret her solitude when it comes down to it? Toward the end of their lives people need to be reminded they are loved, that they have made a mark on the world during their short time here. Chris has not yet met a patient who declined the comfort of loved ones during the last few hours of life. Madeline might not realise it now, but she will want this too. All his patients do in the end.

Chris tucks his thumb under the flap of the envelope and lets his fingers rest on the letter within. There is a waft of stale perfume as he slides the textured paper out and a small square of paper flutters to the floor. Retrieving it he sees it is a cutting from a newspaper: a short article, obviously not the main news for the day, and cut so close to the edge that Chris can't tell when or where the article is from. The newspaper bears the yellow tinge of age that suggests the report occurred some time ago. The headline jumps out at Chris and as keen as he is to read the letter that accompanies it he can't help but read this first.

Local teacher commits suicide after rape charges

Harry Watts, a sociology lecturer at Moor Valley College, was found dead in his cell at Wakefield Prison yesterday following a preliminary appeal hearing. Mr Watts was convicted of raping eight young women under his tutelage at the college over a period of four years. Each victim reported their teacher blackmailed them into exchanging sexual favours for higher marks and positive university references. Mr Watts denied all charges but as a result of DNA evidence his appeal was overturned.

Court proceedings last year revealed Mr Watts had been accused of abuse by a friend of his eleven year old daughter six years earlier. During the trial the prosecution questioned the decision not to have charges formally filed against Mr Watts at the time despite lack of evidence.

Mr Watts' leaves behind a wife, a son and a daughter. The family declined to comment.

Chris wonders what relevance this article has to either the sender of the letter or to the recipient. What caused Madeline to keep such a story? Perhaps he will find answers in the letter.

He unfolds the heavy, cream paper and examines it. At the top, there is a printed section with the words 'From the Hartland's' in thick, embossed lettering. The rest is written in beautifully cursive handwriting. He scans the contents at first eager to capture the most useful information. But, he is disappointed. The letter is dated almost twenty years ago, from a woman named Cecelia asking forgiveness for something that is not defined. Does it have some connection to the article tucked within the envelope? Chris reads the letter over again in an attempt to make sense of it. The last part seems the most relevant:

"I know Eric has been to see you. Please let me explain; I know you'll forgive me. My life's been ruined too Mads, I don't want you to blame me forever. I wish I hadn't let you down but I didn't know any better. Please get in touch so we can talk.

Ever hopeful, Cecelia"

A knock at the door startles him and he stuffs the papers into his pocket. If he's caught snooping at a patient's belongings the board won't hesitate to fire him.

"Come in," he calls.

Betsy peers into the office. "We didn't get a chance to finish our conversation." She steps inside and closes the door behind her. Placing a selection of files onto his desk she takes a seat opposite. It has been some time since they have been in his office together. Not since they were on the night shift in fact.

Placing her elbows on the desk Betsy rests her chin in her hands. It is a moment before she speaks: "So what are we going to do about Madeline Tailor?"

Chris wants to sit up, to lean forward and impress his insistence on Betsy that it isn't their choice to make in spite of the invasion of privacy he's just committed. But he is reluctant to move closer to Betsy who now stares at him with daring blue eyes. He opens his mouth to say it and the ringing telephone cuts him off. Betsy sits back into her chair and folds one leg over another.

"Hello, Dove Break Palliative Unit. Doctor Wright speaking."

"Has Madeline Tailor checked in yet?" asks a woman's voice.

Chris is caught off guard by the unexpected question. He blinks back his surprise and bites his tongue before opening his mouth to say 'yes'. Something about the hasty, direct question strikes him as suspicious. He plays it safe.

"Could I ask who's calling?"

Chris is left listening to a dial tone. A glance back up at Betsy shows her head is tilted to the side, listening. He places the receiver back into its cradle.

"What is it?"

"Someone asking about Madeline..." he trails off. His thoughts return to the letter in his pocket. Has he missed an opportunity to find Madeline a friend?

"Then why didn't you tell them she was here?"

Chris shakes his head. "It could have been anyone." His heart flutters in his chest as he wonders if the board would ever be so under-handed as to set him up. At least one of them would.

"But what if it wasn't? What if it's someone who can help her?"

Betsy is already leaning over the desk to take the telephone away from him. Chris watches as she stabs five digits on the numerical panel.

"What are you doing?"

"Finding out who it was," she says. Her last touch puts the call on speaker-phone.

The telephone rings once, twice and then a woman answers with a familiar voice. Surprisingly for Chris, so is the name.

"Hello, Cecelia Hartland."

Betsy and Chris lock eyes over the desk. Betsy raises her eyebrows and flaps her hands. He needs to speak.

"Ah, yes, this is Doctor Wright at Dove Break, I believe we were disconnected." His palms are clammy. He's never been so nervous about contacting people before. But then, he supposes, he hadn't been caught out and told under no circumstances should he attempt it again.

There is a prolonged silence. Chris and Betsy wait.

"Sorry," Cecelia finally replies. "I was hoping to confirm if you have a patient by the name of Madeline Tailor?"

The incident with the Porters and the letter in his pocket makes him cautious.

"I'm afraid I can only give that information to family members."

"I'm her sister."

Chris smiles wryly, he has been backed into a corner. He looks around the room for inspiration and finds it in the pile of files on his desk.

"We don't currently have any details on file for this patient," Chris says. "But perhaps if you're expecting your sister to arrive I can take your number and return your call?"

He can see that Betsy is perplexed, her cheeks are red and she is pouting.

"No thanks, I must've gotten the wrong place. I appreciate your help."

Cecelia hangs up. Chris immediately dials one-four-seven-one, as Betsy had done moments before, and scrawls the number in his notepad.

"What was that about?" Betsy asks.

"What do you mean?"

"Someone calls for a patient where we have no next of kin, no family or friends and you just fob them off?" Betsy's vowels are elongated, emphasising the slight Irish lilt to her voice that Chris finds so alluring.

"I couldn't pass on privileged information to a complete stranger."

"She might be Madeline's sister," Betsy argues.

"And she might be lying. We don't know the background, so we need to tread carefully."

They sit facing one another, shoulders set back and chins high.

"Since when have you been so concerned with the rules?"

Chris doesn't respond.

Betsy taunts him. "Oh, so you're scared of the board?"

"No," he snaps.

Betsy folds her arms and waits.

"I just think we need to be sure." He flinches as he realises he's said: 'we'.

She unfolds her arms and smiles. "I guess that makes sense. So we're going to work together on it? The two of us?" There's a dimple in her left cheek.

Chris sighs. She is tenacious. Surely they all are at twenty-four? It seems like a lifetime ago for him, though it was only sixteen years.

"If we can." He agrees only to stop her pestering him. "But, let me take the lead. I don't want you getting into trouble."

Betsy stands. "I should be the one doing the dirty work – if you put a foot wrong the board will be on you in a second." She holds out her hand.

He hesitates but then relents. If she wants to put her job on the line for Madeline then so be it. He's hardly in a position to argue. He hands over Cecelia's telephone number.

talk to Madeline again before you go digging," he says. see how she reacts when we tell her that sister Cecelia Ca.. .e pulls himself up from his seat.

Betsy nods, then points. "You'll need to sign those before you do anything. I didn't bring them here as a ruse, you know."

Chris steps back to retrieve the files and wonders how he has been so easily talked into allowing Betsy to help. He knows he should just leave well alone, yet Betsy's zeal reminds him of himself. His mind lingers over the possibility of helping Madeline as he signs off on the orders for his other patients: if they can help Madeline, why shouldn't they?

Betsy hesitates, then stands. "Chris, we need to talk about—"

His final *-ght* skips and his pen jumps off the page. "No, we don't," he replies.

The phone interrupts them, and Chris scrambles for it like a lifeline. Not Cecelia, again?

No, one of the other nurses reporting the death of a patient. Mr Stepping had been with them six weeks and built up a rapport with Betsy, reminiscing about Northern Ireland and introducing her to his family as his favourite nurse.

"I'm sorry," Chris places a hand on her shoulder after breaking the news, but Betsy doesn't meet his gaze. Instead she lets her body give way and his hand slides from its place. Her eyes are already red-rimmed and there are tears on her cheek.

"You'll need to call his family," she says.

"Would you like me to say you'll meet them?"

She shakes her head. "I'll ask one of the other girls to do it. I'm not feeling all that well."

Chris wants to comfort her but resists. It's always a struggle when one of the residents passes, but Betsy seems to be taking this harder than usual.

"I'll pass on your condolences." She nods dourly. "Once I've informed his family and followed up on the overnight notes we can speak to Madeline, if you're up to it?" He speaks gently in an effort to coax her out of her withdrawn bubble. It's odd to see her this way, she's usually so upbeat and fiery. It's what he likes about her.

"Sure, just come find me." She leaves, her shoulders still slumped and head down. Chris hopes it's just the shock of losing a patient that has disturbed her. If he is going to commit to helping Madeline he will need the nurse on his side.

His hand brushes the letter in his pocket and he retrieves it to read once more. Chris doubts they are sisters; the article only refers to one daughter of the abuser Harry Watts and Madeline is adamant about there being no family.

He makes the call to Mr Stepping's relatives, who take the news with heartfelt resignation, and he wonders if a long, drawn-out goodbye is what Madeline is trying to avoid. Perhaps she thinks a sudden loss would be easier to accept by friends and family.

Yet, Chris clearly remembers the shock on his mother's face as the police informed them of his father's death. It was like the grief hit her all at once and she collapsed like one of those thumb push puppets he used to collect as a child. Chris experienced a wave of terror that he was responsible: that he had denied his mother the time to grow accustomed to the thought of a world without his father. He convinced himself that as much as it hurt to see his mother blindsided with the news, sometimes a quick, clean shock had its place.

But is that decision right for Madeline and the friends and family Chris suspects she must have? Before Chris leaves to meet with Mr Stepping's family he makes one more phone call and then returns to work with renewed vigour.

~~~

Within an hour he is searching for Betsy so they can check in on Madeline together. He could go without her, but she's never shied
~~~

away from a patient's family before and he's concerned Mr Stepping's death has hit her hard. This is confirmed when he finds her in the kitchen, stirring a cup of tea that has already gone cold. He is wary of comforting her so he simply states he is going to see Madeline and is relieved when she follows.

As they enter Madeline's room he rests a hand protectively on the letter in his pocket. Using the knowledge he gained from it to try and help his patient is in direct violation of his agreement with the board, but surely he's already committed the offence by reading it?

Madeline is curled up on her bed with a notepad and pen, the room looking altogether more homely than the bare, clinical space Chris is used to. "Good afternoon Madeline." She looks up, her skin pale with a translucent shimmer that he often sees on chemotherapy patients. When she smiles her blue eyes shine and she looks almost healthy again. "Have you settled in?"

"Just about," she replies. "Though I'm not sure there's much point unpacking if I'm not going to be here long. Doesn't that make a job for you later?"

"It's usually tackled by the family." In the natural light coming from the window Betsy is almost as pale as Madeline and it's obvious she's been crying.

Madeline closes the notepad and lays down her pen. "Ah, so you're here to gang up on me?"

"Not at all," Chris says. He stands at the foot of the bed to ensure a clear view of Madeline's reaction. "I was just coming in to let you know that we had a call for you. From Cecelia Hartland."

Madeline raises an eyebrow. "And what did you tell her?"

"Nothing. We're not permitted to give out information to non-family members."

"She said she was your sister," Betsy adds.

At this statement Madeline guffaws. "She's not. We used to be friends, a long time ago. That's all."

The ease at which she lies surprises Chris. He reaches into his pocket to retrieve the letter but before he can lift it out Betsy is talking.

"She sounded concerned on the telephone. We really do want the best for you Madeline, and that includes having someone who cares about you to support you through this difficult time. Sometimes we all need a little help to accept things as they happen."

Chris notices a tear gathering at the corner of Betsy's eye. He clears his throat, drawing Madeline's attention away so the nurse has a discreet opportunity to compose herself.

"I found this on your floor earlier. You were sleeping and I didn't want to disturb you." He holds out the envelope and Madeline takes it with delicate fingers. "I was worried you might be a light sleeper."

Madeline 'hmm's agreement but her attention remains on the letter in her hand. Chris thinks he sees a small smile play on her cracked lips, but with her head bowed it's difficult to tell. It's gone before he can be sure.

"How strange." She waves the envelope at him. "This is from the very same woman who just pretended to be my sister."

Chris allows a little 'oh' to escape his lips, trying to mock surprise.

"We used to be the best of friends, you know. When we were just kids who didn't know anything, like what trust really is." She turns the letter over in her hands. "But, once trust has been betrayed you can't get it back. You can say you're sorry, but it doesn't really mean anything. It won't change what happened." She shrugs and then, in a harsh tone; "But Cecelia doesn't understand that."

She tosses the letter onto her bedside cabinet, the sudden movement sets off a cough, gently at first as if she were politely clearing her throat. But the cough increases rapidly and each one comes with more force. Tears form in the well of her eyes and

Chris can see the muscles in her neck straining. He rushes to her side and passes her a tissue as she grasps for one. He places a hand on her shoulder, easing her upright, and then listens to the wheezing in her lungs. He is just reaching for the oxygen mask attached to the wall when Madeline's coughing fit stops. When she opens her eyes there is terror in them and he holds her gaze until she looks away. As she brings the tissue away from her lips he sees the frothy blood. She does not have time to waste.

Then, Betsy is opposite him coaxing Madeline back onto a mountain of pillows and reassuring the patient that she is okay. Chris watches as Madeline crumples the tissue in her hand and tucks it under her blanket. He offers the oxygen mask to Betsy who secures it on Madeline's face and he withdraws to the end of the bed. Only when Madeline is comfortable again does he present the information he'd collected from his second telephone call.

"Your friend Cecelia, isn't she the one who took you to chemotherapy?" Betsy tosses him an intrigued glance over her shoulder, he hasn't told her he called Madeline's previous physician.

Madeline pulls the mask down to her chin. "Doing your homework," she croaks. "How very noble. You really want me to have that friendly bedside support, don't you?"

"We just don't want you to regret not having the support when the time comes." Betsy rests a hand on Madeline's arm but she is still staring at Chris.

He nods to the place under Madeline's blanket where the soiled tissue is. "Fear shouldn't prevent you from admitting how sick you are."

Madeline looks between them, her gaze slow moving and deliberate. "Very well," she announces with a flourish, displacing Betsy's hold. Though the effect is dampened by her raspy tone. "Bring me the telephone."

Betsy manoeuvres the corded telephone to Madeline's bed and then withdraws. Madeline doesn't make a move until Chris turns to go. They hover outside as she makes the call. Chris purposefully leaves the door ajar so that they can hear, concerned Madeline will fabricate some excuse for not being able to get in touch. Particular snippets of conversation drift out to them.

"Yes, well, if you're going to bother the staff I might as well." She pauses. "I'm willing to listen, and to talk. No doubt that'll be us done then." Madeline sighs and then her voice suddenly gets louder. "What changed my mind? Something my doctor said. I won't have him thinking I do things just because he assumes I'm scared. I've got nothing to lose, after all. So it's about time we talked about it."

There is a prolonged silence from Madeline and they hear her drop the telephone back into its cradle without even saying goodbye. She calls out to them, as if she expects them to be right outside. "There, done. Happy now?"

Chris can't see the point in feigning disinterest. He strides back into the room. "I don't think you'll regret it." Chris moves the telephone back to its usual position.

"I might not, but I'm sure Cecelia will," Madeline replies, letting the words linger in the air. "And I'm going to want one of those forms – you know the one I mean, the one that says you can't bring me back from the brink of it all."

Chris is caught off guard. "Typically we suggest that patients talk through decisions about a 'Do Not Resuscitate' order with their family."

"Excellent," Madeline responds, lifting the oxygen mask back up to her face and taking a shallow breath before continuing. "In lieu of family Cecelia can help me decide. I have no doubt she'll be in support of my untimely demise once she hears what I have to say."

Chris can't quite work out whether Madeline's abrupt cheerfulness is because Cecelia is coming, or because she has surprised him by asking her to come. Madeline is a curiosity, someone who – Chris hopes – is only pretending to be more than ready to meet her maker.

"Should I update her about your condition and decisions about your care?"

"Why not? Save me the job. Wait until after I've seen her to ask about the DNR., won't you? Don't want to pile it all on at once." Her voice sounds distant through the confines of the mask but Chris still detects a veiled smugness that concerns him, as if she is putting on a show. He wonders if perhaps he's made a mistake in pressuring her to call her friend. Distracted by this he responds on auto pilot.

"I'm sure that she'll understand."

"Don't worry, she'll be in favour when I tell her what I need to." Madeline pulls her blanket up over her. "Anything else, doctor? Or can I get some rest before my visitor arrives?"

Betsy is a step ahead of Chris as he exits the room. Opposite them, there is a nurse at the station peering over her glasses. They must make an odd pair, ducking in and out of Madeline's room.

"Can I talk to you?" Betsy lays a hand on his arm and steers him away.

She is upset that he did not tell her about Cecelia. He can feel it in the way her fingers grasp at his sleeve. Chris glances over his shoulder at the nurse who continues to watch them until Betsy has ushered him around the corner.

Chris shakes her off. "What's wrong?"

"I need to talk to you."

"It'll have to be quick. I should check on the other patients before Cecelia arrives."

Betsy is undeterred. She shifts from one foot to the other and looks up and down the corridor. "Not here, in your office."

"Is it about a patient?"

"No, it's—" she stumbles over the word. "—Personal."

Chris tries to catch her eye but she won't look up at him. She has been the only nurse to stand by him in the aftermath of the Porter case. He even overheard her rationalising his behaviour to the other nurses on the night shift. That was when he first decided to talk with her instead of hiding himself away in his office during his probation. She made those long nights bearable. With her warm smile and positive attitude she accepted he had only been trying to do the right thing. He learned about her background in Northern Ireland and how she did a brief placement in a Middle Eastern hospital treating mortally wounded soldiers. But when Chris returned to working days and she switched her own schedule to coincide with his he sensed the shrewd eyes of the other nurses examining them and had kept his distance.

Chris reaches out to squeeze Betsy's shoulder and attempts to conjure some reassuring words. Before he can, footsteps echo in the corridor. Chris drops his hand but they are still stood unnervingly close. One of the administrative staff turns the corner and offers a polite acknowledgement.

"Doctor, Nurse." He dips his head.

Chris responds but Betsy does not. She keeps her head low and he realises she is on the verge of tears. He wants to comfort her but doesn't want his kindness to be misinterpreted, by Betsy or the other staff. He pulls out the key to his office.

"Look, why don't you go and take some time in private. You know how the rest of the staff can talk. We need to be careful." He pauses. "If our concern for Madeline gets back to the board we could both be in trouble."

"I know that, it's just..." She trails off and Chris can see that whatever it is, she is ashamed of it.

Chris recalls another time she looked as vulnerable as she does now. Her body had leaned into him, her pale skin soft against the dark pink of her lips. He blinks away the memory. That situation can't be repeated. "It's okay to be upset about Mr Stepping. We all encounter a few patients that mean more to us than others. Take a break. You look like you need it." He holds out the key.

She sighs but takes it roughly from his hand and then she turns and marches away. He wishes he could do more but he is afraid of making another mistake, of letting his gratitude for her support overwhelm him. He thought he'd made himself clear after that night, but perhaps working together to help Madeline has complicated things. He listens to Betsy's footsteps and as they fade away he returns to work while he waits for Madeline's guest.

~~~

A little over an hour later a nurse taps him on his shoulder and informs him there is a visitor for the patient in room four. He points toward the waiting area down the corridor from the Nurses' Station. Fortunately Chris is on the last of his tasks – inserting the most recent checks into the patient files – and after a brief 'thank you' to the nurse he heads toward the room. He hesitates at the glass door allowing him a moment to examine Madeline's friend as she stands staring out of the window with her back to him.

Cecelia Hartland is tall and thin with shoulder length ash blonde hair that shows darker at the roots. Her jeans cut off at the ankle emphasise long, shapely legs but the effect is marred by the ugly black pumps on her feet. She must sense his presence as she turns and Chris notes that her nose is a little bit too large for her face matched only in size with big, brown eyes. As he approaches he catches the scent of her perfume; a crisp, sharp aroma that brings to mind orchids and sweet peas.

"Mrs Hartland, welcome."

"It's Miss." Her voice surprises him, it is deep and throaty not at all like the light, soft tone from the telephone. "Is she driving you mad yet?"
~~~

Chris smiles amicably. He can see that her eyes are rimmed with dark circles and her mascara is smudged.

"Not quite," he replies. "Would you like to see her?"

Chris gestures the way with a hand and Cecelia scurries to his side. Her footsteps are small but quick, making her walk seem agitated.

"Miss Tailor seems in good spirits—"

"She won't like that."

"I'm sorry?"

"Being called Miss. She won't like it."

Chris slows his pace. "No, you're right. She prefers Madeline."

"And if she's called me I doubt she's in good spirits," Cecelia casts a sideways look at him. "But, go on."

This time he chooses his words more carefully. "While Madeline might seem in good spirits, given the severity of her condition I don't expect that she will be able to maintain the façade much longer."

Cecelia peers into each room as they walk by as if she is worried Chris will lead her astray.

"Madeline doesn't do anything you can expect."

"I'm beginning to see that," he says. "But I'm pleased that she agreed to contact a friend."

Cecelia stops walking and Chris has taken two steps ahead before he realises.

"We haven't been friends for a long time, though she's quick enough to accept my help if she thinks she needs it. Still, she's an important part of my life, whether she admits it or not."

For a moment, Chris is concerned that Cecelia might turn and walk away but instead she catches up with him and encourages him forward.

"How long does she have?"

This time it is Chris who stops. They're only a few metres from Madeline's door.

"I'd estimate a week, two at most."

Cecelia stumbles and Chris has to grab her elbow to stop her from falling. "Are you okay?"

She has covered her mouth with her hand where her manicured nails dig into the skin on her cheeks. "Yes, sorry. I should have expected that."

Chris doesn't mention that without the DNR it could be longer, but once she signs that document any treatment to save her life will be against her wishes.

"This way." He nudges Cecelia on again, forward a few more steps. Then he asks her to wait while he ensures Madeline is fit for visitors. Cecelia has lost any trace of colour in her cheeks.

"Now that I'm here it wouldn't surprise me if she turned me away."

Chris lets the comment hang in the air. Through the small windowpane in the door he can see that Madeline is sat on her bed, writing. The oxygen mask sits next to her and Chris wonders if she has even bothered to use it. As if she knows she is being watched she looks up from her work. Chris raps on the door as if he has just arrived.

"Madeline, Cecelia is here."

The writing accoutrements go away immediately. He steps into the room to stand beside her bed and he can hear the raspy quality to her breath even over the noise of her packing her notebook and pens away. He holds up the oxygen mask.

"This is more useful when it's on, you know?"

Madeline gives him a glare that a school girl would be proud of and snatches it away from him. Holding it up to her face she takes a couple of breaths to make her point. but she is distracted by something over his shoulder. The diversion is enough to interrupt the rhythm of her controlled breaths and she drops the mask in a coughing fit. Within a second Cecelia is rubbing Madeline's back and whispering that it will be okay into her ear. Madeline shakes her head, narrows her eyes and physically holds Cecelia back with an outstretched arm. She regains her composure and then scowls at her friend.

"Couldn't just leave me to die in peace, could you?" she gasps.

"Mads," Cecelia's tone shoots up an octave.

"I only asked you so I could tell you in person, I didn't think it was fair to do it over the phone."

"What?"

Chris dare not move.

"You've been wanting to know what happened for years Cece," Madeline says, lowering her arm. Cecelia shuffles forward. "About me and your father"

"Oh, Mads, not now." Even though her words say no, Chris can see Cecelia leaning in, desperate for the information. He has a sudden urge to interrupt them, to stop Madeline from saying whatever it is that will turn Cecelia against her. He realises it is no coincidence that Madeline asked for a DNR after the call to summon Cecelia.

"No, it has to be now. Otherwise you'll never know." Madeline lifts her chin, looking Cecelia right in the eye and then says; "None of it was true. You were right. It was a story I made up. He never touched me."

Chris watches Cecelia blink once, twice and then the third time her eyes shut but don't reopen. She starts to fall. Chris dashes around the bed to try and catch her but knows he'll be too late. He winces as Cecelia's head catches on the corner of the side table and her lithe body folds to the ground. When Chris reaches her she is sprawled on the floor occupying the entire space between bed and wall. He hits the emergency button and glances up at Madeline who has the oxygen mask back up to her face.

Chris could swear she is only using it to hide her smile.

Betsy and another nurse rush into the room, exchanging a bemused look to be tending to a visitor rather than a patient, but they work quickly. Betsy ignores Chris' attempt to help so he steps back and tries to process what just happened. If Madeline is the girl mentioned in the newspaper article - the ten year old who had accused a man, presumably Cecelia's father, of abuse - then what did she just admit to?

There is a groggy moan from Cecelia and at Betsy's instruction the other nurse goes to retrieve a wheelchair. Betsy glares up at him.

"What happened?"

"I'm not sure." Chris turns to Madeline. She still has the oxygen mask up to her face but there is a sparkle in her blue eyes.

"I didn't think what I had to say would have such a dramatic effect." Madeline leans over the bed to look down at Cecelia. "Will she be all right?"

Cecelia stirs at the sound of Madeline's voice and tries to stand. Even with Betsy's help she sways and threatens to crumple onto the floor. The second nurse swoops in with the wheelchair just in time. Chris watches Madeline's gaze follow Cecelia as she is wheeled from the room.

"Care to elaborate?" Chris asks.

"An old skeleton," Madeline says, discarding the oxygen mask. Her face is slack with a greyish pallor. Chris can see the weariness creep in and dull the shine to her eyes. "We all get what we deserve in the end." She falls back on to her pillow and closes her eyes. "I'm so tired, Christopher."

She calls him that on purpose, he is sure of it. He glances up at her monitor that shows her vitals are stable. He can't imagine what has suddenly made Madeline confess such a startling secret to someone she considers a friend. Right now though, he feels more responsibility to Cecelia; to make sure that she isn't seriously hurt after her fall.

"Get some rest, Miss Tailor. I'll come back to check on you in a while."

Madeline rouses. "Don't forget to ask her about the DNR," she calls out. "I'm sure she'll be all in favour now."

~~~

The nurse who fetched the wheelchair tells him that Betsy has taken Cecelia to the closest lounge, one of two spaces that families can use when visiting. Both are set up to look like a typical living room, but the one around the corner from room four is the cosiest. It has a soft seated settee with huge cushions and a tall back cloth chair with rounded arms. It was painted only last year, in cornflower blue and someone – Chris suspects Betsy – has placed some fake daffodils in a vase on the coffee table beneath the window. It still smells faintly of mildew and egg, but the late afternoon sun streaming in makes it bearable.

He watches as Betsy settles Cecelia onto the sofa and places a glass of water in her quivering hand. When Chris speaks it startles Betsy but Cecelia remains emotionless.

"Miss Hartland, are you okay?" He gentle reaches over to examine her head and is relieved when it shows no visible injury. He checks her vision and as her eyes follow his finger she mumbles.

"No wonder she never forgave me."

"I'm sorry?" Chris leans in to hear.

"There was nothing to forgive. All those years I spent trying to make it up to her when she knew..."

Betsy lays a hand on Chris' shoulder. "Have another drink," she tells Cecelia. "We'll be back in a minute."

She leads him into the doorway and stands with folded arms.

"I thought we were in this together?"

Chris runs a hand down his face and feels the stubble across his chin. Betsy has been a good ally and if he had shared the contents of the letter with her she might easily have convinced him not to encourage Madeline to call Cecelia. Certainly, if the circumstances are as he suspects he doesn't believe Cecelia will want to stay and hold Madeline's hand.
~~~

"From what I gather, Madeline accused Cecelia's father of something when they were children. Cecelia felt responsible, but Madeline has just admitted to it all being a lie."

Betsy opens her mouth, either in incredulity or to speak, but before she gets chance Cecelia's voice – deep and clear – comes across the room.

"Because she wants to show she still has the power to entertain. She's always been a show off. I can't believe she's doing this to me." Cecelia pushes herself up from the sofa. "I have to know why. Why did she lie? What possible benefit could it have had?"

She stands precariously and Chris goes to support her, a hand cupping her elbow and an arm around her waist. The tears come quietly, rolling down Cecelia's cheeks at a quick pace. Chris senses her muscles tense and then release. She lets him ease her back down onto the sofa.

"I'm afraid I can't answer that," Chris tells her. "But you've obviously been a through a lot with Madeline. We know very little about her. If I'd have known she was going to upset you like this I would have dissuaded you from coming."

Cecelia smiles, a tightening of her mouth rather than a grin, and wipes the tears from her cheek. "You have no idea of the past Madeline and I have. It's fraught with disappointment. We were inseparable once, but when everything happened it ruined us. I've spent so many years trying to make it up to her and now..." She sighs. "It should have been the other way around."

Betsy is still standing in the doorway with her arms crossed, waiting for him. But Chris doesn't want to explain himself right now. He perches on the edge of the coffee table and takes Cecelia's hand. If he wants to help Madeline he has to know.

"Can you tell us?" he asks.

Cecelia stares at him, her smudged mascara creating a panda effect around her eyes. Chris hears the sounds of muted footsteps from behind. Betsy doesn't want to hear it.

"She's got to you, hasn't she." Cecelia states eventually. There is no questioning in her voice.

"I just want to know more about her and why she's so insistent to be here alone. I'd like to know if there is anything we can do to help her."

"You want to help her?" There is such surprise in her tone. But the admonishment seems to energise her, and she sits forward with a straight back. "Well then, you deserve to know who it is you're helping," she says. "Let me tell you about Madeline and who she really is."

CECELIA'S STORY

The first time I met Madeline she was shuffling into our classroom just after the start of spring term with downcast eyes and a thick coat with a matted fur lined hood. The vividness of her red hair made me stare. I managed to lower my gaze, but not before Madeline looked up at me with sharp, bright eyes that reminded me of dark oceans I'd only ever seen on television. As the teacher introduced her and then guided her to a chair, I watched out of the corner of my eye. She was so small, like a doll.

It was January, our final year of Primary school, and we'd settled into our established groups leaving no space for newcomers. She had to take the only seat left in the room, closest to the teacher's desk on a single table with Eric, whose Mum had died the previous year and left him with some challenging behavioural issues. Over time I learnt that Madeline had a way of looking at you, from your face down to your feet and back up again that made people uncomfortable. She didn't speak in class unless she was called upon and for the first few weeks I never saw her anywhere but in that classroom, despite searching for her in the playground, the lunch room, and at the school gates at the end of the day. I would pretend I had left something on my desk just to go back and check for her, but by the time I got inside the room would be empty and her things had gone from the cloakroom. I'd end up walking home from school alone, wondering how she managed to get past me.

My friends sometimes talked about her, offering the occasional scathing remark about her clothing or uptight attitude, like children do. She came to school in patterned dresses with bold colours clashing, trimmed with yellowing lace or gypsy skirts that hid her pale, skinny knees and were frayed at the ends. It's no wonder they prefer uniforms nowadays.

"We're going to work in pairs today," our teacher told us. "I'll need a partner for Madeline."

That ended up being me. I was the only volunteer from our entire class of thirty. Once the teacher had laid out our task - to create family trees and compare them to our partner's - I introduced myself to the elfin figure to my right.

"I know who you are," she replied. She had a dusting of freckles across her nose and dark rims around her eyes and she kept her focus on the paper in front of her. I breathed in a waft of sweet smelling lavender that reminded me of my grandma and for a moment I concentrated on sketching out the basics of my family tree.

"Is that it?" I asked her a few minutes later, conscious of the silence that had settled between us in the din of the classroom. I pointed at her crude sketch of three family members on her page; a circle each for her and her Mum, a triangle for her Dad.

"At least I'm not an orphan."

I wrinkled my nose. "What's that supposed to mean?"

"It's why Eric's not here. His Dad's dead too now."

I leaned in to her, my nose acclimatised to her scent, and I strained to hear what she had whispered over the din of the class.

"How do you know that?"

"My Dad's a policeman. He knows." She didn't look up from her page. She started adding grandparents to her diagram and then crossed them out with thick, black lines.

This was by far the most information any one in our class now had about the mysterious Madeline. As it turns out her Dad was the policeman on shift when the car accident that killed Eric's father had happened.

"Did he tell you?"

Madeline shot me a narrow eyed glare.

"Of course not. I heard him telling my Mum."

She put her pencil down and pushed away the paper she had been working on. It represented seven people, only three of which were still alive.

"What does your Dad do?" she asked, pointing at the triangle I'd drawn to symbolise my father.

"He's a teacher, at college."

"Oh."

That was it. Conversation faltered and we sat in silence for ten minutes while I completed my family tree. I could feel Madeline watching me extend my family; my brother, my cousins, my grandparents. When I glanced up she was staring down at my page, pouting. She caught me looking and turned away, pulling out another piece of paper that she hid with one arm as she scribbled on it. The bell sounded and everyone jumped out of their seats. My muscles tensed, as eager to be away as the rest of them out of habit. I turned back to my table of friends but I had been left behind. I forced myself to tidy away my things slowly, so that no one would notice I was hurt by such an easy dismissal.

"Your friends have gone," Madeline swung her backpack over her shoulder. It swamped her.

I shrugged. "I'll catch up with them later."

"Oh, okay."

There was a hint of disappointment in her voice and I realised that this was my chance to find out where she disappeared to all the time. I blurted out the first thing that came to mind. "Do you want to have lunch with me?"

Madeline stopped and turned. Her jaw jutted out from her face and her blue eyes seemed darker than they had been only moments before.

"No," she said. "But you can have lunch with me if you like."

I furrowed my brow. *What did that mean?*

"Come on," she flicked her head in the direction of the door. I followed her blindly.

She took a right turn down a corridor in the opposite direction to the lunch room.

"Where are we going?"

She didn't answer so I kept two steps behind, a nervous flutter in my chest. We weren't supposed to be wandering the school at lunch time. Madeline ignored me, continuing on without a backward look. She turned another corner, left this time, and I heard a click and soft thud. By the time I got to the turning she was gone.

I was tempted back the way I came, to join my friends in the lunch hall, but a whispered voice startled me.

"In here."

It took me a moment to place her fiery mane in the darkness of a crevice in a doorway; a storeroom. With a quick check to ensure no one was around I took a deep breath and slipped in beside her.

"What are you doing?" I took a step in, to better see what she was up to.

"Close the door," she hissed.

I pushed it to and she turned on the light, though it was dim with dust and flickered intermittently. Madeline's face was pinched, her eyes narrow slits and lips a flat line. I towered over her, her head only just reaching my shoulder. She led me to the back, where it was cramped, room enough only for us to stand a few feet away from one another, hampered on either side by tall stacks of shelves with various stationary supplies.

"What's that?" I ignored the musty smell and tried not to sneeze when I disturbed the dust on a shelf with my breath. Madeline ducked under my arm easily and tucked the box I'd spied out of view.

"It's nothing."

But I'd seen something in the box, a glint of light as she pulled it away. She stood like a sentry, guarding the corner with her chin high and shoulders back. Behind her I could just about see the nest she had made for herself, hidden away in gap between shelf and wall right at the back of the room in the shadows.

"If we're going to be friends we need to share stuff."

Madeline's mouth fell open a fraction and her eyebrows knotted together. I'd surprised myself. *Did I really want to be friends with a girl who hid in a cupboard and seemed to dislike everyone else in our class?* But I did. There was something about her. She was so different from everyone else that I was drawn to her. I wanted to know what made her the way she was, why she came to school in such prim clothes and what she was doing in this cupboard all alone.

"My Mum says friends can't be trusted. That they just cause trouble."

"So you're going to through your entire life without any friends?"

"Yes."

"Isn't that a bit pathetic and lonely?"

Madeline bit her lip. I knew she wanted to say yes but couldn't.

"I suppose so." She gave me one last glance of suspicion and then shrugged, letting her grimace turn into a smile. "Come and look what I found."

Inside the box were several items that Madeline had discovered on her walk between home and school or within the classrooms and corridors. Most were unimpressive; a pen lid, a stubbed pencil and two buttons – one black, one red. But right at the bottom was the flash of something I recognised. I reached out to make sure and Madeline snatched the box away.

"You can't have them, they're mine."

"No they're not."

"Yes they are." Madeline held the box to her chest but she wouldn't meet my gaze.

"You're stealing things."

"I am not," she screamed. Although I was a head taller she had such a loud voice for a tiny mouth. "I found them. It's not my fault people lose things. I just pick them up and keep them safe." Her lips curled into a sneer and her cheeks flushed but she lowered the tone of her voice so that by the end of her sentence she was almost whispering.

"Whose was that?" I pointed to the necklace.

"I think it might have been Mrs Lee's."

"And you aren't you going to give it back?"

Madeline threaded the precious find though her fingers. "Why should I? She was the one who lost it. Maybe she'll be more careful from now on."

I didn't question her ruthlessness. It made her more daring than me. I'd have given it back as soon as I found it, or handed it to lost property. Madeline's refusal to conform to such banalities pleased me.

"I think Mr Collins bought it for her. He's always in her classroom, leaning on her desk laughing with her. I bet they're secret lovers."

Madeline put so much emphasis on those last words, letting her tongue sound out the syllables dramatically that I immediately believed her. She set up a scenario whereby Mr Collins had left it in a box in Mrs Lee's desk as a token of his affection and Mrs Lee put it on when she came into work but had to remember to remove it before going home to her husband.

"That can't be true?"

"Well then maybe her husband was having an affair and he bought it for her to say sorry." Madeline chomped on one of my sandwiches which I'd offered to share to validate our friendship. She had no lunch with her.

"Do you think so?"

"Sure," she replied. "Maybe that's why she likes flirting with Mr Collins. It makes things even between her and husband."

I soon realised Madeline was an excellent storyteller. Each of the objects she had collected began a whole series of potential tales, whether she knew their owners or not. Some were more believable than others. She weaved fairy tales and possibilities together and we were only disturbed by the ring of the bell that signalled the end of our lunch hour. Madeline stuffed her box into her rucksack and peered out of the door. I could see hordes of children passing by through the gap over her head.

"Let's go," she whispered, and she slipped out into the crowd before a teacher could spot her. I followed close behind, pulling the door closed as I went and we rushed back to the classroom. We were the first to arrive, and I realised that as the store cupboard was so close to class this was how she managed to appear so early. Our teacher strode in, smiling at seeing us together.

"Miss, can I sit next to Madeline for the rest of the day please?"

I caught Madeline's grin as I asked. It was a commitment to our blossoming friendship.

~~~

Eric didn't come back school after what happened with his Dad. Madeline told me a few days later he was going to live with his grandmother so I made a permanent move to sit next to Madeline in class. We spent every break and lunch time in that cupboard. Each week she would bring a fresh box of found objects for us to examine and we would make up stories about who they belonged to or how they'd been lost in the first place. We weaved fact with fiction and dropped people we disliked into the narrative, creating nasty little secrets about them that would make us smirk when we saw them next. With one look we could communicate, a reference
~~~

to a story already told or a promise to include a detail in the next. We hardly spoke in class, but as soon as that store cupboard door shut we chattered like crickets in summer.

~~~

Two weeks later Madeline came running into class twenty minutes late with red cheeks and an apology for the teacher hindered by panting breaths.

"Where were you?" I whispered, as our teacher resumed her talk.

"Slept through the alarm. My Mum's not well. We were up half the night."

The teacher glared at us and I kept quiet, knowing we would have the chance to talk at break time. But, half an hour before the bell was due to ring the school secretary rapped on our classroom door to say that Madeline's father was in reception waiting to take Madeline home.

Madeline rolled her eyes as she packed up her stuff and gave me a shrug as I watched her walk away. She was gone for three days and I hated every minute. I'd been so busy with Madeline I was now unpopular among my previous group of friends. With Madeline in school I was too distracted to care, but now my isolation pressed down on me and I felt suffocated sitting in the cupboard alone. But it was better than the playground with the sniggers and veiled insults from girls I thought had been my friends. The stuffy air rattled through my nose and the silence was oppressive. I read some of our stories out loud, attempting to recreate the atmosphere we usually had, but Madeline was the one who made them come to life. With me, it was just reading. I didn't have the knack of making it seem believable.

When I went outside it was clear I had no one to sit with or talk to but I did notice how sharp Madeline's observations had been about the people around us: how our Head of Year walked
~~~

with a slight limp, and that a boy from our class had a faint scar that trailed beneath his chin. She must have been excellent at watching other people because in all the time I knew her I never saw her talk to another kid in our school and yet she seemed to know all about them.

Mum got worried about me, asking why I was so quiet all of a sudden. At home I'd been so full of tales about Madeline and the stories she'd told me – relating them to my parents not half as well as Madeline told them. But in her absence I had nothing to report, so I would shrug and sit in my room wondering if Madeline's father might have had to change jobs, worrying I might never see her again and how I'd sacrificed my friendships for nothing.

"Such an over-active imagination," Dad said, ruffling my hair. "Isn't her Dad one of the local police?" I nodded. "Well, I'm sure I saw him yesterday. No reason to worry." He pulled out the checkers board and started setting up. "Want a game?"

I knew he was trying to distract me, to cheer me up, but I felt inconsolable.

"Don't you have to go back to work, like last night?" Exam season was approaching and Dad would often come home for dinner and then return to the college around the corner to mark the mock papers his students had done.

"Not tonight. Tonight I let my girl win at checkers."

~~~

The next day I shuffled into class, my bag hanging limp in my hand, shoulders slumped and gaze on the floor. It was Friday, meaning if Madeline wasn't back I'd have to wait a whole weekend before knowing if she'd return on Monday. But when I saw Madeline tapping her fingers on the desk waiting for me, I skipped toward her and embraced her.
~~~

"Where've you been?" I demanded, grasping on to her arm as if she might escape again.

"Had to look after my Mum. She's fine now though, so I'm back."

Her eyes were duller, with a yellowish tinge beneath them as if she'd had no sleep. Her hair didn't shine as it used to either, nor did it appear to have been brushed. She caught me looking and shook my hand off her arm to smooth out her locks. We didn't have time for any more detail, as the teacher arrived to take the register. Still, as she called out our names I noticed that a group of girls were whispering and pointing with mean little grins on their faces. I glanced at Madeline, but her back was to them. I glared at them in defence of whatever they might be saying about Madeline, but one of them - a girl I used to be friends with - rolled her eyes and looked away.

A second later a screwed up piece of paper flew past my head and landed on the desk next to my hand. I looked back to see my old friend staring right at me and I vowed not to turn away first. But, the teacher called out my name in the register and I automatically shifted my attention toward the front. I unscrewed the paper that had been thrown. Madeline seemed miles away. '*Her mother's a loony*' was scrawled across the page. I crumpled it in my hand and pocketed it, careful to make sure Madeline didn't notice. But I should have known better. The second the store cupboard door shut at break time she called me on it.

"What was written on that note?" she asked.

"Nothing, it was just a piece of paper." I wanted to protect her. I thought that's what friends did.

"Liar." Madeline pushed me. She was stronger than I gave her credit for, plus I didn't expect it, so I stumbled, the shelving breaking my fall.

Anger bubbled up. "Fine," I pulled the paper out of my pocket and flung it at her. But then I remembered what she'd said the first day we met: that friends couldn't be trusted. By lying to her I'd proved that.

"It's not true," she cried, ripping the paper into tiny little shreds. But I could see her blinking back tears.

"It's okay." I reached a hand out to her and she smacked it away.

"It's not true. I can prove it. Come to my house for tea. You'll see. She's fine."

I hesitated, and Madeline must have thought it was because I believed the note. But before I could respond the door of the cupboard opened. We both leapt into the corner, crouching behind the large pile of notebooks we had created out of the organised chaos of the closet space. We watched through gaps in the school supplies, our breath as silent as we could make them and hearts thumping against our chests, as a teacher - a young woman I didn't recognise - stumbled in, closely followed by our Deputy Head. They shut the door quietly and our eyes widened as they began to kiss, their hands all over each other, moaning and groaning.

"Ewww," Madeline exclaimed, stepping out from the darkness. My heart jumped into my throat.

"Oh, my!" The woman gasped as the Deputy Head bellowed; "What on Earth are you doing in here during break time?"

Madeline stood before him and shrugged. "Nothing," she answered, matter-of-factly, following it up with: "What are you doing in here?"

The young woman was beetroot red and started backing up to the door. The Deputy pushed his chest out, asserting his authority. "That is none of your business young lady."

I hung my head low, shrinking behind Madeline's defiant pose. But I was still a head taller than her and closer to the Deputy's anger. Madeline appeared utterly unphased: she stood equally as proud as her enemy, her chin struck out high.

"Do you want us to report to the Headmistress then sir?" Madeline asked.

I exhaled, finally she was being sensible. My parents would be disappointed with my disregard for rules, but they would be angry if they found out I'd been involved in back-chatting to a teacher – the Deputy Head no less. I felt my heart settle but still beating so fast it rattled my rib cage. Tears stung my eyes, but I gulped them down.

"If you want, sir," Madeline continued, her voice even and calm, "we can tell Mrs Ferris just how you found us." She stepped forward and my eyes widened again as she reached passed the Deputy and held her hand out to the pretty woman.

"Sorry, I don't know you. I'm Madeline Fields. Can I have your name so I can report it to the Headmistress?"

My mouth fell open, mirroring the adults in the room. I closed my eyes tight. I didn't want anything to do with this. My parents were going to be furious.

The Deputy cleared his throat. "Gloria, I need to handle this. I'll speak with you later." The door opened and the click-clack of Gloria's heels echoed down the hall. "You two," he ordered. "Out here. Now."

Stepping out into the bright corridor I almost burst into tears. I was shaking. Madeline had crossed the line. We might even be expelled.

Then, quickly, before the Deputy had time to begin his scolding, Madeline said: "Was that your wife then sir?"

I felt the blood drain out of my entire upper body and pool in my lower limbs. I so desperately wanted to run, but I was trapped here with Madeline who seemed to know no fear. I watched her smile sweetly at the Deputy, her gaze holding his. His nostrils flared with each angered breath. Three of his shirt buttons were undone.

"Now, listen here." He took a step forward and leaned into us with his eyebrows furrowed into one big clump of wiry hair. "We do not tolerate students hiding away in store cupboards when they should be outside." He was speaking to me, his eyes unwilling to meet Madeline's steely gaze – still boring into him. "But as this is your first charge I'll let you off with a warning."

I exhaled again, my shoulders relaxing.

"If I hear you mentioning this to anyone," he tossed a glance at Madeline. "Anyone. I will waste no time in informing your parents that you have been flouting the school rules." His tone lowered significantly as he threatened us.

I couldn't believe he was letting us get away with it, especially after Madeline's responses.

"Yes, sir," I stammered, thinking his warning deserved a reply. "Thank you."

Madeline was still staring at him, her arms folded across her chest, hip kicked out and the temptation of a smile on her lips looking much older than she was.

"Now get going," he said.

I reached out for Madeline and had to drag her away, only feeling her scurry behind me once we were out of sight of the Deputy. I continued to a quiet corner of the playground, eventually turning to face her. She was laughing.

"What's so funny?" I screamed. "We could have been expelled. Why didn't you just keep your mouth shut?"

"Don't be stupid," Madeline snapped, her expression darkening. "He would never have sent us to the Headmistress. It would have meant he was found out. My Dad knows his wife – she's a typist at the Station. He wasn't going to risk his marriage for us."

"Oh," I whispered, only now understanding what had gone on moments before. I suddenly felt like a child: Madeline had seen the opportunity and had taken it, using her power to stop us from getting into trouble.

"Wasn't that exciting?"

I gulped a few breaths of the fresh air, letting it dilute my shock at the understanding of our escape and then shook my head emphatically. “It was terrifying.”

“We were just like characters in the story. Stupid Mr Grogon can’t beat us. I told you he was a weasel.”

I vaguely recalled one of Madeline’s adventures where the character reminded me of our Deputy, except he was a love rat who made women fall in love with him so he could spend their riches.

“Don’t you feel like you’re buzzing?”

I started to shake my head and then realised she was right. My entire body was energised. My terror had turned into electricity. I began to appreciate what Madeline was talking about. She skipped around me, laughing and clapping.

“He can’t mess with us,” she sang.

In the spirit of camaraderie I joined in her medley. This was the first time Madeline and I had been seen together out of class. I stopped skipping, noticing my old friends staring at us from across the yard. None of them would have stood up to a teacher for me, especially not one like the Deputy Head. *Did that make Madeline my best friend?*

“Can I still come to your house for tea?” I asked.

Madeline halted and gazed at me with her head tilted. Her long hair fell to one side, almost reaching her waist. The sun rippled through it and created a pink reflection on her cheek. I was mesmerised.

“Really?” she asked. “You’re not scared that my Mum’s crazy?”

The way she asked the question should have made me suspicious. But, I was so elated from our near escape that I just shook my head and threaded my arm through hers, linking us together. “No, of course not. Those lot over there are the loonies,” I gestured to the gaggle of girls with their heads together, whispering again. “They’re just jealous, that’s all.”

"I'll have to check with my Dad." Her eyebrows creased like they did when she was thinking up a new story.

"Me too," I said. "How about Wednesday? My Dad is home early on Wednesdays"

Madeline nodded slowly. "Okay. Wednesday," she repeated.

It was like we'd never had our little tiff. But a tiny part of me looked forward to seeing another side of Madeline, being in her room and meeting her family. I was ready for something different. She rarely talked about her home life, even less about her parents. It was always those stories inspired by the objects in the various boxes she brought to school. I hoped this visit would broaden our friendship and I'd finally get to see the girl behind the stories.

~~~

The rest of the day passed quickly and I raced home to ask permission to have tea at Madeline's on Wednesday, already wishing my weekend away.

"Are you sure that it'll be all right?" Dad asked that night. "You said her Mum was ill recently."

"She's fine now. Madeline said it'll be okay. Please, I really want to go."

Mum came to the rescue. "I'm sure if Madeline's Mum is happy to receive guests then it'll be okay. Why don't I give her a call on Monday to confirm? Can you get me Madeline's telephone number?"

I nodded. All weekend I dreamt about what Madeline's house might look like. I imagined hundreds of boxes in her room, all with strange lost objects hidden away inside. I built up her parents in my head; her Mum a model with pretty blue eyes like Madeline and long strawberry blonde hair that she wore in a long plait down her back. Madeline had once said she got her red hair from her Dad, so I pictured him with a ginger beard and a round face like Madeline's.
~~~

I fidgeted and twitched my way through the weekend and only stopped on Monday when Madeline confirmed I was invited for tea on Wednesday. I had to coax the telephone number out of her, assuring her it was only so our Mums could agree. Madeline seemed not to understand why this was necessary but I convinced her that this was how it always worked. Eventually she shrugged and scribbled her number on a scrap of paper that was indecipherable. Mum ended up looking for it in the phone book. In the end I think she spoke to her Dad.

By Tuesday morning we were both wound up balls of excitement, talking of nothing else except what we would do at Madeline's on Wednesday evening now it had been officially sanctioned by our parents.

"What's your bedroom like?"

"Like a bedroom. With a bed and stuff." Madeline said, tapping her foot on the shelving in the cupboard. Our run in with the Deputy hadn't dissuaded Madeline from using the spot as a place to spend time. If anything, she'd be even more insistent that it was our special space, we'd earned it now.

"Is it painted purple?"

"No. It's beige. Mum wouldn't let me have purple. I have a whole load of boxes though, with all my found treasures in them."

I was getting a bit bored of the bric-a-brac Madeline referred to as her 'treasures' though. "We could play dress up," I suggested. "You must have tonnes of clothes in your wardrobe." I'd never seen Madeline wear the same outfit twice, so it was a natural assumption.

"That's 'cause Mum keeps throwing them out and buying new ones."

"You're so lucky. I have to beg for new stuff."

"It's not really new," she answered. "Mum gets it from the second hand store on Wellington Avenue."

This threw me. Despite asking Madeline where she got various pieces of clothing from before, she'd always dodged the answer.

Sometimes she let me look at the label if I really insisted and I'd be amazed that her parents would buy her jackets and skirts from named shops.

"I didn't know that."

"Now you do. Nothing would fit you anyway, scarecrow." She smiled at me to show she was joking, but she was right. Her tiny clothes would never go over my broad shoulders.

"But I have my valuables box," Madeline said. "I can't bring it to school 'cause I'm scared of losing something. There's some great stuff in there."

"Like what?"

"Wedding rings and necklaces. I've got a money clip and six earrings."

After that first visit to the storeroom when our friendship had been made there had never been another necklace in any of Madeline's boxes. She'd only found it that day, so it had been added to the box for safekeeping. But as soon as she got home, she explained, it went into her valuables box instead.

"That sounds like fun," I said, though I couldn't quite inject the enthusiasm into my voice. I didn't want to go to Madeline's and do what we did in the store cupboard at school. There had to be more to Madeline than hiding out and making up stories about discarded objects. I'd sacrificed my other friends for her and I hoped that a visit to her home would catapult our friendship into something a little less repetitive than the routine we'd fallen into.

~~~

Wednesday came around quickly. At my request we scoured the playground and fields for new finds during break and lunch rather than hide ourselves away in the cupboard. I thought it would be more interesting but mostly I just felt silly wandering around looking for nothing in particular. I couldn't tell Madeline this of course. She revelled in the search; eyes down, scanning the
~~~

ground, stooping low on occasion to scrutinise various hiding places and then, after what seemed like an age, she would announce a find and hold it up for me to admire. It being on school premises the item was typically not very interesting – a pen lid, a few pennies, plastic toys or cards. Mrs Lee's broken necklace was by far the most impressive find and I never actually saw Madeline locate this, therefore my reactions to her petty discoveries were always more muted than her own.

When the final bell tolled at the end of the school day Madeline dragged her feet even more than usual. Our teacher had to shoo us out, impatient for us to leave so she could lock the room up and disappear herself.

"Which way to your house?" I asked as we made it outside, fifteen minutes after the bell.

"This way," she said. Madeline began to stroll toward the back of the school.

"Doesn't your Mum meet you at the gate?"

"I only live a ten minute walk away, behind the fields." She cut a zigzag line through the football fields at the back of the school. I followed, a damp smell of freshly cut grass assaulting my nostrils, picking my way through the sticky blades of grass that clutched at my sandals. Madeline's gaze was down again and we meandered our way to the fence at the far side in what I thought might be considered companionable silence, but was more like boredom on my part.

"Doesn't your Mum get worried if you're not home on time?"

She didn't look up to answer me. "Not really. She tends to lose track of time at home all day." Bending, she brushed away some grass and claimed a key ring for a prize. "Haven't got one like this," she grinned, unzipping her rucksack to add it to her box.

I nodded. We were so close to the fence now I was in throwing distance of the sty that would lead us out into a housing complex. I purposefully walked on Madeline's right side, veering to the left to encourage her toward it. It worked, with a sigh,

Madeline clambered over the wooden structure and jumped down onto the path. Within a few houses she pushed open a rusty gate and announced it was her home.

"Mum, we're home." Madeline discarded her rucksack as soon as she got through the door.

I held back, taking in the hallway of the mid-terrace, a dark blue carpet leading up the stairs with shoes, papers and toys stacked on each step until about half way up. Straight down the hall was the kitchen. Madeline disappeared into it. I went to follow, then glimpsed my grass covered shoes and tugged them off, leaving them next to the stairs. As I entered the kitchen I glanced through the door on my right, which led to their living room, I spied a brightly clothed figure laid out on the sofa.

Madeline was getting us drinks, clinking the glasses and asking me if I wanted biscuits.

"Is your Mum okay?"

She shrugged, handing me some juice. "She'll be up soon. If not, I'll wake her in time to make us some tea. C'mon."

Madeline downed her drink with an audible gulp, put her glass in the sink and left. Not knowing what to do I took a sip of my own juice and then left the rest of it in the kitchen getting to the hall just in time to see Madeline thumping up the stairs. I took the steps two by two eager to see Madeline's room but the small space she occupied was disappointing. Beige walls – like she'd said – a single bed next to the window with an in-built wardrobe in the wall at the foot of it and a set of drawers as a bedside table. The only other thing was a set of shelves, opposite her bed, which left us little room to manoeuvre. On the shelves were several sets of boxes. I recognised some as the ones she brought to school.

"Where do you want to start?" she asked, flinging herself back onto her bed, still unmade from the morning.

Was this it? I'd wanted it to be colourful and interesting, but this was hardly the room of a kid. Even the curtains were dull and bland. It looked more like a guest room. I blinked back my disappointment, reminding myself she'd only been living here a few months – perhaps they hadn't gotten around to decorating yet – and shrugged in response to her query.

"Valuables box?" I suggested and Madeline grinned, pleased with my choice.

She flicked her hair over her shoulder and leaned forward, tipping herself until she could reach under the bed. I noticed a knot forming in her hair at the base of her neck and momentarily wondered where she kept her hairbrush.

She re-emerged right way up with a purple felt box gripped in her hands. It was only small, maybe a hands width each way. Madeline eased off the lid and I peered inside. She was right, all of things inside could be considered valuable, but the singularity of some of the items just seemed sad to me; mismatched earrings, broken chains, tarnished rings. Things that were no longer loved or useful. But Madeline appeared so proud of them. She upended the box, letting the contents spill out onto the bed. Rifling through she picked out one piece in particular, a small ring with what looked like a pearl set in it, fancy metalwork holding it in place.

"This is my favourite," she told me. "I found it in the back garden on our first day here. It was in a little box buried under some weeds. I think it was a present to welcome me to the house." She slipped it on her middle finger. It was still loose but over time she might grow into it.

"Can I see?" I asked, holding out my hand. Madeline let me have it, reluctantly. I tried to put it on myself but my knuckles were too thick and Madeline snatched it away from me.

"Don't get it stuck." She put it back on and held out her dainty hand to show me. I peered at it, losing interest when I realised the band was dark with dirt and the pearl was a dull shade of grey instead of cream-white. As she took her hand away the ring fell, bouncing off the bed onto the carpet where it rolled around and settled. Madeline pounced on it.

"I've been waiting ages for it to fit, but it always falls off. It's so pretty though. You know, I think it used to belong to a girl who lived here before the war. She was given it by the man she was supposed to marry, as a promise before he went off to fight. But I don't think he ever came back and so when she had to go and marry someone else, she buried the ring because she didn't have a body to bury instead."

Madeline started telling one of her stories, elaborating on the summary she'd given me. I could tell it was one she had rehearsed so many times and her gaze never faltered from the ring on her hand, which she twirled around her finger as she spoke. Like a lot of Madeline's stories it centred on a girl who had to be brave and independent because of the lack of reliable men – men who would go off to war and get killed, or be tempted by other women. Sometimes these girls had magical powers and put curses on those who made them miserable.

"Maddy, are you up there? Do you want to come for a dance?"

A light, high voice came up from the bottom of the stairs cutting right into the tragedy Madeline was trying to create for her bereaved character. Madeline furrowed her brow, rolled her eyes and then pulled herself off the bed into the hallway. She stood at the top of the stairs to respond.

"Mum, I told you, I've brought my friend home for tea." She spoke through her teeth, her knuckles white where she grasped the banister.

"Oh you have? That's delightful. Let me come say hello."

I heard her bounding up the stairs and, before Madeline could get in her way, a tall, wispy woman was stood in her bedroom doorway smiling down at me.

"Hello," she said. "I'm Maddy's Mum. So pleased to meet you, it's nice that she has a friend." She offered me a pale hand, which I took though it felt far too formal. Then she curtsied, holding up her tie-dyed gypsy skirt with one hand and pulling me up from my seated position with the other.

"My, you are tall," she stated when I came eye to eye with her.

"Thank you," I said, trying to be polite. "I'm Cecelia."

"Would you like to dance Cecelia? I bet you're a fantastic dancer. Don't you think, Maddy?"

Madeline glowered in the hallway.

Her Mum turned back to me. "Well, do you?"

"No one wants to dance Mum," Madeline answered for me. "Besides it's almost tea time. Why don't you go and make us something?"

Her Mum dropped her skirt and my hand, which she had still been grasping throughout her invitation.

"Of course dear, whatever you say, dear," she said, giving the same flick of her golden blonde hair that I'd seen Madeline perform earlier. "I'll call when it's ready then shall I?"

As she had her back to me, returning to the stairs, I didn't see her mother's face but I heard the sarcasm in her tone. Madeline kept her gaze on her Mum as she passed, letting her head follow so she could stare at her until she was out of sight down the stairs. Then, in a flash, Madeline's expression altered and she smiled at me with a little shrug of her shoulders.

"Sorry about that, where were we?" She skipped back into the room, clambering on to the bed and pulling me back down with her. "Oh right, the day she found out her betrothed had been killed..." And she continued with her story as if nothing had disturbed us.

~~~

Tea turned out to be fish fingers, peas and mash potatoes. It was delayed once because Madeline had to run downstairs with a warning when the smoke from the grill started to seep in through her open door.
~~~

"Mum, you've forgotten again," she yelled as she pummelled down the stairs. I hung back, not wanting to see Madeline's embarrassment or the tense conversation I heard snippets of as I reached the bottom of the stairs.

"...I told you not to..."

"...only being myself, can't blame me for that.."

"...what's she going to think?"

"Who cares darling, I'm sure she'll understand. It's only a bit of fish for Pete's sake."

I dawdled in the hallway. Madeline's Mum must have caught a glimpse of me and smiled. "Sorry dear, bit of a technical problem with tea. Be ready soon though." She pushed Madeline into the hall with me. "Why don't you two watch some T.V.?"

I could see Madeline's bottom lip, protruding as if she were a toddler on the brink of a tantrum. "Come on," she said, pushing open the door and stomping into the living room.

"My Dad burns tea all the time," I said, trying to lighten the mood. "Once, he even set fire to a tea towel."

Madeline looked at me. She paid no attention to what I'd just said but after a moment, sighed and turned on the television. "It'll be ready soon."

"Don't we need to wait for your Dad?"

"He usually eats before he gets home. Or he'll have a sandwich when he gets in."

"Oh," I replied. I thought it odd that they didn't eat together as a family. My confusion increased when Madeline's Mum called us through to the kitchen to eat and she had only set two places.

"Not hungry," she declared when she saw my expression. I glimpsed the empty packet of fish fingers on top of the bin and watched her scrape a measly amount of mash potato from the pan onto Madeline's plate.

"Thank you," I said as I sat down. It felt awkward, not helped by the fact that Madeline and her mother appeared to be ignoring one another; her Mum leaning up against a counter and Madeline pushing peas around her fish fingers.

The sound of the front door opening and closing seemed like sweet relief after listening to myself chew the meal in front of me, trying to figure out if I should make conversation or not. A short, portly man with balding ginger hair strode into the kitchen wearing a grubby shirt. His heavy boots made a thumping sound as he walked. He went straight to a cupboard, retrieved a glass from one shelf and a bottle of liquor from another. It wasn't until Madeline piped up with 'hello Dad,' that he saw us.

"Oh hi there," he said, staring at me. He paused in his unscrewing of the bottle cap and grinned at me. I could see the resemblance between him and Madeline; the pale skin, pointed nose and rounded cheeks, not to mention the hair.

"This is Cecelia, Madeline's friend." Her Mum introduced me, then exited the room. The air felt heavy, as though it had suddenly become static. I felt a frizz of electricity pass between Madeline's parents as her Mum brushed passed her father. Madeline's plate scraped across the table.

"I'm done." It seemed like she had barely eaten. "Want to come back to my room?" she asked, even though I was cutting up a fish finger, trying not to stare at her Dad.

"Give her chance, Madeline," he said, returning to his bottle.

Madeline leaned back in her chair, arms folded. I stuffed in three more mouthfuls and then announced I was done.

"Let's go." Madeline was out of the kitchen and half way up the stairs before I'd even risen out of my chair.

When I got to her room she was already stretched out on her bed, feet swinging in the air, chin in her hands. "Everything okay?" I asked.

"Yeah, just don't want to spend all your time here with my parents." She pointed to a box on the shelf. "Pass us that, would you?"

I retrieved the box, enjoying the way the silver design caught the light and made it shine, and placed it on the bed next to her.

Opening it, she pulled out shells and pebbles and even a pressed flower, wrapped in tissue paper. "All of these things are from places we've lived. This one was when we had a cottage in the country," she passed me the flower. "This one when we lived next to a beach." She held up the shell.

On it went, a list of all of the different houses they had lived in, in various places around the North. I spent a moment counting all of the keepsakes she laid out before me as she spoke and got up to eleven before we heard a knock at the door downstairs.

Madeline collected all of her objects and deposited them back into their box. By the time we reached the landing I could hear Madeline's Mum saying hello to my Dad.

"Well, if it isn't you," she said with a laugh. "Here for Cecelia I presume?"

"Yes, what a coincidence," Dad replied. I had never realised how deep his voice was, but in comparison to Madeline's Mum's sing-song tone my Dad's was resonant.

We strolled down to them stood face to face in the hallway. Madeline put herself between them which only made her appear even more elf-like than usual. I perched on the bottom step to slip my shoes on.

"Have you been good? Did you behave yourself?" Dad asked me, but looked to Madeline's Mum for the answer. She grinned at him conspiratorially as I fastened up my buckles.

"Here to collect your daughter?" Madeline's Dad appeared behind his wife, his gaze resting on my father over her shoulder. My Dad didn't respond.

"Ready to go sweetie?" he offered me a hand and pulled me to my feet. "Thanks so much for having her over."

Madeline still stood between the adults, her head tilted up with keen eyes darting from one to another.

"Any time," her Mum replied, with a gentle touch of Dad's arm. Madeline suddenly gave an exasperated sigh and pushed past both her parents, disappearing into the living room.

"Bye Madeline," I called out, flattered that she seemed to be so upset to see me go home. "Thank you for tea Mrs Fields," I bowed my head in thanks, thinking she would appreciate the show of respect. But, she wasn't even looking at me. Her gaze was still on Dad, until Mr Fields broke it by putting a hand around her waist.

"Lovely having you over Cecelia. Have a good night."

"Night," Dad said, leading me out with a warm hand around my own. "Hope to see you again sometime."

"Cheerio," Madeline's Mum called out. But Mr Fields was already closing the door.

"Good time?" Dad asked.

"Okay," I shrugged. It hadn't been so dissimilar to being the store cupboard at school. Madeline's parents weren't all that interesting, despite her Mum's strange welcome and the odd atmosphere between the two of them. She certainly didn't seem loony, like the girls at school had said – just gleeful and a bit absent-minded if the scene with the fish fingers was anything to go by. Her Dad was a bit of a grump, but I supposed that it might just have been a bad day. Madeline had been happy to tell stories, just like always.

"Do you think you should return the invitation?" Dad opened the car door for me, which made me smile. I felt like such a lady when he did that.

I didn't really want Madeline to come to our house, to inspect our things and change the memories I had made of all the belongings I had, because that's what I felt she would do. As Dad made his way around the car to the driver's seat I considered how I might be able to get out of inviting her back without it seeming rude. But, as the car started and pulled away, I couldn't justify it.

"I guess I could invite her round," I said. "I'll check with Mum first, though."

Dad reached out and tousled my hair. "Good thinking. Check with the boss first."

I giggled, squirming in my seat and thought of a way to prevent the visit. "I don't know if her Dad would be able to collect her though, he works nights a lot."

"That's all right. I can take her if you want," Dad said. "Anything to help my little girl."

~~~

When I asked Madeline if she wanted to come to my house - Mum gleeful at the possibility of hosting my new friend - I was hoping she'd say no. Overnight I'd tossed at turned at the prospect of spending the rest of school year listening to Madeline wax lyrical about ordinary bric-a-brac that she'd found, only venturing outside to search for new finds. She wasn't even coming up with new material anymore. At her house she'd told me two stories that I'd already heard. What had seemed different and interesting before suddenly took on a tiring monotony. I missed the carefree gossip of the group of friends I used to have.

But, with a huge grin on her face and dimples in her cheeks Madeline accepted my invitation with enthusiasm. It seemed the visit home had been a success that validated our friendship. I had no idea what we would do if her parents consented and she could come to my house on Friday evening, so I held out hope that she wouldn't be allowed.

No such luck. Friday morning brought a bouncy Madeline into class and even bigger dimples as she twitched with excitement at meeting my family.

"What's your brother like?" she asked as we sat sharing our lunches in the store cupboard.

"Annoying."
~~~

"How?"

I shrugged. The store room had lost its appeal. I'd realised that we were just hiding now. "Like a thirteen year boy I guess." I hadn't ever really thought much about how Eric behaved, just that he teased me and I didn't like it.

"Well, is he like the prince from the story about the forgotten princess or more like the wizard in the frog tale?"

"Like the kid in the cowboy story, who hides under the hay," I replied.

"Really?" Madeline shuffled through various belongings in a box. "What's it like, having a brother?"

I pursed my lips. Madeline had never asked these types of questions before. "I dunno," I shrugged. "It's okay I guess. We have to share everything, which is rubbish. But sometimes we can convince Mum and Dad to buy us stuff together."

"Does your Dad go out a lot?"

"Not really. Sometimes, I guess. At the weekend, for drinks with his mates. Why?"

"Just wondered," Madeline replied. Despite asking the questions, she didn't seem interested in the answers and she chose an object and changed the subject. We fell back into a routine. I sighed under my breath and zoned out as she suggested that the troll figure had been bought by a teacher as a present for his son, whom he couldn't visit anymore because he'd ruined their family by having an affair. When the bell rang, I was relieved and had to hide a yawn. I was sick of the dry air in the cupboard and the sound of Madeline's voice. But what could I do, I had no other friends.

By the time the bell went at the end of the day, I'd picked myself up in the excited atmosphere that crackled between the class at the prospect of the oncoming weekend. Madeline seemed affected by it too, as she was out of the room and in the corridor before I'd even put my pencils away.

"Let's go," she called out to me as she hurried up the school drive. "Which way?"

I laughed at her eagerness but was puzzled by it too. She scurried along beside me not even bothering to scan the pavement for hidden treasures.

"That's it, on the end there," I pointed to my house, a corner semi, and Madeline's jaw fell open at the sight of it.

"It's so big," she said.

"Not really," I pushed open the gate and made my way down the path. Madeline continued to stand out on the pavement. "Coming?" I asked.

She blinked, then nodded. "Are you guys rich or something?"

I laughed. "No."

Having been to Madeline's house I realised that my family was better off than hers. I put it down to the fact that only her father seemed to work, whereas both my parents had jobs. I let myself in, calling out to Mum as I did so. She appeared a second later in the hall.

"Hello girls," she grinned down at us. "Hi Madeline, I'm Cecelia's Mum."

I took a second to try and look at Mum as Madeline would see her: a slightly plump woman with brown curly hair and a strong, pointed nose. Madeline gazed up at her and mumbled a hello. I hadn't expected her to be so shy.

"We okay to play in my room until tea Mum?"

"Sure thing sweetie. Your Dad will be home in an hour."

Mum nodded at us with a smile still playing on her lips. I poked Madeline in the ribs.

"Coming?"

She was disturbed from her reverie long enough to follow me up the stairs. I led her to my room, banging on Eric's door along the way to tell him to turn his music down. Some indiscriminate sounds were blaring from behind it and they suddenly got louder as the door opened and a pillow emerged from it, hitting Madeline squarely in the face.

"Hey!" I yelled.

Eric appeared at the open door. "Crap. Sorry. It was meant for Cissy." He retrieved the pillow from the floor and hit me with it. "You okay?" he asked Madeline.

"I'll live," she snapped. She cocked her head to one side, listening out for something. "Isn't that Michael Jackson?"

Eric beamed. "Yup. Do you like him?"

"He's a bit weird, but he can dance I guess."

I felt suddenly alienated. Madeline was supposed to be my friend and Eric was monopolising her. I also had no idea that Madeline knew anything about music.

"His moonwalk is spectacular," gushed Eric, attempting – unsuccessfully – to mimic his hero's signature move. Madeline laughed. I had never heard this laugh before; a light giggling that involved her tipping her head slightly and letting her long red hair dangle over her back.

"Just keep the noise down will you," I ordered. I grabbed Madeline's wrist to coerce her into my room.

"Sorry about him," I said. "He's stupid."

"Boys are," she agreed, with a final glance out of the door as I closed it. "Have you ever kissed a boy?"

My mouth dropped open in shock. This was the type of question that my other friends often asked of each other, making it off limits for Madeline. Even in her stories the heroine rarely ended up with the valiant prince in a typical mushy romantic way. There was hardly ever any kissing – unless it was initiated by the girl.

Madeline was awaiting my response, a serious expression on her face.

I answered with an embarrassed shake of my head, then recalled something redeeming that one of my friends had once said to make it seem less so. "But there isn't a boy I want to kiss, so it isn't so bad."

Madeline nodded. "Me neither," she said. "The boys we go to school with are big babies and all they care about is football."

There was a moment of silence as I hesitated to ask the same question back. "Have you ever met a boy you would like to kiss, even not at school?"

"Once, at the train station," she admitted. "He helped me reach a watch someone had dropped down the side of a notice board. It was broken but it was such a pretty watch, it had Mickey Mouse on the front. My Dad thinks it's just the battery that needs replacing."

I urged her on, reminding her of the boy instead of the find.

"He was quite tall, broad shoulders with longish blond hair and these amazing blue eyes. He had really soft hands too." She smiled, nostalgia infecting her.

"What was his name?"

"I don't know. I didn't get chance to ask, 'cause his friends were waiting. I thought he might ask me but..." she paused, looking down at her hands that were fiddling with my blanket. She shrugged.

"Never mind," I said. A silence stretched between us and I searched for something to say that would keep us on the present topic. "At least boys notice you."

Madeline looked up sharply. "You think so?"

"Sure, you're pretty and interesting and you have some beautiful dresses." The lie fell easily off my tongue. It wasn't all untrue, she was pretty in an elfin way but I knew my school friends thought of her as boring and odd, those hand me down dresses not helping her style.

"Wow, really?" she asked again. "Most of the time I just feel invisible. I mean, you have all these friends in school and I sometimes wonder why you'd rather hang out with me than them."

I smiled, pleased that Madeline had seen the sacrifice I'd made for her. We giggled together and started picking out who we might let kiss us.

"What about Eric?" Madeline asked after a few other names had been considered.

I continued to laugh, as we had been in hysterics throughout, and it took me a moment. "Eric? You mean smelly Eric who used to sit next to you? Ewww!"

"No, I mean Eric. Eric, your brother."

I stopped laughing immediately. "What?"

Madeline's face was too serious and her blue eyes met my brown ones for a whole five seconds. I didn't know what to say. *Why would Madeline want to kiss my brother?* Eric was mean and obnoxious and stupid. Then I noticed a slight twitch in Madeline's lip and realised she was holding her breath. Her eyes sparkled and she raised an eyebrow.

"Ewwww," I gasped. "That's disgusting."

She fell back, laughing. "Got ya," she announced triumphantly. "As if I'd kiss a boy who can't even do the moonwalk."

There was a knock at the door and without waiting for permission Eric tumbled in. His sudden presence made us laugh even harder, so much so that Madeline's face turned bright red.

"What's up with you two?" he asked, before shaking his head at our idiocy. "Dad's home."

Madeline stopped laughing first, just as Eric bolted from the room. "Does that mean it's time for dinner?"

"Almost," I replied. "Dad likes to have five minutes peace first. But, we can go down and say hullo." I got up and started out of the room but Madeline didn't follow. "You okay?"

"Where's the bathroom?"

"There," I pointed across the hall. "Want me to wait?"

"No, I'll be down in a second."

"Where's your friend?" Dad asked as I stepped into the living room.

"In the loo," I replied, giving Dad a hasty kiss on the cheek. He gave me a hug back.

"How was school? Any homework?"

"Nope. It was okay, but boring. Work is too easy so I got it all done in class."

"That's my girl," he ruffled my hair tenderly.

We heard the patter of feet on the stairs then a gentle knock on the door.

"Enter," Dad bellowed, and I elbowed him in the ribs.

"Hi," she whispered.

"Hello again," replied my Dad, a big goofy grin on his face. His nose wrinkled when he smiled and his brown eyes sparkled. "How was your day Madeline?"

"Excuse me?" Madeline looked shocked. Suddenly she seemed shy and demure, not at all like the strong outspoken girl I knew.

"Come and sit with us and tell us how school was."

She wandered into the room keeping the coffee table between us but never taking her gaze from my Dad.

"School is pretty boring," Madeline replied.

"Looking forward to starting high school after the summer?"

She shrugged.

"How's your mother?"

Madeline scowled at him. "Fine. Why?"

Dad glanced across at me. I raised my eyebrows as if to mimic his confusion. "Cece told us she wasn't well last week."

"Oh," Madeline's shoulders relaxed. "No, she's better now. Thanks for asking."

"Dinner's ready!" Mum popped her head around the door. "Everyone wash up. It'll be on the table by the time you get back."

Dad escaped to the kitchen. Madeline and I thundered back upstairs to wash our hands. As the tap was running, Madeline said, "Your Dad seems nice."

"He's all right, I guess." I stole a glance across at Madeline, intent on washing her hands. "He's just a teacher. Nothing interesting like a policeman."

Madeline's face changed with a grin widening her cheeks and her eyes lighting up. "Ooh, I forgot," she whispered. "I heard that Mrs Collin's son got arrested."

"What?" I extended my hands, drips of water flying through the air. "Which one?" Mrs Collin's had two sons, one who was fourteen and another at nineteen.

"The oldest one. He hit a policeman. My Dad had to handcuff him and everything."

"Wow," I breathed.

"C'mon slow pokes," Eric cried, banging on the door. "I'm starving."

We slipped out of the bathroom and trundled down the stairs with no time to ask more questions. Eric overtook us in the hall, wiping his hands on his trousers.

"What's for dinner?" he asked, catapulting himself into a chair.

"Nothing special," Mum replied. "Just spaghetti and meatballs." She looked across at Madeline. "Your Mum said you really like them. I hope mine are okay."

Madeline's eyes widened. "You spoke to my Mum?" she asked.

"Last night," Mum answered. "She called to confirm you were coming over. Nothing to worry about," she added when she saw the expression on Madeline's face.

Madeline smiled back, mouth closed and lips slightly pouted. "I'm sure the meatballs will be great Mrs Watts."

"How many?"

"Five, can I have five?" Eric said.

"Guests first dear." Mum spooned three meatballs onto Madeline's plate.

"That's great, thanks."

"Are you sure? I made plenty."

Madeline nodded as Eric insisted he would eat any extra. Mum piled several meatballs on Eric and Dad's plate before rolling some from the spoon onto my own. Madeline's meal looked meagre in comparison. Three meatballs sat atop small hill of spaghetti. I watched as she gingerly brought the first mouthful up toward her delicate lips. Her eyes darted from the plate to my Dad, to Mum and back to the plate again. Just as she placed the food into her mouth our eyes met and I smiled warmly.

I tucked into my own meal. It was delicious and before I was halfway through Eric had already finished and was bothering Mum for more.

"You'll have to wait Eric, until we're all finished," Mum protested, although usually she would have already provided him with more mid-meal.

"Madeline, are the meatballs up to scratch?"

All eyes turned to her, this petite redhead imp that was perched at our family table, looking out of place. Our entire family was tall and both Dad and Eric were broad shouldered. Such proportions made Madeline look even smaller than usual, although it seemed to heighten her features – making her face seem like a porcelain doll, blue eyes stuck open, staring ahead.

Madeline made a dramatic tilt of her head and pursed her lips. "They're great. Thank you."

I glanced at her plate. The contents were spread across it, meatballs decimated and in bits. I estimated that she had eaten one at most.

"I'm glad," replied my Mum, also lowering her eyes from Madeline's face to her plate.

Before Mum could comment further, Dad jumped in with a query. "So, Madeline, your Dad's on the police force, eh?"

Madeline nodded, carefully spooning a small portion of food into her mouth.

"What's it like?" asked Eric. "Having a policeman as a Dad? Do you have to be on your best behaviour all the time? Me and

Cissy do – what with Dad being a teacher." Eric chattered on, oblivious to Dad's glare. "It must be worse with the Law in the house."

My parents laughed. I smiled too.

"It's okay," Madeline answered. "I don't see him much, he's so busy catching bad guys. But I guess he's pretty strict – depends on what you mean by it." She was pushing the food around on her plate, not even pretending any more.

"It's a very noble profession," Dad said, laying a hand over Madeline's. "I'm sure it takes up his time. There are so many bad guys to catch. I bet he does a great job."

Madeline was transfixed on Dad's hand as he patted her own gently then removed it. "What about your Mum? What does she do?"

Madeline's fork slipped from her fingers and clattered onto her plate. "She doesn't work," Madeline whispered. "She's…"

"A housewife?" Mum jumped in, sensing Madeline's discomfort. "That must be nice. I struggle to keep up with all the chores even though I only work part time."

"Ah," Dad smiled. "But you're out saving babies all day," he said. "Housework should take second place."

"I work for a charity," Mum explained. "Helping to find parents for orphaned babies."

It wasn't quite that simple. The charity was one who counselled rape victims and, on occasion, helped to organise adoptions for those who had become pregnant as a result and decided not to keep the baby. It wasn't a fun job, she told me, but she did it because it was rewarding: she felt like she was giving something back. I was proud of her for that. It gave me something to aspire to.

Eric moved on from his request for seconds. "Any dessert Mum?"

Mum shook her head with a smile, glancing at Eric. I noticed Madeline watching her and then following her gaze to my brother. For a second Eric's face fell.

"You're kidding?" he gasped.

Mum laughed then, "Of course there's dessert." She turned to Madeline. "Would you like some ice cream?"

Madeline's eyes dropped to her plate, food still mashed up and then stared back at my Mum.

"Mads doesn't really like ice cream all that much do you?" I said.

Madeline let out the breath she had been holding and shrugged apologetically. "Not really."

"Who doesn't like ice cream?" Eric asked. Madeline coloured, a slight blush to her cheeks.

"All the more for Eric then, eh?" Dad chimed in, glaring at Eric and then patting Madeline's hand again.

"Cecelia can have my share," Madeline said with a smile at my Dad.

"Really?" I grinned. "You hear that Mum?" I yelled through to the kitchen. "I get extra, not Eric."

Mum brought the ice cream out, my bowl filled by the extra scoop. Eric sighed with a dramatic flair until he realised he'd got extra too.

"Whoever finishes last has to help with the washing up," Dad said.

"Harry, I don't think that's such a good idea," Mum replied as Eric and I glared at one another over our bowls.

"They'll be fine," he said. "Ready? Go."

We set to eating at once. I was determined not to lose, despite the brain freeze I could feel creeping across my forehead. Madeline had sacrificed her share of ice cream for me, not to mention saved me from the wrath of the Deputy Head, so I'd win it for her sake. I crammed in another mouthful and the cold burnt my tongue.

"Calm down, Cece," Dad warned. "You'll make yourself sick."

I grinned across at Madeline and shrugged. "Not going to let Eric beat me."

Dad chuckled and Madeline cheered me on. "C'mon Cece, you can manage it."

I watched Eric wolf down his ice cream. A pale yellow drip was making its way down his chin. I glanced into his bowl. Mum had given him more than me after all. This meant I was in with a chance. I shovelled another spoonful into my mouth.

"One more to go Cece," Madeline said. "You can do it."

I scraped the spoon on the dish and licked the final remnants from it. My breath felt cold and my head was pounding, but it wasn't so bad. I had won.

"Eric's my helper then," Dad confirmed. "Why don't you girls go upstairs and play for a while."

Eric groaned, letting the last of his own dessert slip back into the bowl. "No fair, I had more than Cecelia."

Dad shrugged and winked at me and Madeline. "Can't get the staff these days."

I jumped down from my seat and grabbed Madeline's hand. "C'mon, I'll show you my new tape player."

We ran upstairs whispering and giggling about Eric's messy technique. Once in my room I put some music on and we jumped on the bed for a while. I sang along - I knew every word - and Madeline contributed the occasional whoop. Soon though, I began to feel funny. My belly rumbled and churned and I had to stop us both from rocking the bed. I felt like I was out at sea on a ship that was being tossed and turned by storm-fuelled waves.

"I don't feel so well," I managed, before dessert reappeared on my sheepskin rug.

"Yuck," Madeline yelped, retreating to the safety of the doorway. "I'll go get your Dad."

A few minutes later both my parents were shuffling me into bed. Eric hovered in the doorway with a smirk on his face. I saw

Madeline elbow him in the ribs and narrow her eyes at him. He went back to his own room then.

"I'd better get Madeline home," Dad said, as he folded up the rug and carefully placed it into a bin liner.

"Don't throw it away, it's my favourite," I protested.

"We'll have to wait and see if I can wash it." Mum opened the window as she spoke. "I told you that ice cream eating competition wasn't a good idea Harry."

Dad rolled his eyes behind Mum and he smiled at Madeline with an outstretched arm, leading her down the hall. "Come on Madeline, let's let Cecelia rest. I'll take you home."

"Hope you feel better soon," Madeline called out, but my eyes were already closing. Too much excitement and ice cream. I think I heard Dad say that to Madeline as they left, but I couldn't be sure. I snuggled down in my duvet and concentrated on the comfort of Mum stroking my hair.

~~~

When I woke up it was dark and cold. The wind from the open window made my curtains bellow. I pulled a blanket around my shoulders and peered at my watch in the orange glow of the light coming from the lamp post on my street. It was only nine o'clock. I padded my way to the window, planning to close it but wrinkling my nose at the stale, sweet smell of vomit and ice cream. Just as I was considering turning back to bed I heard voices. My parents were talking in hushed tones at the bottom of the stairs and their conversation wafted in through my door.

"Nothing happened."

"Then why would she say it?"

"I don't know. All I did was drive her home."

"You were gone a long time Harry," Mum said. "Longer than necessary."
~~~

There was a long pause and I peered out of the doorway, jumping back when I heard a clap and then a soft thump.

"So you think I did it?" Dad's voice was vicious and thick with accusation. I'd never heard him speak like that before.

"No, no of course not," Mum's voice was muffled, as though she was crying.

I heard a screech of tyres on tarmac and a car pulled up outside. I scurried over to the window, the blanket falling around my feet and I looked down. In the murky light I could see Madeline's father, climbing out of his haphazardly parked car. He didn't even shut the door before storming up to our porch.

"Are you in there, you coward," he yelled, pounding on the door.

My stomach tightened suddenly and I felt sick again. Despite retrieving the blanket and pulling it around me I felt cold and goose bumps rose on my arm. *Why is Madeline's father here? And why is he banging on our door?*

I rushed into the hallway intending to call out for Mum, but when I got there Eric was standing next to the banister, peering down.

"Go home," Dad called out. "I didn't do anything."

The banging became insistent. As Eric looked up our gaze met and Mr Fields screamed through the door.

"Don't you dare deny what you did to my little girl, you monster. You get out here and face me like a man."

Mum was sobbing by then, big gasping breaths that brought tears to my eyes. Eric reached out and grasped my hand. I leaned over the two top stairs to try and catch a glimpse of our parents. Eric tried to pull me back, but I used his grip as leverage and leaned out until I could see Dad. He was holding the telephone out to Mum.

"Call the police."

Mum's face was streaked with tears and she looked pale except for a red stain on her cheek partially hidden by wild hair. Dad was stony-faced and his cheeks flushed. For a moment there was silence and the whole world stopped.

Abruptly, the moment ended and Mr Fields' low, guttural voice sounded from outside.

"I'll get you for this," he warned. "No one should be allowed to do what you did to my little girl."

What had he done? I didn't understand. Eric jolted me back onto the landing and I collapsed into his arms. There was a crack and a bang and we realised Mr Fields was kicking the door. I gripped onto Eric to try and stop myself from shaking.

I heard the distant sound of my Mum on the telephone, repeating our address, telling them about a madman at our door. The kicking became a relentless rhythm of thuds.

"Harry," Mum pleaded with him, for what I didn't know.

"Go and make sure the kids are okay," he ordered.

Eric pushed me back toward my room and I tripped my way back into bed. I squeezed my eyes shut with the blanket pulled up to my chin. I sensed Mum at the door before the click of the handle signalled that it was closed. I hopped out of bed and put my ear to the wood. I could hear Eric asking her what was going on.

"Shhh, nothing. Go to bed," she repeated it twice. I could picture her standing at the top of the stairs, knowing she hadn't moved to go down because of the creak on the second step.

Sirens wailed from outside and I covered my ears. They were so close my head thrummed with their rhythm. The kicking on the door stopped a beat after the sirens did. The sudden quiet felt weighty and the air in my room felt thick in my lungs. A gentle rapping started up and I heard the front door opening. I strained to hear, closing my eyes to better focus on the voices below.

"Mr Watts, we'd like to speak with you about an incident being reported by Mr Fields' daughter. Can we come in?"

He must have taken them into the kitchen, at the back of the house, because I didn't hear any more than that. Mum rushed downstairs and then I darted to the window to see Mr Fields being folded back into his car by a young policeman. Their voices drifted up to my window but I couldn't make out what they said.

"I think Madeline's being telling stories," Eric whispered behind me.

He startled me so much I nearly fell out of the open window.

"What?"

"She's told the police something about Dad," he said.

"She wouldn't do that." The image of her standing with her chin jutting out, threatening to tell the Headmistress about Mr Grogon's activity in the store cupboard flashed in my mind. She had been so different when faced with that danger, not the shy little girl I'd brought home for tea.

"She lied about Tom."

"Who?" I gripped onto the blanket around my shoulders.

"Earlier on, when she said Tom Collins was arrested for hitting a policeman. He wasn't."

I pushed passed him to clamber back into bed. Eric stood stoically in the middle of my room. Madeline was my friend, he didn't know her. "How would you know?"

"I'm mates with his little brother." Eric's eyes narrowed at me. "Tom saw some copper beat up a guy with a prossie. He went to the Station to give a witness statement. He never got arrested."

I opened my mouth to defend Madeline but no words came out. Eventually I pushed some out: "Maybe she got mixed up?"

"Maybe she's mixed up about what happened with Dad too." Eric's jaw was taut and he spoke through clenched teeth.

"She wouldn't say something that wasn't true," I said, trying to convince myself. *But how many stories have I heard her tell?*

"Whatever," Eric threw his comment over his shoulder as he went back to his room. "She's said something he's in trouble for."

I listened for more voices on the landing, but almost forty minutes went by and there was nothing except the occasional gruff tone I recognised as Dad's when he was angry. Something serious had happened, but I didn't understand what, or why Madeline would want to get my Dad into trouble. I crawled back into bed, the exhaustion from the day and weariness from my earlier bout of sickness making my eyelids heavy.

I must have slept, because the next thing I knew it was morning and Mum was tapping on my door telling me to wake up.

"There's a policewoman down stairs who wants to ask you some questions, Cecelia," she explained. My breath caught in my throat. "You're not in trouble. It's just," Mum sighed. "Your friend has said some things about your Dad that need clearing up."

I remembered the shouting and banging from last night. The fear of it rose in my belly again and the thought that Madeline had lied about Tom settled in my mind.

"But she's always making up stories about people," I explained. "She does it all the time at school."

Mum scrutinised me, her eyes red and puffy and cheeks rosy as she knitted her eyebrows together at my comment. "Is that true?" she asked.

I nodded until my neck hurt. "All the time. She said our Head of Year was a witch and that the gardener killed the class pets for fertiliser."

"Well," Mum replied, her pace slow. "You tell the policewoman that and maybe it will help your father."

I jumped out of bed and pulled on some clothes eager to help Dad not be in trouble.

"As long as it's true," Mum added.

"It is. I promise," I said, rushing down the stairs. All I wanted was to help Dad, to make sure he didn't get into any trouble. And it was the truth. I didn't ever think that telling the truth would harm anyone. I told the policewoman how Madeline and I became friends, the stories she'd tell and how she'd stood up to the Deputy Head when he caught us in the store cupboard –

although, I left out the part about him being with a woman, I didn't think that was important.

"Do you have any proof that Madeline likes to tell stories sometimes?" the woman asked, fiddling with the buttons on her blouse. Her voice was soft and she talked at me by looking through her eyelashes as she bent in front of me.

"Yes, back at school," I said. "Sometimes we write them down in notebooks."

It had been Madeline's idea to record them, to use the spare books to make notes about the adventures she would tell so we could pick up where we left off each day.

"That's good, Cecelia. Thank you for telling me." She stood up, Mum behind her with a blank expression.

"It's not much, but it something," the policewoman told her. "It could help." Mum just nodded and I noticed a tissue crumpled in her hand.

"What story did she tell about Dad?" I asked. But I never got an answer, not from my parents.

That weekend Eric and I were sent to our grandparents, the trip being presented as a treat for good behaviour. I knew that's not what it was, because of the surprised stare I'd endured when I told the policewoman Madeline and I spent every break and lunch time in the cupboard instead of outside, like we were meant to be. I tried to talk to Eric about it, but I think he'd been instructed not to say anything. He got irritated when I asked.

"Leave it alone, Cissy," he sneered. "They're sorting it out. It'll all be fine." Every time he looked at me I could tell he was imagining needles in my eyes. "No thanks to your stupid friend." He checked Grandma wasn't looking then shoved me with his shoulder, harder than if he was playing. "Don't you dare hang out with her any more. I told you she was a liar."

We didn't go to school on Monday. Instead Grandma and Grandpa took us to Whitby for the day. I tried to enjoy the fish and chips but they left a greasy film in my mouth and the gulls were vicious as they ripped leftovers from my fingertips.

"Do you want ice cream?" Grandpa asked.

Eric glared at me. "No," I sighed. "I got sick last time I had ice cream."

Grandma put an arm around me. "Oh dear, when was that sweetie?"

"On Friday. It's why I couldn't take Madeline home with Dad."

The wind whipped off the sea and disturbed the papers on our knees. Out of the corner of my eye I noticed my grandparents exchange a glance and then a slight shake of the head from my Grandpa. No one would say anything about Madeline again.

PART II

THAT WHICH IS LEFT

There is a gentle tapping from behind and Chris turns to see Betsy hovering in the doorway.

"My family was never the same after that." Cecelia is crying and Chris leans forward to pass her a tissue. She takes it but carries on talking, having not raised her head to the sound of Betsy's knock. She is still anchored in the past.

"It wasn't hard to figure it out: when I went back to school I had to deal with snide remarks and the embarrassment that came with an accusation like the one Madeline made. The fact my father was a teacher made it all much worse. We moved away a few weeks later because we couldn't handle the rumours. Then my mother left him and changed our names to her maiden name, which made us all wonder."

Betsy takes a step inside the room. "I'm sorry, Doctor." She bites her lip. "Your wife is on the phone."

Chris looks between Betsy and Cecelia and then shakes his head. "Tell her I'm busy. I'll call her back."

"It's the third time."

Chris tenses.

Betsy cautiously clears her throat. "She said something about dinner tonight."

Cecelia sniffs and forms an apologetic smile. "I'm fine. Go."

"No." He places a gentle hand on Cecelia's shoulder and he feels her trembling. "Tell her you couldn't find me," he says to Betsy.

As soon as Betsy closes the door Cecelia's tears flow like miniature streams down her cheeks. She pulls at the tissue he offered her. "How can I possibly forgive her for tearing my family apart?"

Chris remains silent. There is nothing he can say that will make a difference.

"My Dad didn't help himself, he spent so long trying to convince us that what she said wasn't true and we just ignored him. And after he was jailed for abusing those college girls," she shrugs. "Well, that just seemed to prove everything. I didn't even go and see him before he died. Eric did though. He said Dad still protested his innocence about Madeline though he admitted all the rest. Eric believed him, but I couldn't." Cecelia's expression hardens. "I took Madeline's side after his conviction. I always felt obligated to help her. But now I see she must have been using me. Like she used my father; to get attention, to tell a story, to be remembered in some sick, twisted way."

She collapses back onto the sofa, stretching her neck to look up at the ceiling. Chris lets the stale truths hang over them for a moment and then takes a deep breath.

"Cecelia, Madeline called you in response to our insistence that she needs some support, a friend to help her through these last few days and to help her make medical decisions about the end of her life. I'm sorry for the difficult situation that this puts you in but Madeline would like your opinion on whether she should sign a Do Not Resuscitate order."

Cecelia raises her head and narrows her eyes at him, they still have the sheen of sadness but the tears have dried up.

Betsy slips back into the room carrying a tray with two steaming mugs: a peace offering, perhaps, for storming out earlier. Chris nods his thanks and Cecelia pounces on the packets of sugar and begins to tear them up to pour several into her tea. He glances up at Betsy and slots in a brief conversational marker for her.

"It means that we wouldn't pursue extraordinary measures to preserve her life were those circumstances to arise."

"I know what it means," Cecelia snaps. She stirs her over-sweetened drink with a ferocious clatter. "Will she die anyway?"

Chris nods. The mood has changed. "Another round of radiation and chemotherapy would extend her life, but not save it. Without these I would estimate she only has a week at best."

"Will it be painful?"

Cecelia's eyes are focused firmly on the swirling motion of the tea. Betsy gingerly takes the seat next to her. "We can keep her comfortable for the most part."

With a quick swipe of her hand the tearful stains are brushed away and Cecelia sits up straight and squares her shoulders. "What would you suggest?"

"As her doctor he can't recommend one form of treatment over another. It's is a discussion you should have with Madeline, in order to ensure you both realise the consequences of the outcomes available."

Chris has to stop himself from wincing. Based on what he's just heard, Cecelia is unlikely to want a conversation with Madeline ever again. So when Cecelia takes a long swig of her drink and stands it surprises him.

"Then let's go see her," she announces.

Betsy smiles, ignorant of the magnitude of what has just been revealed, but her smile falters when Cecelia adds: "I'd like the opportunity to tell her to rot in hell face to face. I'm done helping her."

Chris pulls a hand down his face and the stubble on his chin prickles his palm before he rises to his feet. Is this what Madeline wants? He has no idea.

Chris leads them to Madeline's room. The only sound is the stark tapping of their feet against the tiled floor. Cecelia lips are drawn in and her eyes stare downward. Her footsteps slow as they approach and Chris can hear short gasping breaths that lengthen as they reach Madeline's door.

"I can't do it," she says. "I want her to die. I can't help it. I don't need to see her again to know that I hate her."

"Cecelia," Chris lays a hand on her arm. Beneath the long-sleeved shirt she has stopped shaking but is now rigid, with rage or fear Chris can't tell. "If you have questions, now might be the only chance you get for answers."

This buoys her on and she strides forward into the room after Betsy. Chris takes a moment with his head bowed. He hopes he's encouraging her to do the right thing.

"Cece," Madeline makes an attempt to sit up in bed and smiles at her friend as though their last meeting never happened. Betsy rushes across to help her.

"Why, Mads?" Cecelia pushes the words out through a tight jaw. "Why lie?"

Madeline shrugs. "It would have happened eventually. It did happen eventually. He was a paedophile Cecelia. When I accused him he was just a terrible, terrible man." She sucks in a breath through her mouth. "You thought you knew him but you didn't. He proved me right in the end, so what does it matter now?"

Cecelia throws her arms out. "It matters to me," she yells. "It mattered to my mum and to Eric and to the school he worked for. It mattered to the press and the police and the entire neighbourhood." She growls the last two words; "It matters."

Madeline casts a glance at Chris. The corners of her mouth twitch upward. Could she be enjoying this?

Madeline refocuses her gaze on Cecelia. "It's the past Cece. It's not going to change anything. Harry's still going to be remembered as a man who abused young girls. You're still going to hate your mother for leaving him and I'm still going to die." She pauses for another breath and tilts her head to the side. "I can do that quickly, if you'd like. If I sign that piece of paper they won't be able to save me, would you like that Cece? To see me go without being saved?"

Betsy raises a hand to her mouth and her wide-eyed gaze travels from Madeline to Chris. Chris is only surprised at how direct she is.

"He killed himself Mads, can you understand that? He died because he couldn't face what you drove him to do."

Madeline closes her eyes and shakes her head, as though frustrated that Cecelia can't comprehend her reasoning. A white pallor creeps across her face and tiny beads of sweat appear on her forehead. "He wasn't the man you wanted him to be Cecelia, I didn't want you to have to learn that too late."

"How dare you say this was for my benefit." Cecelia lunges for her, but Chris catches her around the waist before her outstretched hands reach his patient. The worst she is able to do is tug at Madeline's IV line.

Madeline flinches as the needle is yanked out and cradles her arm, but it doesn't stop her from talking. "Accept the truth Cece. You were lucky I was such a good friend."

Cecelia strains to escape Chris' grasp. An elbow catches him in the ribs, winding him. For a second his focus is lost. Cecelia breaks away and screams in Madeline's face.

"You deserve to die all alone with no one there to help you, just like my Dad." Her face is red and wet with tears. Chris clutches at her arm and is relieved when she yields and takes a step away from the bed. But her glare remains fixed on Madeline who sits steadily with a self-satisfied smile. "Sign the damn papers."

Madeline's smile suddenly becomes crooked and her blue eyes widen in panic. She pushes back into the pillow gasping for breath. Her pulsometer marks out an erratic tune as her heart beats wildly. Chris shoves past Cecelia.

"Is it happening?" Cecelia shrieks. "It is isn't it?" It feels like she is screaming right in Chris' ear. "Good!"

He pushes her back and appeals to Betsy. "Get her out of here."

He is grateful that Madeline hasn't yet signed the DNR and does everything he can to ensure that Cecelia's words are not the last she ever hears.

~~~

Half an hour later, Chris exits Madeline's room with a tired sigh. Madeline is in critical condition, her lungs slowly filling with fluid. Some might argue that his decision to drain the fluid is one to extend her life. Chris feels it is justified given the circumstances.

Cecelia is waiting on a chair down the corridor, her knees drawn up in front of her. Her hair is tangled and face pale. When she sees Chris she stands, though she doesn't look like she will be able to remain upright for long.

"Is she...?"

Chris shakes his head. "No, she's stable for the moment."

There is a mustiness to the air, like the taste of regret. Cecelia keeps her head bowed and she fidgets, pulling at the hem of her shirt, readjusting her watch strap and scratching her cheek.

"I need to see her again. I didn't mean…"

Chris cuts her off so that she doesn't have to say the words. "I don't think that would be a good idea. For either of you." He can see Cecelia wants to protest so he hurries on. "I think you need to go home and rest. You've had a shock. Give it time." He tries to speak gently, but it comes out cold and clinical. He can understand why Cecelia needs to know the reasoning behind Madeline's choices, but he has to put his patient first and Madeline might not survive another heated discussion.

Cecelia's shoulders sag and her knees finally give way. She falls into the chair again.
~~~

"After everything I've done for her over the years. Whenever she needed help I always let her take advantage of me. And it was all a lie."

He takes the seat next to her and places a hand on her knee.

"It can't be easy, knowing that you were betrayed, but you can't change the past. Even now, talking won't bring your father back, it won't change that she lied." These are words he wishes he could accept himself but even as he pauses to let the words sink in for Cecelia he knows they won't do any good. "You should go home and rest."

Cecelia nods. She looks haggard now, not at all like the woman he met earlier that day. He is the one who brought her here, even in spite of Madeline's warning that she wanted to be alone. Madeline may have made the call herself in the end, but if it wasn't for him none of this would have been revealed.

He helps Cecelia up and walks her to the exit. She thanks him on the way.

"I'll be instructing my staff not to allow visitors for Madeline." Cecelia opens her mouth to disagree, but Chris shakes his head. "No visitors. She's not strong enough."

She gives a final shrug and shuffles out of the building.

~~~

A little later, he taps on Madeline's door and is relieved to find her being cared for by Betsy, who is helping her sit up. Madeline's skin is ashen beneath the oxygen mask, but her blue eyes are open and her gaze unnerves him as he approaches.

"Glad to see you're okay."

"Thanks to you, I understand." Her voice is croaky and breathless, her pitch deepened.

He stands just a little bit straighter and raises his chin. He can sense Betsy is looking up at him too but Chris refuses to break eye
~~~

contact with Madeline. He doesn't need to defend himself for doing his job.

"I sent Cecelia home."

"And she went?" Madeline asks, pulling the mask down to her chin.

Chris nods as Betsy lifts the oxygen mask back to Madeline's face. Madeline tries to bat her hand away but the nurse keeps the mask held firm. Eventually Madeline relents with a roll of her eyes, allowing Betsy to position the elastic around her head.

"I told you I deserved this," Madeline says, her voice muffled by the plastic mask. "I heard what she said. I didn't think she had it in her."

"People often do or say reckless things in the heat of the moment."

Betsy brushes down the sheets. "Why did you tell her? She didn't have to know."

"Because she should know. I was the only one that knew the truth, now she knows it too."

There is a moment of quiet while Betsy re-tucks the corners of the bed sheet and Chris wonders if Madeline's motives were so pure.

"What did she say in the end, about the DNR?" Madeline asks.

"She doesn't want you in any more pain that you have to be." It is the nicest way he can think to phrase it.

"So you'll bring me the paper work?"

"I'll go and get it," Betsy offers.

Chris watches her go and then turns back to Madeline.

"Is that the answer you were hoping for?"

Madeline makes an attempt to shrug and her head shifts on the pillow. "I honestly didn't know what she would do. I'm glad she had the courage to make a decision. That's not like the Cece I know. It's good to know she's got a bit of fight in her."

"Betsy is right, you didn't have to tell her. You just wanted to push her away."

Madeline coughs. It sounds light enough, but Chris is conscious of the rattle that indicates her lungs are tight. She shifts the mask and wipes her mouth before speaking.

"It was for her own good. I couldn't die knowing I'd lied to her. I'm not that terrible, Christopher."

Chris grimaces at her use of his name. It reminds him of his wife, and how angry she will be at his ignoring her phone calls. A penny dropped into the well of his mind.

"Are you still married, Madeline? Or are you keeping secrets from Mr Tailor too?"

When Madeline repeats her cough, Chris knows he's hit a nerve. This cough comes from her throat and is dry and weak, not at all like the previous ones. It also gives her an excuse to hide her face from him.

"Cecelia told me what happened. She referred to you as Madeline Fields when you were a girl." Chris waits for a response, but nothing comes and so he must be right. "Does your husband know you're here? Don't you think he'd like to know his wife is dying?

"Oh, I'm sure he'd be fascinated to know just where I am," she says with a crooked smile. Her blue eyes widen as she raises her eyebrows at Chris, as if daring him to ask more.

"So perhaps we could—"

"Call him?" Madeline asks. "If I knew where he was, perhaps."

Chris takes a step closer and reaches out to place a hand on Madeline's arm, a bruise already blooming in the crook of her elbow where the IV was pulled out. "We might be able to track him down, if you gave us some more details."

Madeline laughs, but it turns into a hacking cough half way through and specks of blood appear on the mask. Chris takes it and swiftly cleans it out before settling it back on her face.

Madeline continues as if nothing happened. "No, that isn't necessary. He wouldn't come anyway."

"Are you sure?"

Before Madeline can answer Betsy reappears. She carries a clipboard with the papers to sign. Madeline shuffles herself back into a sitting position and reaches out for the form as if it were a life raft.

Chris intervenes, clasping the clipboard before Madeline can take it. "You do understand this means that we can no longer perform resuscitative measures and that, were you to suffer another incident similar to the one that occurred earlier today, we can't intervene to save your life?"

Madeline nods and snatches the papers from his hand.

"I would very much recommend that you discuss this with your husband, regardless of the situation between you."

"Husband?" Betsy asks.

"We've seen cases where the next of kin turn up once it's too late. It's not an easy situation to manage. You should think about it."

As if in defiance, Madeline signs the sheet with a flourish and then collapses against the bed with a long, rasping sigh. "He'd probably say just the same as Cecelia."

Chris shakes his head. He isn't sure what else he can do to help her. He slides the clipboard and pen out from her slack hands and gestures Betsy away. "We should leave you to rest."

Madeline nods faintly, her eyes already closed. Chris leaves with the worry that she might die in the night alone, regretting her decision to put Cecelia's words in her husband's mouth.

Betsy turns on him as soon as the door is closed. "She has a husband?"

"Educated guess." Chris hands the DNR paperwork to Betsy.

"That's it? We're not going to even attempt to contact him?"

Chris hesitates. He doesn't want to encourage Betsy to get involved any further, she still looks pale and there are dark rims beneath her eyes. "She didn't want to talk about it. And I didn't want to push."

"Because Doctor Gregory is in?"

Chris' stomach flips. There is no board meeting scheduled, which is the only reason Chris can think of that his predecessor would be at Dove Break. Betsy responds to his panicked look.

"I thought you knew. Isn't that why you sent Cecelia home?" He shakes his head. "We can't just let Madeline die alone, she thinks she deserves it, that it's her own fault she doesn't have anyone." Betsy's green eyes lock onto Chris' and her gaze remains on his for a fraction longer than she speaks. Then she lets her eyelids drop and keeps her vision fixed on his shoes. Her voice breaks. "One mistake shouldn't force her to be alone."

Chris gently takes her elbow and steers her away from the Nurses' Station.

"We shouldn't do anything while Doctor Gregory is here. Since the board suspended me, he's looking for any excuse to get rid of me. Someone must have called him." Chris doesn't doubt that Doctor Gregory has allies in some of the long-term nursing staff. He tries to think who might have heard Cecelia screaming at Madeline.

Betsy reaches out to place a hand on his arm. "Then let me help. At least let me look for her husband, make sure we know how to contact him if she changes her mind."

Chris shakes his head.

"Don't worry about Doctor Gregory," Betsy reassures him. "If anything happens, blame it on me. I'm thinking about leaving anyway."

"What? Why?" Chris isn't at all ready for the small kernel of disappointment that settles in his chest.

Betsy glances up and down the corridor and Chris automatically does the same. Another nurse is approaching them. "Could we talk in your office?"

Chris examines the wide-eyed stare of Betsy as she looks up at him through her lashes. *Why would she put her job on the line?* Doctor Gregory probably doesn't even know who she is, she's only been at Dove Break eight months and the first six of those were spent on night shifts. Yet, as soon as Chris completed his two month stint of enforced night shifts Betsy transferred to days. He realises he should have addressed it then.

Chris opens his mouth to say 'yes', intending to encourage her to leave. He doesn't need another distraction. But he doesn't have chance to speak. The nurse, who is only a few steps away, anticipates his movement and she calls out to him before he can guide Betsy to his office.

"There's a telephone call for you, Doctor. It's your wife. She says it's urgent."

Chris frowns. He can't dodge Holly all day, when Betsy interrupted Cecelia's story he recalls that Holly had already called three times.

"We'll talk later?" Chris directs this toward Betsy who has already begun walking away. As he approaches the Nurses' Station telephone he momentarily wonders if she will try and find Madeline's husband on her own. He picks up the receiver.

"Holly?"

"Finally, I've been waiting for ages."

"What's the matter? The nurse said it was urgent."

"I need to know what time you'll be back for dinner tonight."

Chris furrows his brow. "That's it? That's your urgent need to speak to me?" Along the corridor he sees a short, hunched over figure approaching.

"It's important, Christopher. I think I've found—"

The name rankles him and he cuts her off. "You've taken me away from a patient to ask me when I'll be home for dinner?" Chris keeps his gaze on the person nearing Madeline's door. Despite the curve of his back Doctor Gregory's movements are swift and purposeful.

"We need to talk about last night."

"I'm sorry Holly, I'm busy here. You must realise my patients come before dinner plans?"

Holly's breathing is strained. Chris imagines her stood in the kitchen, the phone to her ear and her lips in a tight line.

"This is our marriage. Surely it comes before your job?"

Chris watches Doctor Gregory knock on Madeline's door with a sharp tap and then enter without waiting for permission. Chris glimpses the ring of grey hair that punctuates his liver-spotted head as he disappears into the room. He tightens his grip on the phone as he tries to concentrate on answering Holly's question. But, why does the Vice-Chairman of the board want to speak to Madeline?

"These people are dying, Holly. When I'm here they're my priority."

Chris remembers using the same justification during his board hearing. His mind flashes back to the moment, almost three months ago, when he was disciplined over the Porter case. Doctor Gregory championed his dismissal.

"This is hospice care," Doctor Gregory had stated. "Not social services. You are employed to treat the patient's physical symptoms, their emotional ones are not your concern. You're certainly not expected to identify family members that will interfere with the condition of those patients."

Chris hung his head, even though he hadn't agreed with Doctor Gregory's position. Fortunately, the other - more conservative - members of the board had tempered Doctor Gregory's narrow view. Chris was suspended for seven days and relegated to night shifts for eight weeks thereafter to minimise his contact with patient relatives.

"You're always there, Christopher." Holly's tone is now clipped, caustic and low. "I'm not asking for much, just an answer about dinner. It's not like you're saving lives, is it?"

He bites back his distaste at Holly's comment, his gaze still on Madeline's door which is now firmly shut. With each passing moment Doctor Gregory will be probing for reasons why he should be dismissed. He needs to intervene before Madeline mistakenly says the wrong thing.

"Well?" Holly snaps.

"I'll be home when I'm home," he replies. "I have to go."

He hears Holly yelling his name as he hangs up on her, regretting it almost immediately. But Holly will have to wait. He rushes to Madeline's door, repeating the quick knock and entry he saw Doctor Gregory perform a moment before. Once inside he feigns surprise to see his colleague leaning over the foot of Madeline's bed.

"Doctor Gregory," Chris offers his hand. Doctor Gregory looks down at it with a sneer and turns back to Madeline.

"You contacted Miss Hartland yourself?"

Madeline is laid back on her pillow with a shocking white pallor that contrasts with her short red hair and blue eyes. She glances at Chris and makes an attempt to clear her throat which only serves to start a coughing fit. Chris moves forward to offer some assistance and, once she settles, holds up the oxygen mask that is discarded by her side.

"You're supposed to wear this," he chastises.

Madeline gives him a weak smile. "Doctor Gregory here just popped by to see how I was after my supposed decline following Cece's visit." Her voice is thick and croaky.

"You were warned about interfering on your patient's behalf again, Doctor Wright."

"I was acting on my patient's instruction."

"It's true," Madeline adds.

"Is it also true that your visitor screamed - loud enough for those outside this room to hear - that you deserve to die alone? And that after you recovered from the stress of this visit you immediately signed a Do Not Resuscitate form?" He glares at Chris. "Hardly looking out for your patient, is it?"

"She's my oldest friend. We had a disagreement."

Doctor Gregory ignores Madeline's comment and remains stoically focused on Chris. "You were hired based on your credentials and recommendations, not on your capacity to insert yourself into the lives of your patients. Last time we spoke you had wilfully contacted a patient's relative when specifically instructed not to by his wife. This time I see that you neglected to protect your patient from a similarly tumultuous visit. Which is it Doctor Wright; caring too much, or caring too little?"

Chris holds his tongue knowing that whatever he says will aggravate the elderly doctor further.

"No defence I see," Doctor Gregory shakes his head as he speaks and his lips upturn into a smile.

Chris tries to relax his tensed muscles but they contract with each intake of breath. He's damned if he does, damned if he doesn't. He straightens his posture, allowing him to look down at Doctor Gregory. "I can't be held responsible for the relationship between patients given the emotional difficulty of the situation. Mrs Tailor spoke of signing a DNR since admission and speaking with a friend about this decision - as advised to us by the board - only served to bring into focus the severity of her condition."

Chris glances down at Madeline who looks like she might be sleeping, but beneath half opened lids her keen blue eyes are directly on Doctor Gregory whose smile twitches and flattens out. Chris wonders if she is unnerving the senior physician.

"The board advises a family member be consulted, not simply a friend," Doctor Gregory says, jutting out his chin.

"I don't have any family," Madeline snaps. "Thank you for that reminder."

Chris bites back a smile at Madeline's obvious contempt.

"Which is why we suggested a friend be called into discuss it," Chris adds, concerned that Madeline's short statements are only making her more weary. "You can confirm this with Nurse Murphy if you like." He positions the oxygen mask back on Madeline's face.

"I'm sure that won't be necessary," he replies. He turns and strides out of the room, Chris only sighing in relief after the door is closed behind him.

"Sorry about that," Chris says.

"What a nasty little man. If anyone's interfering, it's him."

"I'm glad you see it that way."

"He was referring to the misunderstanding that was in the newspaper?"

Chris recalls how she questioned him on it on their first meeting. He nods.

"He doesn't like you." Madeline's voice becomes weaker with every word.

"You should rest," Chris says, making to move away. Her hand comes out and tugs at the sleeve of his doctor's coat.

"He doesn't approve of you trying to help?" She doesn't let go of his sleeve.

"He thinks it's reckless and inappropriate and it almost got me fired. Fortunately, the rest of the board understands it to be a mistake." Madeline inclines her head, her hand falling away. "Get some rest," he tells her, and leaves her to sleep.

~~~

Seeing Doctor Gregory has put him on edge and he goes about the remainder of his shift with distracted intent. He checks in on other patients, offering polite but inconsequential chit-chat to relatives and visitors. Every so often he glances over his shoulder certain he will see the elderly physician glaring at his back, but Doctor Gregory has disappeared. Instead, Chris finds Betsy at each turn; reading files, chatting with another nurse or darting into a patient room. Then, for the last hour of his day she is
~~~

nowhere. He wonders if she will go ahead and try to track down Madeline's husband on her own, particularly if she plans to leave Dove Break. She is a good nurse, it would be a shame to lose her, but perhaps it would make things easier for him.

As he leaves the hospice at the end of the day he checks for Doctor Gregory's car. He doesn't see it. He can't decide if he's relieved or disappointed. Perhaps if his adversary had stayed he would be late home, as he had indicated to Holly.

But as he nears his car he sees Betsy leaning up against it, her arms wrapped around the thin jacket she is wearing. He slows. Could she have found Madeline's husband already? Or is this about her leaving: is she doing it because of him?

Betsy looks up. "Is now a good time?"

He wants to tell her no, that it will have to wait, yet he doesn't. He pushes the button on his key and gestures for her to get in the car. Beginning to feel the chill of the autumnal air too Chris puts the engine on and turns up the heat.

"You haven't been looking for her husband have you?" Chris asks.

Betsy's face pinches in confusion, her eyebrows low and mouth down turned. She has no idea what he is talking about.

"Madeline. You wanted to look for her husband?" He pauses, but Betsy doesn't say anything. "Doctor Gregory was with her earlier. We need to be cautious. I wouldn't put it past him to try and fire us both if he thinks we overstepped the mark."

She shakes her head. "That's not why I'm here."

She sits facing forward, her gaze locked on the hedge in front of the car. She is picking at some imaginary dirt under her impeccably clean nails. She once told Chris it's a nervous habit of hers and that the routine of it calms her, the steady check of cleanliness before every nursing shift makes her feel rooted in the moment and distracts her from whatever might be on her mind. She must feel him staring because suddenly she clasps her hands together as though she doesn't want him to know she is nervous. This, in turn, makes Chris anxious. He waits.

Still without turning his way she takes a gulp of air and begins a speech that Chris suspects she has been practising for some time.

"I realise that we haven't known each over very long, Chris, and after Mrs Porter made all those accusations it must have been terrible. To have everything scrutinised by the board and have Doctor Gregory criticise you. Then when you were transferred onto the night shift, where nothing ever happens, I was so relieved. I mean, for myself. I've had a hard time fitting in here and you were just so lovely to me. You are lovely. I mean…"

With every garbled sentence Chris' heart pounds in his chest. He knows where this is going. It isn't the first time a nurse has confessed to having a crush on him. Usually it is silly and flippant. Once it had been awkward and uncomfortable. But the way Betsy is talking, he recognises it is more serious. He knows he's sent out mixed signals. She was his only support when he started the night shift, so welcoming and interested in his approach to looking out for the patients. He can't deny the attraction, she's a pretty girl.

"Betsy," he says when she is forced to take a breath.

"Chris, I need—"

He cuts her off. "No, you don't. I thought I'd been clear and perhaps the situation with Madeline has muddied the waters." He recognises now why she offered to put her job on the line to help Madeline. "I'm married." He curses himself for not adding in the prerequisite 'happily' in the middle of those words. But Betsy will know it isn't true. That much they established through their conversations over those long nights.

"I'm very flattered. And I should never have let it get as far as it did. That's my fault."

She tries to interrupt, facing him full on, her torso twisted in the passenger seat and her hands outstretched. Chris holds out a flattened palm and continues regardless.

"I'm sorry. But it needs to be said. Nothing will happen between us. We are work colleagues. Nothing more. Do you understand?"

She shifts in her seat again and returns to staring out of the windscreen. Chris can see she is on the verge of tears. He feels a twitch in his cheek. His insides are writhing. It has never been this hard before. He isn't sure if it is the closeness that he feels with Betsy or the fear he has that his marriage is breaking down that makes him feel so vulnerable, but he doesn't want Betsy to know either of these things. It might give her some hope that there could be more and that would be cruel.

"I understand that," she says. "But -"

"No buts. We need to put this behind us and move on. Can we do that?"

"That's how you want it?" she asks.

"I'm afraid so."

Betsy presses her lips together and slowly opens the car door. A wave of cool air floods in and Chris is grateful for it. He's sweating. She clambers out of the car and pushes the door shut with a measured click. Then, she turns and flees. She runs across the car park with her hands up to her face. He feels like a jerk. All his recent memories of Betsy pass through his mind: late night coffee breaks and intimate conversations. He remembers laughing and the warmth of her hand on his arm. He shakes his head.

He has a wife. A wife he must go home to and apologise to for not wanting to adopt a child. She is the one he needs to focus on. She deserves that much at least. He opens the window, turns down the heat and pulls out of the parking space. All the way home he silently rehearses what he might say to Holly.

~~~

When Chris pulls up outside the house the blinds are still open and no lights are on. Holly must be at the back of the house
~~~

cooking dinner in the kitchen. He checks himself, after he hung up on her earlier he doubts she'll be making him dinner. He picks up the flowers from the passenger seat and makes his way up the path. How many times has he walked up to their door with a desolate Holly behind him, clutching her belly? Can he really disappoint her by admitting he cannot adopt? The cellophane around the lilies crinkles in his grasp.

"Holly?" He calls out as soon as he steps inside. There is a musty odour like that of unsettled dust. It is silent and heavy and Chris knows immediately that Holly is not here. He tosses the flowers onto the narrow sideboard and takes the stairs two at a time. The airing cupboard door is ajar and his shoulder catches it on the way to the bedroom. The bed is made, neat and taut, with nothing out of place. He yanks open the wardrobe doors and pulls at the drawers. The majority of Holly's things are gone.

He stumbles across to the bed to sit down. Is this it? He thinks back over the last few months, then further, over a year and longer. Holly has always been desperate for a child and yet since they stopped trying Chris has refused to acknowledge it. He didn't want to admit that he is terrified of being a father, of failing as his father did or being unable to forgive a mistake like Mr Porter. Except, Porter had been right not to trust his adopted daughter and in the chaos that ensued afterwards Holly had lost the one thing distracting her from a baby; her job. And Chris had been too wary of Holly's wrath to pay attention. He'd slipped and forgotten what it meant to be partners.

He realises that Holly has seen past his 'let me think about it' response to adoption. The phone calls this afternoon must have been her attempt at an olive branch and he dismissed her three times before finally hanging up on her. Chris falls back onto the crisp sheets – so like Holly to change the bed linen before she left him – and wonders what he can do.

"I'm going to stay with my parents."

Her voice startles him into sitting upright and a muscle in his back twinges with the sudden exertion.

"You're still here?"

Holly leans against the door frame with her arms crossed. Her hair is pulled back in a neat bun and she wears a crisp white shirt, expertly ironed.

"The flowers are a nice touch, but they won't change my mind."

He gets up and crosses the room. Holly shakes her head and takes a step back into the hallway. They stand like this, a chasm of space between them, for a few minutes. Chris fights an urge to drop to his knees because he knows Holly will just roll her eyes at his melodramatic plea. He can almost hear her say 'too little, too late'.

"Let's at least just talk about it."

She scoffs. "That's what I've been trying to say for a long time. But you won't listen."

The stairs creak as she goes back downstairs. Chris follows, using the opportunity to close the gap between them until he is a step behind her in the hall.

"It's not been an easy time for either of us. But we can get through this. Please, Holly, don't go."

"How would you know if it's been difficult for me, Christopher?" She turns on him, manoeuvring her shoulder away from his outstretched hand. "I've spent weeks waiting for you, waiting to talk to you, for you to hand me a morsel of attention wasted on those patients of yours. And I have nothing to show for it. And, why? Because you're too damn selfish to put us first."

The scent of the lilies slowly wilting on the sideboard sweetening the air makes Chris feel nauseous. A horn sounds outside and Holly's glances to the door behind him.

"Then stay and let me try."

"What's the point? You're not going to change your mind, are you?"

"I—" He can't make himself say it. He doesn't want to make false promises. The fear that the child would love Holly and not him prevents the words from forming. "I'm willing to talk about it."

She sighs and disappears into the kitchen, returning with a suitcase that she pulls behind her.

"Please Holly?"

"Just move out of the way." She won't even look up at him now. The horn blares again from outside. Chris knows that if he doesn't let her go his mother-in-law will get out of the car and insert herself into their argument. She is a staunch supporter of Holly, no matter what the issue. Each time they lost a potential grandchild she would sneer at Chris as though it was his fault. He could never take care of her daughter well enough.

"Later, then? Tomorrow? I don't want this to be the end of us Holly. I love you."

She shakes her head and steps around him, the suitcase rolling up and over his shoe. He shuffles back and knocks the framed collage on the wall – the one with their photographs over a map of all their favourite places. It wobbles and then falls, dropping behind the radiator as Holly closes the door, leaving him alone.

~~~

Three hours later and Chris has convinced himself that Holly is right to leave. Sat at the kitchen table, he has concluded that as much as he wants to be a father, realising that Holly would not be the woman to father his child caused him to pull away. He questions whether he shouldn't have let her go then, allowed her to move on and find someone who would be able to settle for what she wanted. But then, he can't imagine life without Holly.

They met when Chris was twenty-two, Holly only seventeen. Early into their engagement, when they were still infatuated with one another, she met his mother - before the decline of her
~~~

disease stole her away. Chris was proud to report to Holly that his mother had approved, that she told him to keep hold of such a strong, genuine girl that would steady and support him. And so he did, Holly being exactly what his mother had suspected she would be. When he advanced to senior physician at the Unit, Holly congratulated him, buying him balloons and a cake to celebrate even though she'd lost their baby girl only two months before. By the time children had become the topic they would not talk about, she was helping him find support for his patients, understanding his need to help those who could not help themselves.

When they first discussed adoption she understood his reasoning for not wanting to be a father to a child that wasn't his own. She admitted she could sense the effect the lack of a real father had on Chris.

"You keep everything bottled up, but I see the way you look at your step-father," she told him once.

"He's not my step-father. He's just Mum's husband. That's all."

"They've been together since you were thirteen, haven't they?"

He nodded. "Doesn't make him my step-father though."

"Did he ever try to be?"

"Not even a little bit." He realised his voice was too deep, that his bitterness seeped out and spread out across his words. "But I didn't want him to. He's not related to me. It isn't like he had a lot to live up to anyway. Dad wasn't perfect, by any means, but he was the only father I'll ever get."

Holly reached over and placed a hand over his. "Do you miss him?"

"No." It was a lie, but Chris didn't deserve to miss a man he hadn't liked as a child, a man who'd been denied a last chance to be with his family. This was before Holly knew what Chris had done. Even when she teased it out of him, years later, she hadn't wavered in her love for him.

"You did what you thought was best," she said. "It was brave of you to protect your Mum. That's one of the reasons I know you'll make a brilliant father." She caressed his cheek and kissed him on the forehead. "You're not ashamed of how much you love your Mum."

And now, he isn't even prepared to learn how to love a child that is not his own to save his marriage. No matter how much he tries to convince himself it could be a possibility, a knot forms in his stomach and expands outward until he feels sick with the thought of it. He isn't that good of a man. But while the admittance of it pains him, it doesn't change how he feels.

Perhaps it's better this way? It isn't Holly's fault things are difficult between them; he was the one to offer up her name as an accomplice to the board, the words slipping out before he could gulp them back down. It was so easy to talk about Holly supporting him then, explaining how she found Mr Porter's adopted daughter through council records and they never expected the betrayal of one who seemed to adore her father.

There it is again: the deceit and falseness of a relationship not tied by blood. If he and Holly adopt, will their child turn out to be so embittered against them? Chris knows what it is like to have a parent forced upon you, to discover that a man you have nothing in common with is suddenly expected to be referred to as 'dad' simply because he married your Mum. Chris doesn't want to repeat that same absence of kinship with a child meant to be his own. Even if they adopt a baby, Chris will always know that it isn't truly their child. How are you supposed to build a loving relationship if you start out with a lie?

Of course, Chris doesn't feel he can absolve himself from the lie of omission he's already told. He draws a hand across his forehead, shadowing his eyes from the stark kitchen light, brighter now that it has become dark outside. Betsy's wide-eyed admiration had buoyed his confidence and reminded him he'd been trying to do the right thing, even when it had all gone wrong.

At a time when he should have been working on his marriage with Holly he was charmed by the flattery of another woman. If anything, Betsy's misdirected attempt to confess her feelings has only made him realise how important Holly is. He was right to dismiss Betsy. He just wishes he had done it sooner.

Slowly he pushes himself up from the chair and pours another drink. Could he win Holly back? He sighs. But he has nothing new to offer, so any attempt would be an empty gesture. He takes the glass into the living room, but turns back for the bottle after he drains the first drink on the way there, enjoying the burn of the alcohol as it trickles down his throat. He deserves the burn the spread outward, to set him alight and turn him to ashes.

A memory flickers. A letter in the fire, flames engulfing the page, destroying a dying man's wish for forgiveness. Is that how his own life will end too? Alone, unloved, and bearing a responsibility for too many mistakes made.

He pours another drink.

~~~

Chris wakes with a start, his face plastered to the arm of the sofa and his hand clasped around a glass. For a moment he wonders why Holly has not chastised him for falling asleep in the living room. Then he remembers Holly isn't here. His knuckles turn white around the glass. Is this his life now? His hand grows weak and he lets go. The tumbler falls with a gentle thud onto the carpet and clinks against an empty bottle.

It's a familiar noise, though not one he's heard in a long while. It propels him up and off the sofa, a rising swell in his stomach. He will not become his father, trapped in a circle of self-pity and turning to drink to drown his sorrows. It may only be one night, but Chris is painfully aware where this road leads.

He collects the glass, washes it and returns it to the cupboard, throwing the vacant bottle away as he passes, grateful it was only a
~~~

third full when he retrieved it. Perhaps he will end up like his father. Perhaps one day someone will realise he hasn't turned up somewhere and will come to check on him, only to discover he has died days beforehand, clutching a picture of people he supposedly cares about but done nothing by which to prove it.

The day Chris found out about his father's death comes back to him so abruptly it seems like he can feel a hand on his shoulder.

Two officers on their doorstep with grim faces and their breath white clouds of pity and dismay at the chipped paintwork and broken glass in the door. Chris remembers feeling hungry, there had been no breakfast that morning.

The policewoman had softly held him back with a tight lipped smile as his mother followed the uniformed man into the kitchen. Chris had tried to sit as still as possible on the sofa to minimise any noise so he could overhear their conversation.

"Are you cold?" the policewoman asked with a shiver. Ice crystals were sparkling on the window panes from the morning frost, and a gold-embossed birthday card on the windowsill caught the sun. It has been his twelfth birthday three days before.

He shook his head and shuffled to the end of the sofa. Peering through the gap in the door he glimpsed his mother leaning against the sink. Her hand was at her throat.

"You're shaking." The sofa sagged as the policewoman sat beside him. "Your Mum's not in trouble. My partner just needs to…tell her something."

He wriggled out from the gentle hand she placed on his shoulder. "I'm fine."

The policeman held out some papers for his mother. They were dirty, wrinkled pages with thick, black ink marks. Chris had felt suddenly sick. It couldn't be. He'd burned it.

"How about I light the fire? This place needs warming up."

Chris didn't respond to the patronising tone. They didn't have a lot of furniture; only the sofa, the black and white T.V. and the wood burning fire, which his mother hated. His father had spent two weeks trying to install it, adamant that it would make them cosy in winter. A specialist had to be called in to fix the mess his father made. It took the guy less than two hours to get it all working. There was no need to guess why his father hadn't been able to do it. Chris was the one to move all the lager cans out of the room before the gas man arrived.

The policeman's deep voice carried. "So you didn't know he was sick?"

Chris leaned over the arm of the sofa and almost tumbled off, but it was worth it to hear his mother's reply.

"No, I haven't heard from him in months."

There was a rustling of paper and some under-the-breath murmuring from the policewoman. She was rearranging the fire-tinged logs. Chris darted towards her.

"No, don't do that."

"You know how to light this?"

Chris glanced over his shoulder. The kitchen door was closing. He turned his attention to the fireplace. He could still see charred bits of paper on the stonework.

"Mum doesn't like it, she said it's too dangerous." The policewoman looked at him. "My Dad once fell asleep and a spark jumped out and set fire to the rug."

The policewoman nodded slowly, as if she was underwater, and grunted as she pushed herself back to standing. When she turned Chris brushed the burnt paper as far back as he dared. Hopefully it was out of sight. Before he could check the policewoman hadn't seen the remains of his father's letter there was a deep, guttural groan from the kitchen. Chris was through the door in a second, smudged fingerprints on the doorframe that wouldn't be wiped off for weeks.

"Mum?"

She was on the kitchen floor. Her hand had moved from her throat to her mouth. Her eyes were squeezed shut and her face was wet. The policeman stood to one side, papers in his hand.

"What did you do?" Chris yelled. He threw himself on the floor with his mother and pulled her into his arms. The policeman had a furrowed brow and his lips were a tight thin line. He looked over to the policewoman now stood in the doorway.

"Mum, what's wrong? What is it?"

She didn't answer, instead burying her head into his shoulder. Her tears soaked through his shirt to his skin. Chris knew, of course. He'd been forewarned.

"It's your father," the policewoman said. She stepped into the kitchen and helped Chris coax his mother to the living room. "I'm afraid he passed away."

Chris let his mother's arm drop from around his shoulder as she slumped onto the sofa. The letter Chris had intercepted said as much would happen, in time. But Chris had never really believed his father wouldn't simply turn up on the doorstep again. His vision started to blur. Then his cheeks were wet too and he lifted a hand to wipe them.

The policewoman caught his wrist. "You've got soot on your hand." She held it out for him to see the black smear across his fingers. Chris stood there in the living room, the policewoman rubbing at his face with a tissue, and stared at his mother curled in a ball sobbing at the news his father was dead.

"How?" Chris managed to croak.

"Do you know what pneumonia is?"

He shook his head. The letter had said cancer.

Chris shakes the memory away. He wouldn't have been able to do anything for his father, even if he had told his mum that dad was sick; that he needed money; that he wanted to come back. What he knows now about pneumonia suggests that his father could have died before the letter had even been received. Still, it doesn't dilute his own fear of dying alone, just like his father. Without Holly, what does he have left? They were supposed to have a family, be happy, and enjoy life together. But those plans are spoilt now. Maybe he will die alone, like his father or, at the very best, like Madeline Tailor - in a specialised ward where he will be just another patient and no one will remember him after he's gone.

He pushes himself up off the kitchen counter where he is leaning and closes the blind to the darkened night sky. He needs to give Holly time. Right now he can't promise her anything that she wants and so any attempt to win her back will be an empty gesture. What he can do though, is ensure that Madeline Tailor doesn't die alone, leaving behind a husband who - in all likelihood - doesn't even know that she is sick. He buries the thought that he is trying to help Madeline because he hopes that one day someone might do the same for him. He goes straight to the cramped study – no trace that it was once a nursery - and switches on the computer.

He knows that when Holly tracked down various friends and relatives for his patients in the past she didn't always resort to the Wills and Probate company records. Sometimes she simply let the internet do the work for her. He struggles to recall how she did her research, she had tried to teach him a few times but he had feigned ignorance because…Well, because he thought the joint effort of helping people might keep them together. Except, of course, it all went too far and Holly lost her job.

He sits back in the chair, a list of 'Tailors' on his screen. Is he interfering? Madeline made it clear that she wanted to be left alone. Yet, she called Cecelia of her own accord less than a day after asserting herself. She said that she deserved to die, but Chris can't believe that is related to a single childhood mistake. Her inclination to come clean with Cecelia must be symptomatic of a larger desire to ask forgiveness for something else. He lets his fingers hover over the keyboard: is there any harm in looking? As

Betsy said, it would be better to have the husband waiting in the wings in case Madeline changed her mind rather than have to contact him when it was too late.

He spends the rest of the night searching, making notes and eliminating possibilities. Occasionally he stops, questioning if it is the right thing to do. But he always talks himself back to the screen. With the exception of Mr Porter and his ostracised, adopted daughter who was apparently disowned for good reason, helping his patients in this way rarely backfired. He can't quite match Holly's speed at the search and it is dawn when he realises he will have to use a paid service to examine the public records he really needs. By the time he has mistyped his debit card number three times and is finally able to access the information regarding Madeline's marriage, he is late for work.

~~~

The moment he arrives at the Unit Betsy homes in on him and tells him she needs to see him in private. He shakes his head with a pointed look at the senior nurse at the desk.

"It's about Madeline," Betsy hisses. She brushes past him with a glare.

He immediately turns and follows, hoping that no one notices what looks like him coming to heel. She leads him to his office and then waits as he places the key in the lock. She is standing a fraction too close so he can smell her perfume and the hairs on his arm stand on end.

When they enter Chris leaves the door slightly ajar so a thin shaft of light creeps in from the corridor beyond. Betsy makes a point of closing it. He is already at the other side of his desk and suddenly thinks that this might not be about Madeline. He discards his coat and sits down, placing his hands together over his lap. Betsy stands opposite and says nothing.

"So, how is she?"
~~~

"Not good."

The words hang in the air between them. Betsy's face is still and Chris can't read it. When she parts her lips Chris jumps in to stop her speaking.

"I found her husband."

He doesn't know why he tells her. It doesn't seem to change her stiff posture but she blinks and looks across at him.

"And?"

"He's remarried, with three children." He waits for her to take a breath. "From what I can tell, they're still married."

"What?" Betsy finally lets her guard down, the surprise showing on her face. Chris gestures for her to sit down and is relieved when she does.

"I looked it up online. There's a marriage certificate for Madeline to a man named James Tailor when she was seventeen. He married again three years later, no record of a divorce that I could find."

"I wonder what happened."

"Without asking Madeline we have no way of knowing. But she was adamant about not contacting anyone. Perhaps this explains why."

"A bigamist husband from half a lifetime ago, that doesn't make sense."

"She might still love him." Chris recognises a wistful tone to his voice. If Madeline could still love a man from almost twenty years ago, then perhaps Holly still loves him, perhaps he has a chance.

"What else did you find out?"

"Hardly anything," he admits. "A few articles about her artwork, one that said she was up for a prestigious award once." He hesitates, a vague niggling at the back of his mind. "Both her parents are dead. Her mother a few years ago…" he trails off. There it is. The kernel of something interesting that he's barely had time to register in his rush to work. "But her father died right around the time she got married. There's no mention of her in the public record for a few years after that."

"Maybe we should ask her?"

"If she wanted him here she would have contacted him."

"What if he doesn't know where Madeline is? What if he still cares? There's a chance Chris, and it might be her last one." This is the Betsy he recognises, the one with a determined passion for patient advocacy, not the stony faced woman who marched him here. "She's had a rough night. There might not be much time left."

Chris uses his computer to check the night shift notes. As Betsy suggests, Madeline has been struggling with pain and breathlessness throughout the night. At least one entry notes her disdain for wearing the oxygen mask, though Chris wonders if such basic measures will help any more.

"Where does James Tailor live?" Betsy asks.

Chris purses his lips, not wanting to answer because he knows exactly what Betsy's response will be. She remains stoic until he relents. "About two miles away," he murmurs.

"That's not a coincidence. There's no way Madeline checked in here by accident. Her old school-friend less than a stone's throw away and now a husband down the road?" Betsy shakes her head and a blonde curl escapes from behind her ear. "It's too perfect."

Chris doesn't know what to do. There might be a good reason why Madeline is here instead of other facilities, but Betsy's point is a valid one. He remembers Madeline commenting on the Porter case on her arrival; she knows his record, is she using it to her advantage?

"No," he waves off the possibility. "She probably just wanted to be in familiar surroundings. We can't interfere like this. Not without Madeline's knowledge."

Betsy offers him a cool stare, similar to the one with which she began their conversation. "Are you willing to stake her life on that?"

She is purposefully baiting him, he thinks. After their last conversation she is colder than usual, as if she secretly hates him for not reciprocating her feelings. Is she angry enough to set him up with the board? Will she call Doctor Gregory the moment he makes the mistake of speaking to James Tailor? He pinches the bridge of his nose between finger and thumb, the exhaustion from lack of sleep settling over him like a warm blanket promising comfort.

"I don't know," he admits, not realising until Betsy replies that he's spoken out loud.

"Well then you'd better be damn sure," she says. The softness in her Irish accent emphasises the harsh statement.

He nods and stands up, intending to speak with Madeline again. Betsy examines him with her green eyes and remains seated, staring up at him with fierce determination.

"Chris."

He senses intimacy in the undercurrent of her tone. He pretends not to have heard and moves around the desk toward the door. Betsy's hand reaches out and she grasps his arm.

"I'm pregnant."

Chris stumbles, but does not fall. Betsy stands to steady him, and with a sudden light-heartedness, stifles a chuckle at his reaction.

"It's not funny," Chris says, brushing her hand away. She stops smiling.

They are less than a metre apart. Chris' height gives him an advantage but Betsy is calmer, she's had time to adjust. His palms are clammy and his heart skips a beat. He can hear it, as the whooshing of his blood cascades around his head. A question flickers in his mind but he will not ask it. Betsy answers anyway.

"It's your child, I'm certain of that."

"When did you find out?"

Betsy takes a step back, her gaze fixed on the floor. "A few days ago. I wasn't sure until—"

"Who else knows?"

"No one, I wasn't even sure if I should tell you."

"Why not? I'm the father. I deserve to know." He leans back on the desk, unsteady. "Are you considering…" He can't say it.

"No."

The answer is immediate and Chris exhales, not realising he's been holding his breath. He holds up a palm to appease the glare that came with her answer.

"When my mother finds out I'm pregnant out of wedlock she'll be disappointed. When she finds out the father of my child is married she'll be furious. But if she ever, ever found out that I'd terminated a life inside me..." Betsy trails off, anguish in her voice. "I could never. A life is a life, Chris. Wanted or not."

"I'm in full agreement," he says, just in case she thinks he might not be. The dread that accompanied the thought of losing his only child settles and re-emerges as a swirling fear of what to do next.

"What do we do?"

"I was just going to leave, maybe go back to Ireland. But you had a right to know. I couldn't just go without telling you."

Chris concentrates on taking a deep breath in and letting it out in a slow, measured way. He doesn't know how to feel.

"The thought of being a single mum is terrifying, but not as terrifying as having to go back to Ireland and ask for mum's support. She won't be surprised, it'll just prove I fall below her expectation, but there isn't any other option."

"You could stay," he offers.

"And what, be your mistress?"

Chris shakes his head. "What happened was a mistake. We both know that."

"Right," Betsy nods. "Maybe this doesn't have to change anything. No one will know."

"We will," he says, and he remembers he said the same thing to his wife. "I want to be a father Betsy. I know this isn't what you imagined for yourself, but I'll take the burden of responsibility. I need to be in my child's life."

"But I don't want to ruin your marriage."

Chris remembers all of the plans Betsy had for herself and how she had been so determined and hopeful about her future when they talked over those long night shifts. Now his mistake has cost her those dreams and she's worrying about his already failing marriage. *Failed*, he corrects himself.

"You don't need to worry about that," he tells her. "I'll support you however I can."

Her eyes are glassy with tears but, before she can respond, there is a knock at the door and Chris - his mind elsewhere - automatically invites them in.

A nurse opens the door a fraction and peers in through the gap, her flickering gaze takes note of Betsy now stood staring out of the window, her back to the nurse. She is trying to wipe the tears from her cheeks without being noticed.

"Mrs Williams in room fourteen has passed away, Doctor." The nurse doesn't meet his eye. "They'll need a signature."

He nods but the nurse waits. He gives Betsy a sympathetic look and catches the surreptitious inclination of the head in response; she understands. He walks down the corridor on the heels of the nurse, his head still whirling at the news he has just been given. He should celebrate. He will be a dad, have a child he can call his own who he will have a natural bond with.

But, Holly.

It might have been possible to reconcile if it was just a single mistake, but Betsy's pregnancy is too much of a betrayal. How can he ask Holly to forgive him this?

He goes through the motions of his role using the routine to distract him from thoughts that bounce around his mind. Once he has dealt with Mrs Williams the nurse takes the paperwork from him and points down the corridor.

"You might want to check in on Mrs Tailor, she had a difficult night."

He recalls Betsy told him the same thing and that she didn't believe Madeline had much longer to live. He desperately wants to see Betsy but his patients don't have the time to spare and so he knows he has to focus and put his patient first. As he strides down the corridor he remembers that he is on a half day and relaxes his tense shoulders. He will have the afternoon to talk things over with Betsy.

Madeline's deterioration is enough to distract him from any of his previous thoughts. She lies on the bed, sheet pulled up to her shoulders and oxygen mask firmly settled on her face. Even against the stark white of the pillow her red hair is dull. She doesn't open her eyes until he is stood next to the bed.

"How are you feeling?" He listens to her breath sounds which are full of static. The cancer is eating away at her lungs.

"I've been better," she croaks. Her eyelids droop closed again.

Chris respects her desire to make a joke but worries about what it means. "Madeline, are you sure we can't contact anyone for you? Someone just to sit with you, so you're not alone?"

She opens and then narrows her eyes at him and lifts a limp hand off the bed to half-heartedly wave him away. Chris can't stop himself thinking that is watching a woman die alone because she is too proud to ask for help and the threat of the empty room haunts him. He reveals his hand.

"Not even your husband? We know he lives close-by."

Madeline's eyes widen and she drags the mask down from her face.

"You've been doing your research."

Chris places a hand over hers which is cold and stiff.

"He wouldn't want to see me now," she tells him. "Such a long time ago." She tries to smile but it forms into a grimace. "Wasn't a good wife," she jokes. "He deserved better. And got it, from what I hear."

Chris winces at her dismissal, but it's clear she knows he has married again. Bringing up James Tailor hasn't panicked or distressed her and so Chris doesn't think there's any hard feelings. It makes him curious as to what happened between them and why Madeline is so sure he won't want to see her again. He replaces the mask on her face.

"Are you in pain?"

He sees the mask move, up and down, signalling the inclination of her head.

"I'll add a morphine drip," he tells her. "You can manage the dosage."

Again the mask wobbles on her face. There is brightness to her eyes that makes him think she might be smiling. Chris squeezes her hand and she reciprocates with a gentle clasp of her own. He lets go and calls through the door for a nurse and is relieved when he sees Betsy dart out from behind the Nurses' Station.

"Can you set Madeline up with a morphine drip please?" he asks her, though it isn't the question circling his mind. He glances over to Madeline, her eyes now closed, and takes a step further into the room away from the corridor. Betsy mirrors his movement. He lowers his voice to a whisper.

"Tell me you're going to stay?"

Betsy bites her lip and shrugs. Chris swallows down the urge to tell her that Holly has left him, that he has nothing to lose by her staying, but he doesn't want her to stay out of pity.

"Have you been to see a doctor at least? Made sure everything is alright?"

"Yes, it's all fine. I had my ultra-sound yesterday. That's why I wanted to tell you."

Chris replays the conversation from the day before in his mind. How foolish he was to think that she was trying to seduce him.

"I have a copy if you want to see?"

Chris' heart thrums. "Yes, of course." He expects her to produce it there and then, but she whispers that it is in her locker and she'll show it to him later. He isn't expecting the swell of disappointment even this small delay causes. Betsy looks across at Madeline and Chris follows her gaze. Their patient is still sleeping; the only sign of life the rhythmic jump of the line on the monitor.

"She's not doing well," Betsy observes. "She needs someone here for her."

Chris nods. She doesn't have long, he is certain of that, and the only lead they have is her previous husband. At the very least perhaps he could offer other suggestions for who might remind Madeline her life has been worth living.

"I'll see what I can do."

Silently, Chris hopes that helping Madeline will keep Betsy close for long enough for him to convince her to stay. But he knows that he would follow her to Ireland if necessary. He is ashamed that he let Holly go without a fight but he cannot give up his child. Channelling the fierce desire to do the right thing, he leaves Betsy to administer the morphine drip and goes directly to his office where the notes he's made about Madeline's husband are still on his desk.

~~~

Chris re-reads the few notes he's made about James Tailor from last night. They aren't much, just that Madeline's former husband is a mechanic who appears to have remarried three years after the date on Madeline's marriage certificate. Perhaps he isn't even the right James Tailor. Chris' gaze flickers up to the notice board, as it so often does, and he diverts his attention away from Tony Porter and fixates on another photograph, then another, until he reassures himself that he's helped far more people than he's hurt. Before his resolve can abandon him he picks up the telephone and punches in the number that is scrawled on the page in front of him.
~~~

A man picks up on the second ring and for a moment Chris is unsure of what to say.

"Hello? … Hello? Anyone there?" It's a gruff voice, but a warm one.

Chris clears his throat. "Is that Mr Tailor, of Tailor Mechanics on Thornby Way?"

"Yes, but this isn't my business number."

"Oh, no, of course. My name is Doctor Christopher Wright, I was hoping I might be able to take a moment of your time?"

"With what?"

"Well, I work at Dove Break Palliative Care—"

"We've heard enough. Stop trying to interfere in our family. If you call again I'll have your license."

Chris is so surprised to be interrupted that it isn't until he hears the dial tone buzzing in his ear that he registers the anger in James' voice. Should he risk ringing back to try and explain the situation? From the abrupt dismissal, Chris doesn't think James will take kindly to another attempt. Did Madeline's previous doctor tried to get in touch, perhaps put James' second marriage in danger? But then why would that give James the right to take their license? Something doesn't sit right.

Chris' left hand sits on the telephone receiver and he spots the glimmer of his wedding band as it catches the light. He should get used to being dismissed, because when Holly discovers his betrayal she won't ever speak to him again. He allows himself a moment to take in the enormity of his situation and considers how alone he will be in future. Even with a child, he will only be a part-time dad at best. With Holly gone the house will be cold and empty, if he's still living there. He imagines Holly will be back at her parents, settled into one of their three spare bedrooms that remain decorated for guests rather than grandchildren. They'll hate him too, probably already do. And their friends, what few they have, he doubts that they'll take his side when they find out.

The phone rings while his hand is still resting on the receiver and it jolts Chris out of his reverie. He answers it with a secret hope that it might be Holly, calling to say she wants to talk. Betsy's distinct Irish twang rattles down the line.

"Just thought you'd want to know Madeline's more comfortable now we've got the painkillers in. She's resting now, but I don't think it'll be long before she leaves us."

"Have you told anyone?"

"About her husband? Of course not."

"About the pregnancy."

"Why would I do that? It's not something I'm that proud of."

Chris lets out an audible breath.

"Relieved are you?" Her accent isn't so soft now. "Worried I'll blab and it'll get back to your wife?"

"Betsy, please. Not over the phone."

"What in case a colleague hears that you knocked me up?"

"No. I— just— please calm down." He struggles to back track.

"I am calm. I told you because you had a right to know. That's all. Besides, I'll be leaving soon and then you can stop worrying I'll disrupt your life."

"That isn't why I asked," he lies.

"Look, can we focus on our patient? Madeline's scared and doesn't have long left, so get her husband here and do it fast. Everything else can wait."

Chris swallows down the lump in his throat that has appeared with the thought of Betsy leaving, his child with her. "Her husband hung up on me."

"Then go get him, you said he was local."

Tony Porter's photo seems to double in size. "I don't know if that's a good idea."

"Well, we can't just give up. He's our only lead. It's your half day today isn't it? Go talk to him."

"I was hoping we could talk."

"I'm on until six. So you've got plenty of time."

"You'll be here when I get back?"

"I don't have anywhere else to go, do I?"

He hadn't realised how angry she must be. He needs to tell her that Holly has already gone so that she doesn't think he's got anything to protect other than their baby. But she doesn't give him chance.

"I'll check Madeline's old medical records, see if there is anything in there that might help us."

"Good plan," Chris agrees. "I'll see you when I get back then."

"Probably," she says, and then hangs up.

~~~

When the time comes to leave Chris gathers up his coat and notes on James Tailor and briefly considers going to see Holly once he has been to see Mr Tailor. If he tells the truth now perhaps there might some hope the marriage can be repaired. Or is that wishful thinking? Would it be better to wait, determine the future with Betsy before he attempts to win Holly back? He doesn't want to hurt her all over again.

As he approaches the automatic doors he swings on his jacket and catches sight of a hunched figure curled in one of the wingback reception chairs. He sighs, taking any opportunity to divert his thoughts from the complicated situation he finds himself in.

"Is that a relative of someone?" he asks the young woman shuffling papers at the welcome desk. He keeps his voice low so as not to draw attention.

The receptionist looks up and then reddens as she yanks a set of ear phones from beneath her hair. "Sorry?"

He gestures to the other side of the room. "How long has she been waiting?" Chris can see now that the person huddled in the chair is a woman with frizzy blonde hair. A woman he recognises.
~~~

"She's been here since I unlocked the doors this morning," the receptionist says. "Said she didn't want to see anyone, just needed to be here in case the patient in room four passed."

Chris strides across the room and stands over Cecelia Hartland, who is squeezed into a chair sleeping, still wearing the same clothes that she had arrived in the day before.

"Miss Hartland?" When she doesn't respond he reaches out and gently touches her shoulder. "Cecelia?"

She wakes with the ease of someone pretending to sleep.

"Hello," she murmurs as she stretches out.

"Are you here to see Madeline?"

Cecelia shakes her head. "No."

Chris waits for her to explain. Instead the silence solidifies between them. He sits in the chair opposite. The receptionist has already returned to her music.

"Then why are you still here?"

Cecelia wraps her arms around herself and offers a half-hearted shrug. "I got in my car to leave yesterday and just couldn't drive away. I hate her for what she did to my family but…" She shrugs.

Chris finishes the sentence how he hopes Cecelia would. "You don't want her to die alone."

"She'd deserve it."

"I can ask if she will see you again, if it will help?"

Cecelia cackles. "Oh, she'd love that. Madeline adores the drama she creates." Cecelia reaches out a pale hand to Chris, and lowers her tone as her big brown eyes stare into his. "Please don't tell her I'm here. I just can't leave, not yet. Not until—" She breaks off again withdrawing her hand and turning to look out onto the car park. "Is she in much pain?"

"We're keeping her as comfortable as we can. But she doesn't have long left. She could really do with the support."

She shakes her head once, then again in a slow movement, as though she is telling herself not to give in. "I won't. Not after everything that's happened."

Chris sighs and then stands. James Tailor it is then.

"Are you not taking care of her today?"

"Actually, I'm going to see Madeline's husband, James Tailor."

Cecelia leans back in her chair but Chris catches the subtle raise of an eyebrow.

"Madeline asked for him?"

Chris is careful not to answer.

"Curiosity alone might get him here, I suppose," Cecelia says.

"Why do you say that?"

She offers him a wry smile. "Not my story to tell. But, I can't imagine he's forgotten his first love." Cecelia gets to her feet and asks him where the bathrooms are. He points behind the reception desk and watches her saunter away.

He wonders if Cecelia's desire to stay has anything to do with the drama she blames Madeline for creating. Madeline intimated that Cecelia wasn't really a friend but someone who was always there to help. Maybe Cecelia will miss the attention. It certainly seems as if she is looking for further disruption, otherwise why wouldn't she just tell Chris about James? He ponders how curiosity might be James' drive to visit. Whatever the reason, he simply hopes that it will be enough to get him here and support Madeline before it is too late.

~~~

It takes five minutes to drive to the leafy cul-de-sac where James Tailor lives and Chris suspects Betsy is right: Madeline has chosen Dove Break on purpose. He examines the cream painted semi-detached house with a slightly overgrown front lawn and his jaw tenses at the sight of a tricycle embedded in the grass. This is what he and Holly had wanted their life to be.

He half expects the house to be empty, after all who would be home at two o'clock in the afternoon, but a truck is parked in the driveway with 'Tailor's Mechanics' emblazoned down the side.
~~~

Chris taps his fingers on his steering wheel for a few moments trying to decide what to say. He hasn't approached family members on behalf of his patients in some time, not in person anyway. Given James Tailor's attitude over the telephone he doesn't expect a welcoming response. As he clambers out of the car he briefly wonders what would happen if Doctor Gregory discovers this visit. Would Betsy be angry enough betray him? Chris doesn't think she is, but if she plans to return to Ireland then she won't be worrying about her own job. He needs to make sure she stays and knows he won't abandon his child under any circumstance, that he isn't that type of man. Of this much he feels certain.

Confident of his decision on the situation with Betsy, Chris strides up to James Tailor's door. It is painted a vivid cerise. A quick glance across the street and at the neighbours' houses and he realises that three out of the four doors he can see are painted in the same shade. He uses a lion-faced knocker to tap out three rhythmic beats.

The door is opened by a man, tall and broad with a thick, brown beard tinged with greying edges. He has creases lining the corners of his brown eyes which are alert, but the bags beneath them demonstrate fatigue.

"James Tailor?"

The man nods and Chris continues.

"My name is Doctor Chris Wright, I was hoping that I might speak to you about a patient of mine that I think will interest you."

James' lips turn pale as he presses them together. He puts a hand up, closing the door by a fraction as he does so.

"No more," he says. "I love my daughter, but we've made the decision to keep her at home." The door starts to close.

"No, no," Chris wedges his foot into the gap. "It's not about your daughter."

James peers through the few inches of space that Chris' foot permits.

"Then what do you want?"

"My patient is Madeline Fields."

James' hold on the door loosens and it swings open to reveal a neat hallway with carpeted stairs. A small child, about three or four, stands on the landing clutching a teddy bear. Chris assumes she is a girl because of the pink pyjamas, but the short, patchy hair is unmistakable. The child stares down at him and her glare makes him unbearably sad. She takes advantage of his silence.

"Daddy, I want a drink."

At the sound of her voice James turns and trots up the stairs and gives her a swift kiss on the forehead as he bundles her up into his arms.

"I told you to stay in bed, sweetie. I'll bring you a drink."

James disappears and Chris stands awkwardly on the step, unsure whether to go in or leave. But this is obviously the right house and the right man. Chris cranes his neck to look inside, trying to get a sense if there is anyone else home. It seems that James and his daughter are the only occupants. Chris is relieved, perhaps it will give him opportunity to talk candidly with him.

James comes back down the stairs with narrowed eyes.

"What did you say before?" he asks.

"Madeline Fields." Chris repeats. "I'm here about Madeline Fields."

James takes hold of the door and Chris braces himself for it to slam in his face. But James is steadying himself and he brings his other hand up to cover his mouth. In the quiet Chris can hear the bristles of his beard scratch against his calloused hands.

He doesn't look up at Chris but says, "I haven't heard that name in years."

"She's a patient at my Unit. I'd like to talk to you about her if I may?" Chris speaks gently. James appears vulnerable, despite his heavy-set figure. His gaze remains on Chris' feet, one arm out to lean against the door and then, slowly, he invites Chris in with the other.

"It'll be an hour or so before Hannah's back with the kids," he says, showing Chris to a living room that has a cosy, lived in feel to it. "I just need to get the little 'un a drink."

Chris perches on the sofa, the cushions dented and flat, and examines the photographs around him. He recognises James, even without a beard, in almost all of the pictures where he is surrounded by family; first with a bride, then a pregnant wife before it jumps to a scene with one toddler and a baby and, finally, a photo of all four of them surrounding a hospital bed with a fifth member of the family. This is the girl Chris has already seen. In this photograph she is a small, smiling child with outstretched arms despite the nasogastric tube in her nose.

Chris hears footsteps pounding down the stairs and automatically stands as James returns.

"What's the condition?" Chris asks.

"Leukaemia." James answers without even missing a beat. "What do you know about Madeline?"

Chris nods, straight to the point then. "Madeline is a patient at my Unit. She's gravely ill and all alone. I was hoping that I could find some support for her," Chris pauses, looking around him. As he does he feels his shoulders slump and a fist-like mass in his stomach. He can't upset this man's life when Madeline herself doesn't even want him by her bedside. James has a more important patient to tend. He starts back to the door. "But I think I've probably come to the wrong place."

"Not the wrong place," James replies. He places a hand on Chris' chest to stop him from leaving. "I spent a long time wondering what happened to that girl. Her being sick and alone was not what I expected."

"I work for a palliative care facility Mr Tailor. I'm afraid Madeline's prognosis isn't good. I'm sorry to say that your wife will die within a matter of days."

James' guffaws. "She's not my wife. Never has been."

"But she has your name, her friend referred to your wedding and there's a marriage certificate." Chris doesn't share how he knows there is paperwork on their nuptials.

"Oh, there was a wedding," James explains. "A little over twenty years ago now. I haven't seen Madeline since."

"Why?" he asks.

"You'd do better asking her. She disappeared after the ceremony. Never saw her again." Chris glances at the photograph of James and his new wife. "I was granted an annulment."

Disappointment swells within Chris. He wonders if Madeline had good reason to leave James, something he doesn't know. Coming here was a mistake, now James will want answers that Madeline may not want to give.

"I've no interest in seeing her," James says, as if reading his thoughts. "I put that question to bed a long time ago." He picks up a frame with a picture of his three children flanking his wife. "Wasn't given much choice but to move on. I've got bigger things to worry about now than why a teenage girl ran away on her wedding day."

Chris lets out the breath he has been holding.

"I'm sorry for disturbing you," he says. He holds out a hand to shake, James takes it with a wry smile.

"Did she send you?"

Chris shakes his head. "I'm concerned she's alone. Someone mentioned she was married so we looked you up. You being so close, it was easy to come by and see..." He shrugs. "Never mind I can see it wasn't the right thing."

"Beggar's belief she's not got anyone," James comments. "Never met a girl so magnetic. She must still have it, if she's got you running around after her."

Chris stops, mid-step, on the way back to the hall. Cecelia said much the same. James is right, there is something about Madeline he can't quite put his finger on. He knows he can't leave then without asking:

"What happened between the two of you?"

James purses his lips and stares at Chris, though Chris gets the feeling James isn't actually looking at him. His eyes glaze over, just for a second, and then he blinks and invites Chris to re-take his seat. For the next hour, James Tailor answers Chris' question in more detail than he could hope for.

JAMES' STORY

I was nineteen. I'd just started my apprenticeship in mechanics and was enjoying my first few years as a young adult. Madeline turned up at one of our late summer parties; a petite, slim young girl dressed in denim shorts. She caught everyone's eye because her red hair clashed with the bright orange shirt she wore, tied in a knot at the front.

My friend, Aiden, gestured with his beer bottle. "Who's that?"

I looked over to where he'd pointed. From our vantage place on the back wall we could see the mix of people hanging around Aiden's back garden.

I shrugged. "Didn't you invite her?" Aiden was the type to host parties as often as he could, which meant every weekend his parents went away.

"Nope, but I'm gonna find out who did."

He strode away and I watched as he approached Madeline. He got her attention by grazing the small of her back with his hand still cold from holding the beer. She didn't even flinch. They had a short conversation and then Aiden weaved away through the crowd taking every opportunity he could to brush up against various scantily clad girls. I admired his confidence.

"Do you think he'll let me stay?"

Her voice startled me. She'd crept up beside me and was leaning against the wall, her arms folded. I had to clear my throat before I spoke.

"I expect so."

She offered me her hand. Her nails were painted a deep pink and there was a charm bracelet around her tiny wrist small enough to be a child's. "I'm Madeline."

"James." My clammy palm swallowed up her hand. I saw Aiden at the other end of the garden, near the house, he tipped his bottle to me and winked. I turned back to Madeline: "Who're you here with?"

"No one."

"Do you always turn up at parties uninvited?"

She smiled then and a dimple appeared in her right cheek. "Not always."

She faced forward, examining people on the lawn. I studied her face while I had the chance: small button nose, pixie like chin and soft, pale skin with a few freckles. Her hair fell down one shoulder and reminded me of ribbons tied to a balloon. She must have been around five foot two, every part of her miniaturised when compared with my six foot figure. Perhaps this was what made her seem so perfect and doll-like. She made the word beautiful seem dull.

"Like what you see?" she asked, that dimple still in her cheek. She was staring at me too out of the corner of her eye.

I looked away. My cheeks burned. I put my efforts into keeping my gaze forward and thinking of something to say. "What college are you at?"

"I'm not in college."

"How old are you?"

"Sixteen. I just finished school this last term."

I must have looked shocked because she tipped her head back a fraction and laughed. It was a peculiar tone. She actually chuckled with a 'ha-ha-ha' sound. I'd never heard any one laugh like that before.

"The look on your face: Priceless."

I offered a sheepish grin. She made it seem like I'd just told her a joke rather than done something embarrassing. I took a swig of beer. It was warm from being clasped in my hand but I noticed that my palms were no longer damp, nor my face hot. Somehow she'd put me at ease.

We talked until the sun went down, sharing music, books and stories like we were old friends who hadn't seen one another in years. I discovered she'd only moved into the area a few weeks ago after leaving school. Her Dad was retired and she was waitressing, trying to figure out what to do with her life. Mostly, though, she let me talk. I told her about my passion for taking things apart and then putting them back together again to see how they worked. I even shared my carefully thought out plan about buying the auto shop from my boss after I'd completed my apprenticeship and had saved up enough capital working for him. I forgot about the rest of the people at the party.

"Want to walk me home?" Madeline asked a few hours later.

I checked my watch, it was past midnight and we were the only ones left in the garden. The remaining light was the yellow glow coming from Aiden's house, every window illuminated. A handful of people were still lounging in the living room or picking at the remains of the food in the kitchen.

"Sure."

I ran inside to grab my jacket, terrified she'd leave before I returned. Fortunately as I tripped out of the door, Madeline was pottering around on the pavement outside Aiden's house, her head down as if looking for something.

"What've you lost?" I asked, scanning the tarmac next to her feet, searching for whatever it might be.

"Oh, nothing." She smiled at me again and threaded her arm through mine.

It was odd to be standing next to her after being sat on the wall together. Her head barely reached my shoulder. It felt like I was taking a kid home despite the connection we'd made through the night. We walked on in silence. My disappointment that this girl was too young for me kept me quiet. I didn't want to invest any more feeling into her. I couldn't believe that someone so young could have made me reveal myself so openly.

Madeline didn't seem put off by my quiet mood. She walked with her eyes on the pavement and I listened to the sound of our footfalls – two of Madeline's for every one of my own. I slowed my pace. Her arm was warm on mine. We were a gallery of opposites; me tall, her petite; me tanned, her pale; me broad shouldered next to her thin form.

"Just around this corner." Her voice struck out clear and deep in the murky orange of the street-lamps. She pulled a key out of her pocket in front of a hairdressers and inserted it into the blue door just inside the porch.

"You live here?"

"Yeah." She fiddled with the key in the lock until it gave and she kicked open the door.

"Hope we don't wake your Dad," I took a step back to stand on the pavement instead of in the confined space of the doorway with Madeline.

"My Dad lives round the corner. This is my place."

She said it with such a simple shrug that I almost didn't believe her. I stood for a minute with my mouth hung open, not sure of what to say.

My mind was overloaded with questions. What parent allowed their daughter to live alone? How did a sixteen year old rent a bedsit? How could someone so young have their own place while I was still living with my parents?

"How can you be living alone when you're only sixteen?"

"It's complicated."

Stood a step away, on the threshold of her own place, and knowing she had a full time job at a café a few streets away I saw her as a young adult like me. She didn't talk like a sixteen year old. Until we'd started walking home I hadn't even considered her as any different to me

"Thanks for walking me home," she said, turning away from me with a sigh.

I reached out and caught her elbow to spin her around. I had to bend low to kiss her, but she anticipated my move and raised herself onto her toes to meet my lips. She tasted of fizzy raspberry sherbet. When I released my grasp on her I saw my giddiness reflected in her eyes. Her pink lips curled into a satisfied grin.

"Maybe you could walk me home again sometime?"

"Most definitely."

We stared at one another for a minute before untangling ourselves. I watched Madeline disappear back into the shadows, glimpsing a final sparkle of her blue eyes as she shut the door. I waited until I saw a light go on upstairs before wandering away, in no rush to get home, replaying that kiss in my mind.

~~~

I walked Madeline home at least a dozen times before I ever ventured up those stairs to her bedsit. I was too afraid of what might happen, of misreading the signals and taking advantage. Instead, I'd go to the café on my lunch break to talk about our day and stop by after work for a mug of tea waiting for her shift to end. We'd hold hands as we walked, glancing at one another without speaking and smile each time one of us got caught looking at the other. Conscious of the difference in our age, and wary of circumstances, I didn't want to rush things. But when she invited me up one Saturday afternoon, tugging at my sleeve with a provocative glare, I followed.

Had she been nineteen, I imagine we would have ripped one another's clothes apart in our lust for one another. Instead, she led me to a lumpy sofa bed and offered to get me a drink. I sat, taking in the room around me to cool my desire. It was a basic set up; a single room with a corner kitchenette next to an old gas fire and a doorway leading to a short corridor, at the end of which I
~~~

could see a tiny bathroom. It smelled of fresh linen and the slight sting of lemon that lingers in the air after a clean. The sofa was in front of the window with light straining through yellowed net curtains and next to this, taking up an entire wall, were a set of shelving and a single wardrobe. There were a few books amongst the shelves but the majority of space was taken up by boxes of varying size. I counted at least forty by the time Madeline had brought me my lemonade.

"Want to see what's in them?" she asked, reaching for one before I'd even said yes.

When she lifted the lid I peered inside. It looked like a knick-knack box, full of random things. Madeline began to remove items and placed them on the coffee table next to my glass. The early autumn heat wave we were having made the glass sweat, little beads of condensation clung to it making it slippery and cool.

"These are all things I found on the street along the way to work," she explained.

I understood then: every time we walked somewhere together, her eyes would scan the pavement and road rather than where she was going. In the three weeks since we'd shared that first kiss I'd grown used to steering her around obstacles. Occasionally she would stop, bend and retrieve something from the floor. When I asked she'd always shrug and say it was a penny or a button, something for good luck. Now I realised they ranged far more than just coppers and buttons.

"You found this?" I asked, holding up a feathered ear ring.

"Caught in the bushes next to the park," she said. "This one," she picked up a beaded bracelet with a broken clasp. "I found at the side of the road next to my door."

She had more than just bits of jewellery and tat. She showed me the wedding ring she'd discovered outside an art gallery, fallen in a gap between paving tiles. She had key-rings and tennis balls, pens and badges, watches and umbrellas. In one box she had a selection of playing cards all with different backs.

"Is this a full deck?" I asked, flicking through them.

"No, there's fifty-eight in total. Five jokers, three jacks of hearts and a couple of two of spades. I'd love to get a set though, that's the aim. I've collected half of those from the park this summer."

I raised my eyebrows, simultaneously impressed by her collection and dismayed by the things people often simply left behind.

"Why keep all this stuff though? What are you going to do with it?"

Madeline fiddled with a key-ring in her hands as she answered, not looking me in the eye. "I dunno. I fix what I can. I haven't bought any jewellery, ever. I have this idea that I could make something from it all; a huge sculpture of lost mementos that people would recognise as their own. I just can't bear to see it all abandoned, not when it could still be used or kept." She half-shrugged, placing the key-ring back in a box with such care I knew immediately how important this collection was to her.

"I think it's great that you save all this stuff," I said, laying my hand over hers. "If you think that you can make something of it, you should."

I looked at her with new eyes after that, realising that some of her mismatched outfits stemmed from wearing clothes she brought home from the lost property box at work. Each piece of jewellery she wore was unique. I remembered commenting on her wearing only one earring a few days ago and her response was that it was meant to be that way. There was a Mickey-mouse watch she hung from the belt buckle of her jeans, the strap beyond repair, which I'd assumed was a gift when she was a child. All her belongings took on new significance. It was what made Madeline, Madeline.

I left before it got dark that night. We'd done nothing more than kiss, deep, sensual kisses that I pulled away from panting with desire. As I walked away I turned to wave knowing she'd be at the window watching me and I saw another man, much older than me, stumbling up the road. He was short and round, with a balding head and a crescent of ginger hair over each ear. His chubby face was half hidden by a beard that was flecked with grey, though I could detect the reddish tinge it used to be. He had to stop every few steps, hunched over and breathing heavily. As he reached the hairdressers, he steadied himself on the window frame. I stopped to watch him; he was in no state to even notice me half way down the street.

He disappeared into the porch where Madeline's door was and my gaze lifted to her window. The net curtain was down. I hurried back to her doorway, afraid that this man might cause her trouble somehow, and was just in time to see her pushing his bulk up the stairs as the door was swinging closed.

"Madeline? Are you okay?"

The door re-opened and she appeared with a furrowed brow and pink cheeks.

I could see the man clambering up the stairs behind her mumbling something under his breath. The air was infused with body odour and stale cigarettes. Madeline glanced over her shoulder and closed the door so all I could see was her face. "He's my Dad, James. It's fine. I'll be all right."

I stopped the closing door with my hand. "Are you sure?"

Up until this point Madeline had managed to dodge most of my questions about how she came to be living apart from her Dad. She hardly mentioned him. Even without meeting him it was easy to suspect the obvious: the musty stench that was settling around us both was proof of that.

"I promise you, everything is fine," she said, her eyes wide. She was embarrassed. I would have felt the same if circumstances had been reversed.

"Okay," I removed my hand from the door. "Call me if you need me though."

She nodded before slamming the door shut and I made out the patter of her feet racing up the stairs. I hung around in the porch for a few minutes, ears pricked, but heard nothing so I wandered back home and spent a sleepless night wondering about Madeline's relationship with her father.

~~~

"Tell me again why your Dad left the police force."

We were sat at a corner table in Cups and Saucers, Madeline on her lunch break, and I was pestering her for information about her father. So far, she hadn't been forthcoming.

"Medical reasons," she replied, picking the salad out of her sandwich.

"What's wrong with him?"

I watched Madeline re-bread her ham sandwich next to the discarded lettuce and tomatoes on the plate. She took a bite and chewed leisurely before answering.

"Stress. Heart palpitations, that kind of stuff."

"The alcohol can't help."

Madeline stiffened. She dropped her sandwich and pushed her plate away. I was about to apologise but realised her gaze was focused just over my shoulder. I shifted to examine the man who had entered the cafe. I didn't recognise him; stocky, with floppy brown hair and slouched shoulders. He seemed to be in his early twenties. The second he saw Madeline he smiled and inclined his head, though he took a seat in the furthest corner, next to the window. I nudged Madeline with my foot.

"Everything okay?"

She blinked and smiled – though not enough to create her dimples. "What? Yes, sure. I should get back to work."
~~~

"You've only had ten minutes." I placed my hand over her own as she reached for the plate. "It's not like the place is busy."

Except for the man, there were only three tables occupied and Susie, the other waitress, had them covered.

"You're right," Madeline took my hand and squeezed it.

The guy clearly made her skittish, but I put it down to him being a difficult customer and changed the subject.

"I was wondering if you might like to come over to mine for dinner tomorrow night? My Mum's interested in meeting 'this girl' I've apparently become besotted with." Madeline had refused the first time I'd asked only a week or so after we'd met. I didn't blame her then, but now I felt we were ready.

"I don't know. I promised my Dad I'd pop in this weekend."

"Oh come on Mads," I said. "You can still see him. Invite him along if it'll make you feel better."

I didn't really mean it, but the look of horror on Madeline's face panicked me. Was her Dad so bad he couldn't be trusted through a meal?

"Let me think about it." She leaned over to give me a kiss on the cheek. I got a distracting glimpse of her cleavage. Before I could coerce her into giving me an answer, the café door swung open and a group of pensioners ambled in. "I'd better give Susie a hand." Madeline swiped our plates up and tossed me a quick smile.

I stayed for a few minutes watching her work. She flattered the pensioners as if they were all beloved grandparents and the feeling seemed mutual; they laughed with her and nodded their heads at her polite and helpful manner. I could love that girl, I thought.

Just as I was getting up to leave I glanced across at the man that had come in during our lunch. He was sat sideways on his chair, his back against the wall, with his feet crossed in front of him. Susie must have served him the cup of coffee that sat steaming next to the newspaper at his elbow. He was observing Madeline just as I had been only moments before. I recognised the lopsided smile and softness of his expression. My stomach tightened into a fist, one that I wanted to smash straight into his face.

Instead, I shrugged my jacket on and made a bee line for Madeline on my way out. As she was walking between the pensioners and the counter, I wrapped an arm around her waist and bent down to kiss her on the mouth. I left her with a bemused but affectionate expression. As I passed the window outside it was satisfying to see that the guy was now turned to his coffee and flicking through his newspaper.

~~~

Madeline came to dinner with my parents the next day. I could tell she was nervous by her constant need to fiddle with things – from twirling her hair to tapping her fingers. She dressed in more conventional clothing, though they were all charity shop buys. Still, the blouse she was wearing was her size and the jeans she wore didn't have rips at the knees.

After polite introductions, Madeline's gaze stopped at a photograph on the mantle. She gravitated toward it and I readied myself for the embarrassing stories Mum was bound to tell. But, instead of picking out the one of me in my scout uniform at the age of six, she pointed to my parent's wedding photo.

"This dress is beautiful."

Mum beamed. "It was my mother's. I had it altered to marry Brian, it didn't originally have the lace sleeves or train." A flicker of sadness crossed her face and her smile faded into a nostalgic one. "My mum died before I met Brian, so it was like having a bit of her with me on my wedding day."

Madeline was transfixed. "You look amazing."

"Still does," Dad interrupted.

"I'd better get dinner out," Mum said, and she disappeared into the kitchen.
~~~

Dad followed, calling over his shoulder; "Do you two want to get settled at the table? James, tell your sister dinner's ready."

I took Madeline into the dining room, a space usually full of junk reserved for special occasions. Mum had cleared the room and had arranged the table like it was Christmas – a vase of flowers in the centre flanked by candelabras. I glanced down to see Madeline's expression, slightly awed with wide eyes.

"I think Mum went a bit overboard," I whispered, offering her a seat and then ducking out to fetch Sarah. At thirteen she was just settling into her drama queen phase and was sulking because Mum and Dad had told her she wasn't allowed to go to the cinema with her friends. I banged on her door.

"Hey pipsqueak, dinner."

I left it at that. If she chose to ignore me, so be it. But curiosity about Madeline must have won out, because she appeared in the dining room with a shy smile a few minutes later. We all sat in silence until my parents came in with platefuls of Yorkshire puddings swimming in gravy.

"Whoops, almost forgot." Dad jumped up out of his seat and brought back a bottle of wine. He started pouring and I was just about to point out the obvious when Sarah piped up.

"Can I have some? Please?"

"Sorry sweetheart, you know you're not old enough," Dad said.

"That's not fair. James' girlfriend isn't old enough either."

All eyes fell on Madeline whose glass my Dad was just about to fill. "Oh, ah, erm..." Dad floundered.

"That's okay Mr Tailor," Madeline replied with a hand over her glass. "I'd prefer juice if you have it."

"Of course." Mum bolted out of the room and came back with a jug of orange juice.

For the next few minutes we all ate, the scratching of knives and forks on plates making up for our lack of conversation. By the time we were half way through the main course it got too much for Mum.

"I hope you don't mind me asking," Mum started. "But James tells us you live in a flat on your own rather than with your Dad."

"Yes."

"Why is that?"

"It's a long story."

"Doesn't your Dad worry, with you only being sixteen?" Dad asked. "I mean, I know I would if it were Sarah."

Madeline stopped in the midst of her cutting up her food. "What if it were James?" she asked.

"If what were James?"

"If James was living on his own at sixteen. Would you still worry then?"

Mum chuckled. "I'd worry he'd never have any clean clothes."

Dad and I smiled but Madeline didn't lower her gaze from Dad's face. Eventually he had to answer. "I think that's a bit different."

"Why?"

My parents exchanged a glance. Sarah caught it and waded in for herself. "Yeah, Dad, why is it different?"

There wasn't even the sound of knives and forks to hide the silence this time. We'd all stopped eating to stare at one another, looking for an answer none of us wanted to hear.

"Parents have a duty to care for their kids and I'm not convinced that sixteen is an appropriate age to shrug off this responsibility." I could tell by the way my Dad pronounced each word with precision that he was choosing them carefully. "I think any child living alone at sixteen would be considered questionable."

None of us could make eye contact with one another. When I glanced toward Madeline she had red cheeks though she held her chin high.

"Excuse me." She stumbled out of her seat and rushed past Sarah to the door. I followed, with a glare at my parents on the way out.

"Where are you going?"

"I'm sorry James, I don't think this was a good idea. Your parents hate me." Her cheeks were stained with tears.

"No, no they don't," I said, folding my arms around her. "They just don't get your independence, that's all."

"So I'm not normal?"

"That isn't what I meant." But she'd already wrestled out of my embrace, pulled the door open and was on the driveway. I tripped down the steps after her, but felt a hand on my shoulder.

"Wait here, I'll go." Mum shuffled passed me and jogged after Madeline who strode down the pavement. I watched as Mum caught her arm and spoke, though I couldn't hear what was said. My stomach was churning and the wine had made me light headed. I think it was stood on that top step in our doorway that I realised I loved her. When I saw Madeline nod and accept a hug from Mum I could breathe again. They began walking back to the house, Mum's arm around Madeline's shoulders.

"You okay?" I asked.

Madeline nodded and wiped the tears from her face. We all filed back into the dining room, Dad standing as we did so. "Madeline, I apologise. I'm afraid I'm a bit conventional when it comes to these things, but of course I don't know your family's situation and I've no right to judge."

"Thank you." Madeline's voice was low and quiet and she couldn't quite look Dad in the eye. Her shoulders moved up and down, like she was taking a huge breath in, and then she said; "If it helps any, I turn seventeen next week."

Her gaze moved up to Dad's face and she gave him a lopsided smile with a little shrug. It was just what was needed to lighten the mood and we all started laughing, nervously at first but then as conversation slipped into what Madeline might do to celebrate her birthday we all settled into a more relaxed state.

~~~

As I walked Madeline home that evening I felt a new closeness had developed between us. My parents asked questions I'd never thought to and as a result I knew Madeline better. When we got to her door she tugged at the front of my shirt so I had no choice but to lean down and kiss her. She pushed her body up against my own and I struggled for breath, a deep urge swelling.

"Madeline." I whispered into her ear as she kissed my neck.

"It's okay," she said. "I'm ready."

She took my hand and led me up the stairs. I hadn't wanted to pressure her into having sex with me but I was desperate for it. When we reached the bedsit I realised she already had the sofa bed prepared, with soft new sheets that smelt of lavender. It occurred to me this was why she had been so upset at dinner. But I didn't get chance to ask because she pulled me down on top of her and started unbuttoning my shirt.

Afterwards, in the dark shadows cast by the street light at the window, I told her I loved her and she curled into me repeating my words.

~~~

The next couple of months were amazing. Long, lazy Sundays tangled up together in sheets and lustful nights where I felt so hungry for more of her I could hardly stand it. I started staying at the bedsit, wrapping myself around Madeline, breathing in sync with her and savouring the taste of her on my lips. We attended a few parties, Madeline clinging to my side and me with an arm slung around her shoulders. My parents commented on young love and took Madeline under their wing. In her, Sarah found a new friend, someone who would side with her in discussions with our Dad and Madeline showed her some of the things she collected, starting Sarah off on a similar hobby.

I briefly met Madeline's Dad out on the street one evening when I arrived early to pick her up for dinner with friends. The two of them were standing under the porch together deep in conversation. I noticed Madeline's hair was a deeper russet colour when compared with his. I hung back. When I'd brought up the topic of meeting her Dad she always went pale and shook her head; a firm no. I decided to create the opportunity instead.

When Mr Fields turned to leave I stepped in front of him. Madeline saw me and rushed to greet me with a smile.

"Is this him then?" Mr Fields asked.

I offered my hand and he shook it with a loose grip; once up, once down, and then dropped it.

"You better be looking after my little girl," he said staring up at me.

Mr Fields wasn't much taller than his daughter. Together they looked perfectly proportional but I seemed like a giant.

"He is, Daddy, don't worry." Madeline gave me a squeeze then stepped away to give her Dad a swift kiss on the cheek. "You should get going, before the shop closes."

He stood up straighter then, a definitive nod to his head.

"I've just got to get my coat, be down in a sec." Madeline hopped up the stairs and I studied her father as he walked away.

He seemed like an ordinary man, but something wasn't right. I expected more questions, an inquisition about who I was and how I deserved his daughter's attention. After all, I was the nineteen year old who had captured the heart of his 'little girl'. I watched as he headed down the road and disappeared into the corner shop. A few minutes later, as the sound of Madeline's footsteps pattered down the stairs, he emerged with a bag weighing him down on one side. Whatever his purchase was, it was heavy and rectangular and I immediately suspected two six-packs of beer.

"What does your Dad do for money?"

"Police pension," Madeline answered. "Can we go now?" She marched off, away from the corner shop, and I took two long strides to catch up with her.

"What's wrong?"

"Nothing."

"Something obviously is."

She sighed, one long breath combined with a roll of her eyes. "So I lend my Dad some money now and then, so what?"

"Exactly," I agreed. "So what?"

"Well you obviously don't think much of him."

"I hardly know him. I only just met him tonight."

"Exactly."

I wiped a hand down my face and tried to think of what to say. We walked on a few feet in air that felt cold and tense.

"Look, I have no idea what I did, but I don't want us to fight. I don't know your Dad and if you lend him some cash now and then to look after himself, then that's your choice. It's good that you're able to help him out."

I hadn't realised until then that Madeline's eyes were filled with tears. "I'm sorry. Stuff between me and Dad aren't the same as with your parents. We've been through a lot, okay? I don't want to talk about it. I just want you to understand. Can you do that?"

I moved so I could wrap my arms around her, stooping to kiss her forehead as I did. My answer was the polar opposite of how I really felt but what else could I say?

"Yes, of course I can."

~~~

The run up to Christmas was busy. Madeline and I were both working extra shifts to earn more and while I was getting up to go into the garage early, Madeline had taken on evening shifts at the
~~~

café. I missed her but when I offered to visit her at work she shut me down.

"No, you're working long enough hours as it is. You don't want to be sitting in the cafe waiting for me to get a break. Not that I get one any more, it's busy with all the late night Christmas shoppers. It wouldn't be worth it. Go home, get some rest and we'll spend some time together on Sunday, okay?"

I liked that she cared enough about me to sacrifice her time with me. I was usually dog tired after spending ten hours fixing 'urgent' jobs and trying to find time to do my own family Christmas shopping. Yet, I worried that it had more to do with questions about her Dad. When she agreed to spend Christmas day with me I was relieved.

"So I'll go see Dad in the morning and then come across to yours for dinner at two?" Madeline said as we lounged about in her flat on a rare Sunday off a week before Christmas. She was settled on the floor in front of me with a selection of objects as gifts for my parents and sister: A leather wallet for my Dad, whose initials she'd stitched into the front; A silver necklace with the letter 'L' hung from it for my mum and a bracelet for Sarah made from a selection of her found beads.

"Sounds like a plan." I tugged at the jumper she was wearing and wiggled my eyebrows.

She slapped my hand. "Not now, pest. I'm wrapping presents."

"Why do you need the extra shifts if you aren't spending money on Christmas presents?"

"I'm saving."

"For what?"

"A rainy day?" she answered with a smile, indicating the water-streaked window from the sleet outside.

"We should go on holiday."

"Fat chance, where would we go you could afford?" She wrapped Sarah's present in tissue paper and then deposited it into a makeshift bag.

I shrugged and wrapped my arms around her. I kissed her and she wriggled free, giggling. "Anywhere with you," I told her.

"You should get home. You'll miss dinner."

"Aren't you coming?"

"Have to go check on Dad. Promised him I'd cook."

I wrinkled my nose to show my disappointment as I disentangled myself from the cushions on the sofa.

"We'll get to spend all of Christmas afternoon and night together," Madeline said, giving me a kiss on the cheek. "Now go, before I make you stay."

"Make me stay," I joked, and she pushed me toward the stairwell in response.

~~~

I arrived home just as Dad was serving up and grabbed myself a plate to take into the living room to balance on my knee – the way we usually ate when we didn't have guests. I was halfway through shovelling food into my mouth when Mum told me she'd invited Noah Fields for Christmas dinner. I nearly choked on my mashed potato.

"What?"

"I saw him, in the local supermarket and I introduced myself," Mum said. "He seemed to think you and Madeline had broken up because she hadn't mentioned you in a while."

"Well, I doubt she talks to him much about me."

"Anyway, he was pleased to know you were still a couple and when I found out he was going to be all on his own on Christmas day I invited him over."

"I don't know if that was a good idea Mum."

I hadn't told my parents about my suspicions that Noah Fields was an alcoholic, or that his and Madeline's relationship appeared to be backwards – with her looking after him rather than the other way around. But I knew that Dad had heard a few stories in
~~~

the pubs, mainly centring around why Noah was barred from them all.

"It was a spur of the moment thing. He said he'd love to. We can't ask him not to come now, can we?"

"I guess not."

Inside I was already worrying what Madeline might have to say about all of this. Although, perhaps it would be good for them to interact with another family, maybe we could get to know her father a bit better. If Madeline and I were as serious as I hoped we'd be, it would be worth it.

~~~

"She did what?"

"She invited him along," I explained for the second time. "Didn't he tell you last night when you went over?"

We were walking back to her place after I'd picked her up from her shift at the cafe. She had been so desperate to leave she was waiting for me outside when I got there. The cold must have been welcoming, as when I arrived the window in front was steamed up and Madeline had rosy red cheeks and was gulping in big breaths. Now she was hyperventilating over her Dad coming for Christmas.

"It's not a good idea. He'll drink you dry, then cause a scene. James, we have to do something."

"What can we do?" I shrugged. "We'll just have to keep an eye on him and hope for the best."

"How's he going to get home? We can't afford a taxi and I bet he'll be in no state to walk back on his own." Madeline threw her hands up in the air, taking one of mine with it as we were holding hands. "I'll just have to come back with him, make sure he's all right."

"I'll talk to my parents, see what we can work out. I might be able to drive him, you never know."
~~~

I was hoping my parents would treat me to a car for Christmas, as I'd been hinting for months by pointing out old bangers that needed a bit of work. When I'd spoken about getting one myself a month before they'd talked me out of it, so I thought that was a good sign.

"I wonder why he didn't tell you last night?"

Madeline picked up her pace and I had to stride to keep up with her for a change. Her answer was framed in a cloud of cooling air above her head as she spoke. "I dunno. He's a man, he's forgetful. He was drunk?"

She added the last one on as a question, but I could tell it was probably the truth. I spent the next few days reasoning with her, convincing her it would be all right.

~~~

By the time Christmas day came around Madeline had figured out a way to deal with her Dad's drinking – low alcohol beer always poured into a pint glass. I was actually looking forward to meeting the strange man whose daughter I was pretty sure I wanted to spend my life with. I was glad Madeline identified a solution to Noah's fondness for drinking, because by the time the meal came he'd already gone through eight cans.

"Told you we'd need at least twelve," Madeline whispered to me as we passed in the hallway. I shrugged. We'd bought eighteen. Dad had raised an eyebrow but not commented when I'd lugged them all home earlier in the week.

So far, the day had gone well. We'd exchanged presents, everyone thrilled with their lot: most especially me with my beat up Golf GTI. I think Noah would have been happier with a six pack rather than the rather smart watch Madeline offered him. He'd bought her a wool jumper, still with the tags on. Madeline kissed him on the cheek and folded it away. I never saw it again.
~~~

"So, Noah," Dad began as we sat down for dinner and the novelty gifts in the crackers had been discarded. "I understand you used to be an officer of the law?"

"That's right," he said, wolfing down the turkey whilst piling his fork with roast potatoes.

Dad glanced at me before continuing. "How are you finding retirement?"

"Not too shabby." He went to drink from his glass but it was empty, the froth sliding down the inside. I swiped it up and fetched him another.

"You seem awfully young to be retired Noah," Mum commented as I came back.

Noah glared across at Madeline, their eyes meeting for a fraction of a second before Madeline looked down.

"Fifty-six." Noah patted his chest. "Heart gave out on me. Bit dodgy now."

"Madeline says you've lived in quite a few different places the last few years. Anywhere you'd recommend worth visiting?"

Again, I caught a look between Noah and Madeline, no more than a glimpse but I saw it.

"Don't think we stayed long enough to take notes, did we Maddy?"

Madeline stopped with her fork in mid-air and mouth open. "Erm, not that I remember," she said. "We're pretty settled now though." She put a hand under the table on my thigh and squeezed.

"Little things tend to spoil a place," Noah said. "Rotten neighbours, stray dogs, crime. It's hard to find a place called home."

"Where are you from originally?" Dad asked.

Madeline shot up from the table, spilling her drink in the process. "Oh, god, I'm so sorry." She began mopping up the mess with her napkin.

"Sarah, go get a tea towel," Mum ordered, adding her own napkin to the mix. We all passed napkins forward to soak up the mess. By the time Sarah came back it was mostly cleaned up.

As we tidied the mess, Noah scraped the last remnants of gravy from his plate with a piece of potato and winked as he put it in his mouth. "Fantastic grub, love."

"Thank you," Mum said, though I'm not sure she was all that flattered.

After dessert we all slouched in the living room to watch T.V. Noah, as guest of honour, got the chair where Dad usually sat so Sarah was relegated to the floor.

"But it's not fair," she protested.

"Sarah," Dad warned her with a scowl. I was fed up of hearing her name said in such a tone.

"Stop being a brat," I added. Sarah narrowed her eyes at me and pushed out her bottom lip.

Noah chuckled to himself.

"What, Dad?" Madeline asked. She reached out to place a hand on his arm. It was the most contact I'd seen between them since the gift-exchange.

"You used to be just like that as a kid," he told her. "Butter wouldn't melt, still don't."

Everyone smiled except Sarah, who flounced out of the room and stormed up the stairs. A door banged.

"Whoops, sorry 'bout that."

"I wouldn't worry, she's quite the drama queen just lately," Mum said.

"Aye, you were one of those too, Maddy. Remember?"

I wanted to continue smiling and ask for more details, but a shadow passed over Noah's face as he spoke and Madeline was staring at him. I could see her fingers digging into the flesh on his arm. I nudged her with my foot and she darted a look at me then released her Dad.

"Why don't we go start on that washing up for your Mum?" she suggested to me in a breezy voice.

The kitchen was organised chaos, plates and dishes stacked high next to the sink, foil covered leftovers on the counter tops and utensils lined up next to the cooker, all dripping with Christmas ooze.

"What's going on with you and your Dad?" I asked, shutting the door behind me.

Madeline turned on the taps in the sink and kept her back to me. "Nothing."

"Is there something you're scared he's going say?"

"Always."

"Like what?"

"Like how he misses my mum, or that he had to look after me when she left, or that it was my fault she went, or that everything was my fault."

I stepped behind her wrapping her up in my arms. "Hey, don't get upset. It's okay."

"It's not okay James," she said in a low voice. "It's really not."

"Sure it is," I spun her around and put my hands on her shoulders. She was so small. "You've got me now. Everything will be fine. I promise."

She guffawed at my promise and shrugged my hands off her. "It won't be." She made it sound like a threat.

"What do you mean?"

She glanced up at me but couldn't hold my gaze. Her face scrunched up and she put her hands over her eyes and whispered something.

"What?" I leaned in, stooping so I could hear her over the whooshing of water into the sink.

"I'm pregnant, James."

The water sloshed over the side of the sink and wet my feet. I rushed to turn the taps off and then threw a tea towel on the floor to soak up the excess. Madeline stood there, the water not quite touching her toes. Her face was sill hidden and her shoulders were stooped. She was smaller than ever, like she was trying to fold herself away. I pulled her into me and although I got some resistance, she relented just as the door to the kitchen opened.

"What happened?" Dad was holding Noah's empty pint glass.

"Nothing." I released Madeline and went back to tidying the mess we'd made. Madeline bent to help me.

"Don't get my Dad another," she said. "I think it's probably time we took him home."

"You sure? He's welcome to stay longer." Dad saw the glance that passed between me and Madeline and no more needed to be said. "Okay then." He put the glass on the side and left us scrambling about on the kitchen floor.

Noah appeared in the doorway, sneering. "Apparently I'm off home."

Madeline immediately jumped up. "Yes, Dad. You are."

They stood face to face, Noah marginally taller than Madeline but Madeline with by far the fiercest stare.

"Can I take the rest of my beer then?"

"It's all gone," Madeline lied.

"Was rubbish anyway. Hardly feels like I've had a few." As if to disprove his point he swayed and had to grab onto the door frame for support.

"I'll be ready to drive you home in a minute, Mr Fields."

"Noah," he said. "Call me Noah."

~~~

Twenty minutes later Noah had his coat on and carried a Tupperware box full of leftovers. While our parents said their goodbyes Madeline and I hung back at the end of the hall.

"We'll be fine, it's only around the corner," I told her.

"No, I'll come with you. You don't know how he can be sometimes."
~~~

"Seriously, Madeline, I'm sure I can get your Dad home without you." The news that she was pregnant had filtered through my mind and I had already made my decision. I just needed to get Noah alone for a minute.

"He's right," Noah called from the door.

"Fine," Madeline folded her arms. "I'll finish the washing up. Bye Dad." She gave him a wave and disappeared into the kitchen with a scowl.

As soon as we were in the car I knew I only had a few minutes with him. "I'm really glad you and Madeline were able to spend Christmas with us, Noah."

"Wasn't so bad in the end was it? Bet Maddy told you to expect worse."

I hesitated, not knowing who to side with. I settled on avoidance. "Your daughter is a great girl," I said, cringing inwardly at the awkwardness of it.

"She can be. But you be careful there lad, she's not always as prim as she makes out."

"I was actually wondering if you, well, how you might feel, or if…" I was garbling. My hands were sticky on the steering wheel. I was relieved the roads were empty.

"Spit it out."

"I'd like to ask her to marry me."

Silence settled on us like fresh snow. I risked a glance at Noah. He was staring ahead into the darkness, his lips a thin line. His hands rested on his knees and he was tapping with one finger. I pulled into his street and slowed to a halt outside the selection of council houses where his flat was. I waited for him to respond, to move, to do anything, but he just sat there.

"Noah?"

"Fine, yes, do what you want," he said, fighting with his seatbelt. He shouldered the door to push it open and fell into the road as it gave way. "You don't need my permission. She always does whatever she wants anyway."

I jumped out and ran around the car to help him up, but he slapped me away.

"You do know what you're getting yourself into, right?"

"I...I do. I love her."

"Good for you."

He threw this last comment over his shoulder as he slunk into the shadows. I heard a door slam and assumed he'd got inside safely. I drove home without even paying attention. I hadn't expected a response like that. I thought he'd want to ask me questions, or tell me it was too soon, but to hand his daughter off like that; I was surprised.

~~~

When I got home, Madeline was curled up on my bed reading the book Mum had given her.

"About earlier," I said.

"I know," Madeline sat up, bundling me to one side. "I'm sorry, I shouldn't have told you like that. It just, it all got too much. I was going to wait. I mean it's Christmas, we're supposed to be celebrating...."

"We're not celebrating?" I asked with a sly grin.

"You mean...?"

"Madeline Fields," I dropped from the bed to the floor so that I was on one knee holding her tiny hand in mine. "Would you do me the honour of being my wife?" Then I leaned in and whispered, "And the mother of my child?"

She whipped her hand away and put it over her mouth. I was terrified she was going to say no. But finally she spoke.

"Yes, of course."

We hugged and kissed and I hoped Madeline felt a lightness in her stomach, just like I did in mine. The start of a new life together; a family. It was exciting and exhilarating and scary all at
~~~

once. We chatted over one another, our emotions bubbling up like fizzy pop.

"No, wait." Madeline grasped my hands. For a petite girl she had a strong grip. "I don't want everyone to think we're getting married because you knocked me up." Her brow furrowed. "I want to marry you because I love you and I can imagine a life with you. But that's not what people will say if they know I'm pregnant."

She had a point. It happened all the time. "Then let's keep the baby a secret," I said. "We'll tell people that now we've decided on getting married we just can't wait and we'll do it as soon as we can."

"But I'll still be pregnant James, people will start to notice. Plus, they'll soon realise once it's born."

I bit my lip, thinking and pondering. Then smiled as I hit on a solution. "So we tell them that in the whirlwind of the wedding we didn't realise. That we only found out after the wedding." I shrugged. "What a happy coincidence."

Madeline laughed. I loved that sound, a light tinkling 'ha-ha-ha' that made my heart pump with happiness.

"I guess that's possible," she said, and we curled up together to whisper plans to one another as the night faded into morning.

~~~

We told my parents the following day. Their smiles didn't quite reach their eyes and their hugs were gentle but supportive. The moment they got me alone they expressed their concerns.

"Are you sure about this James?" Dad said. "You're both still young. You don't have to rush into these things."

"I love her and want to spend my life with her. I don't want to have to wait to do that."

"Madeline's Dad might not be as supportive," Mum pointed out. "She is only seventeen."
~~~

"I asked him, he seemed fine with it."

"You did?" Dad sounded surprised.

"On the way back to his last night. I wasn't going to risk asking Madeline until I knew her Dad was on board. I'm not that dumb."

We laughed together, my parents more at ease knowing that Noah Fields had given the go ahead. Madeline went to tell him on her own, she thought it would be easier, I didn't tell her I'd already asked for her his permission. We both knew we'd need his support if we were going to get married soon: he'd have to sign the papers to allow it.

~~~

"You'll need a dress," Mum said to Madeline the next day when she came over to discuss our plans.

Madeline scrunched up her face. "A dress, oh God."

"You're supposed to be excited."

"I am," Madeline said. "I just can't imagine this big fuss over me in a massive white dress. They're not easy to come by second-hand."

"You want to wear someone else's dress for our wedding?" I asked.

"It will be my dress when I'm wearing it. Then I can pass it on and it can be worn again, rather than sitting in a wardrobe somewhere collecting dust."

Mum excused herself possibly thinking we were going to disagree. I took Madeline's hand and kissed the soft skin on her palm. "Sounds sensible to me."

"It'll take ages to find one though," Madeline said. "Especially if..." She brushed her hand over her stomach. I opened my mouth to respond but Mum came sweeping back into the living room carrying a huge white package.

"Mum?"
~~~

"Madeline's right," she said, laying the package down on a vacant chair. "They do just collect dust." She unzipped the plastic cover and carefully pulled out her own wedding dress.

"Wow," Madeline breathed. "It's even more stunning than the photograph." She reached out to caress the silk skirt and lift the lace arms.

"Better see if it fits then, eh?" Mum said.

"What?"

"Well, you're right," Mum said. "Something this beautiful shouldn't only be worn once. It deserves more than that. I've been selfish to keep it in a wardrobe all these years. Now it's time to show it off again."

Madeline glanced between me and Mum several times before speaking. "You mean you'd let me wear it for our wedding?"

"Why not? You said you liked it right from the moment you saw our picture," Mum gestured to the photo on the mantle.

"I...I'm speechless."

"Good," I said, grinning. "No arguments then. Go, try it on."

Mum and Madeline disappeared into the dining room while I tapped my feet waiting for them. Twenty minutes later they were back, self-satisfied smiles on their faces.

~~~

The New Year passed in a blur, and by mid-January everything had been arranged. We would be married on the first of February, three months into Madeline's pregnancy. We booked the registry office – managing to fill a cancellation slot – and organised a reception at the local pub. We decided only to invite close family and friends to the ceremony – my parents, Sarah and Noah plus Aiden as my best man and his girlfriend, with a few more of my relatives and friends to the reception. I asked Madeline about her mum, but she avoided my gaze and shook her head. I knew her relationship with her mum was difficult – that she'd left when
~~~

Madeline was eleven because of some huge argument that her parents had got into. Madeline never wanted to talk about it, so I let it go.

We managed to find a ground floor apartment to share, a five minute walk from the garage I was working at. It was perfect; two bedrooms, a bright, sunny lounge with clear glass doors and a tiny patch of garden. The landlord was reluctant at first, his dark eyes on Madeline's youth and scrutinising the cash I offered as a deposit. But his daughter, a girl about my age, was more accepting, questioning Madeline about the wedding plans and encouraging her father to nurture young love.

Eventually, he scribbled us a note on some cheap paper to prove we'd paid our deposit and first two weeks rent. I took it with a smile and he reminded me that rent was due every fortnight from the day we moved in. We nodded and hurried away - so many things to organise - but I couldn't wait to get back to that apartment. I couldn't wait to start my life with Madeline.

~~~

The night before the wedding, I lay on my bed and gazed at the suit hung on the back of my door imagining what our child might look like – a boy or a girl? There was a commotion downstairs, and as soon as I opened my door Madeline hurried past me in tears, sobbing like a child into her hands. Mum wasn't far behind, her mouth hung open and her arms reaching out to try and catch Madeline to comfort her and to ask what was wrong. When she saw me in the doorway, she shook her head in bewilderment.

I wrapped my arms around her and could feel her shaking. Her face was hidden in her hands and I peeled back the layers of her coat to find that her skin was on fire. "Madeline, what's wrong, are you okay?"

The answer was muffled and forced from behind her hands. "No."
~~~

I pushed the door closed. "It's not the baby, is it? Is everything all right?"

Something in my voice brought her around. She clutched onto me, and showed me her red, blotchy face, wet with tears.

"No, no, it's fine. The baby's fine."

I felt the breath I had been holding escape and my shoulders relaxed. I couldn't imagine what else would upset Madeline so much. "Then, what is it?"

"My Dad knows," she said, in between short gasping sobs. "He went mental."

My face suddenly went cold and numb. I couldn't move. I did not want to be on the bad side of Noah Fields. Especially not the night before I married his daughter.

"What did he say?"

"That he wouldn't let me marry you, that I was stupid and irresponsible. That I was just like my mother."

"Shhh," I stroked her hair, rocking us back and forth trying to soothe her, though I had no idea how to calm her down when the panic was rising in my own gut. I manoeuvred us onto the bed and sat with her until her weeping had become gentle moans and she allowed me to slip free from her grasp.

"I'll go and talk to him," I said. "I'll make it right. It'll be okay."

"No! You can't."

"But the wedding's tomorrow."

"It's fine, he's not coming. He said he never wants to see me again."

Madeline suddenly seemed calmer and more focused than when she'd arrived.

"But you said he found out, that he didn't want us to get married," I stood up, towering over her. I knew she couldn't stop me if I wanted to go.

"He doesn't. But he can't dictate what I want to do. He won't come, it'll be fine. We just had a big argument and I'm upset." She took a step toward me and threaded her arms around my waist and lay her head on my chest. "He needs time to calm down, that's all."

"Are you sure you don't want me to speak to him?"

"Definitely not," she whispered as she unbuttoned my jeans. "If he can't be happy for us, then I don't want him there anyway. He's already signed the papers, it's agreed. It'll be fine."

She pushed me back onto the bed and clambered on top of me. She was so different to the girl who had come running in moments ago in floods of tears. Now she was Madeline the temptress, reminding me why I loved her so much, running her fingers across my bare chest.

"I love you," I said.

I felt the buzz of her words on my ear as she reciprocated with "I love you too," then started to nibble on my earlobe.

That was the last night we ever spent together.

~~~

As Madeline walked down the short aisle of the registry office, I didn't take my eyes off her. She looked stunning. My mother's dress was just her style; slightly out-dated but classic all the same. There had been a minor moment of dread when the sewing scissors were needed because Madeline had put on a bit of weight. And, when we arrived at the registry office Mum teased me about my bride's new appetite for life and biscuits.

"Thank goodness the dress had a lace-up back," she chuckled. "You'll have to keep an eye on her. I think your wife-to-be is a stress eater."

When Madeline came to stand beside me I saw her gaze take in the scene behind me with a flicker of fear.

"Don't worry," I leaned in to whisper. "Aiden sent his little brother to keep an eye on your Dad's place. Just in case."
~~~

Her expression went blank for a moment then she smiled. She gave a slight nod and then the ceremony started.

I choked on my last phrase, but Madeline repeated her lines in a loud, clear voice without her gaze ever wavering. My hand shook as I pushed the ring on to her steady hand. When she placed the ring on me, her skin felt smooth and soft, in stark contrast with my clammy palms - it reminded me of the night we'd met. I felt the pressure in the moment before the registrar announced us as husband and wife and understood what I'd committed to and what those vows meant. Right then, I honestly believed that I would never love another woman for the rest of my life.

We filed out of the registry office with our paperwork, Madeline holding it up in the February sun and marvelling at it. "We did it," she said, squeezing my hand.

"Yes we did," I said, bowing down to kiss her – my wife – again. But I was distracted by a blur of a boy running towards us. It was Billy, Aiden's little brother, who doubled over in stitches the moment he got to us.

Between gulps of air he said; "There's police outside Fields' house, an ambulance too. Think something's happened, taken him to hospital."

Despite the short, sharp sentences Billy got his message across and we all flew into a panic, firing questions at him. It was Madeline who became the voice of reason.

"He's probably fine," she said. "You guys go to the pub and start without me. I'll go to the hospital, find out what's going on and meet you there."

"Don't be silly," I protested. "I'll come with you. You don't know what's happened, it could be serious. I don't want you to be on your own if you need me."

"James, I'm not letting him spoil this for us. He's probably got punch drunk and called the ambulance himself, hoping that it will stop the wedding" She took my hands. "Fortunately it's too late."

She kissed my knuckles and in a low voice said; "It's not the first time he's been taken to hospital. Just let me go see him, make sure he hasn't done anything too stupid. I promise I'll meet you at the pub."

I didn't answer. How could I let my new wife go and face her sick father alone?

"Our guests need at least one of the happy couple to show up the reception," she added.

My instincts screamed she shouldn't go on her own, but she held me at arm's length and her eyes urged me to agree with her. So I let her go. My father offered to take her, so did Aiden, but she declined – a pointed glance my way to warn me that her father might reveal her pregnancy. We called a taxi, she recovered her bag for our honeymoon trip from the boot of the car and changed in the registry office toilets, promising to sneak into the pub and get changed back into the dress within an hour.

We went onto the pub and explained what happened; everyone understood. We all waited for Madeline to reappear. Instead, a female police officer marched into the pub after an hour and a half and asked to speak to me in private. My immediate response was excuse myself to throw up. I was so convinced that something terrible had happened to Madeline and the baby. Once I'd recovered, I gingerly made my way back to the, now muted, party.

The police woman and I went to the back of the pub, where the tables had been set for our wedding meal. I cast a furtive glance over my shoulder at my father before we disappeared and saw him nod and smile weakly.

The arrangement for the meal was magnificent. Sarah and my Mum, along with a few of their friends, had created a wonderful centre piece for the main table – origami paper flowers, bursting out of a tall, thin vase. Smaller bouquets of paper flowers sat neatly in the middle of each of the other six tables. I found it ironic that these flowers would not wilt whilst I waited patiently for my new wife to arrive.

The police officer guided me to a few spare chairs that had been left around the fringes of the room and indicated for me to sit. But, I couldn't stand it any longer. I blurted out: "Is she all right? Is Madeline okay?"

The police officer smiled at me and took a seat opposite. She pulled out a little black pad and pen from one of the many pockets in her vest. "I'm afraid I have no idea where your wife is Mr Tailor. In fact, we were hoping you might be able to tell us."

The knot in my stomach expanded. "She went to the hospital, to see her father: he was taken there this morning"

"May I ask why you chose not to accompany your wife to the hospital?"

"Madeline and her father were going through a rough patch. He had decided not to come to the wedding. She wanted to make sure he was all right on her own, and sent me here to let our friends know and continue the celebrations until she got back."

"And when was this?"

They were all legitimate questions, after all it was odd that I hadn't gone with Madeline. I squirmed in my chair, having to admit that it had been longer we'd agreed and that I was concerned.

"Mr Tailor, I'm sorry to have to inform you of this, but Mr Fields died at his home last night. A neighbour reported it to us this morning."

I slumped into the chair: no wonder Madeline hadn't returned. I jumped up onto my feet. "Oh, God. She'll be devastated."

"Mr Tailor. Madeline did not show up at the hospital, nor has she been seen at her apartment or her father's home. We've also checked your own residence, but there is no one there either." She paused to let this news sink in. "Do you know of any other place where Madeline might go?"

Our new apartment flashed into my mind. But I didn't want the police to disturb her. I wanted to be the one to comfort her. It was my job to hold her while she grieved. I shook my head in numbed disbelief.

"Mr Tailor, it's imperative that we locate your wife. Although Mr Fields died of a heart attack, he also sustained a blow to the head and had injuries consistent with having been in a fight. Neighbours have reported that was a loud disturbance; an argument that occurred approximately half an hour before Mr Fields' estimated time of death."

"Madeline told me that she had had an argument with her Dad. He was an alcoholic."

"We know, the neighbours have corroborated the assertion that Mr Fields was a heavy drinker. Still, we need to locate Madeline to clear up the events of last night. I'm sure it's nothing to be unduly concerned about and there is a rational explanation for things. We just need to speak to your wife."

"I don't know," I mumbled. "I don't know where she is."

My entire life was crumbling before my eyes. This was my wedding day; my father-in-law had died under suspicious circumstances, my wife had gone missing, and I was feeling the burden of carrying around the secret of our child. My body was exhausted and my mind confused. I kept re-playing the last twenty four hours over and over again. The sound of Madeline's voice in my ear telling me she loved me.

My father suggested that we move to our home and wait for Madeline there. He said those very words – 'wait for Madeline' – as if he believed she would come back. But, by this point, six hours after we had committed our lives to one another as husband and wife, I had considered that Madeline wouldn't return, though I couldn't believe I might never see her again.

I asked my father to stop at the apartment on the way back. I peered in through the windows, seeing the shadow of the furniture we had picked out together. Nothing new, but none of it from Madeline's bedsit. We had decided that we would start afresh and choose everything together. But that furniture was the only thing in the apartment that night.

The following day, the police came back to question us all again. They told us that her bedsit above the hairdresser had been cleared out. I suggested she had packed up in anticipation of our move, but they seemed unconvinced. And so, I began to doubt it too.

~~~

After a week - the week that would have been our honeymoon - I moved into our apartment. My parents were against it: I was depressed and withdrawn, mourning for the loss of Madeline, but also that they didn't know – the loss of my child. I could only hope Madeline would contact me somehow, let me know she was all right and the baby was still okay. I couldn't explain why she had disappeared but I believed if she did try to make contact, it would be at our new home.

I hung around for days, not unpacking anything, relying on family to bring me meals. My parents both attempted to convince me to come home, but I was adamant: if I couldn't be with Madeline, I wanted to be alone. Three weeks passed and I heard nothing. The police closed their enquiry and stopped searching for Madeline. They told me about a final sighting of her with another man, holding hands with him and getting into his car. I refused the idea that she had run away with someone else. I insisted she had been taken against her will.

The police officer who had spoken to me at our wedding simply placated me with empty words. There was no evidence she was under duress. She left a number for me to call if I heard from Madeline, but I threw it away as soon as I shut the door. Madeline wasn't coming back. Even if she hadn't left with another man, if she wasn't here with me now, she mustn't have wanted to be here
~~~

in the first place.

~~~

The landlord came around every two weeks to collect rent, and eventually I went back to work. A month after the date of the wedding I started back up at the garage. I unpacked my belongings and made the apartment my home. After eight weeks a parcel arrived; a large box with a black ribbon tied around it. I ripped it open and lost my hands in a sheath of white material that was my mother's wedding dress. With it was a small card. I had high hopes that Madeline would ask me to meet up with her somewhere, but it wasn't even from her. It was signed 'Patricia' and then, beneath that to clarify: 'Madeline's mother'.

I must have read the words over a hundred times, there were so few of them. The note simply stated that Madeline had been to see her, said she'd got into trouble and asked for money. Then she requested her mother send the dress back.

She didn't want to write to you herself, Patricia wrote. *It's just like my daughter to lead people down troublesome paths. She miscarried the kid, and took my money. She won't be back again. Count yourself lucky.*

I didn't feel lucky. I felt hollow. I stuffed the dress in the back of my wardrobe and said nothing. The next day, at my parents' instruction, I applied for an annulment of the marriage. It was accepted with speed and suddenly I was a bachelor again. If it hadn't have been for that letter, I might have pined after Madeline for years. But when I read it I couldn't bear to love her any more. Her mother seemed to think I'd had a lucky escape, that her daughter was a mean, cruel girl that would have destroyed my life. I wasn't sure that Madeline hadn't already destroyed it.

~~~

I moved on, as well as I could. Within six months the pain wasn't so bad, more of a general ache. Somehow I recovered, started smiling again and forgot. Eventually I was soothed by the gentle care of the landlord's daughter; that same girl who had congratulated me and Madeline when we secured our home. I've never told anyone else that Madeline was pregnant. That's been my secret to keep all these years and now I'm done with it. I have more important things to worry about than a woman who discarded my child like an old coat, despite all her supposed morals about rescuing what others had left behind.

PART III

THAT WHICH IS LOST

Chris listens to James' final words and thinks that it seems like a story of forgotten hopes and faded dreams.

"Now I've got a real baby girl who's sick and the only thing I can do about that is be here for her. So, no, Doctor, I ain't visiting Madeline. I don't need to know why she did what she did. The fact she did it is enough for me."

"I'm so sorry." Chris knows he can't ask this man to spare any compassion for a woman he has not seen in twenty years. "I hope your daughter fights through," Chris says, as he stands up.

"We had hoped for a bone marrow donor but she can't wait much longer. We're being bothered by the doctors to keep her in, that's what I thought you were calling for."

Chris nods, understanding James' desire to protect his girl from the melancholy of a hospital environment at such a young age. They walk toward the hall together and James' footsteps seem weary as he glances up the stairs where his daughter sleeps. The door opens before they reach it and a small boy darts in followed by a soft, fair woman and a teenage girl hiding rounded cheeks behind a long fringe.

"Oh, hello darling." The woman looks to James and then glimpses Chris over her husband's shoulder.

"Dad, Dad, look. I made this at school. It's for Emily." The boy waves a papier-mâché model up at James who bends down to see.

"Hannah, this is Dr Wright," James says as he looks over his son's handiwork.

His wife's warm expression disappears and Chris watches her eyes widen. She drops the bag she is holding, but the girl, who looks about thirteen, rescues it.

"It's okay Mrs Tailor," Chris says. "I'm not here about Emily. She's fine."

She visibly relaxes. The girl rolls her eyes and takes the bag away into another room. James stands, his hand on the boy's shoulder.

"Sorry. I should have explained."

"Dad, can I go give this to Ems? Is she awake?" The boy hops from foot to foot.

"Sure kiddo." The second he is given permission the boy races up the stairs. Chris watches him go. What stamina would you require to keep up with a son so energetic?

"The doctor here came to tell me my wife was dying," James tells Hannah.

"But, I'm fine."

"Not you, Mrs Tailor. We have another Mrs Tailor at the Unit." They suit one another, thinks Chris. He wonders if people think the same about him and Holly.

Hannah looks between them and waits.

"It's Madeline, Hannah. She kept my name."

Hannah's mouth falls open a fraction and the recognition in her eyes tells Chris that she knows the story that James told, at least about her husband's previous love, if not the lost chance to be a father.

"I'll get out of your way. You've got much more important things to worry about." Chris says. He shakes James' hand and thanks him for his time.

"I hope you find someone to be with her," James says. "No one deserves to die alone." He pauses. "Even Madeline."

As he shuts the door, James is still shaking his head as if he doesn't believe the girl he spoke of could possibly be on her own. Chris is beginning to understand though. Madeline has made a lot of mistakes in her life, the glimpse he had been given by Cecelia and James prove as much.

Chris walks away from James' house with the image of a young boy repeating 'Dad' in his mind. The relationship between James and his son, even in such a brief moment, demonstrates the bond between them; the excitement of the boy and patient respect of the father. Chris wants that. He doesn't want to experience the pain and regret he witnessed as James spoke of Madeline running away and of the child he had lost. The thought that Betsy might feel she has to run away from him crushes any eagerness he may have at being a father.

He is just about to pull away from the curb in the car when the notification for a text message buzzes through. He so rarely uses his mobile phone that the sound makes him jump and he has to dig it out from the inside pocket of his jacket.

It's Betsy: '*Found something. You need to get back here. Now.*'

He turns the car back to the Unit, glad for the reminder that Betsy is still there, waiting for him. He is less interested in what she has found relating to Madeline than he is in convincing her to stay and raise their child together. Seeing James and his family reinforces how much Chris wants to be a father. He may never have the family that James has – so crucial for support in such difficult times – but he does want something, and he is too afraid of losing what might be his only chance at it.

~~~

Chris hurries through the automatic doors of the Unit intent on finding Betsy so that they can talk. On his way back he imagined what it would be like if Betsy did choose to return to Ireland. He can't bear the thought of never seeing his child, or only visiting once a month, once a year even. As he slows to a more reasonable pace to enter the corridors of the hospice a booming voice calls his name from behind.
~~~

"Doctor Wright?"

Chris stops momentarily, calculating what would happen if he continued on, pretending he hadn't heard.

"We need to have a conversation."

He relents and turns to face the hunched figure of Doctor Gregory. He stands in the doorway, a beady set of eyes with eyebrows pulled low. Despite this thunderous expression there is the evidence of a satisfied smirk twitching on his lips. Over his shoulder Chris spies the ghostly face of Cecelia with a hand over her mouth.

"Doctor Gregory," Chris pushes his shoulders back in an effort to tower over the old man. He doesn't offer his hand this time.

"This young lady was telling me that you went to visit Mrs Tailor's ex-husband." There is a pause. "Without your patient's permission."

Cecelia disappears from behind Doctor Gregory. So, she knew the situation between Madeline and James and had let Chris go anyway. Did she let him go because she had expected James to come, or because she knew he would not?

"I was under the impression that they were still married," Chris explains, glancing across at the receptionist who no longer has her ear buds in. "Therefore I felt it pertinent to make her husband aware of her decision to sign the DNR." He knows this won't satisfy Doctor Gregory, but he says it anyway.

"You've been warned repeatedly about interfering in the lives of your patients, Doctor."

"I don't believe I was interfering," Chris replies. "I was simply doing the best I could for my patient. As I always try to do."

"But your patient isn't aware that you planned to visit her spouse?"

Chris says nothing.

"Perhaps we should consult with your patient?"

Doctor Gregory strides past Chris, turning a few steps away to hurry him along. "Well? Let's see what she has to say then."

~~~

Chris follows him to Madeline's room with a dejected stride. Either Madeline will back him up and dismiss Doctor Gregory, or she will tell the truth. Chris glimpses Betsy in the corridor as they turn toward Madeline's room Her eyes are wide and he just catches the drop of her jaw as they stop at Madeline's door, as if she wants to call out to him. Again, Doctor Gregory knocks and enters without waiting for permission to do so.

"Mrs Tailor, apologies for the intrusion, but—"

Doctor Gregory stumbles in his speech. Chris' skin suddenly turns cold and clammy, his breath catches. Holly is perched on a chair next to Madeline her face turned expectantly toward the two of them.

"I'm sorry, I didn't realise you had visitors, Mrs Tailor." Doctor Gregory composes himself. "I just came to ask if you were aware Doctor Wright here contacted your previous husband about your condition?"

Chris can't take his eyes off Holly. She sits with a cool expression, showing no recognition of him. Chris is relieved Doctor Gregory never met his wife, god knows what he would think if he did. Chris trips over the reasons why Holly might be here but he can't think of any, and that scares him.

"You know very well he didn't," Madeline's voice is a whispering croak. At the statement he is looking for, Doctor Gregory smirks at Chris. "But I called in the cavalry." Madeline gestures to Holly, who takes her gaze from Chris to smile at Madeline and then reaches out to clasp her hand. She refrains from introducing herself. Chris feels every set of eyes in the room settle on him.

"I—" he begins, not quite sure what to respond.
~~~

"It's my fault." Betsy's voice comes from the doorway. "I told the doctor about Mrs Tailor's husband. I said the patient had asked for him. She didn't have anyone to support her and I thought I was doing the right thing." She hovers half in and half out of the room, her face flush with the lie which only serves to extenuate her guilt.

Doctor Gregory throws his hands up in a dramatic fashion. "Excellent, just what we need. More social workers in the department than medical professionals."

Chris catches Holly's eye. She resumes her scrutiny of him with a blank, calm face that looks through him rather than at him. Only when Holly blinks and then begins to stand, slowly and deliberately, does Chris recall that it was Doctor Gregory who insisted on informing Holly's previous employer of her misuse of company resources.

"I'm sorry," Holly addresses the older doctor with an upturned nose. "Who exactly are you?"

Doctor Gregory squares his shoulders and lifts his chin in the air. "I'm a key board member here, and I have concerns that your…" He fumbles over the word, not knowing how to describe Holly in reference to Madeline. She stares at him with crossed arms. "Concerns that Mrs Tailor is not getting the best care. It appears her physician and primary nurse are more concerned with finding errant family members than they are in providing quality care."

Doctor Gregory switches his gaze from Holly back to Chris. "This is exactly why I wanted you gone," he says, spittle forming at the corners of his mouth. "Now you've gone and made an impression on the staff who think they can get away with this sort of behaviour. You'll be out before the end of the month, Doctor Wright, mark my words. As for you, young lady—"

Holly intercepts before the old man can continue.

"How dare you," she says, moving into his personal space. As a result, she towers over him. "How dare you come into this room, where my friend is dying," she bends over Doctor Gregory and lowers her voice. "Dying," she repeats. "And try and settle some score you have with one of your staff. Have you no respect?"

Doctor Gregory takes a step back. Chris sees his Adam's apple bounce as he swallows back the indignity of being confronted in his own hospice.

"From what I understand Doctor Wright here and his nurse have been exceptionally kind to my friend, despite some personal issues she is experiencing with her support system. It's a good job I arrived before you stripped them from her care and let her pass away in this room alone and without compassion."

"I apologise," Doctor Gregory's voice is high and squeaky as he wrings his arthritic hands before him, his head hung. Chris senses the traces of a smile twitch at his mouth. He is unashamedly proud of his wife.

"Well, that's enough of all the excitement," Madeline pipes up. "Not sure I can take much more, thank you."

Holly eye-balls Doctor Gregory and he bows his head to Madeline and shuffles out of the room. Chris sees the surreptitious glare that he aims toward Betsy though, and suspects the confrontation is not yet over.

"Thank you for that," Chris leans forward to offer Holly a reassuring squeeze on the arm but she ducks his touch.

"I didn't do it for you," she states, sitting back down.

Chris glances back at Betsy, who raises her eyebrows and inclines her head. She doesn't want to be alone outside with Doctor Gregory. Still, he can't leave without knowing.

"Why are you here?" he asks.

"I called her," Madeline says with a grin. The hollowed out cheekbones and pallor of her face give the expression a ghoulish quality.

"Madeline and I are old friends," Holly explains. "She was my art teacher - remember that piece, Christopher? The one with the photographs and the map of all our special places?"

It dawns on Chris why Madeline's work seems familiar. The piece in the hall, the one he passes every single day as he drops his keys in the bowl below it bears a striking resemblance.

"Madeline was the tutor. It's been, what? Eight years? I had no idea Madeline was the patient you were referring to the other night, if I'd have known—"

"Doctor?" Betsy is still at the door, caught between two awkward situations. He can't leave her to face Doctor Gregory's wrath on her own.

"Are you staying?" Chris asks.

"If you want me to?" Holly asks Madeline.

At the question Madeline nods a slow deliberate movement her gaze fixed on Chris with a smile.

His shoulders are tense and he concentrates on trying to relax them. Holly is here, Madeline is no longer alone. But, Betsy is also here - pregnant with his child - and Chris doesn't know how long he can keep such a thing secret. If he doesn't confess to Holly soon, the betrayal will only puncture deeper into her heart when she discovers what happened.

Chris stares at Madeline - has she known Holly was his wife all along? The question lurches around in his stomach so he turns away. He ushers Betsy into the corridor. As expected, Doctor Gregory stands waiting with a red face and flaring nostrils. He hasn't appreciated the dressing down he's received and is no doubt going to take it out on them.

"Let me explain—" Chris speaks but Doctor Gregory cuts him off.

"If you think you're going to get away with this." He pokes a finger under Chris' chin, which is about as high as he can manage.

"Stop." Betsy inserts herself between the two men, facing Doctor Gregory. She comes eye to eye with him. "This is my fault, Doctor. I lied to Doctor Wright. I told him Madeline had asked for her husband."

"No, Elizabeth—" Chris interjects but Doctor Gregory raises his voice once again with a self-satisfied sneer.

"Don't you have any control over your staff, man? They don't even respect you enough to tell you the truth."

"It's not that, I just wanted to make it clear that it was me who made the mistake. Not Doctor Wright. You can't punish him for something he didn't know was wrong."

Doctor Gregory's eyes shrink to slits and he peers over Betsy to Chris.

Is Betsy really going to take the blame here? Is this her telling him that she plans to leave, take his child away and go back to Ireland?

"Is this true?"

Doctor Gregory's voice pulls Chris back into the moment. If he tells the truth he will lose his job. If he lies he will lose his child. But Madeline has someone now and so he doesn't need to be here anymore. He can always find another job. He opens his mouth.

"Is this yours?" Cecelia barges past him, elbowing him to one side holding a small black book up in the air.

Doctor Gregory shakes his head at the interruption, his cheeks wobbling, and then snatches up at the notebook. Cecelia purposefully holds it just out of his reach.

"I can only assume it belongs to you Doctor Wright," Cecelia continues, in a strange, wired voice. "After all, your name is scrawled over all the pages." She flashes him a smile and offers him the book. Chris flicks through it as Doctor Gregory protests.

"Ah, no, that would be mine. Confidential notes. Pass it here Doctor." He reaches out for it again, but Chris deftly swoops it out of his reach.

"Are these notes on how to fire me?" he asks. They are. Dozens of minute scratchings in Doctor Gregory's cursive writing detail the various ways he might catch Chris out in order to reinstate himself as senior physician at the Unit.

For a few moments the four of them listen to the static sound of Doctor Gregory breathing; a rapid intake of air followed by a snort of dismissal as he exhales. They all look at him and their collective, constant glare breaks his resolve.

"They forced me to retire, didn't even ask if I approved of you," Doctor Gregory spits. "Now give me that back. And let's hear how you supposedly knew nothing about your nurse's little plan."

Chris pockets the book and folds his arms. His heart hammers in his chest. "I don't think so. I'd appreciate it if you would leave now, Doctor Gregory, before we have to bring this matter to the board."

"Oh yes, by all means, let's go to the board. They'll be waiting to hear how I was right about you."

"I had quite an entertaining read while you were in Madeline's room, Doctor Wright." Cecelia says. "I imagine your board would be very interested in reading the musings of their most respected member."

Doctor Gregory's face flushes an even deeper red and he pulls his lips into a tight, white line. Betsy copies Chris' stance, folding her arms over her chest and they stand in silence. Doctor Gregory faces up to Chris, Betsy and Cecelia until finally his shoulders slump and his bottom lip begins to protrude ever so slightly.

"This is not over," he warns.

Chris shrugs, though he feels vindicated. He doesn't understand why Cecelia rescued him: redemption for informing the old man about his visit to James perhaps? Chris watches as Doctor Gregory grumbles away, his back humped and his gait uneven. He feels a glimmer of pity for the old man then. Will he eventually end up in his beloved Unit without any friends or relatives to count on? Chris internally vows to be kind to his predecessor if it ever comes to that. He won't share the notes with the board unless he is forced to.

Cecelia begins to back away, but Chris stops her. "Why give it to me?"

Cecelia drops her shoulders and keeps her gaze on his shoes. "When he asked me about Madeline, I thought he'd been put in charge of her care while you were away. He told me I couldn't stay. That if I didn't want to see her I couldn't just take up space in the waiting room." She takes a breath. "After all she's done to me, I still can't bring myself to leave her behind. I won't be in the same room as her, but until she's gone I'll be here, just to make sure."

"You knew James Tailor wouldn't come to support her, didn't you?"

She half-smiles and shrugs. "I suspected. She never saw him again after their wedding ceremony, did he tell you that? I thought he might come just to confront her."

"And you're disappointed that he didn't?" Chris asks.

Cecelia raises an eyebrow at his question, but this is the only response he receives. Perhaps Cecelia admires James' ability to cut Madeline out of his life and not get drawn back in. "He had other priorities," Chris adds.

"Shouldn't everyone?"

"Was James the father of the baby then?" Betsy asks.

Chris is taken aback. How does Betsy know about the pregnancy? Perhaps Madeline has finally opened up. "He was," Chris says. "I think he was more devastated about the death of the baby than he was about his missing bride."

Cecelia is backing away and Chris catches a glimpse of something in her eye as she slinks off down the corridor. He is about to call her back, to ask her what she knows, when Betsy grabs his arm and pulls him back to the Nurses' Station.

"Death of the baby?" Betsy repeats in a whisper. "According to Madeline's medical notes, she had a healthy baby girl."

"What?" Chris' attention is immediately drawn back to Betsy, Cecelia disappearing from both his view and his mind at the revelation.

"James Tailor told me he got a letter after Madeline disappeared saying that she had lost the baby. He thought that was why she'd left. Are you saying that she lied to him?"

"When were they married?" Betsy scrabbles through a thick file on the desk.

"Early 1991 according to the certificate I found."

"Well, according to this she gave birth at full term in June, so I imagine it's the same child." Betsy glances up at Chris and he smiles down at her. It was smart to request Madeline's full medical records, prior to her diagnosis, the kind of thing Holly would have thought of.

"Holly." Chris suddenly exclaims, reminded by this thought that his wife is in the room across the corridor.

Betsy's face falls and she closes the file and puts it back in a drawer. As she slides it shut the sound it makes emphasises a change in mood.

"I'm sorry, Betsy," Chris pulls over a chair and they both sit. Betsy pinches together her lips and Chris realises it is his responsibility to speak. He decides to start slowly.

"You were going to take the blame with Doctor Gregory?"

She shrugs.

"Because you don't think you have anything to stay here for?"

No answer.

Chris' heartbeat increases threefold. This isn't what he intends. He wants Betsy to stay, to be a father to their child.

"Betsy, I—"

"I don't want to cause trouble Chris. That's your wife in the other room. I don't intend to break up a marriage. And I won't be responsible for it. I'm ashamed enough as it is."

He holds up a hand. "Betsy, Holly has already left me." Saying the words out loud makes it feel real and he has to swallow down the fear and uncertainty that it pushes into his chest.

"You told her?"

Chris shakes his head. "She said she wasn't happy." He exhales an ironic laugh. "She wanted me to agree to adoption. But..." He shrugs.

A sound escapes from Betsy: a surprised, squeaky gasp.

"This was before," Chris hurries to add. "I didn't make the decision because of you and the baby."

"It's not that," she says. "I think - oh god - I think Madeline already knows about us."

"What? How?"

Betsy rummages around in the pocket of her tunic and produces an ultra-sound scan image. "I had this, to show you like we agreed." She holds it out to him and they both take a moment to stare at the white, fuzzy evidence of the night they spent together. "It fell when I was replacing her drip and she saw it. She asked me all these questions about what I was going to do. I just thought that she needed the distraction."

Chris detects a swell of anger in the pit of his stomach. His chest tightens as he asks, "And you told her it was mine?"

"No," Betsy barks at him, her expression horrified. "I said it was an older man, a mistake, a one night stand. She just sat there and smiled and then asked if it was someone like you. I didn't respond but she knew, Chris. It's like she could read it on my face. The next thing I know she's asking for a telephone and she calls in this woman, saying she's a friend. I didn't know she was your wife until she introduced herself."

Chris has no idea why Madeline has brought his wife into the Unit, especially if she suspects Betsy is pregnant with his child. Has she done it on purpose? She made it clear when she first came to Dove Break that she knew who he was, and what he'd done. Can he accept it is a coincidence that she knows his wife from so long ago? Chris lets out a long breath, trying to think of what to do. His mind is muddled between the situation with Madeline and his relationship with Holly. How have they become so intertwined?

Somewhere in the corridor behind them a door opens. Betsy stuffs the picture back into her pocket and tucks her legs under the desk, as if she is working. Chris stands but he doesn't take his eyes from Betsy until he hears the voice.

"Christopher, I think we might need to talk."

When he turns he sees that Holly's face is drawn and pinched, the way it gets when she is contemplating a serious issue. He wonders what Madeline has told her but daren't ask her outright.

"Yes, okay. This way." His mouth is dry and his tongue sticks to the roof of his mouth as he speaks.

He leads her to his office, their footsteps echoing loud in their comparative silence. His feet get heavier with each step, as if they are reluctant to lead him to the final confrontation of his married life. As he opens his office door to allow his wife in first she murmurs an automatic 'thank you'. He will miss her courteousness. A child would benefit from the small, everyday detail such as the social necessity of polite behaviour. He enters and shuts the door.

Holly sits with her legs crossed and arms folded: a fortress of disinclination. Chris waits, perched on his chair, but she says nothing. She is staring at a point just over his head, out of the window, blinking at the light. Then he realises that she is attempting not to cry.

"Holly."

She jumps and closes her eyes and at the same time a tear rolls down her cheek.

"I'm so sorry."

"Don't."

"What do you want me to say?"

"Have you got anything new to say, Christopher? Suddenly decided that you'll accept a child in need to be worthy of your fatherly love?"

He winces at the fierceness in her tone. "Holly, you know that's not why—"

"Does it matter why? I can't convince you that not all sons will end up hating their step-father, or that all adopted daughters won't swindle the man who loved them as their own." She unfolds her arms to flick an imaginary piece of dust from her pencil skirt and then deftly brushes the tear from her face. "There's nothing for us to discuss there. I'm here to talk about Madeline."

Chris back-tracks in his mind; so Madeline hasn't revealed his secret. Yet.

"Madeline?" The name is a shock between them.

"Yes, we need to do something, Christopher. She doesn't have anyone. She told me a few minutes ago she has nothing left to live for." Holly's body language alters as she speaks, her hands dance in the air and she leans toward Chris with urgency. "I thought I was being kinder by not helping you anymore, but seeing Madeline all alone, that's not how it's supposed to be. We need to find someone to help her."

Chris falls back into his chair. This is what he has been trying to do. But it seems that, wherever they look, Madeline has made too many mistakes to call in any favours now. There is the possibility of a daughter, thanks to Betsy's inquisitive persistence, but given the last situation he dealt with involving an estranged daughter he isn't inclined to get involved.

"You're here," Chris points out. "When it came down to it, you're the one she called Holly. We haven't been able to convince her to contact anyone else."

"What about the woman in reception? Madeline says it's an old friend, why is she just hovering instead of supporting her?"

"It's complicated."

"Then un-complicate it."

If only it were that simple. "Look, Holly. Madeline lied to that woman about a very serious issue. Cecelia Hartland is wandering these halls to make sure that Madeline does die alone, as retribution for her father." He hasn't thought of this until he says it out loud. Is this how he thinks of Cecelia? Is she so heartless given the lie to which Madeline had confessed? Chris forces out a frustrated breath, would Holly come to visit him if, on his death-bed, he confessed to getting another woman pregnant and then abandoning his child? He wouldn't do that, he knows, but he also wouldn't blame Holly if she never wanted to see him again.

"I doubt that," Holly replies. "You don't prowl the halls of a hospice to get revenge on a poor woman who's dying. Madeline didn't even know she was here."

"And now that she does, will she see her?" Chris already knows the answer and Holly confirms it by glancing away.

"There's got to be someone who cares about her. What about the husband Doctor Gregory mentioned?"

Chris catches Holly's distaste at saying the name and smiles at the memory of how she chased him away.

Their eyes meet and Holly smiles back, just for a second. "Yes, I did rather enjoy that." Her smile vanishes. "But what about him? Why isn't he here?"

"They're not married, never really were."

"There must be somebody else?"

"There's you," Chris repeats. He won't mention the daughter. He's been burned too many times, not just by Mr Porter's situation, but by the people he's spoken to from Madeline's past. There's probably good reason why Madeline hasn't mentioned a daughter and Chris now realises he is willing to respect those wishes.

"I'm not the person she needs. I barely know her. We bonded years ago over the fact we both miscarried our babies, Christopher. It's a terrible connection to have with someone."

"Madeline miscarried?"

"When she was seventeen," Holly tells him. "Perhaps that's why she and the man you thought she was married to never lasted? Perhaps he didn't want a defective wife either."

Her words sting him because they are so unexpected. "I don't think that of you," he says gently, examining Holly with fresh eyes: is what she really thinks of him? No wonder she left.

"Sorry," Holly shakes her head and her hair falls forward. "This is about Madeline, not us. I shouldn't have said that."

Chris tries to think of something - anything - else to stop him focusing on the deep sense of shame he feels, knowing the sin he has committed will corroborate Holly's assumption of him. He will have to tell her, eventually.

His mind veers back to Madeline. "Madeline didn't lose a baby when she was seventeen."

"She told me she was pregnant, that her father died and the shock of it must have caused the miscarriage."

Chris moves his head from side to side and repeats the words Betsy uttered only ten minutes before. "According to her medical records, Madeline gave birth to a healthy baby girl."

"Then we need to find out what happened, if she's still alive Christopher then we have to contact her."

A day ago, Chris would have agreed. A day ago, Holly would have rallied against him.

Yet, here they are.

"She doesn't want that. If she did, she would have told us already."

"Don't be ridiculous," Holly leans over his desk and swivels the computer monitor to face her. She reaches out for the keyboard, now so eager to do that which she refused to do since she was fired. Chris places a hand over it.

"I think we need to take a step back Holly. I've already spoken to two people who aren't interested in supporting her. If there really is someone else, don't you think she would have mentioned them already? I need to respect my patient's wishes." Doctor Gregory would be proud, Chris thinks with disdain.

"Then maybe she's scared that her daughter won't want to see her either, but we have to try. Can you imagine having a child out there in the world while you die alone in a room, wondering what they made of themselves?"

Chris' hands quiver and he quickly hides them beneath the desk. Did Holly say that on purpose, to goad him? But she swipes the keyboard across the desk and starts tapping keys rhythmically. This is Chris' exact fear: of Betsy leaving and having his child, of never knowing them, of never being able to be a dad, of him alone in a room, with no one. Just like his own father.

Holly's voice disturbs him. "And how do you think that young woman would feel if she finds out her own mother died alone and she wasn't given the chance to visit her?"

Chris doesn't have to imagine that, it almost happened to him.

He watches Holly work, searching as she was trained to do, trying to find more out about Madeline Tailor and the child she lied about; not just to them, but to James too. He leans back in his chair with a hand up to his face, letting Holly take the lead. Too much is happening all at once. If there even is such a person as Madeline's daughter perhaps Madeline hasn't mentioned her because she no longer exists. But the idea seems to have given Holly back a verve for life he hasn't seen for weeks. Save that one moment when she appealed to him to reconsider adoption. He bites down on his lip to prevent the words from escaping. He can't tell her here, now. It isn't fair.

After all, what if he did confess? Holly would leave and Madeline would be alone again. It could take days to locate a daughter and Madeline doesn't have that long. Chris convinces himself it's a coincidence that saving Madeline from being alone prevents him from hurting the woman he loves.

"You should go and talk to her," Holly says, as she searches through internet records. "Make her see that contacting her daughter is the right thing to do."

Chris doesn't agree, but he pushes himself out of his chair and leaves the room. He can't sit there knowing he is concealing a truth from her. But he has no idea how long it might be before Madeline reveals it for him. He finds it interesting that she hasn't mentioned Betsy's pregnancy to Holly, especially given the stories he's since heard about her. But perhaps she isn't certain. There is no better way to find out than to talk to her. Chris returns the way they came and heads back to Madeline's room.

Chris is surprised to see Madeline propped up in her bed writing in a hardback note book on her knees. The oxygen mask is by her side and Chris shakes his head at her when she looks up.

"It's very unflattering," she says, snapping the book shut and putting them to one side. Then she picks up the mask to take a breath, raising her eyebrows at Chris to make her point.

"How are you feeling?"

"Unusually bright," Madeline replies, letting the mask fall again. "Though I think that might be down to the drugs." She nods toward her morphine drip with a grimace.

"Probably." It is a well-known phenomenon that patients tend to get better before the final decline. But Chris doesn't mention this to people, it ruins their last chance to enjoy life.

"You want to know something." Madeline's breathing is stilted, but stronger than earlier. "You want to know why I called in your wife."

Chris thinks he notices her chin arc upward and a devilish shine to her blue eyes but he says nothing. He props himself across from her on the set of drawers. He never likes standing over his patients – he is too tall for that – but sitting seems informal, almost contrite. Leaning gives him the appearance of calm authority.

"You met with my husband, I only thought it fair to even the scale." Madeline smiles at him. "It was why I chose you, you know, I read about that incident with the Porters. I suspected you might take my loneliness as a reason to help me. Discovering that I'd met your wife a long time ago made it seem like fate."

His jaw drops, but he catches himself as his lips part so he looks only partially stunned. So she has been manipulating him. Did she plant that letter on the floor for him to find? As if reading his mind she answers his question.

"I didn't mean to have you contact Cecelia. Wrong bloody letter, would you believe?" Madeline pauses to suck in a breath through the mask. Chris waits with curious patience.

"I hoped you'd get to Penelope eventually."

"Penelope?" Chris' voice squeaks on her name and he clears his throat. "Who's Penelope?"

"Not found that part out yet, eh?" Madeline chuckles.

"Apparently not." Chris is perplexed by Madeline's sudden optimism and honesty. He's been trying to get her to open up and share the details of people who might support her since she arrived and now she is giving it to him without obstacle. She's moving too fast for him, he needs time to catch up.

"Why don't you tell me Holly's part in all this?"

"How could I not invite her into this, Christopher?" Madeline mimics his wife's tone and then laughs. But the chortle catches in her throat and she begins to cough, weak little gestures that betray how exhausted her body is. Chris moves across and holds the oxygen mask up to her face. Her eyes water and it spills over her taut cheekbones creating miniature streams down her face. A few deep breaths later and Madeline bats him away.

"Serves me right," she croaks.

Chris doesn't respond. He listened to Cecelia and James explain how Madeline inserted herself into their lives, drew them in with her mystery and intrigue and then ruined them. Is this what she plans to do to him?

"Serves you right too." She slumps down into the pillows with her gaze piercing him from beneath her lashes. "Does your wife know about your dalliance with your nurse?"

Anger rises in his belly and runs across his body, electrifying his limbs. He consciously relaxes his fists. "I'm not sure that's any of your business."

"I could say that my affairs were none of yours, but that didn't stop you."

There it is: the truth. The one that Chris consistently puts to one side to convince himself he is helping those who need it. Madeline is playing him at his own game and now she has his secret. The only reassurance he has is that Madeline is adept at keeping secrets.

"Your wife is the icing on the cake, Chris." Madeline picks up their conversation. "I didn't think I'd get another chance at being remembered by anyone else, yet here she is. Now none of you will forget me when I'm gone."

"That's what this is about? Being remembered?"

Madeline shrugs. "The ancient Egyptians believed as long as your name is said after you're gone that you'll live forever in the afterlife. I like that idea, Chris, of being talked about when I'm gone."

Any frustration he experienced in discovering Madeline has manipulated him disappears. Chris is surprised to discover that, at the heart of it, they share the same fear. She may have gone about it in a different way to Chris, but he understands her desire not to be forgotten or leave no lasting memory on the world. He glances around her room and his gaze comes to rest on the artworks propped up against the wall.

"Wouldn't your artwork speak for you?" he asks. It is clear now, the connection between Madeline's approach and the piece that Holly hung in their hallway years ago; the maps that cover the canvas, the picking out of specific locations. Madeline collects physical remains, his wife, memories.

"Once, perhaps." She shuffles back up to a sitting position with a wince but immediately slides back down once she settles again. "There's too many doing the same now. Besides, people who are good at something don't get remembered in the same way as people who do terrible things. Think of Hitler or Stalin, even Judas gets a mention in the Bible, not for doing good but for the trouble they caused."

"I wouldn't want to be remembered alongside those names."

"Are you sure?" Madeline asks. "If it's a choice between being remembered for the mistakes you'd made versus leaving this life leaving no impression at all, which would you rather?"

Chris wants to say that he'd prefer to be lost in obscurity but when he opens his mouth no sounds come out.

"It doesn't really matter how you're remembered, just that someone remembers you. Make an impact, change someone's life – but if you change it for the worse, you'll be remembered more often."

He listens to the whine of Madeline's breathing and realises that, once his wife discovers what he has done, she will not remember him as a good husband. He will be remembered not fondly, but vehemently, because he's ruined the life she thought they had. He will have taken what she wanted and left her with nothing. Perhaps the same could be said of Betsy too, he hasn't made her life any easier. James Tailor hasn't set eyes on Madeline for twenty years and yet he can still recount every detail of their courtship.

"Happy endings are forgotten, Chris. They're inconsequential." Madeline's eyelids flutter and her words begin to slur. "But no one forgets the awful tragedies in life." The last few words are just a breath before she closes her eyes. She is struggling, despite the bravado. As she slips into sleep, Chris checks her thready pulse and positions the oxygen mask securely on her face. He supposes he can't refute her rationale, but to use it as justification for making the lives of others more difficult seems disrespectful. He doubts this is what she was thinking when she lied about Cecelia's father or left James on their wedding day. Chris wonders if it might be her way of trying to make peace with what she has done.

There is a tap on the door and he sees Holly's face at the window. He steps out, leaving Madeline to rest. She will need it, based on what she's said there is still one more visitor to come.

"Did you find anything?" Chris asks as he pulls Madeline's door closed behind him. Betsy is still sitting at the Nurses' Station, her head down, presumably avoiding his wife. Further down the corridor, at a bank of chairs he sees Cecelia, her foot bobbing at the end of a crossed leg.

"Lots," Holly holds up a sheaf of papers, not dissimilar to the ones she proffered him about adoption. She looks almost as disappointed too. "But nothing linked to a daughter. I can't find any family for her at all. There was her mother, but she died six years ago and there was no mention of Madeline in the obituary. Most of this is about her artwork and how she won a prestigious grant of some sort for it." Holly shrugs. "Even that was over ten years ago. There's little about her after that."

Chris collects some of the sheets from Holly's overflowing hands. One flutters to the floor and he bends to pick it up. There is a picture of Madeline in a striking green dress shaking hands with another woman. Madeline was clearly a beauty before the cancer, in this image she is stunning, drawing the eye despite her petite stature, as though she is the centrepiece to her own work of art. The woman next to her is a little bit older, but also admirably sculpted though she seems stiff in comparison to Madeline's relaxed grace. Chris reads the caption beneath it.

'Artist Madeline Tailor accepting the award from Penelope Fraser.'

Penelope.

Isn't this who he was meant to contact right from the start?

"Christopher?"

He realises he is still squatting with the paper between his fingers. He stands and hands it back to Holly along with the rest. Madeline is too physically weak and mentally stubborn to give him the information he needs, he has to work for it. Cecelia knew about James. Perhaps she will know about Penelope too.

"Miss Hartland?" He strides down the corridor toward her and she jumps up out of her seat as he approaches. She glances up and down the corridor, as if trying to find a way out of speaking with him, but he reaches her before she can move.

"Is she…?" Cecelia asks.

"No."

Cecelia closes her eyes and lets out a breath. Without the worry of Doctor Gregory, Chris decides to be direct.

"Do you know where Madeline's daughter is?"

Cecelia's posture stills and she refuses to meet his gaze. Holly joins them and catches his question, along with Cecelia's discomfort.

"You knew all along then?" Holly comments, dropping the papers into the chair where Cecelia had been sat.

Cecelia licks her lips and studies her shoes.

"Madeline told me she wants me to find Penelope for her," Chris says, scrutinising the effect Penelope's name has on Cecelia. Her hands twitch as he speaks and he detects a slight nod of her head. "Does Penelope have something to do with her daughter?"

Cecelia throws up her hands. "Always so damn mysterious," she exclaims. "Why she can't just do her own dirty work I'll never know." She flings herself back into the seat, crumpling the papers Holly has set down.

Holly takes the seat next to her and places a gentle hand on Cecelia's arm. "If she's so frustrating, why are you still here?"

"Because I can't leave, can I? Her life is practically my life. I've spent so long running after her, fixing her messes because I thought she was so damaged by what my father did, more fool me. But I don't see why I should help her now. Let her die by herself in that room; my dad did, alone in his cell thinking no one would ever believe him - all because of her."

He and Cecelia have that in common, both of their fathers have passed away without their family, disgraced and alone. Of course, he had a hand in ensuring his father didn't have any support by burning that letter when he was eleven years old instead of showing it to his mother. Does Cecelia also harbour some guilt for bringing Madeline into her father's life, even though she could not have predicted how she would influence it?

"Perhaps that's what she wants," Chris muses.

"And what about her daughter? What do you think she might want?" Holly snaps. "Cecelia if you know what happened and can help us find Madeline's daughter you should. Not for Madeline's sake, but for the girl. Imagine how she might feel if she discovers her own mother died alone in a room, just like your father, when it could have been prevented. Would you want someone else to go through that?"

Cecelia slumps back in the chair, forcing more papers to dislodge and fall to the floor. Chris has to admit Holly makes a good argument. He can't bear the thought of another person carrying the burden of shame he feels for abandoning his father in those last hours. Isn't that why he tries so hard to advocate for his patients?

"She's right," Chris says. "At least give her the option. She might not even be interested in seeing the woman who had to give her up for adoption."

"Ha," Cecelia sneers. "Had to?" She straightens herself up. "Madeline couldn't wait to get rid of that child. She told James she'd had a miscarriage, but that wasn't true - god, why didn't I see through her then?"

Chris and Holly exchange a glance. Holly doesn't know the background between Madeline and Cecelia and knows even less about James. The only source of her information is Madeline, and as Chris is learning, she cannot be trusted.

"She got herself into a right mess," Cecelia continues. "Young, single, pregnant. Said she had no one else to turn to, that I owed her, that my father had turned her life upside down. So of course I did what I could. But she wanted rid of that baby, I can tell you that much. Sold it to the highest bidder."

"Penelope Fraser," Chris surmises.

But at the same time Holly screeches; "Why?"

Cecelia nods up at Chris and then turns to Holly. "Because she could. I've sat here for a long while now and gone back through our supposed friendship. I only hope that poor girl she gave birth to isn't interested in seeing Madeline. Neither of them deserve it."

Chris realises that Cecelia has omitted a huge chunk of her relationship with Madeline. "How did all this happen?" he asks.

She sighs and leans back, speaking with a weary tone. "My Mum worked for a charity that dealt with victims of rape who had become pregnant. Sometimes they'd organise private adoptions - because, really, what woman would want a child conceived from a situation like that? Anyway, I was helping out when I was in college and had access to the records of all those who had applied for parental status. It was easy to find a couple who had a rejected application and let Madeline make them an offer. They nearly snapped our hand off."

Holly lets out a long breath as she shakes her head from side to side, her hair bouncing. Chris watches her and reminds himself how beautiful she is. He knows she is thinking about the vulnerability of the couple who bought Madeline's child, of the potential suffering Madeline might have gone through giving up that child. She catches his eye and he spots her tears. He lifts a hand to reach out to her, but she breaks off their gaze. Of course, he denied her the possibility of adoption and she's left him.

"Well, let's contact them and see if this girl wants to come and see Madeline," Holly says.

"Madeline only mentioned Penelope, I don't think she intends to see her daughter."

"Don't be ridiculous." Holly springs out of her seat and hurries down the corridor.

Chris angles a worried look at Cecelia who just shrugs and stays in her seat. He sighs inwardly and follows his wife. Just as she disappears into Madeline's room he passes the Nurses' Station. Betsy glares at him and he holds out both hands in a gesture of apology.

"Things just keep becoming more complicated," he tells her as he sweeps past.

"With your patient or your wife?" Betsy asks.

Chris can't answer. He darts into the room with another apologetic look at Betsy, who rolls her eyes and turns away. He knows Holly is going to try and convince Madeline to contact her daughter, but equally he is aware this is not what Madeline wants. What Madeline wants is to make sure she is remembered for something and Chris can't shake the feeling that although she is a woman who can keep secrets if they serve her, she might easily use what she knows to make a permanent impact on their lives. He should have told Holly while he had the chance. Instead Madeline now has it in her power to emotionally destroy his wife and his relationship with her.

As he enters the room he sees Holly standing over Madeline with her hands on her hips.

"You have to see her Madeline, she's your daughter."

Madeline's gaze flickers to Chris. Her eyes look dull and jaundiced but there is a keen hatred in them. Chris immediately knows that she hadn't counted on him discovering a daughter.

Madeline reaches up with a clumsy grab to pull the oxygen mask from her face.

"You can't tell me what to do." Her breathing is jagged, interrupting every other word. She lifts the mask back to her face with concerted effort.

"Holly, please, leave her be. It's her choice."

Holly turns her attack on him. "Now you advocate for patient choice? You've been fine up until now to choose for your previous patients, and from what I understand, for Madeline herself when it was at your convenience. Now, just because Doctor Gregory tells you so, you've decided to fall into line?"

Madeline attempts to chuckle. It is more a cough than a laugh but Chris can see she is pleased by the friction between them.

"You're no better." Holly points at Madeline. "You've got a child out there in the world, one you tossed aside because you were young and stupid. Well, you should know better now." Holly catches up Madeline's hand and perches on the edge of the bed, softening her tone. "No mother should abandon her child. You need to see her before you go."

"Why should I?" Madeline yanks her hand away.

"You owe it to her. She'll want to know who her mother is eventually."

"And she will," Madeline replies. "But she doesn't have to watch me shuffle off my death bed, does she?"

Chris steps in to hold the mask up to Madeline's face ordering her to take some deep breaths in. Holly grabs the opportunity.

"You can't make that choice for her. If she doesn't see you now, she'll never get another chance." Holly sits down, pulling the chair up close to Madeline's bed. "Oh, Madeline, when we first became friends I thought you understood what it meant to be a mother without a child. I never realised that you'd given up your own. You must regret it. You can't tell me you don't."

Chris brings to mind the image of Madeline and Penelope Fraser. He doubts that meeting was a coincidence. Did Penelope know then that Madeline Tailor is the biological mother of her adopted daughter? Before he can think to ask, Madeline forces his hand - and the oxygen mask in it - away from her face.

"Not that it matters, but the only thing I regret is getting pregnant in the first place. I wasn't cut out to be a Mum, neither was my own come to think of it. I can't think of anything worse than having to apologise to a stranger for making the right decision."

Her speech is delivered with vehemence, which is more than her health can handle. Madeline snatches back the mask for herself and sucks in the air that her lungs need.

"Don't do this, Madeline," Holly says. "If I could have, I'd have given up my life for any one of my children to live. It changes you. Don't deny yourself the opportunity to see what you made."

Chris' heart aches at the desperation that Holly displays. She can't understand how a woman would ever give up their child through choice, just as she can't believe Madeline doesn't want to see the child she gave birth to twenty years ago.

"I'm not you." Madeline stares at Holly from behind her mask and narrows her eyes.

"Well," Holly declares, standing up and tossing her hair over her shoulder. "I know what it's like to lose a child, and it's terrible." A single tear rolls down her cheek. "I can't believe you would turn your back on your daughter. I won't believe it. You're just being stubborn. But you do have a choice, Madeline. You can see your daughter again. I'll find her, Madeline. We'll get her here."

Madeline is shaking her head. "Just get me Penelope. That's all I need."

"I can do that," Chris offers, placing a hand on Madeline's and squeezing it in support.

Chris wants to take Holly in his arms and tell her it will be okay, that this is Madeline's decision and they have to respect it. He understands that now. After all, what could be more painful than giving up a child only to see them in the moments before you died, when you could do nothing more for them? He looks up to see Holly's eyes bearing down on him from the end of Madeline's bed.

"You should make sure her daughter comes too," Holly says. Her voice is cold and her stare icy. "She might want to see her mother, just once. Don't tell me you don't understand that."

Chris feels a stab in his heart as Holly uses what she knows about his own father against him.

"Doesn't she deserve that chance?" Holly adds.

Chris glances across at Madeline and for a split second, as she takes a vengeful intake of oxygen, he knows exactly what is coming.

"As you deserve the chance to know that your husband has impregnated his nurse?" Madeline speaks in a false, high tone of a voice that mimics Holly's. It is childish and mean but more spiteful is the smile on her lips beneath the plastic mask, the same smile he is now sure he saw when Cecelia fainted on the very spot he stands.

"What?" Holly's voice hits an octave higher than usual. "Christopher? What is she saying?"

He can't deny it. He can't even lift his gaze to meet her brown eyes. He hears the clack of her shoes walking toward him, and yet still the slap is a shock. The way her hand ripples across his cheek and his face takes the force of her anger. She screams at him, but he only picks up every other word, her fury is tumbling from her mouth at such speed. But he takes it, because he loves her and he deserves her resentment.

He keeps his gaze on his shoes, though he is tempted to look up at Madeline. He imagine she must be enjoying this, it is certainly distracting Holly from her situation.

Holly lets out a sob and covers her mouth. "No wonder you didn't want to adopt a child with me."

Chris knows that this is his opportunity, he meets her eye. "It was a mistake. One single mistake."

"That's all it takes," Holly spits back at him.

"I'm sorry." He tries to take her hand, but she rips it out of his reach. "I didn't want you to find out like this, I wanted to tell you. I just didn't—"

"How long have you known?"

"A couple of days."

Holly's face twists into a disgusted smile. "I bet you were relieved when I left then. After everything, I made it so easy for you."

"No, that wasn't it." He steps toward her, now desperate to explain.

"Stay away from me." She jabs a finger toward Madeline. "At least she had the decency to tell me the truth."

The movement diverts Chris' attention away from Holly and in that moment he catches a glimpse of Madeline, slumped against her pillow, eyes barely open and her lips tinged purple. Her hand is laid on her chest and Chris imagines she clutched at it only a second ago. He pushes past Holly and snatches the pillow from beneath Madeline, laying her prone on the bed. He listens for breath sounds but hears nothing, but she still has a heartbeat – the screen shows it is erratic but there. He punches the emergency button and Betsy is there within seconds, working with him without even the need for a glance. He places the oxygen mask back on Madeline's face and Betsy turns the dials on the wall. Slowly Madeline regains consciousness. Her eyes flutter open and Chris smiles with relief.

But then he remembers what she has done and his smile vanishes. He looks around the room. Holly has gone.

"Everything okay?" Betsy asks. She reaches over to place a hand on his arm. He pulls it away.

"Holly knows," he says. "Madeline told her."

"She would have found out sooner or later."

"Did you see where she went?"

Betsy shrugs. Chris starts to move away, but something tugs at his sleeve. Madeline's fingers are curled around his doctor's coat.

She forces the words from her lips. "How long?"

Despite the trouble she has caused, the terrible things she has done, Chris can't help his compassion. He tries to tell himself it is his job, but that isn't true. Madeline intrigues him. What she believes is right; he will remember her. Was he not such a coward Madeline wouldn't have been able to hold his betrayal over him. He gave her that power and she had used it to insert herself into a painful moment, a memory he nor Holly will likely ever forget.

"Not long," Chris responds. "Perhaps it's time to contact Penelope?"

Madeline nods, then closes her eyes. Chris glimpses up at the monitor, her heartbeat is steady. The oxygen is doing its job.

"Who's Penelope?" Betsy asks.

"Her daughter's adopted mother."

They lapse into silence. Betsy checks the I.V. line and then gently lifts Madeline's head to place the discarded pillow beneath it. Chris tries to collect the carnage of his thoughts. So much has changed in three days. He is going to be a father. Holly has left him and, given her reaction, it is unlikely she will ever come back. His patient - the one whom he has tried so desperately to help - has been manipulating him all along and with only a few hours to live he is to contact the woman who adopted her child. He considers not doing it for a moment, letting Madeline pass away quietly in this room without ever mentioning her to Penelope Fraser or her daughter. But this isn't his decision to make.

"I'll have to speak to Cecelia to get the details to contact her." Chris looks at Betsy who avoids his gaze. "But then I think we should finish our discussion. I don't want you to leave Betsy."

She sighs and purses her lips. "I'm not sure I should stay. I heard your wife, Chris, she's devastated."

"I don't think you need to worry about my marriage." He offers her a weak smile and wonders if the whole hospice knows their personal business now, given the shouting that went on "Please don't make any decisions without me."

As Chris speaks Madeline's eyes open, her blue irises contrast against the pupils that focus in on him, and despite being dulled they are still the most vivid thing about her. Her pallor is yellow and the skin on her face is puffy, as though she has been crying.

"I'll go and ask Cecelia for those contact details." Betsy leaves and Chris feels a pull to go after her. But she is an exceptional nurse, while Madeline is still their patient he senses she won't go far.

Madeline parts her cracked lips and whispers something. Chris bends down to her and she repeats herself with a breathy sigh.

"Gave you quite a shock there."

"With my wife, or your condition?"

Madeline is too weak to smile but he sees the twitch of her mouth. Chris puts everything she has done to one side. Laid out on the bed before him is simply a woman about to die.

"If you can, you should let your daughter visit."

Madeline turns away from him. He carries on, regardless.

"This is it, Madeline. You won't get another chance. There's a possibility even Penelope might not make it here in time."

She shifts her head back to glare at him and then rolls her eyes.

"If she doesn't make it," Madeline whispers. "The wooden box is for Rachel." She lifts a weary hand and points to the corner of the room where there is a small carved wooden trunk. Chris thinks it is the one he found her carrying when he first met her only three days ago. She has hidden the depths of her cancer well. She was much sicker than they realised on admission.

He presumes Rachel is her daughter. That she knows the name suggests to Chris that there is another story to be told; that Madeline does care more than she - or even Cecelia - will admit.

Chris stands upright and towers over Madeline's tiny form. After being manipulated by her for all this time, the information he has discovered, the secret she has revealed to his wife, he feels it is about time he took charge.

"You rest. I'll see to it that both Penelope and Rachel get here." Madeline's eyes widen. Chris puts a hand up to calm her. "I doubt it will be in time to make conversation, but at least she'll believe you wanted to give her the box yourself."

Madeline nods with closed eyes and Chris leaves her to rest.

In the corridor Chris is surprised to see Holly sitting bolt upright in one of the waiting area chairs. She stares straight ahead at the wall opposite, the one with the scuff mark Chris can't help but see every time he walks past. She is pale, but there is a flush to her cheeks that Chris knows he is responsible for. There is an anguish in the way she holds herself so formally, stiff and taut on the outside when Chris can see the fear in her eyes. He hovers for a moment, his jaw taut with the shame at making a mockery of their marriage. As if sensing him watching her, Holly shifts her focus to him. She stands up as soon as he makes a move toward her.

"Is she okay?"

"Holly, I—"

She presents him with the palm of her hand. "I don't care for your apologies or explanations. I'm asking about Madeline, my friend. Is she okay?"

Chris nods. Holly's voice is cold, each word pronounced with such precision and when she lowers her hand he glimpses the slight shake it has.

"Is her daughter coming?"

"I'll make sure of it," Chris says. He steps toward her, his instincts wanting to embrace her, but she backs away. She will not look him in the eye. Instead she looks just below and beyond his right shoulder. In contrast, Chris can't take his eyes off Holly for fear he might never see her again.

"Can I sit with her until then?"

"Are you sure?"

"Does she have any more of your secrets left to tell?"

"No."

"Well then. Can I stay?"

He is caught off guard. But Madeline isn't the one who's betrayed her. She may have lied, have done something Holly could not conceive of, but Holly is compassionate and fair. She won't let Madeline die alone out of spite.

"Of course, I—"

But as soon as he affirms she can stay Holly swishes past him. He pushes a forefinger and thumb onto his eyelids. He is tired, confused and angry. He'd like to blame Madeline, but she is only part of the turmoil that has been created over the last three days. Chris can't help but feel that he might very well end up just like Madeline one day; alone on his death-bed with a selection of disappointing memories the only thing to keep him company. The question is, can he say he is any better than her, that he wouldn't deserve such a fate?

He lets Holly return to Madeline and goes in search of Cecelia. He finds Betsy with her in the reception area. They appear to be arguing.

"Why not give it to me?" Betsy's words rolls out of her mouth in one long drawl. "If we have to go looking, it will waste more time. She doesn't have it, you know that."

Cecelia shrugs and makes eye contact with him over Betsy's head. The nurse turns and throws her hands in the air and rolls her eyes.

"She won't give me Penelope's details."

Betsy begins to storm away, but Chris catches her arm. They exchange a look and he lets his grasp on her arm drop. She remains next to him but with her back to Cecelia.

"We really need those details Cecelia," Chris says. "Madeline won't make it through the night. I'd like at least to suggest to her daughter that we attempted to contact her."

"Are you sure?" Cecelia fronts up to him, her eyes wide. "She'll be dead by tomorrow?"

"In all likelihood, yes."

Something in the way Cecelia is standing changes. Chris can't be sure what it is, but he notices the difference; a slight lowering of hunched shoulders, a softness in the knees. It is as if every muscle in her body was stretched tight and the news that Madeline is, indeed, in the process of dying has released something.

"Fine," Cecelia swipes up her faded black handbag from the seat. "I'll tell her."

Chris steps closer. "I don't think that's a good idea."

"I can have her here before midnight."

"That soon?" Betsy asks. It is already nine o'clock.

"I happen to know she's visiting Rachel at York University." Cecelia grasps onto a black pocketbook, her knuckles white. "Otherwise she'd be in France."

"Madeline's daughter is in York." Chris simply states the fact. He can no longer be surprised by how well Madeline has managed to place herself at the facility. "I still think it's better if I—"

Cecelia is shaking her head. "She won't come if you ask. I can get her here. I promise."

He hesitates. Can he trust Cecelia not to lie? She shuffles backward and drops into a seat.

"Or you can find her yourself. Though from what you've said it will be too late by then."

Betsy, as suspicious as he is, turns to ask: "Why would you do that? I thought you wanted her to die alone like your father?"

Cecelia sticks out her chin. "No. Not anymore. She should face up to what she did. Penelope will make her do that. She won't forgive."

Something in her tone makes Chris believe her. Whatever she may say to get Penelope to Madeline's bedside, at least Madeline will get what she wanted.

"Okay, I'll let our staff know that we're to let them in. In circumstances such as this we can make exceptions for visiting family."

"She won't bring Rachel."

Chris doesn't want to argue with her, it wastes time, as Betsy stated. "Just tell her to be here as soon as she can."

Cecelia grins at him as she stalks away to make the telephone call. She is pleased about something. He can't quite imagine Cecelia to be so callous as to enjoy the demise of Madeline, even if she believes her to be partially responsible for her father's suicide. But, as long as it gets Penelope here so Madeline can tell her to give the box to Rachel, this is all he needs to care about.

He lets the night guard know they are expecting someone and then turns back to Betsy.

"Could we talk?" Chris asks Betsy.

"So now you have time for me?"

"It's been a hectic afternoon. And, we've got a lot to discuss."

"Not really, I've made my decision."

A weight suddenly presses down on his chest and he has to catch his breath. "You told me about this for a reason Betsy, at least give me chance to change your mind."

"Fine. But I need something to eat."

She leads the way to the kitchen area, where there is a small round table with four rickety chairs. It is late in the evening and the hospice is quiet but not peaceful. Staff are settling the patients for the night, ensuring they're comfortable and tending to the insomnia that often results from a fear of sleeping but never again waking up.

The lights in the kitchen are turned off but a yellow brightness from the corridor spills in. It is only used to make cups of coffee for the night-staff, so they shouldn't be interrupted, but it reminds him of the nights they spent here two months ago talking and getting to know one another. The conversations they shared then had been a precursor to that one night that led them here. He wants a neutral space, somewhere that doesn't remind him of the echo of Betsy's laugh or the long hours they've spent together. His office would be just as bad, if not worse.

Betsy, illuminated by the harsh white brightness of the fridge, reveals some sandwiches. "You want one?"

"Sure." Chris doesn't much care, though at the sight of them his stomach dances. "Can we go and sit in one of the family lounges?"

"Let's use the one opposite reception," she suggests. "We can keep an eye out for Penelope."

Chris takes the proffered sandwich and nods. It isn't the nicest of rooms, a floral explosion of chintz with worn cushions. The wall it shares with the corridor is one half glass, so anyone can see in or out. Settling themselves in individual chairs Chris suddenly feels awkward. Betsy takes a bite out of her sandwich and then a swig of the orange juice she's brought with her. The noise of him opening his own sandwich packet seems loud and invasive. He wants to get this right, he needs to get this right. If he makes a mistake now he might never see the child he so desperately wants.

He thinks of the ultra sound scan and it occurs to him how hopeful he already is about the baby. He has wanted to be a father for so long, a better father than his own or even his step-father had ever been to him. It's important to let Betsy know that he intends to support her, not to walk away and leave her to deal with the situation if things get too hard.

"Chris?" Betsy's voice startles him and he realises he is sat with the sandwich half to his mouth, just staring at the table.

"Yes, sorry."

"Look, I know you said you wanted to be a father, but you don't have to be. It's a messy situation and I should never have let my feelings get the better of me."

Chris tosses the soggy bread onto the table, appetite gone. "We have equal parts here, Betsy. Please don't feel that you are to blame."

"Oh, I know that." She shuffles forward to sit on the edge of the seat. "But, your marriage, it's too complicated. I never wanted this."

"Being a father is all I've ever wanted."

"You could still have that with your wife."

He realises Betsy cannot have heard Holly's screaming so clearly if she does not know why her suggestion is not possible, otherwise he would not have to tell her: "Holly can't have children."

He's never said it out loud before. In fact, he and Holly have never really discussed it at all. They've been pregnant numerous times - six, in fact - but Holly was unable to carry any of them to term. It was obvious to both of them that the problem was not conceiving but keeping the pregnancy.

"Oh," Betsy's understanding of the implication is clear. He knows that she will read into those words just how much of a betrayal their dalliance has been. "Then I should go. I can't think of anything worse than to stay and be the reminder of what your wife can't have."

"Holly won't be a problem. I know her. I didn't expect to be a cheating husband. I never even saw it coming until it happened. But, Holly, she's caring and understanding and accepting." He gulps back his shame. "She'll let me go because she knows what it means to me to be a father."

"Then, what do you want me to do, Chris?" Betsy blows a stray hair from out of her face. "I didn't expect to be a single mother at twenty-six. I'm not even sure if I want children yet at all. But I'm here, pregnant with your child: a man I hardly know and certainly can't see myself growing old with."

Chris catches her eye. Compared to her, he is already growing old. In his forties and his life is a mess.

"I'm not suggesting we get married, Betsy."

"Good, because that's not on the table. But, Chris, this isn't my life. I don't want it."

His flesh goes cold. "But you said—"

"I don't mean the baby." She places a hand on her stomach, as if protecting the child from her misinterpreted words. "I meant the life. I don't want to be a single mother. If I go back to Northern Ireland and confess my sins to my mother, I know she'll do the right thing for the baby. She'll raise it herself, it'll be part of a family, with cousins and aunties and uncles. You could still have contact if you want, I'll make sure of it."

As she speaks he places a hand over his mouth to stop him from begging her not to do what she is suggesting. His chin is scratchy with stubble against his fingertips.

"I'll take the baby," he offers. "I can be a single father, I'm ready for that. I can't imagine not spending every day with my own child, Betsy. I want the chance to bring him up, to watch her grow. I don't want to be some man that visits twice a year who they hardly even know and that they're forced to call 'Dad'."

"How are you going to be a single father Chris?" Betsy leans back in her chair. "You don't have a support system, no parents or siblings to help you. I've known you for three months and never even heard you mention a single friend."

She's right. He and Holly have withdrawn from friends, those who've moved on with children of their own. They were too difficult for Chris to deal with when he had to comfort Holly in the wake of another miscarriage. Over the last two years they have become isolated until he and Holly were the only ones left. And now, it's just him.

"I'll make it work."

"Don't you think our child deserves better?"

"Better than a father who will love them and protect them and do everything I can to make them happy?"

"You know what I mean Chris." She sits up again and folds her hands together so she can lean her chin on them. "A child needs a family."

Chris thinks back to his own childhood. Could he be both father and mother? His own Mum tried to be both for a time and it exhausted her. He remembers her crying to a friend, distraught that she couldn't be everything for her little boy. He felt burdened by a responsibility that should not have been his then. Growing up with just Mum had been lonely because, on her own, she hadn't been enough, even he will admit that. He had considered, more than once, that the relationship with his step-father - started so soon after he saw her crying to that friend - had been a solution to that problem in his mother's mind. Yet it only served to remind him how much he was missing out on because that man would never be his father, or even pretend to be one.

It takes him a moment to get the words out and overcome his fear of saying them out loud. "If you go to Ireland, I'll have lost everything."

"But I don't have a reason to stay."

Chris presses his lips together. He can't force her to stay just so he can be the father he has always wanted. He settles for diplomacy.

"You don't have a reason to go, either."

She shakes her head at him and then rakes a hand through her hair, pushing it back. "If I go then I know that this baby will be in good hands, that it'll be brought up in a loving environment with plenty of family." She sighs and looked across at him. "You could still be a part of that."

Chris lets the possibility stretch out in front of him. He would move to Northern Ireland - nothing would stop him from doing this, certainly not Holly. He would see his child not every day perhaps, but frequently, if Betsy's mother permitted it.

"Your mother would be happy to share her grandchild with me? The same mother you said you came to Yorkshire to get away from? The mother that's going to judge you for becoming pregnant out of wedlock to a married man?"

A sob escapes Betsy. A moment ago she seemed composed, calm and rational. But now Chris can see she must be flailing wildly in the dark, trying to find the best way out of her situation and attempting to see the one she has settled on as best she could, ignoring any faults.

"What else can I do, Chris? I can't have the baby here and then just give it to you. How will you cope? What will happen? I might not want this baby myself but I couldn't face just walking away. I'm not that selfish."

"No, I didn't mean to imply..." He trails off, but he had thought Betsy was trying to absolve her responsibility. She must want to go back to her mother's so she can maintain a link. Hadn't Cecelia said something similar about Madeline; that she couldn't wait to get rid of the child? Yet, she knew her daughter's name and has met the woman who adopted her. Is it possible to give a child away and not be tempted to return and find out if you made the right decision?

They lapse into an uncomfortable silence.

Did Madeline make the right decision, thinks Chris. Had she met Penelope Fraser and believed her daughter was better off? This would be his own fear if he and Holly had been to adopt. The child would never truly be theirs, there would always be a danger of the biological parents wanting to stake a claim, to move past their earlier regret and forge a relationship with the child that they had brought up as their own. What about Madeline's daughter; she will be twenty now, is she curious about her heritage? Has she ever looked for Madeline, asked her adoptive mother about her? Perhaps that is what happened all those years ago when Madeline met with Penelope, perhaps she was turned away, having discovered a daughter who didn't care to see her knowing she has been abandoned at birth. This would account for Madeline's reticence about seeing her.

Betsy takes a final swig of her orange juice, the movement disturbing Chris from his thoughts. It seems so much easier to contemplate Madeline's predicament, to watch the complications from afar and not be directly involved. When it comes to his own life, Chris can't quite make it seem like the one he has pictured for himself.

"I'm sorry Chris, but I have to do what is best for me and the baby. Right now we're one and the same, and I feel like my only choice is to go back home. At the very least I'll need the support." He opens his mouth to protest, but Betsy holds up a hand. "I know you'd support me here, if I stayed, but I don't just mean one person. I need people, more than one, another woman who knows what it is to go through this and be able to reassure me I'll be okay. You can't do that, not alone."

There it is. Betsy sees him as an individual, as someone who is alone without a support network, with no one else to rely on or to care for. His greatest fear is coming true, bleaker than he ever anticipated it because it is happening alongside the possibility of his greatest joy. In a year's time he will be a self-fulfilling prophecy; he will be his father, holed up in a bedsit somewhere having lost everything that is important to him in the world.

"Madeline will be my last patient. I've already handed a notice letter to Doctor Gregory." She gives an apologetic smile and a shrug. "He was pleased, to say the least."

"No, Betsy." He sweeps himself off the chair and onto his knees, any shame in begging her to not to go cast away by the thought he won't have the time he needs to persuade her to stay. "Don't leave, not yet. Let's talk about this some more: find a solution. There must be one that doesn't involve me being a part-time parent. I couldn't bear that."

He grasps at her hand but she pulls it away from him stiffly. "I don't know…"

She sounds uncertain, more so than she had a few moments ago. Maybe he stands a chance. "Betsy, really—"

A gruff voice cuts him off. "Doctor, nurse, there's someone at the front desk asking for you. Says she's here to see a Madeline Tailor?"

It is the night guard. Chris picks himself up off the floor, his face flush with both the exertion and the embarrassment of being seen kneeling in front of a young woman. But what does it matter? The important thing is to make sure Betsy doesn't go. If he can just convince her, find a way to make her see that he can be a suitable father for their child, that she doesn't have to participate but would be welcome to share in the experience. It is unconventional, perhaps, but it could work, it has to work. Chris can't bear to consider any other option. He stares down at Betsy, who is slumped and sad. He appeals to her one last time.

"Please don't go until we've talked again."

He wants to stay, to ignore his duty to his patient, but Madeline has less time than him and he can't argue with that. Betsy nods with a closed mouth smile, a weary gesture but he believes he can hold her to it.

~~~

In the reception area Chris examines the tall, lithe woman who could be a similar age to himself, but in the slight elevation of her chin and the tailored cut of her clothes she is clearly not of the same upbringing. Her style is one of simple elegance and it is striking. Chris finds himself standing straighter as he introduces himself.

"I'm Doctor Wright," he says, offering a hand.

"Penelope Fraser." She has the barest hint of a French accent that lingers on her pronunciation of the 'r's in Fraser. "I came as soon as I heard." Chris doesn't question her on this, but from the formal tone to her voice and the porcelain expression on her face, he doubts whether she has come out of concern for Madeline.
~~~

Chris tries to read her, but the skin is too perfect and the stare cold. Based on the clean cut of her godet skirt and the cashmere jumper that emphasises the curve of her shoulders and slim waist, alongside the Chanel handbag that dangles from her forearm, the only thing he can be sure of is that she is a wealthy woman.

"I'm not sure how much you know?"

"That Madeline is dying and she wants to see me."

Chris nods and glances up to the clock above the reception desk; eleven forty-five. Cecelia was true to her word. "She is very weak and we don't believe she has much longer left with us." He examines Penelope's face but there is no change, not even a twitch or tightening of the lips. "I understand that you have a…" he stumbles over the word, "…relationship with her."

"Not a particularly pleasant one." For the first time since their meeting Penelope drops her gaze and Chris takes a breath. He didn't realise how stiffly he has been standing, nor how tight his chest has become with the effort of trying to mimic Penelope's stillness.

"Then why did you come?"

Her brown eyes flicker back up to pierce him. "To make sure that it is true."

Chris gestures back to the family room where he and Betsy were moments before. Betsy has disappeared. "Why don't we sit down to discuss it?"

Penelope surveys the area he's invited her to and he identifies the first change in her face, a slight narrowing of the eyes. She moves past him and chooses one of the chairs, laying her coat on the arm with care and perching on the seat with skill. She sits with her back rigidly straight, her shoulders set back and chin parallel to her thighs where her crossed hands rest.

"I can tell you are not shocked by what I said, Doctor."

"Please, call me Chris."

"Well, Chris," Penelope smiles at him and he is relieved to see the crosshatching of lines that appear beneath her eyes, the first sign of real life on her sculpted face. "We have a complicated past, Madeline and I."

"You adopted her daughter?"

A slight raise of a neat eyebrow is all he receives. "I did not know Madeline until my daughter, Rachel, was seven." She pronounces Rachel like Raquel, a French emphasis.

"She has something for her, something that she would like to pass on. My wife and I have been trying to convince her to see Rachel, but—"

Penelope cuts him off with a deep, guttural protest. "No."

"We understand that it might be difficult—"

Penelope stands up, brushing away invisible remnants of the cheap furniture from her skirt. "I will not let my daughter see that woman. Not after what she did to us."

"But, it's true: Madeline is your daughter's biological mother?"

Penelope nods, sweeping dark blonde hair from her face. "And she ruined us because of it."

"But Rachel is looking for her?"

Penelope fixes him with that cold stare again.

"I told Rachel at fifteen that she was adopted. When she came here to university she began to look. There was very little evidence of her real mother, so I assumed she would not be found. Now, this-" Penelope looks around her breaking the gaze she held with Chris, "-changes things."

"How?"

"If Rachel discovers her mother is dead, then the search can be over. Madeline can never hurt us again."

Chris rises from his own seat and takes a step to the side, subtly blocking the door. "What about the gift Madeline has for Rachel?"

"I can assure you that we want nothing from her."

"Would Rachel say the same thing?"

Penelope's lips go pale with the pressure she exerts on them, presumably trying to hold her tongue and Chris knows he's discovered a flaw to her argument.

"Does Rachel know that her real mother is so close? That she wants to reconnect with her child before she dies?" It is a lie, of sorts, Madeline is too fearful of rejection to admit to wanting to see Rachel, he thinks. But Penelope doesn't know that.

Penelope stands with her coat over one arm and her handbag over the other. Her shoulders move up and down as she breathes and for a moment Chris thinks she might not answer.

"If you know your patient at all by now, Doctor Wright, you will know that she is not one to look back or give a damn about how anyone else feels, now or in the future. As far as I am concerned she had her chance and she forfeited it for money."

Penelope moves forward, forcing Chris to take another step back, but he maintains his position in front of the door

"That was twenty years ago, she was a young girl afraid of making more mistakes." He isn't quite sure why he is arguing for Madeline, knowing what she has done to both Cecelia and James, not to mention his own marriage. But he feels a part of him is fighting for himself, the fear that perhaps he might end up just like Madeline one day. It takes him a few seconds to realise that Penelope is laughing at him.

"Oh, she has fooled so many of us." She places her bag and coat down on the sofa, shaking her head. "You are just the last in a long line." She claps her hands together softly and inclines her head. "Well done to Madeline, the actress down to the last moment."

She is right, and Chris knows it. Madeline appears to have played out her life at the centre of dramas that she herself created, but he can't believe that she would do it on purpose. He hadn't meant to get Betsy pregnant, ruin her life, destroy his marriage, and break his wife's heart, but it happened all the same. He feels anger stirring in his belly at the thought that one of his patients will die having been reminded of all of the mistakes she has made, rather than get the chance to fulfil her last wish; to give that box - whatever it is - to her daughter, perhaps the one thing she has done right in this world.

"What if Rachel finds out you were here? That you had a chance to introduce her to her mother and you chose not to?"

Penelope halts her patronising charade. "How would she ever know that?"

Chris remains silent and still.

"I should go, you have told me what I needed to know." Penelope bends to retrieve her handbag. Chris jumps forward, grazing her arm with his hand.

"Please don't," he says. "Your daughter might never know you were here, but you will. Don't deny her the opportunity she has been waiting for. Madeline won't be with us much longer, she can't do any more damage. Not unless you let her, by lying to your daughter."

Penelope stops mid-stoop and then straightens herself with slow, measured movements turning her head to regard Chris with haughty derision.

"You think you know my situation? You believe to know what is best for my daughter?" She shakes her head at him. He thinks he sees the glimmer of a tear reflect in her eye. "I love my daughter, Doctor, more than anything – she is all I have left. If I thought that meeting Madeline would help her, I would do it. But it will not. Circumstance guarantees it. There are too many skeletons in that closet, many more that Madeline could choose to reveal. I do not want that for my daughter."

It sounds to Chris that Madeline may possess of a few of Penelope's secrets, secrets that she does not want her daughter to know. Chris considers the damage that Madeline has done and his attitude to Penelope softens; she is right, he has no idea of what Madeline might have put Penelope through.

"I don't presume to know your situation Penelope. But I do know about regret, I see a lot of it here. I also know about the lies that families perpetuate to keep their loved ones safe."

His stomach still turns when he thinks of that letter. Even though his mother is dead he still wonders now what would have happened if he had told her about it. Would she have let his father back into their lives, only for him to abandon them again once they had cared for him in ways he could never return?

"The truth will out," he continues. "It's a cliché, but it will. Don't stand in your daughter's way, let her decide. She'll respect you more for it."

Penelope stares at him. He can hear his heartbeat as blood rushes past his ears. Will she be convinced? There is a ticking clock on the wall and he counts the rhythmic beat up to forty before she speaks.

"Sit down," she instructs. "I can see Madeline has seduced you, just as she did when I met her. But, she is not to be trusted. Let me tell you why."

He does as she asks, even knowing that Madeline may not have the time. He does it to keep Penelope at Dove Break and perhaps convince her to take the box Madeline so desperately wants Rachel to have. In order to do that though, he needs to know just what Madeline has done to this family to break them apart.

PENELOPE'S STORY

Madeline was one of several artists who had been awarded a grant by a Foundation that my parents had been integral in setting up. As their only heir, I was expected to take over, especially as this Foundation had its base in England. Both my parents had died a few weeks before – my father of a stroke and my mother of a heart attack. Given my grief I paid little attention, but when I saw Madeline's artwork I was touched, moved even.

She had on show jewellery that she'd created from multiple sources and materials not often found together: plastic beads on a silver chain with earrings as droplets; leather gloves mended with buttons and bright stitching; and hair pieces with playing cards as features surrounded by feathers and fake flowers. The simple intricacy of the pieces she had made from lost items was breathtaking.

Each artist was obliged to make a presentation about their process and during hers Madeline's passion spoke to me. Five judges and I, crowded inside her small, temporary studio in London listened to her describe her work. She did so with such confidence and, despite her diminutive frame, she stood tall amongst the tools of her trade.

"All of the work is made from found objects and where possible everything is recycled. Each piece represents a selection of misplaced memories that belong not just to the original owner of the object, but to us all as individuals who lose part of ourselves as we go about our daily lives."

Madeline's long skirt billowed out in the draft that crept under the wooden door and her simple blouse with gold, mismatched buttons demonstrated that she did not just work for her art, but she lived it too.

"Experiences are fleeting but the physical remnants of those moments are often the only tangible reminder we have of our lives and yet we often discard them. While I don't subscribe to materialism as a way of life, the things we lose by accident are more telling than anything we can choose to dispose of. My pieces are an exploration of those objects – objects that people forget have significance or momentarily lose sight of. I believe by cherishing these pieces not just as art work, but also as practical items we can reignite the core emotion of what it means to be connected to others through objects – whether that be an accidentally misplaced earring or a purposefully left umbrella. These are the stories of every single one of us, told in minute detail by the things we leave behind."

As she finished she flicked her flaming red hair over her shoulder and gave a small bow. We applauded her, the noise echoing around the old shop space that she had transformed into a studio.

"Please," she said, "take a moment to examine the works in progress. I'm happy to answer any questions you may have."

Madeline had intrigued us by choosing to present within her studio. All the other artists had taken us to a gallery space or – in the case of one – a hotel where their work was displayed. There were six artists in total and Madeline was the only one whose work captured my interest. Something about the sad, lost nature of every item she used appealed to me, and by creating new things from them she made me believe that perhaps there was hope in every forgotten object and by extension, myself.

"How many pieces are you planning to donate to the auction?" asked a judge.

Each artist, as a condition of their substantial grant, was asked to donate a minimum of two pieces to a charity auction each year. Most only offered two, some – seeing the opportunity to demonstrate their skills to an audience of wealth and, therefore, potential commissions – donated three. No one before had ever given more than that.

"Five," Madeline answered, gesturing to a table where the pieces stood.

We all raised our eyebrows. Only one artist would be commissioned by the Foundation to create a final piece, usually worth up to three hundred thousand pounds. In my eyes, just then, Madeline had already proved her worth.

"How long does it take you to collect all these things?" I asked her.

"It depends, some things I can find easily, if I know where to look. Other items are more difficult, some are unique." She led me over to the back corner of the studio. Opening a small box she showed me a diamond ring, a worn gap in the band that presumably had caused it to fall from the owner's hand. "This I found in a restaurant. Despite waiting three months, no one ever came back to claim it."

"What will you do with it?" I let my gaze fall onto her work station, scattered with buttons, pins, glasses, keys and other paraphernalia I imagined we all ignored every day.

"I haven't decided yet," she tucked the ring back in the box. "Some items have to be put back together, I might just repair it and send it back out into the world, hoping it brings happiness to someone else."

I smiled. I liked that she didn't see the need to make art out of every item she found. Not that her pieces were art in the traditional sense. It distinguished her from the other candidates of the grant; she created practical pieces, not works to be left and admired, but pieces to be worn or treasured. I spotted an ornate key hung on the wall above her desk. "Is that waiting for a home in one of your pieces?"

Madeline laughed, a light sound like that of a piano imitating the rain.

"No, that's just a key for one of my favourite keepsake boxes," she pointed to a wooden chest, a little bigger than a traditional suitcase. I wondered what surprises lay within.

"You seem to have quite a collection," I said, indicating the various other boxes and hampers she had stacked around the place.

"I used to be a bit of a hoarder," she told me, leaning in to whisper. "Creating pieces to sell was the only way I could ever get rid of the things I found."

She didn't look the type. Small but slender, she walked with an air of grace not usually associated with someone so young. I put her at about twenty-three, though her blemish-free skin and bright blue eyes could have made anyone seem youthful. Her hair was the colour of terracotta, natural and full with long waves that covered her small, rounded shoulders. She wore one earring, a long dangling chain with a feather and curled ribbon that I recognised as her own work. If she had been a foot taller I could have imagined her on the catwalk, where I belonged before I made my mistakes.

"How long have you been collecting?"

"Since I was a little girl," she said, nodding farewell to my colleagues as they filed out of the studio. "I used to only make things for myself, then a few friends and eventually, the work grew from there."

I looked around, we were the only ones left. I suspected the rest of the panel hadn't appreciated the modern, fresh outlook that Madeline presented in a world so often dominated by static traditions.

"Am I keeping you?" she asked.

"No, no." I was reluctant to leave. Her work had roused in me an interest I hadn't felt for some time. I wanted to prolong it. I was afraid if I left I would step out of the studio and straight back into the melancholy I realised had become my life. "Can you show me some of your other pieces?"

She tilted her head to one side and scrutinised me. As a member of the Foundation's board I was not permitted to commission or buy any of her work, at least not until after the final announcements in a month. But she humoured me. Perhaps she saw the nervousness in the tapping of my fingers or the sadness that, only that morning, had streaked through my blusher leaving a pale stain on my cheek. Whatever it was, she spent the next half hour giving me a personalised tour of her workshop and with every piece she showed me was the story of how the elements had been discovered and, then, possibly, how they had been lost.

"This is all fascinating," I mused as she made me a cup of tea in the tiny kitchenette hidden behind a curtain.

"Sorry about the cup," she said, handing me a chipped porcelain mug. I waved her apology away.

"Who did you say you were again?" Madeline asked. "I'm terrible with names. I know I should have been paying attention to who was who at the start, but I was so nervous."

She giggled and her cheeks flushed. I didn't mind at all that she'd forgotten my name, I preferred it. When I answered her smile dropped and she spilt her own tea on the work surface in front of her.

"Penelope Fraser, as in *the* Fraser Foundation?"

I nodded, taking a sip of my drink. I hadn't taken Laurence's name, I couldn't, my parents wouldn't allow it and I hadn't been in a position to argue.

Madeline covered her mouth with her hand and stared at me. Her face was pale and she stood as still as I'd seen her all afternoon. Eventually she spoke from behind her hand, her eyes still fixed on me.

"I just served double dipped tea in a chipped, old, stained mug to the owner of the Foundation who makes all this possible?"

I furrowed my brow. "Double dipped tea?"

"Two cups, one tea bag." Madeline's eyes widened further and I could see the tiny red blood vessels within them.

I laughed. I couldn't help myself. It was the first genuine amusement I'd felt since my parents died. I lay a hand on Madeline's arm, which was trembling, and shook my head still chuckling. Madeline didn't join in.

"Don't worry about it," I said. "It's nice not to be pandered to. Who did you think I was?"

This time Madeline's face reddened, right from her neck up to her forehead. "One of the PA's."

I grinned at her to show I wasn't offended but I could tell she was thrown. Her gaze hadn't dropped from my face since I'd told her my name.

"I didn't think you actually attended these." she said. "I mean, I was told the Fraser's wouldn't be here."

Any joy I'd felt was extinguished by the reminder that, when Madeline had been granted the bursary by the Foundation, my parents had still been in charge. They wouldn't have come, not from France, not for this. They were people of ball gowns and tuxedos, an environment I still struggled to find comfortable.

"They – we – usually aren't," I stumbled over the words. "My parents died not too long ago, they wouldn't have been involved at this stage, but since I inherited the Foundation I wanted to see what it was about, where the investment was going..."

The words slipped out of my mouth as if I'd heard Laurence say them minutes before. It had been Laurence who suggested I scope out the nominations for the award – to get me out of the house. At the time I hadn't been interested in any of my parents' money, I couldn't have cared less where it was being spent. But,

Laurence had talked me around. He didn't come from money. In fact, without my parents' generous donation to his own cause, he would never have been able to afford medical school or been close to getting his dream job as Head of Cardio-Thoracic surgery. He felt a responsibility to make sure that my parents' fortune was not being mishandled.

"You should have received a letter." I looked away, blinking back the tears I knew would surface if I could not control them. Madeline's stare began to unnerve me.

"I..erm, I had to move," she stuttered, then dropped her gaze.

"It doesn't matter." My chest was tightening. I had to get out into some fresh air. A car would be waiting for me. There always was. "I should go."

I placed the mug on the side and rushed out, gulping in air as I pushed open the studio door and stumbled out into the bright afternoon light.

"No, wait," Madeline barged into the back of me not realising I'd stopped at the stairs.

"I'm sorry," she rambled, grasping my arm to ensure I didn't fall. "That was awful of me. I didn't know. I'm really sorry. Please, come back, sit down."

She must have thought that offending the name of the Foundation would cost her the award, or at least that's what I suspected at the time. She gripped onto my arm with desperation and I realised I'd scared her. I couldn't leave the poor girl with such a bad impression; my parents taught me better than that. If anything, the one thing I knew was that we had a reputation to uphold.

So I let her guide me back inside and make me a 'proper' cup of tea. Her northern accent was soothing and I found myself smiling at her stories as she babbled about how lucky she felt she had been to receive the initial stipend. I hadn't realised that the studio in London was rented, that she had come down from Sheffield to ensure that the pieces to be auctioned off in the city were comprised of genuine London-finds. That was what she'd spent the grant on, she said, moving to London to prepare for the auction. She didn't need to say it, but I glimpsed the camp bed in the back room as she took our cups to the sink and noted the suitcases I had assumed were part of her 'collection' but were, in fact, too new to be part of it. I admired her. She had come all this way just to prove her worth. I didn't have the heart to tell her that the board she had been speaking to earlier made all the decisions and that my vote wouldn't count in the final discussions. I had been allowed to attend as a courtesy. They could hardly refuse: I controlled the money they depended on.

"What about family?" she asked me as we watched the last patch of golden sunlight move across her studio floor.

"I have a little girl, Rachel."

"How old?"

"Six," I said, then had to correct myself, wincing at Madeline's confused glance. "Seven, she turned seven last week."

I'd made an appearance at her birthday party, long enough to give her a kiss and show her the bouncy castle in the back garden that Florence, our housekeeper, arranged for the day on my instruction. But there were so many high-pitched screams of girly exaltation that I crept upstairs to look through photo albums of my own childhood and wallow in my memories.

"You must love being a mother," Madeline commented, looking up at me through tendrils of hair.

"I do."

"What's she like?"

Speaking of Rachel with Madeline made me realise I'd been focusing on all the wrong things since my parents' deaths. Being asked question after question about my daughter I discovered how little I knew about the little girl I'd neglected whilst caring for my parents.

A light tap on the door interrupted our conversation and the face of my driver peered into the murkiness of the studio.

"Mrs Fraser," he called, spying us sat in the dark. "Just checking that you were still here, it's been some time."

I glanced at my watch. "Oh." We had been talking for hours. "I really should get back," I said, slipping off the stool.

"Of course," Madeline embraced me, and I leaned down to do the same. She planted a small kiss on each of my cheeks as she stood on tiptoe.

"We really should do this again," I said, out of habit.

"I'd like that," she replied, a huge grin on her elfin face.

I pulled a card out of my handbag and offered it to her. "Call me and we can set up a lunch perhaps?" I caught a flicker of something in her eyes. "On me. It's the last I can do after wasting an afternoon I'm sure you had planned to work in."

She let out a breath, her shoulders relaxing. I guessed right: she was out of money, finances never did stretch as far in London as they did up North, even I knew that.

~~~

When I returned home that night, I was just in time to put Rachel to bed and I did so with energetic resolve. Unfortunately, she picked up on it and we ended up playing in her room until Laurence got in at eleven o'clock.

"You really should be in bed, monster." He swooped into the room, gathering Rachel into his arms and launched her into bed glancing at me with an intrigued smile. He tucked her in with calm patience. I kissed her on the forehead and withdrew, a satisfied buzz throughout my entire body.

"You're in better spirits," Laurence said, in our bedroom a few moments later.

I told him about my visit to Madeline's studio and how her work had resonated with my current state. Then, I gushed about our long talk, leaving Laurence chuckling to himself.

"What?"
~~~

"If I'd known you'd just needed a new girl friend I'd have set you up with one of the consultant's wives."

I wrinkled my nose. "Not my type," I joked, but it wasn't far from the truth. Perhaps it was because of my background, but I – rightly or wrongly – judged those with wealth as shallow and boring. It was what I had been afraid of as a teenager, which I suppose explains why I ran away. I'd become even more fearful of it since my parents died too – becoming one of '*those*' women. Talking to Madeline had reassured me I was not, she had said as much when she commented how 'normal and down to earth' I seemed after her confession about thinking I was a P.A. I never wanted to be considered as 'entitled' and had gone out of my way to prove I was not.

"Well, I hope you invited her over for coffee one day." Laurence clambered into bed. "Seems like she's done you the world of good."

I murmured my agreement as I snuggled into him, and it was with this encouragement that Madeline and I started spending almost all of our time together.

~~~

It was early afternoon and Madeline and I had just eaten lunch. It had been two weeks since I'd been to her studio to see her work and we had seen one another almost every day since. Initially she had been concerned our friendship might constitute rule breaking and cost her the Foundation prize, but when I assured her I was not involved with the committee she nodded and let it go.

I watched Madeline gather up the dolls that Rachel had left sprawled out on the sofa. She picked each one up and scrutinised it, turning it over in her hands before discarding it with a bemused expression.

"Did you always want children?" she asked.
~~~

I considered her question as she settled into a seat. She sank into the opulent, cream cushions just like Rachel, her feet only just touching the floor.

"I'm not sure I really thought about it until I met Laurence. I don't suppose you do, really, until you find someone to have them with."

"Mmm," Madeline murmured. She looked far away, a small figure nestled in the huge expanse of sofa with a glazed look over her eyes.

"What about you? Have you thought about having children one day?" Madeline blinked back her surprise at my question and tears began to form at the corner of her eyes. "Oh, Madeline I'm sorry, I didn't mean to bring up old wounds."

"It's okay," Madeline waved a hand at me. "It was a long time ago. A mistake. But one that I've paid for." She took a breath and wiped her face. "I can't have children anymore."

A well of empathy spread through me. I sat forward in my seat, placing a hand on her knee. "Neither can I."

Perhaps it was the wrong thing to say. Perhaps it was the obvious fact that, despite our similar troubles, I had Rachel. Perhaps it was that she knew then what I did not; that Rachel was her child. Whatever it was, it caught something in her and she flopped into my arms and began to sob. I stroked her hair and made useless soothing noises until she calmed, then I extracted myself and brought her a glass of water.

"I'm sorry," she said, as she took the glass from me with trembling hands. "That was completely inappropriate." She sipped at the water. "I just— I always imagined my life going a different way."

"I think we all do."

There were ten years between us and I felt like I was talking to a younger sister. I'd been in her position once: young, naïve and afraid for my future. I thought that I'd made more mistakes that she could possibly have experienced. I wanted to reassure her that life was a journey whereupon we did not know the destination and so we could never rule things out. I believed, because of our shared pain, I might be able to trust her.

"I tried so many times to become a mother," I said, slipping my hand in to hers and squeezing it as reassurance. "I lost so many. I thought it was my fault, that I didn't want it enough, and that I was too afraid. But then I managed to carry Daniel to seven months." I felt the warmth of my own tears on my cheeks then and was not ashamed of them. "He was kicking right up until the day of the scan. And then, nothing."

Madeline shuffled closer to me and wrapped both of her hands around mine.

"I had to give birth to him. My beautiful baby boy. But there were complications, bleeding. I almost died myself. I would have, if it meant he could have lived instead." I swallowed my despair. So different from the agony of losing my parents, yet keenly connected to grief. "After that, well. There was Rachel. I was a mother without a child and she was a child who needed a mother."

I let the implication of my statement hang in the air between us. Madeline stared at me. I could see the faint marks where her tears had washed away whatever make-up she had been wearing. I wondered if my own face looked the same and withdrew my hand to dab a tissue on my cheeks.

"So Rachel isn't yours?"

"Oh she is," I said. "But, biologically, no. Rachel is adopted."

Madeline shifted and then stood up to pace the room. "Wow. Does everyone know?"

I shook my head. "A few people, but it's not something we broadcast. We see Rachel as our daughter the same way Daniel would have been our son if he'd survived. We adopted her when she was only ten days old."

"What about her mother? What happened to her?"

"She was young, too young really I think. We never met her."

Madeline opened her mouth to ask another question and I flinched. I hadn't wanted to tell her the full story. I didn't want to admit that we had needed to buy an unwanted baby. I was ashamed of my past, just as Laurence was of his. She must have seen the look on my face, because she didn't ask any more questions. Instead she gave long nod downward, as if it explained something she had already suspected. Even if she had wanted to ask something else, she couldn't. A second after that nod Rachel burst in through the door announcing she was home from school.

"Hello darling," I jumped up to greet her, embracing her so that I had a chance to wipe any remnants of sadness away from my face. Madeline stopped moving, staring at the two of us.

"Rachel, this is my friend Madeline. Madeline, this is Rachel."

I scrutinised her as she bent to meet my daughter. So few people knew about the adoption that I was intrigued to see if it made any difference to how people would treat us as a family. Madeline reached out with both hands gripping Rachel by her shoulders and smiling so much dimples appeared in her cheeks.

"Well, aren't you beautiful?"

Rachel did have the most luscious strawberry blonde hair that I'd ever seen on a child. I glanced at her trying to see what Madeline would see. A small, skinny seven year old with freckles across a button nose and deep, soulful blue eyes. My heart filled with pride at her.

"You're hurting." Rachel squirmed in Madeline's grasp and pulled away. I stepped forward, a flash of panic contracting in my stomach, but Madeline released her, still smiling.

"Do you like secrets?" she asked.

Rachel immediately leaned back in, any memory of the sting of Madeline's grip evaporating at the intriguing question.

"What kind of secrets?"

"Magical ones," Madeline breathed.

I remembered mentioning Rachel's current obsession with fairy tales and the wonder she had at how easily magic was accepted in those stories. She adored the Disney franchise because they made it all seem so real: the possibility that princess could sing and attract animals, that even without a voice they could still make the prince fall in love with them; not to mention the idea that animals could actually talk.

Rachel's eyes were wide and she glanced up at me to see if I had heard Madeline's words. I raised my eyebrows at her and waited. What had Madeline got in store? Rachel's attention whipped back to Madeline at her next question.

"Can you keep a secret?"

"Yes," Rachel's head continued to nod all the way through Madeline's words.

"As long as you can keep a special, magical secret I want to give you something."

Madeline looked up then to ask permission. I couldn't have said no even if I'd wanted to, she had Rachel mesmerised.

"I promise I can." Rachel leaned in to say something in Madeline's ear, but I overheard her dramatic whisper. "Can I tell Mummy though, she can keep secrets too."

Madeline nodded and winked at Rachel. Their two heads bowed together reminded me of sisters. I marvelled at how easily Madeline seemed to slot into our family – my confidante or Rachel's, she was suited to either role.

Madeline reached into her pocket and slipped out a necklace; a silver chain with the miniature ornate key hanging from it, fixed in place by three tiny beads.

"This belonged to a princess," Madeline said. "It opens a box full of all her secrets. Secrets that she has to keep hidden from her evil step-mother, otherwise terrible things will happen."

"What kind of secrets?"

"Well," Madeline sat down on the floor next to where Rachel stood. Rachel immediately followed suit. I stood over them. "In the box are pictures of the princess' real mother, who was banished from the kingdom by the king when a spell was cast on him by the evil step-mother. Now these are all the princess has left to remind her that her mother ever existed, so she wants to keep them safe. She asked me to look after this key, so that no one else can open the box and destroy the pictures."

"But won't she want to look at the pictures?" Rachel asked.

Madeline shook her head, tapping a finger against her temple. "The princess keeps her mother's memory up here, even though she hasn't seen her in a very long time. But one day she might need the pictures to remind other people who she was."

Rachel fingered the necklace. "It's so pretty."

"Do you think you can look after it for me?" Madeline asked. Rachel's jaw dropped so that her mouth formed a tiny 'O'. "I think the evil step-mother knows I'm helping the princess. But she'll never suspect I would give it to you."

"Really? Could I?" Rachel gazed up at me. "Can I, Mummy?"

I put on a pretend serious face, playing along at what I thought was a game. How foolish I was. "She won't be in danger, will she?"

Madeline knelt next to my daughter and smiled. "No, I'm sure you will keep her safe."

"I can keep it safe," Rachel stated, crossing her arms.

"I bet you will," Madeline said. Then she clasped the necklace around Rachel's neck. "It's very important that you don't lose it, okay?"

"I won't, I promise. I'll never take it off." She touched the key as it rested between her collarbones. "And I won't tell anyone what it is, ever."

"I knew you were the right girl for the job," Madeline grinned and offered up a palm for a high five. Rachel struck it with gusto.

"How will I know the princess when she comes back to get it?"

Madeline winked. "You'll know her, I promise."

Rachel leapt into Madeline's arms, almost toppling the both of them. "Thank you," she whispered and then she scurried off to show her toys.

"That was very kind of you," I said.

"It's was nothing, I thought she might like it," Madeline shrugged, her gaze still on the doorway where Rachel had disappeared. "I should go." She clambered up from the carpet and brushed herself off. Her smile was replaced by a weary look and I thought it must be hard for her to see me with a daughter, given our similar situations.

I walked her to the door and was startled by the handle turning as I was reaching out for it.

"Hello darling," Laurence walked in, giving my shocked face a kiss on the cheek. "Final surgery cancelled, so thought I'd come home to my girls."

Laurence rarely got home before dinner. At the time he was doing his best to put in the hours to prove he would be a top candidate when the time came to announce a new Head of Cardio-Thoracic surgery. I realised Laurence and Madeline were stood staring at one another with bemused smiles. I hurried to introduce them, sweeping my thoughts about Laurence's unexpected appearance away. It was flattering that he'd come home early for once.

"Pleased to meet you," Madeline shook Laurence's hand with a grin, gazing up at him with her bright blue eyes. A flicker of tension passed across Laurence's face, like a minute wince. I could see the outline of a sweat mark on the back of his wrinkled shirt and smell the feint odour of his cologne in the hall.

"I'll see you later, Penelope." Madeline leaned in to kiss me on the cheek, but I was too distracted by the flat expression that came over Laurence's face as soon as Madeline turned her back. I bustled her out of the house with as much politeness as I could, a mild panic increasing my heart rate as I realised Laurence would never come home early just to see me and Rachel.

"What is it?" I asked as soon as I shut the door. Laurence made no attempt to hide the concern on his face now Madeline had gone.

"Someone knows," he stated, handing me a crumpled piece of paper and then turning to his study.

I looked down at the typed note.

"Do you want your socialite friends to know that you bought your child? I bet they don't know why. To keep your secrets safe I want £150,000. You have 24 hours to decide."

I scrambled after Laurence, catching my elbow on the dark mahogany bookshelf next to the door in my hurry. He was pouring himself a drink from the decanter on his desk and I watched as he knocked the first one back and then poured another.

"How did you get this?" I had so many questions, but forced myself to stay calm. I cupped my bruised elbow. £150,000 wasn't that much.

"It arrived on my desk at work in a plain envelope with just my name on the front. No one remembers putting it there."

"Who could know?" I tossed the note onto the desk and Laurence drained his drink and put his glass over it.

"I have no idea. But if we give into this demand, what's to stop them asking for more?"

A wave of dizziness hit me and I reached out for a chair to lean against. It was so long ago, almost fifteen years had passed since I had made the biggest mistake of my life. Meeting Laurence had been my redemption. He pulled me out of the distorted world I had fallen into after running away from home. My parents were grateful to him for rescuing me and in return erased his own regretful error. As we stood facing each other, our eyes locked, both desperate to put our past behind us, yet it looked possible that it might just ruin us instead.

"But if we don't pay—" I started, moving toward him, my hands shaking but my resolve stronger.

"No," he snapped. "What happened to us were mistakes. That's all. We shouldn't have to pay for them anymore." He turned away. His shoulders hunched and his head low. I knew his shame. He had cried in my arms during his early medical training after one of his mentors had taken him to one side and highlighted that an 'issue' had arisen on his record. No matter that he had not known the girl was only fifteen, that she had turned up at a University party dressed and made up to fool every boy there. It had happened two years before Laurence met me and he had thought he had dealt with it by moving to the other side of the country. But a file had been set up by the police and his university had been informed prior to an internship required for his qualifications. What was he supposed to do?

I'd done the only thing I thought I could. I went back to my parents and begged them to save him, like he had saved me. They managed to hide my unfortunate arrest from the records after I'd been caught with cocaine in my modelling days – drugs that belonged to my agent, who refused to acknowledge me thereafter. If they could do it for me, they could do it for Laurence. And they did. But their influence only went so far, and the rigorous adoption checks for us to acquire a child would have unearthed them for nothing: because they would not give a child to a "reformed drug-dealer" and "child molester". So like every wealthy family we used our money to fix the problem.

"It's only money, Laurence," I said. "What does it matter if they want more, we have plenty."

He cast a dirty look over his shoulder at me, his eyes narrowed and black. "You have plenty of money," he replied. "I'm sick of being bailed out by your family's finances. That's what got us into this mess."

"That's what allowed you to be the man you are today, that's what got us a daughter we love and cherish, that's what given us everything we ever wished for. Don't blame the money when it was our choices that got us here."

"Some of those weren't choices, Penny," he spat back. I winced. He hadn't known about my fortune when he fell in love with me. He'd only discovered who my family were after we'd already saved him.

"I thought I was doing the right thing when we buried that charge," I shot back. "I didn't know then that we wouldn't be able to have children, that we'd consider adoption. But we stuck together, we made that choice when the time came. Would you have it any other way?"

We glared at one another, my breath coming in short, sharp gulps. Why were we fighting? I drew my gaze down to a photo on Laurence's desk; the three of us huddled together with great big grins – a family, no doubt about it. When I glanced back up he too was looking at it. His expression softened, the furrow in his brow flattening and his lips slackening from that tight line that had been there as he grit his teeth. He sighed and threw his hands up.

"I don't want to pay," he said. "We'll be paying forever if we give in now."

I opened my mouth to argue but the door creaked open and Rachel crept in.

"Daddy," she called and she broke into a run as soon as she saw him. He was ready for her as she jumped into his arms and swung her around as he caught her.

"Hey sweetheart, what are you up to?"

"Looking for you," she said, burying her face in his shoulder.

We looked at one another over our daughter's head. Laurence's expression was soft but firm. He didn't want to surrender. It had been the same attitude he'd had with me when we'd met, so determined to coerce me away from the people I'd depended on who had betrayed me. He wasn't one to bend easily and I admired that in him. I stared back, knowing that he saw the same stubbornness in my eyes, not for resistance but for freedom. I just wanted it to go away and if a hundred and fifty thousand pounds would let me live in peace with the family I had created, then so be it.

~~~

The following morning I woke up with an empty place beside me in bed. Laurence had shielded himself from any further discussion about the note the night before by playing with Rachel until her bedtime and then sat in her room while she slept so I could not interrupt his thoughts. I expected him to come to bed eventually. I found him downstairs in the kitchen nursing a cup of coffee and a glass of orange juice; his hangover cure.

"Rachel up?" I asked, wary of saying anything if she were close.

"It's barely six," Laurence answered. "Even the maid's not here yet."

I blinked at the clock. I hadn't even thought of looking at the time. The sun had woken me because I'd neglected to close the curtains. That hadn't happened in so long that I didn't question the light streaming through the window.

"Look, Laurence, I think—"

"I'm sorting it."

His tone was unnecessarily harsh. This wasn't like him. We made our decisions together. Or at least I thought we did.

"How?" I asked.

"You said money wasn't a problem, so I'm using it to find out who's blackmailing us." He gulped down his coffee and placed his cup in the sink. "I'm going to take a shower. I have surgery at nine."

I grabbed his arm as he passed. "Who?"
~~~

He stopped to look at me. "Who else?" he said. Then he shook off my hand and I was left listening to the soft pad of his feet going upstairs. I wouldn't have thought he would have the courage to go back to the source of our deceit. But, George was the one who had kept our secrets, therefore he was in a position to identify who it was that had discovered them.

~~~

An hour later, while I was sipping a cup of coffee of my own, there was a gentle tap at the back door. A rapping pattern that was familiar and brought back memories of my father. That was how he'd always knocked on my door as a child. I hadn't known then that this was also a signal he used with his personal private investigator.

I opened the door to George. He was getting old. His hair had thinned out and was now grey all over, even his beard had succumbed and the flecks were brown in white instead of the other way around. His eyes had aged too, diluted down by the years into a watery grey to match his hair. But his strong jaw and Roman nose were impenetrable by time.

"Mrs Fraser," he nodded at me. "Sorry to see you again under such circumstances. You look in good shape though."

I smiled, intending to compliment him as best I could, but Laurence appeared in the doorway. "Thanks for coming," he told George. "I have to be gone in twenty minutes. What do you know?"

No pleasantries or catching up. Straight to business.

"Not much, she's a slippery one."

"She?" I repeated.

"It usually is," George replied. "But I have her on film, in the hospital on her way to your office." He spoke to Laurence, not me.

"You know who it is?" Laurence asked.
~~~

George shook his head. "Cameras aren't that good. But it's a start."

"Keep on it," Laurence checked his watch and pulled a face. "Anything else?"

"Nothing conclusive. I'll let you know."

Laurence nodded and leaned in to give me a brisk kiss on the cheek. "See you tonight." I stayed silent, not daring myself to speak. I watched him walk away.

"How's the girl?" George asked.

I took a breath and turned to the man who had arranged our adoption and I smiled. "She's great, George. Thanks for asking. Coffee?"

He hesitated. He had work to do but I'd guessed he'd been up most of the night already, he needed a pick me up.

"Sure," he said, coming to sit at the breakfast bar while I put the kettle on.

We heard the maid arriving and I excused myself to ask her to get Rachel up after she'd tidied the living room.

"Sorry about that," I said to George, shutting the kitchen door behind me. "We should have half an hour of peace and quiet."

"You don't agree with Mr Fraser about the situation?"

The cups clinked together as I got them from the cupboard, unprepared for his directness.

"I'm not sure," I admitted. "What if she reveals all before we find out who she is?"

George shook his head. "Won't happen. Blackmailers are in it for the money."

"Then if we don't pay, what happens?"

"You buy more time."

I let his logic try and reassure me while he sipped at his coffee seemingly unaffected by the heat of it.

"How safe are we?" I asked after a long silence.

"Your record is practically invisible. Misfiled, and after, what is it – fifteen years? - it's unlikely to be discovered."

"Seventeen." George looked at me. "It's been seventeen years," I said.

"Your husband's," he continued. "That's a different matter. The change of name helped distance the charge but it isn't gone, not like yours. Someone who knew what they were looking for could find it."

I winced. Laurence hated taking on my name when we married. It was unorthodox and suspicious and no matter how many times he towed the line of 'my wife's family name is precious to her' I knew it stripped him of some of his pride as a man every time he needed to say it. Fortunately there were few people in our lives that knew us back then, so people just assumed the usual and, unless they knew my family history, were none the wiser.

"Could it be her?"

"The teenager you mean? From back then?"

I nodded.

George slurped his coffee, tipping back his head to get the dregs from the bottom of the cup. "No, I've already checked. Married with two kids and living in Ireland now. No connection there."

"So then, who?" I sloshed my coffee over the side of my cup and watched the liquid spread over the counter. I felt helpless to stop it.

George took a handkerchief from his pocket and mopped it up, as he was used to doing. "Have you or Mr Fraser told anyone anything recently? Even the smallest mention of anything?"

I kept my gaze on the counter top where the coffee had spilt only moments before. George knew instantly.

"Give me a name and I'll check them out."

"I didn't mean to," I said, tears stinging my eyes. "It was someone I thought I could trust. A friend."

"It always is." George pulled a notebook from his shirt pocket along with a tiny, knife-sharpened pencil. "Name?"

"Madeline Tailor."

The pencil point snapped and graphite skittered across the floor. A dark silver dot marked the notepad paper beneath George's hand. I waited for him to move, to write the name down. He didn't. He sat with that blunt pencil hovering over his page for far too long.

"George?"

At the sound of my voice he put the pencil down and ran a hand over his beard. His face appeared paler, his eyes a sharper shade of blue rather than the grey I'd seen earlier. He stood up and placed a hand over mine. It felt clammy and warm against the coolness of my own. I realised I was holding my breath waiting for him to speak. George had only touched me one other time and that was by accident as he handed me a baby girl, his hands brushing my arms as Rachel nestled into me.

"That's the name of the mother," he said.

My world went dark.

~~~

When I opened my eyes again George and the maid were crowded around me, the maid fanning my face with a magazine. Sprawled on the kitchen floor I must have looked pathetic and weak. When I tried to sit up black spots appeared. I remembered sitting at the table at dinner the night before, too worried to do anything but push my food around my plate, listening to Rachel and Laurence jabbering away as if there was nothing amiss. The last time I ate would have been lunch yesterday. With Madeline.

I grabbed onto the maid and levered myself to my feet. "Will you take Rachel to school?" I asked.

"Of course, of course," she said, leading me to a chair. "But are you all right? Should I call the doctor?"

"No," I dug my nails into her arm and she squirmed away. "I just need something to eat." My eyes met George's, who was still
~~~

stood in the middle of my kitchen looking down at where I'd fainted. "Please," I told the maid, "Get Rachel to school and to the breakfast club. It starts at eight-thirty, you should have time."

"Yes Ma'am, I'll be back in an hour if you need anything." She scurried out. She'd have to rush to get Rachel ready now, but I knew she'd do it.

"You okay?" George asked, coming to sit beside me.

"I don't know." I had no reason not to be honest. "I've put us in jeopardy because I couldn't keep quiet." I slipped out of my seat and headed to the fridge. Now that I'd remembered, I was suddenly ravenous.

"Sit," George commanded, overtaking me. "I'll get you something."

I watched as he put together some breakfast things – croissants and toast with jam. He moved around my kitchen effortlessly, as if he already knew where everything was. When George put down a glass of orange juice in front of me I downed it in one.

"Tell me what I should know," I said. "Give me the answers to the questions I didn't ask back then."

"I never met her," he told me. "I knew her name but the contact was someone else, Celia Heart-something I think. She got your name from her mother apparently."

I stared at George, devouring not just breakfast but his words. Why hadn't I known all this when it was happening? I thought back to the grief I had experienced over the loss of Daniel, of giving birth to a child already taken away. Then I remembered the weight in my arms of a different kind; one that was warm and shifted with my smile: Rachel. I had been far too grateful to have her to question the specifics of where she had come from. What did it matter to me? I was her mother from that point forward.

"Did she know us?"

"I don't know. I thought not. This Celia girl, barely eighteen herself, handled all the details. All she said was that Madeline didn't want the baby."

The food I'd eaten turned to lead in my belly. "Could she take her from us?"

George shook his head, a firm no. "You and Laurence are named on the birth certificate. Only a DNA test would prove you're not her real parents and it'd be tough to get that legally."

I exhaled a long breath and my shoulders dropped an inch. As long as Rachel was safe. That was what mattered. "So how did she find out about the other stuff?"

"Like I said, with enough digging she could have put together Mr Fraser's past."

"But that would have depended on her knowing who we were," I pointed out.

"Maybe she wanted to see the kid?" George suggested. "See if she could squeeze some more money out of you? I'll go and take care of it."

I snatched at George's cuff as he moved. "Don't." He furrowed his brow at me. "I'll go. It's my fault."

"All due respect, Mrs Fraser, I don't think that's a good idea."

I stood up, swallowing down the anger that was stirring so he wouldn't be able to recognise it and have a real reason to prevent me from going.

"All due respect, George, you're paid with my money. I'm going. I doubt she'll react well to strong arming. If she's Rachel's biological mother, she's hurting. Maybe I can make this all go away by just being honest with her."

George shrugged. "Not the way I'd handle it."

"If she can't take my daughter away she can't hurt me."

I walked out of the room repeating that line over in my head for courage. I collected the car keys and handbag from the table in the hallway and strode out of the house with purpose. I figured I'd work out what to say on the drive over to Madeline's studio. But by the time I arrived there I had no idea how to bring the subject up. I couldn't understand how she had been so close to me, fooled me into trusting her and then tried to blackmail money out of us. Not knowing didn't stop me though. I went straight in to the studio without even knocking. It turns out I didn't need a way to ask her the truth. She must have seen it on my face the second she looked up from her work table.

"So you know," she said with a wry smile. She tossed away the tool she had been using and stood to face me. I couldn't take another step forward. I was afraid I'd hurt her.

"How could you?" I asked. My voice was low and didn't sound like my own. The sound of my heart pounding masked it and made it seem muffled.

"How could I what?"

"Give her away like that?"

"I didn't give her away. You gave me a price. Now I'm just asking for another instalment."

She was heartless. That's what I decided as I stood in the middle of her studio amongst all the junk she collected. She didn't really believe in remodelling lost things into more precious items to be coveted. She just wanted a way to worm her way in, and I'd given her the opportunity.

"You can't hurt me," I said. "You gave away your rights when you gave away your child. She's my daughter. You can't have her."

"You think I want her?" Madeline snorted. "I've run out of money, Penelope. Had it not been for your piddling grant I wouldn't even have managed to get to London to track you down. It was all too easy, especially when you showed up here."

So she'd known who I was all along. I recalled what Laurence had said about the never ending demands for money. I saw now that Madeline would bleed us dry if she could. The fact that she'd only asked for a hundred and fifty thousand meant she hadn't realised how much my parents had been worth. But I had no doubt then that once she found out, it would increase exponentially.

"Well, you're not getting any more money."

Madeline glared at me. Any hint of amusement about my confrontation gone from her face. She looked fierce now with all the hard lines of her elfin face drawn into a point that was aimed at me.

"I can ruin you," she said.

"What are you going to ruin?" I asked, throwing my hands in the air. "My reputation? My standing in the community? You can't prove she isn't my daughter and people aren't going to give a damn about a trumped up drugs charge from when I was seventeen, a naïve run away from my French parents. It'll blow over in less than a month."

Madeline tilted her head one inch to the right and pressed her lips together in a smile. "Maybe it won't ruin you. But what I know, what I can prove, will definitely ruin your husband's career."

I suddenly felt like I was in a lift that had plummeted to the ground. The contents of my stomach swirled and my brain felt cold in my head. How had I not seen that? I'd been so sure of myself. So foolhardy in my assertion that we could not lose Rachel I'd forgotten everything Laurence had worked for.

"Now I want double," Madeline said. "The look on your face just told me you'll pay."

"This would destroy Laurence. He is what he does. Are you really willing to ruin the man who cares for your daughter, who loves the child you gave birth to?"

"I don't have to," she stated. "It's your choice, not mine."

I waited in a panicked beat of silence. Laurence would be furious. I steadied my trembling lip and forced some words through: "Give me until this afternoon."

~~~

I took the car that I'd parked haphazardly on the road, and headed straight for the hospital. I had to pull over on the way to
~~~

throw up in a side street. Laurence would blame me for this, and rightly so. But unless we took action now, this would never stop. We'd have to do something she would never expect; we had to neutralise the effectiveness of her threat. I abandoned the car in a disabled bay and ran all the way to the department. It was just before nine o'clock, and I prayed Laurence would not yet be in surgery.

I latched onto the first nurse I recognised in the corridor. "Debra, hi."

"Mrs Fraser, how are you?" She smiled at me, though it didn't quite reach her eyes.

"I need to speak to Laurence immediately. It's an emergency, can you get him for me?"

It took her a second but she nodded and told me to wait. I perched on the edge of a plastic chair jiggling my knee. I watched the hands of the clock move until they were at four minutes past nine. It felt like a lifetime.

"Penelope?"

Laurence's voice pierced my bubble and I jumped up to meet him. He looked handsome in his scrubs but his face was etched with concern.

"I'm sorry," I said. "I know who it is, I tried to put things right, but I only made it worse. We need to do something Laurence. You're right, we can't just give into her demands."

He glanced at Debra who was just over his shoulder in ear shot of my ramblings. "Debra, can you get Walters to step in?"

The nurse nodded and Laurence guided me down the corridor to his office. Once inside he locked the door. "What do you mean you know who it is? How did you make things worse?"

My breath was coming in short, sharp bursts and I was afraid I might faint again. I sat in one of the chairs. My foot immediately started to tap.

"Madeline."

"What?"

"Madeline is Rachel's biological mother. She's the one who wants the money."

Laurence all but collapsed into the chair behind him. He ran a hand through his hair. Then his head snapped back up and his eyes were wide. "She doesn't want Rachel?"

"No," I answered. "She doesn't give a damn about Rachel." I allowed Laurence a moment of relief then came clean. "But she does want three hundred thousand pounds to keep quiet about your arrest."

His face fell. As much as he didn't want to pay and as firm as he had been the night before, he looked devastated. There was a knock at his door. We both jumped. Laurence got up to open it and found himself face to face with his boss, the Head of Cardio-Thoracic surgery who was a year away from retiring.

"Sorry to disturb you," he said, nodding at me from the doorway. "But something just came through on the fax that I'm a bit perplexed about." He held up a piece of paper. Scrawled across the top in big capital letters it said: 'Isn't this who Laurence Fraser used to be?' I didn't need to be able to read the rest. I knew what an arrest record looked like. I'd once had one of my own.

"Do you think we could have a word, Laurence?"

Laurence shot me a look. "I'll be there in a minute," Laurence answered. He waited for the sound of his boss' footsteps to fade before he turned to me. His face was ashen. I could see dark circles around his eyes that I could have sworn weren't there before.

"Laurence, I—" He held his hand up, cutting me off.

"I got the note yesterday morning. George transferred the money less than half an hour ago." He let his hand drop.

"What? But? I just spoke to her." I stammered.

"She never intended on keeping quiet," he said. "She just wanted you to be here when I got fired."

I didn't understand. How could she hate us so much? We had taken in her child, loved and cared for her. We'd been the family that she could not have provided for Rachel. What more could we have done? But then it hit me. We were the family that Madeline would never be. As much as Madeline might not want her daughter back, I considered what it must be like to see your only child happy with someone else. We were being punished for what she had done.

"Go home," Laurence said. "We'll talk when I get back."

He didn't give me chance to defend myself, to offer support or apology. He simply walked away, leaving me in his office while he went to explain why, when he was nineteen, he had been charged with statutory rape under a different name.

~~~

When Laurence finally came home that evening George was already at the house with me. Rachel had been given permission to stay at a friend's to allow us our privacy and I was certain we could save Laurence and his career. But when my husband saw us he just shook his head. He reeked of booze and cigarettes. I swear I saw smoke rise from his jacket as he tossed it onto a chair.

"It shouldn't cost you your job," I said.

"It already has. Unpaid suspension pending review." He made a beeline for the liquor cabinet, stumbling when George stood in his way. He regained his footing and shouldered passed George who, after a glance at me, stepped aside.

"So there'll be a review. You'll be back at work in a month."

"I committed fraud, Penelope. I lied on my application, I withheld information. I was hiding who I was." With each line he raised his voice. "I will not be allowed to work in any hospital again." He was clearly mirroring what he'd been told.

"It can't be that bad, can it George?" I looked to him for help. He had been quiet when he arrived, only telling me that Madeline's studio had been abandoned and the money received.
~~~

When I asked him why he hadn't stopped me earlier that morning he answered that he assumed she would already be gone.

"The way we had to hide his misdemeanour was different to yours," George explained. "We built him an entirely new identity, closely enough related to his old one that he could keep his medical training but removed enough the charge wouldn't be caught during checks." He watched as Laurence downed one drink and poured another. "Once Pandora's Box is opened, it can't be closed."

I winced at the inaccuracy of his metaphor but accepted it all the same. I hadn't realised just how illicit the cover up to protect Laurence had been. But then, I was young and I trusted my parents to rescue the man I loved. A tiny crevice opened up in my heart where I'd plastered over the pain of my parent's deaths, how much they had done to prove their love for me.

A shrill ring echoed from the hallway. I looked between George and Laurence and sighed, leaving them together. When I answered the call it was the mother of Rachel's friend.

"Hi Penelope, I hope you don't mind me calling, but I just wanted to check."

"Check what?" My mind was still in the room with Laurence, trying to think of a way to solve his problem.

"That Rachel knows someone called Madeline?"

My panic swirled, and I focused all of my attention to the telephone call. "What? Why? Is Rachel okay?"

The mother laughed down the phone at my over-reaction. "Oh, yes, Rachel's fine. It's just she was telling us about her new necklace, the one with the key, and apparently her friend Madeline gave her a note today at school to tell her always to wear it because some princess needs her to keep it safe?" She seemed amused by the tale. "But, well, I realised that there isn't anyone in their class called Madeline and when I asked she said it was a grown up, one of your friends?"

My knuckles were white from gripping the handset and I had to remind myself to breathe. Rachel was safe, she'd already confirmed that.

"Yes," I forced myself to speak. "She's not really a friend, more like an acquaintance. She's gone away now. Rachel won't be seeing her again."

I don't think the mother knew what I was really saying, but I needed to hear the words out loud to reassure myself that they could be true. I knew I wouldn't feel safe with Madeline out there, ready to reappear again at any moment to befriend my daughter. So when I rang off, I went straight back into the living room with a determined plan to leave the country. We could move to France. Rachel was still young enough to adapt. We could move into my parent's house – the one that hadn't yet been sold, the place where I grew up. Laurence could learn French and get a job at the local hospital. If George could hide the truth once, he could hide it again.

And he did. But Laurence didn't learn French. He didn't get another job or even apply for any medical positions. He moved to France with us and lost himself. When Madeline received the grant from the Foundation for her innovative vision for art as reimagined memories it was a slap in the face. Her scheme had resulted in her taking even more of our money, and I had to be the one to hand it over. That photo opportunity from the gala was sickening, but I had to do it, lest anyone realise what was wrong.

When I returned to France and Laurence saw it, we fought; he blamed me for bringing Madeline into our lives. I defended my ignorance and accused him of shutting me out of the details of the blackmail. Rachel cried a lot and missed England.

After a year Laurence was a different man, a different father to Rachel than she was used to. He told me once that he could see Madeline in her features, and that she reminded him of everything that he'd lost. Sixteen months after we fled from the U.K. Laurence got into a brand new Porsche and ran it off the road.

The autopsy report stated he had three times the alcohol limit in his blood stream. I had to tell our little girl that her father had died when she was only eight years old.

All of that I can blame on Madeline. Can you tell me I'm wrong?

PART IV

THAT WHICH IS LEFT IS LOST

Chris shifts in his seat uncomfortably, taken aback by the story Penelope has told. Is Madeline really so callous? But, he thinks, Madeline can't be held responsible for the way Laurence handled the situation, she certainly didn't force him to drink and drive. Yet, he understands Penelope's insinuation.

"I don't know," he answers honestly.

"Do you have children?"

He starts to lower his head to shake it – no – but then remembers and lifts his chin. "Not yet. But I will soon."

"They change everything you thought you knew about the world. They're precious in ways you can hardly imagine, especially when you have imagined being a parent for many years. I don't want to destroy the relationship I have with my daughter, or have her think that I betrayed her over all these years. Rachel is the only family I have left. Madeline has already taken so much from me. I won't let her to take Rachel too."

Chris presses his lips together. He knows what it is to keep secrets from those you love, of finally having the one thing you want in life in reach but at the cost of something greater.

"I understand your reluctance," he says. "But while you think you're protecting Rachel, when she finds out she'll think you were hiding things from her and you won't be able to argue the point because she will already have evidence that she shouldn't trust you." Isn't this exactly what he has done to Holly? What his step-father did to him? "This is her one chance at meeting Madeline and if you waste it for her, she may never forgive you."

Penelope lets her gaze drift just to the right of Chris. He can feel her retreating, trying to discover a polite way of extracting herself from the conversation so she can leave and be done with it. He is surprised when she speaks again in a light, textured voice.

"She still wears that necklace, you know? Hardly ever takes it off. She thinks it's romantic, some emblem of her childhood. If only she knew."

"Perhaps she does?"

Penelope's eyes widen in panic, her mouth forming a tiny 'o' shape and a manicured hand moving up to cover it. Then, she blinks, and accepts Chris' meaning: perhaps Rachel knows that the necklace is special, but not that woman who gifted it is her mother.

"I cannot trust Madeline. She will only hurt my daughter."

Chris takes a chance and gathers up one of Penelope's hands in his own. She has warm silk-like skin. "You can't protect her forever. And she deserves to know. The truth that you don't tell when the chance comes eats away at you. I know. I once kept a secret from my mother, trying to save her from herself, and for years I questioned my actions. It isn't worth the heartache."

"But your mother was better for not knowing?"

"I don't know," he replies. "I never got the chance to tell her. But I wasn't." He doesn't have to admit to the guilt that comes with that fact because he is sure Penelope can read it on his face. He understands now that it changed him, created a man who could not bear to see others suffer with their regret. He may have helped some recover their lives but at what cost to his own? For the first time he wonders if palliative care is truly the right thing for him.

Penelope's voice draws him back to the conversation. "You think my daughter will forgive me for lying to her all these years? For watching her struggle to find her birth mother when I knew who it was all along?" Penelope shakes her head in slow, measured movements. "I will not risk that."

"So it's better that she never find out at all?"

"Yes." Penelope snatches her hand away from his grasp.

"Better for her or for you?"

He isn't arguing for Madeline any longer, but rather for Rachel. He wants her to have the opportunity to meet her biological mother and receive a gift from the woman who abandoned her. Despite all of Madeline's past behaviour, Chris wants to believe that she can redeem herself, that she is able to have someone who cares for her by her side when the time comes. He keeps his eyes on Penelope as he speaks and she stubbornly refuses to drop her own gaze. But, as the silence stretches out he can sense her questioning her resolve. Her eyes become glassy and the intensity of her stare weakens. Does she realise how selfish she is being, pretending to protect Rachel when really she is hiding behind her own fear?

"Rachel doesn't have to know the whole story, just that her birth mother once cared enough to check up on her and see the daughter she gave up, and gave her a gift that she's cherished ever since."

Penelope closes her eyes and leans back into her seat. She pinches the bridge of her nose and shakes her head as she responds.

"I suppose you are right. But she cannot know that I had knowledge of Madeline's position. I will discuss that with her once this is over. One revelation at a time."

"That sounds like a fair plan. Do you think she can be here soon? I'm afraid Madeline may not have much time."

Penelope nods, eyes still closed. "I will need time to explain and prepare her for the worst. I shall fetch her myself." She hesitates, opening her eyes to stare at Chris with a slight scowl. "Will the morning be soon enough?"

Chris looks at his watch. Two hours have passed since Penelope arrived and it is almost two o'clock. Chris hopes Madeline is still battling on. He isn't sure if anyone knows where he is save for Betsy and he can't be sure she has stayed.

"I hope so." He escorts Penelope back to the reception area.

Chris watches Penelope leave the building wondering if she will be back. He wants to trust her to do the right thing, if not for Madeline's sake then for Rachel's, but she is a difficult woman to read. He starts to make his way to Madeline's room to make sure she can make it until morning, but a rough voice calls out to him: Cecelia.

"Told you she wouldn't bring Rachel."

She sounds pleased, as if his meeting Penelope and learning of her story vindicates her own desire to ensure Madeline dies alone.

But, strangely, it hasn't. What Chris heard in Penelope's accented words is that Madeline went back to see her child. She wanted to meet the daughter she gave away. She chose this hospice, and him as her doctor, for a reason: this is a place at the centre of her biggest mistakes. Telling Cecelia the truth about her father rather than letting the secret die with her might be seen as an attempt to make amends. That Madeline has a gift ready for the daughter she only briefly met demonstrates at least some regret for the anguish she caused. Madeline might be remembered for all the wrong reasons by Cecelia and James and Penelope, but Chris is beginning to suspect that knowing she has not been forgotten is enough for her. He can't say she is necessarily a good person, but is she really as bad as those memories make her out to be?

Chris stops beside Cecelia. Spending her days at the hospice, prowling around waiting for Madeline to die has taken its toll. She is dishevelled and limp.

"You should stop being angry at her, it would be a lot easier to move on without it."

"Without her, you mean."

"Soon she'll be gone and you'll have no one else to blame for how things turned out. She offered you the truth; I don't think you have anything left to stay for."

"I want to know that she got what she deserved. My father sure did after what he put those college girls through. He might not have molested Madeline, but that doesn't make up for what she did. He died alone for his crimes. Madeline should too. She's hurt enough people."

Chris thinks back to his own father. The words he has just offered Cecelia are true for him too. If he hadn't been so angry and disappointed in his father for consistently choosing alcohol over his own family then perhaps that letter would have made it into his mother's hands. She would have known that her husband loved her and that he was sorry for his faults. The written scrawl comes back to him as if it were inked on his own mind:

I failed you and I failed our son. You both deserve better. But I'm asking for one last chance. I may not get another, from you or from God, but I have to ask: can you forgive me?

As a boy, Chris' immediate reaction had been 'no'. He lit the fire and threw it on before his mother could return from the fish shop with their dinner. He had known then his mother's answer would have been different and so he stayed quiet. And then it was too late to take it back.

Chris examines Cecelia. Her hair is flat at the roots but knotted at the ends. She has acquired a blanket from somewhere, a thin, pale blue polyester that Chris knows itches the skin. She stares off into the distance with a determined expression.

"Would you see her again, if she asked?" he says.

Cecelia shakes her head in a flurry of movement. "Just tell me when she's gone."

"How long have you known?" He pauses. "Not about Rachel, but about where Penelope was, how to contact her? We could have done this a day ago, given Madeline the chance to make her peace with what she did."

"I've been working for the same charity Mum worked at for years. The Fraser family have been generous benefactors for two decades. I've always known where Madeline's daughter is."

Does Cecelia not realise that she is just as devious as Madeline?

"And you would let her die before Rachel has the chance to see her?"

Cecelia shrugs. "I just can't wait to be free of her."

Chris gestures to the door. "Then go, now. Be free."

"If only I could," Cecelia sighs. "But after almost thirty years, I've spent more of my life protecting Madeline and her secrets than I have without her." She looks up at him. "Besides, who else is going to collect her things and arrange the funeral?"

Chris furrows his brow. "You would do that?"

"If only to know that she's dead and buried and can no longer hurt anyone." There is a strangled laugh. "And so I can visit the grave, make sure she doesn't claw her way back out. I wouldn't put it past her."

Chris can imagine Madeline making that same remark and so he smiles before admitting defeat and nodding a farewell to Cecelia. He makes his way back to Madeline's room listening to the sound of his footsteps smothered by the silence of the corridor. He recalls his relief when he reached his own mother in time to hold her hand and reassure her that it was okay and she could let go of the pain. If only he'd given his father the same chance and forgiven him whilst he was still alive. He's held on to his guilt for too long, he sees that now. He does not want to be Madeline, alone in a bed trying to make amends – as his father did – and nor does his want to be Penelope, blaming others for mistakes they cannot be held accountable for. Her accusation that Madeline was at fault for Rachel not having the chance to say goodbye to her adopted father is a step too far.

He pauses, mid-step. Rachel might have lost her adoptive father and she might even arrive too late to meet her biological mother, but her real father is still out there. James might not know that he has another daughter in the world but he certainly deserves to. Chris alters his course to take him to his office. He can check on the system that Madeline is still stable. Late though the hour may be, Chris can't imagine there is a good time to reveal that the child you thought you lost was actually still alive.

~~~

Resuming his path to Madeline's room, he chastises himself for the call to James. Chris was only thinking of himself when he called. James Tailor has other things to worry about than a legacy from twenty years ago. A ringing phone in the middle of the night when your youngest daughter is waiting for a bone marrow transplant is an entirely different kind of hope than the discovery of a daughter you thought did not exist. Still there could be hope, Rachel might offer a match for Emily.

As Chris nears Madeline's door, Betsy appears beside him.

"What's going on? Where's Penelope Fraser?"

"Gone to fetch Madeline's daughter, I hope." Chris pauses at the door. "I need to convince Madeline to see her if she does. How is she?"

"Holding on," Betsy replies. "She still thinks Penelope's coming."

Chris takes a deep breath, he suspects that Madeline will not be happy that the woman she asked for has been and gone. Yet, Chris feels Madeline owes it to herself to make a gift of the box personally.

"And how are you?" Chris asks, examining Betsy's face. There is redness around her eyes, possibly from crying but just as probably from being tired. Chris' own eyes are beginning to sting.

She shrugs.

"Can we get Madeline through this before we make any decisions?"
~~~

She must sense him tensing whilst waiting for an answer because she lays a hand on his forearm - his fingers resting on the door handle - and squeezes.

"I suppose we have time."

A weight drops from between his shoulder blades and he can breathe again. "Thank you."

He pushes the door to Madeline's room open. Holly isn't there, perhaps she's gone home for some rest or stepped out to let Madeline sleep. Despite checking Madeline's vitals on the computer system Chris completes another brief examination. She doesn't wake, but her breathing is laboured, even with the mask clamped securely over her face. It seems as if every breath in is a battle, every exhale potentially her last.

Betsy tidies the bed linen, tucking in the sheets and pulling up the low side bars so that Madeline can't fall out of bed. Chris doubts this is necessary but it's protocol so he doesn't interfere.

"I told the staff on duty that I'd keep an eye on her," Betsy whispers. "Doesn't seem right to leave her, especially if Penelope doesn't make it back on time."

At the sound of Penelope's name Madeline opens her eyes. Immediately the gaze arrests Chris who is leaning over to balance the oxygen output. She reaches up a limp hand to try and capture the mask, but Chris lays her arm back down by her side. He doesn't know how long she will stay conscious so he gets straight to the point.

"Rachel is coming. Penelope agreed to contact her."

Her mouth goes slack with the shock. Her eyes widen enough so that the blue of her iris is fully visible and Chris counts the seconds until she gasps in another breath.

"You need to see her," Chris says. "I doubt Penelope would do as you asked."

Blinking, she simply lets her neck slacken to mimic the effect of a nod and whispers. "I didn't think you'd be able to convince her."

"You should save your strength." Chris gives her hand a gentle squeeze. "She'll be here in the morning."

Madeline, for possibly the first time, does as Chris instructs. He looks up at Betsy, across the bed, and they share a moment of acknowledgement that perhaps they have managed to help Madeline after all. The quiet is broken by the splash of a liquid and a muffled thump and Chris' gaze moves from the Styrofoam cup rolling about on the floor up to his wife's face.

"This is her isn't it? The one that's giving you what I can't?"

"Holly," Chris lets go of Madeline and takes a step forward.

"Don't you dare," Holly warns, holding out her index finger. She turns to Betsy. "You thought you could seduce my husband? Steal him away?"

"No, I—" Betsy stumbles on her words. "It isn't like that. It was a mistake. We didn't mean—"

Betsy's voice shakes and Chris tries to interject. Holly is quicker than he is.

"So you sleep with him and then take away the one thing he wants the most out of life? Oh, Chris, I thought you'd choose better than this." She gestures at Betsy as if she is a shirt for sale. "I thought you'd at least betray me with a woman of integrity, someone who understands what you want. Instead she's nothing but a stupid girl who doesn't realise how lucky she is."

Holly's mouth wraps around the insult with measured rage and grief. Chris sees then just how much he's hurt Holly; this woman verbally attacking Betsy isn't the wife he knows. She's never begrudged another woman for being able to have children. But then, those women were never having his child.

"You don't even deserve it." Holly moves closer to Betsy, a minute step with each word. "Look at you, you're terrified. Do you know what I would give to be able to have this man's child?" She flings an arm out toward Chris. "I bet your whole pregnancy will be easy for you, fertile ground that you are." She pronounces the word 'fertile' like an abomination. "And you don't even want it, I can tell."

A tear slides down Betsy's cheek. Holly is giving a voice to all of the fears Chris knows Betsy has. Everything he has said to try and convince her otherwise Holly is undoing.

"Holly. Stop."

But Holly leans in and manages one final retort.

"I bet you can't wait to get rid of it."

Betsy, tears flowing freely now, pushes past Holly and runs from the room. Chris leaps forward and catches the door as it swings back, calling after her.

"Christopher Wright. I am still your wife. Don't even think about running after her."

"She's terrified," Chris says. "She and I made a mistake and you—"

"I, what?" Holly snaps. "You slept with another woman Christopher. Am I not supposed to be hurt by that?"

Chris hovers in the doorway, uncertain. "You left me, Holly. Last night you packed up your things and walked away, before you ever even knew about any of this. I was devastated."

"Really? So devastated you decide to shack up with your mistress." Holly holds up her hands, palms facing up. "What a fool you've made of me."

Chris is suddenly angry at Holly for wanting to talk now, instead of earlier, before she left him. He lets the door slam shut.

"That woman is pregnant with my child. I don't love her, we aren't planning to run away together but she is carrying my child. You know that being a father is all I've ever wanted Holly. I can't sit back and pretend the mistake I made doesn't have consequences. I can't let it become the regret I live with for the rest of my life." Chris stops to take a breath but is stunned by the palm of Holly's hand across his face. They are the only people in the world in that moment. Their pain, anger, and hurt all that exists for either of them.

"Your regret?" She screams as Chris recovers from the sting of her slap. "That's all I ever wanted too. But you wouldn't let me. You couldn't stand the thought of a substitute for your own flesh and blood, even if it meant I got what I wanted. Well, now you have your chance Christopher. What about me?"

Holly collapses into a chair, sobbing with her head in her hands. Chris stands over her. She is right. He is about to get not just what he wants, but what they as a married couple had been unable to achieve together for years.

"It used to take us months and months. Two rounds of IVF. And for you and her it takes one night." Holly murmurs from between her fingers. "I knew it was me: that I was the problem."

Chris kneels down beside her and places a cautious hand on her knee. "I didn't stop loving you because of what we couldn't have."

"I thought I might be able to change your mind, but I couldn't. So I left. It hurts so much to know I'm not enough and that you can have what you want so easily with another woman."

"I'm so sorry Holly. I still love you. I still want to be with you."

Holly's hair shakes back and forth. "I wish I could have given you what you wanted. I wish I could be happy for you now." She looks up at him, tears still staining her cheeks and her eyes full of more, ready to overflow. "But I can't."

She sniffs and pulls a tissue from her cardigan. The two of them remain there, staring at each other until Chris breaks the silence. "So this is it. We're over?"

He swallows down the lump in his throat. Holly doesn't disagree. He doesn't know what else to say. Perhaps if Betsy wasn't pregnant it wouldn't be over. He might have come around to the idea of adoption eventually. But not now. Holly made her mind up even before she knew about him and Betsy. And now he has a child to worry about. It still seems like there is so much unsaid in the air between them, but Chris doesn't think that any words can repair the damage done to their marriage. He has been stupid, unfair to both Holly and Betsy, and he is ashamed that his wife is right. In the end, he will have what he wants: a child; someone to love him as a father; a legacy to leave behind when his time comes. He won't leave this world having not made a mark upon it.

Madeline's shaky voice echoes in the silence. "Not necessarily."

They both look over at her. Chris has forgotten they are even in a patient's room. He knows Madeline is slipping in and out of consciousness but he is surprised to see she is awake. Has she heard everything?

"I think you've interfered enough," he tells her. Chris stands up but Madeline holds out a trembling hand.

"Hear me out," she says.

Chris is about to refuse. He's heard the turmoil she's caused for others in the past and so far she has already upset his own in her short time at the Unit. He can't imagine what she might have to say that could make Holly forgive him.

"No, let her speak." Holly shuffles over to Madeline and takes her hand. "I want to hear what she has to say."

"The nurse, Betsy," Madeline wafts her free hand at the door. "She's young, she doesn't want to be a mum."

Holly intervenes as Madeline takes a long, drawn breath from the oxygen mask in between sentences.

"Getting rid of the baby won't save our marriage. I shouldn't have said such an awful thing. It's Christopher I'm mad at. Not her." She places Madeline's hand back on the bed and leans back into the chair.

"Betsy wouldn't do that." Chris states. And he knows Madeline is aware of this.

"No," Madeline says. "I'm saying she doesn't want the baby." Another breath in. "But you do," she points at Chris. "And so do you." Madeline turns her outstretched hand to Holly whose mouth falls open.

"You said you wanted to adopt," Madeline is struggling more with every word. "Adopt this baby. Be a mother to your husband's child."

Chris scrutinises Holly's face as the idea settles over her. Early into their problems, after the second round of IVF one doctor suggested surrogacy: Holly immediately refused. Chris agreed and although it was never said he knew it would be cruel for his wife to have to watch another woman carry his child. It is why he is certain their marriage cannot be reconciled by such an absurd suggestion. Still, he holds his breath as Holly's mouth turns downward considering Madeline's proposal.

When she sets her shoulders square and takes a deep breath, Chris mimics her. His kernel of hope deflates at the same time as his lungs.

"I didn't want to believe that I was the reason we couldn't have children, Christopher. I should have accepted it sooner. But I understand now, even before I knew about this," her lips pucker in distaste as she refers to his monumental betrayal. "It's why I left."

"It's okay. I can't expect you to forgive me. I—"

"No. Wait. I'm not done." Holly scowls. "I couldn't have agreed to surrogacy, not back then. But Madeline's right. This is our - my - option now. If we want to be together and have a child, this is the only way."

Chris falters. "I'm not sure it is."

But he knows it's too late. He can see Holly is already building cots and swing sets in her imagination. He glances across at Madeline who smiles beneath the mask reminiscent of a ghoul.

"It's not that simple," he says. "It isn't up to us."

Holly's face, a moment ago ravished with betrayal and anger and jealousy has transformed, her eyes are now bright. "But we could do this, Christopher. If she really wants the best for her child we can do that for her. You've said it before, I'd be a fantastic mum." She grasps at his hand, and he relishes the warmth of her touch again. "Tell her that. Tell her I'll love the baby like my own. Please, Christopher, if you love me, let's just ask her. We could end up being a family together."

Chris takes a breath and closes his eyes, trying to imagine how Betsy might respond to the suggestion. Even as he considers it he can feel Holly holding him hostage and without meaning to, hope burrows its way inside. Betsy doesn't want to be a mother. He could get not just what he has always wanted, but his wife too?

He opens his eyes, shaking his head. "Betsy will never agree to it," he says. "She doesn't want to give the baby up completely, she could never just leave her baby behind, no more than I could. It's why she wants to go back Northern Ireland and have her mother raise the child."

Holly sweeps herself out of the seat and moves her hand to his chest. It reminds him how long it has been since they have been so close. How their relationship has been centred on what they lack for too many years. The glimpse of happiness on Holly's face is maddeningly real.

"She doesn't have to. We can do this Christopher, we can make this work. We just need to show her that it can." Holly begins to push him back toward the door.

"Now?" he asks.

"I should apologise." Holly says. "What I said, it was…terrible. I was so angry. I still am. But we can't let her go Christopher. If I were her I'd be half way home right now."

Chris' heartbeat skips and he clasps his fingers into fists. "Not you," he tells Holly. "She won't want to see you."

Holly makes a face, her brows pulled down and mouth contorted. But this is his responsibility and he doesn't want Betsy to feel forced into this same corner he is trapped in by his wife. "I'll talk to her." He reaches the door and senses Holly on his heels the moment he turns. "Please, stay here and keep an eye on Madeline."

He waits until Holly nods and returns to the chair. Madeline makes clear eye contact with him before he leaves and he senses her smile hidden beneath the mask. This is exactly what Cecelia said she did, only this time she is creating drama in his life. Can Holly really forgive him the betrayal if Betsy gives them the baby? It's an absurd suggestion. Yet he feels the tiniest sliver of possibility within it and he can't decide if he hates or is grateful to Madeline for voicing it.

He doesn't know if Betsy will see the logic in it, but he has no reason not to try. Sighing, he wonders where she might have gone and prays she hasn't left the building. But then, he remembers, and he thinks he knows where she'll be. They've been there before.

~~~

Chris pulls his coat on and pushes at the old door out onto the quad. It sticks, so usually it needs a hefty shove but now it gives way with a creak.

"Betsy?" he calls into the darkness.

The quad is neglected and has been taken over by the few trees and shrubs that once formed part of a planted garden where patients could be brought to sit quietly. In the late spring and early summer, when he and Betsy were getting to know one another, she invited him to sit with her in the fresh air. The sharpness of it would wake them up and give them a moment's peace outside the melancholic tone of the hospice. When the corridors around it were dark the view up to the clear skies was spectacular.

Clouds have begun to gather on this night and the quad is thick with shadow. He picks his way through the overgrown weeds and finds their old foot holes like stepping stones. He doesn't come out here anymore but he can tell Betsy must still
~~~

visit the old bench, hidden by low branches and a grove of high foxgloves, because the weeds still haven't grown through the frequented patches of dirt where he places his feet.

"Betsy?" As he rounds the tree in the centre he lowers his voice to a whisper out of habit. It gives him opportunity to hear the quiet sniff of someone ahead and he hurries across to the bench, catching his toe on a broken paving slab and almost falling into Betsy's lap.

"Please just leave me alone." She pushes him up and away by his shoulder, which only serves to steady him.

"I can't do that." He takes a seat next to her and the old bench bows under his weight. "I'm sorry for what Holly said. She shouldn't have—"

"You should have stood up for me. Why didn't you say anything?" she mumbles.

"I know, I'm sorry. Please Betsy, let me explain."

When she lifts her head from her hands her face is streaked with blackened tears from her mascara and her cheeks are flush, despite the chill in the air. Her bare arms are goose-pimpled and Chris pulls off his coat and puts it around her. He is relieved when she does not immediately shake it off.

"There's a tissue in the pocket."

Betsy takes one to wipe her face. "I feel like such an idiot."

"You're not. It's me. I'm a coward. Madeline told Holly and I thought my marriage was over. I didn't believe Holly would ever forgive me."

Betsy tilts her head and examines him. "What do you mean?"

Chris takes a deep breath, sucking air in from between his teeth. "Look, I don't quite know how to suggest this. It isn't even coming from me. It's Madeline, and by this point I can't quite trust what she says."

"What is it Chris?"

The tone is acerbic and he knows he'll just have to come right out and say it:

"Madeline suggested that if you don't feel ready to be a mother that perhaps Holly and I can adopt the baby."

He can't bear to look at her. He is afraid of seeing the horror of what he is asking. It is selfish of him to ask this of Betsy. But what are his alternatives? He loves Holly and doesn't want to lose her. But neither can he bear the thought of not being a father to his child. Still, he doesn't expect Betsy's cool clam voice to respond: "Your wife would do that?"

There is only confusion on Betsy's face when he gathers the courage to look up. She doesn't seem insulted or horrified by the idea. In return, Chris feels he owes her the truth.

"Holly would do anything to be a mother. It's all she's ever wanted since I met her. She'd love any child in her care like her own." His eyes sting in the night air and there is a gentle breath of a tickle on his cheek, as though a spider has landed on him. "We both would. We've been waiting a long time, Betsy. So long that we'd given up hope. She understands that I can't let our baby go, that I need to be a father to them no matter what you decide." He wipes his face and is surprised to find it wet. "She was angry before, scared and resentful. But she can put it behind her if she can be a mother."

He keeps his eyes focused on Betsy, who stares at him with a face that goes from bemused to intrigued and back again. Chris places a hand over Betsy's where it rests on the bare, flaked wood of the bench.

"I don't know how it would work. But please think about it. For us, for Holly and most of all for that baby of ours you're carrying."

Betsy slowly slides her hand out from under his. It takes him all his strength not to clamp down onto it and beg her to consider this offer. Yes, it is complicated and impulsive and strange. But it might just work. And he wants Betsy to see that.

"Please," he whispers.

She shuffles further down the bench, into the shadows so he can't see her face and he swallows down the words he wants to say. She needs time to think but he grasps onto the vain hope that she hasn't yet outright refused. The silence stretches out between them and Chris listens to the measured breaths that Betsy takes, one after the other not saying 'No'.

The snap of a twig has both of them whipping their heads up and peering into the gloom ahead.

"Who's there?" Betsy's voice travels softly through the air.

"He's right you know," Holly says as she appears from the darkness. Betsy shrinks back and Holly pauses, holding her hands out to demonstrate she is not a threat. "I'm sorry for what I said. I had no right to accuse you of those things. You aren't to blame for the state of my marriage." Holly's eyes flicker to Chris and he looks away out of guilt. "But we've survived worse."

She moves to one side, standing at the far end of the bench next to Chris. She reaches out for him, holding her hand out next to his lowered face. When he looks she offers him a tempered smile and nods. He places his hand in hers.

"I'm sorry you don't feel ready for what's happened. But I've been waiting to be a mother for a long time. Christopher too; it would be such a shame if he didn't get to be a father. Such a waste. He's telling you the truth when he says I can put whatever friction there might be between us behind me. If there is any possibility that we can help bring up this child please know that I'd welcome it with open arms."

Chris feels a spot of wetness brush his hand and realises Holly is crying too. The clouds part for a moment and the moon casts an eerie light over them. Holly's face is bright with a sheen on her that brings out the truth in her eyes. Betsy sits staring straight forward, picking at the tissue leaving a white sprinkling on her lap. Her skin is dull, not bright like Holly's, but marked out like dark scars on each cheek are the tracks of the tears she's cried.

Chris squeezes Holly's hand signalling for her to stop. They can't talk Betsy into this. She has to make this decision for herself or it will never happen. They have months to sort out the details if she agrees to it. He licks his lips, which have gone dry in the night air, and thinks that will also have months to track her down if she decides to go back to Northern Ireland to seek out her mum. Whatever decision she makes Chris vows to stand by her for it, even if it means losing Holly.

He is just about to speak, to prise Holly away from the possibility of motherhood, when Betsy speaks. Her voice is husky and her Northern Irish accent thick with emotion, but what she says pierces right through Chris' heart.

"Let me think about it?"

He holds Holly's hand fast, preventing her from leaping forward to misinterpret that answer as a yes. He wants it to be an agreement as much as his wife does, but they have to be sensitive.

"Okay," Chris whispers. He reaches out to pat Betsy's on the shoulder. "We have time."

She glances up at him, as if his touch has disturbed her, and half-smiles at the familiar words. "We have time," she repeats with a nod.

The three of them pause for a few minutes, listening to the night air. Once an owl hoots, startling Chris into looking at his watch. It is just after three. In another five hours he'll be expected to be back on shift in the hospice, Betsy too.

"We should get some sleep," he says.

As if in answer, Holly yawns and he stands.

"Who'll stay with Madeline?" Holly asks.

Betsy stands too. "I will." She senses Chris' look. "No, it's okay, I offered my resignation to start immediately. I won't be needed here tomorrow."

"You really should reconsider," Chris says. "I'm sure we could get Doctor Gregory to alter his position." He thinks about the notebook in his pocket; how he swore to himself not to use it against his old mentor without provocation.

"No," Betsy shrugs off his coat and offers it back to him. "I think I'll need a change anyway. Whatever happens."

Chris takes his coat back and silently agrees. He's become complacent at the hospice and Madeline's audacity in seeking him out to do her bidding has him questioning his own motives.

"Go home" Betsy ushers. "I'll still be here in the morning. I promise."

He nods and leads Holly back through the quad to the hospice corridors.

Chris checks in on Madeline a final time before leading Holly out to his car. Madeline appears to have stabilised somewhat and providing she has the oxygen mask he suspects she will make it until morning. He doesn't, however, believe she'll see another morning after this. She is weak, her body is shutting down and there is nothing he can do to prevent it. Had she not signed the DNR perhaps he would be able to extend her life a little more - give her and Rachel time together. But he doesn't believe that Madeline or Penelope would allow that and can he blame them? Penelope has only agreed to bring Rachel because Madeline's time is so finite. Even Madeline knows this. Like the old lady who died just as Madeline arrived, she is holding on now to see Rachel and give her that box that seems so precious. He wonders what might be in it but shakes his head to loosen the thoughts as he clambers into the driving seat. After this, there will be no more interfering.

"If you don't mind," Holly's voice seems too loud for the confined space of the car. "I think I'd prefer to go back to my parents."

Chris realises he has turned out of the car park on the familiar route home. Holly's parent's house is in the opposite direction. He catches the undertone of concealed anger and can't blame her.

"Sorry."

But as he says this he realises that if they plan to make the suggested situation with Betsy work they have to discuss their marriage first. He pulls up on the side of the road, as if he is about to turn around, but then kills the engine.

"We need to talk. I need to apologise. After everything that happened it's been easier to deal with my patients that it has to deal with what I did to you. I accept the responsibility Holly: it is my fault you lost your job. I got you involved. And then I betrayed you. I'm so sorry for that."

Holly examines him. But he can see from the set of her chin she is biting down on her response.

"But what I can't be sorry for are all those people we helped before the Porters. I understand now why you wanted to stop though. If anything, Madeline herself has proved I'm looking for problems to solve at work because I could never solve the one at home."

"You mean me?" Holly sits staring at her hands, her left clasped in her right, letting Chris see that she is examining her wedding ring. He reaches out to place his own hand over hers, so she will see his own ring, his promise to her.

"I mean our situation. It's been too difficult for us to face. We've suffered so much loss, I'm frightened that if Betsy doesn't agree to this adoption that our marriage won't survive."

He waits, willing her to allay his fears. But Holly stays silent. He removes his hand from her lap and places them both on the steering wheel.

"I thought so."

"It's not that I don't love you Christopher—"

"Please," he grips the wheel, his knuckles turning white. "Stop calling me Christopher. Everyone else just calls me Chris. Have you not noticed that?"

He glances across at Holly, shocked that he's voiced something so insignificant at such a crucial time. Her bottom lip shivers and

Chris turns up the heating in the car. Too late he realises it is because she is trying to hold back the tears.

"Anything else?" She fixes her gaze on some unknowable spot out in the darkness that Chris can't fathom.

"I'm sorry, it's just…" He isn't sure why it bothers him so much, at least not enough to explain it to Holly.

"No," she holds a hand up. "If we're going to move past all of this then we have to be honest." She shifts in her seat so she is facing him. "I've not felt like your wife in a long time, Christ-" She stops herself. "Chris. I started helping with your patients because it seemed like the only way to get your attention. You were so distant." She bites down on her lip before she continues. "I know you blame me for not being able to give us a child."

"No, never." Though he knows it isn't quite the truth. Her brown eyes hunt the honesty out from him. "Not like that. I wanted us to get some help, to try and find out what the problem was, but I was scared to bring it up. You were always so sure that we'd make it right the next time and so devastated when it didn't happen. I didn't know how to ask."

Holly nods and her hair falls over her eyes. She pushes it back with a habitual gesture that makes Chris feel nostalgic.

"I was scared too," she admits. "I hoped and hoped that it wasn't really me, that my body wasn't betraying my needs, but I can't really deny it can I? Six babies, Chris." She sighs and lets her head drop. The hair regains its position over her eyes. This time Chris tucks it behind her ear and he feels, in his gut, just how long it has been since he and Holly have talked so openly and honestly with one another.

"If we're going to make this marriage work then some things will have to change." He's about to outline the changes he'd like to make but Holly responds.

"Both of us."

"I wish you'd stop blaming yourself for all of our loss. It isn't your fault."

Chris has to stop in order to take Holly in his arms as she unexpectedly breaks into raw, wrenching sobs. It is awkward in the space of the car and he doesn't know what else to do except wait until she calms down. "What is it?" he whispers.

"It is me," she mumbles into his shirt. "After the last..." she can't say the word, but Chris understands. "The doctor recommended some more tests. I didn't want to tell you. I thought you'd leave me." She gives one last sob. "There's nothing they can do. They said given my history it's always more likely to go one way, rather than the other. And I couldn't put us through it all again Chris. I'm not strong enough to have it happen all over again."

Chris rubs her back in even circles and curses himself for not noticing. He thought it had been grief, like before. To discover Holly kept such a secret from him is heart-breaking. The distance between them for all those months, the trouble that the Porter case had caused, their marriage had been on the way to ruin well before he slept with Betsy. Still, that doesn't make him feel any better.

"I don't know what to say," Chris moves back so he can look his wife in the eye. "Except that I forgive you anything and everything. Our lives haven't been easy Holly, they've been touched by more tragedy than I ever wanted to see, and I stupidly chose to specialise in palliative care."

She smiles, just slightly, and Chris is relieved his terrible attempt at a joke is received with weary acceptance. If Holly has been holding on to this for so long she must be exhausted. The adoption papers, he realises now, are what she turned to as a last resort because she knew what Chris didn't. He should not have been so dismissive and unavailable when she needed him. If they get through this he promises to himself that he will pay more attention.

"I suppose we're not going to solve it all in one night," he says. "We're both tired." He acknowledges the deep-set weariness in his bones, the ache in his lower back and stiffness in his neck. The last few days have all been too much. "Perhaps we need to know where we stand with Betsy before we make any decisions. Yes?"

He tacks the 'yes' on the end, as if inconsequential, but he knows he is too curious. Would Holly consider staying with him even if he has to chase his pregnant mistress across the country?

"I don't like to think of our future in the hands of someone I barely know."

"She's a good person. Believe me on that."

"And what if she decides to keep the baby, Christo-. Chris? What then?"

He is certain she would leave him, but is she asking now if he would leave her? He scrutinises her face but can see no semblance of an answer there.

"I don't know," he answers, truthfully. Her eyes flicker, blinking back tears he knows must be just below the surface. "But I'd like you to be with me, no matter what." She opens her eyes wide and he sees the ring of gold around the brown. "Do you think that's realistic?"

"It's too soon to tell."

As much as he appreciates her honest answer his shoulders slump and his eyes darken at her response. He wants to believe they could make it. Yet, while she might have kept something from him, he slept with another woman. He has to keep their digressions in perspective. Holly can't forgive him so easily, not unless it gives her what she has desired for so long. If they could raise the baby together, then she will see the mistake for what it is. If he has to uproot them only for her to be a bystander as he becomes a part-time Dad he can't be so sure.

He reaches back to the keys to start the engine. "Let me take you back to your parents so you can get some rest. We can talk more when we know Betsy's decision."

As he pulls into the road Holly swings around to put her seatbelt on. He hears it click into place and then her warm hand is over his on the gearstick.

"I hope she makes the right choice. For all of us," she says.

~~~

After he drops Holly at her parents - a chaste kiss on the cheek as a goodbye - Chris drives straight home and doesn't even make it up the stairs to bed. He falls asleep on the sofa still wearing his shirt and loosened tie. A little after six o'clock in the morning the sun creeps in through the open curtains and stretches over the carpet, advancing on the sofa and baking Chris in such an intensity he wakes up sweating.

He's been dreaming of his father, his mind piecing together an imaginary scene where he did not burn that letter but instead his father came home and they made peace with one another. Even though he knows it's not true, and that things may never have turned out that way, Chris feels settled. It's time to leave that past behind. He showers and gulps down a cup of coffee before clambering back into his car and returning to the hospice.

He knows Betsy would have called if anything happened to Madeline, so when he arrives he doesn't immediately rush to Madeline's room. Instead, he makes his way to the reception area and looks down on Cecelia, still there, curled up on the uncomfortable chairs as she sleeps. On the floor beside her is her bag, the zip gaping open. Inside it Chris can see a collection of odd things – buttons, pen lids, lollipop sticks and even a marble or two.

"I offered her one of the family rooms," the night guard says as he pulls on his jacket. "Said she was waiting for someone."

Chris thanks him and then gently shakes Cecelia's shoulder. She wakes up languidly, like a cat, and stretches out her limbs
~~~

before she realises it is Chris who disturbed her. Then, she darts upright.

"Has it happened? Is she gone?"

"No," Chris sits down where, moments before, Cecelia's feet were. "I came to ask if you wanted to see her again, before…" He isn't sure if he means before she dies or before Rachel arrives. All he knows is he feels he owes it to her to give her the opportunity to see her old friend one last time.

Cecelia shakes her head. "She isn't going to tell me what really happened, or why she lied. She's done with me. And once she's gone I can be done with her."

Chris glances back down at her handbag. Seeing where his gaze has wandered Cecelia reaches down and pulls it up to her lap to close it.

"Will it be that simple, do you think?"

To avoid his question she fiddles with the bag, examining the stitching with studious concentration.

"When I was a boy I thought that once my father was gone that my mother and I would be able to move on. But I did something that I couldn't take back that meant my father died alone without a chance to ask for my forgiveness for the hurt he caused. But it meant I couldn't be forgiven for my actions either."

"So?" She dumps the bag back on the floor with a thump.

"I just thought you might want to see her again to forgive her before it's too late."

"I will never forgive her. And once she's dead it won't matter anymore."

Chris realises he can't argue with her, and so he just sits with her for a few minutes in case she changes her mind. They listen to the receptionist unlock the main doors and prop it open, so that the warm September air can permeate the cool atrium that is still in shadow.

"They're here," Cecelia says abruptly.

He has to follow the line of Cecelia's pointed finger to understand what she means. There is a Bentley parked in the far corner of the car park with its engine idle and the windows tinted so Chris can't make out who is inside. Still, he knows who it is.

"I honestly didn't think she'd be back."

"Me neither," Cecelia stands up and presses herself against the window. She focuses on the car with an expression of intent. The Bentley remains where it is. Its door firmly shut.

Chris approaches the reception desk with a courteous smile. "Mind if I use the telephone?" he asks the girl. She passes it up to him with a shrug. The phone at the Nurses' Station just outside Madeline's room rings three times before someone answers it.

"Is Nurse Murphy there? It's Doctor Wright at reception."

"One second."

As Chris listens to the background noise of the hospice the Bentley's front driver door opens and he watches as a rugged, older man with grey streaks in both hair and beard opens the back passenger door. He wears black trousers and a short sleeved white shirt. Penelope Fraser unfolds herself from within the car with a nod to the driver, who nods back and returns to his seat. Penelope stands with her hand on the door, then leans forward and says something directed into the backseat.

"Chris?" Betsy's voice jolts him back to his thoughts. "Are you here?"

"Yes, in reception. Penelope Fraser has just arrived." A young woman scrambles out of the car to stand beside Penelope. She is slender and petite with long, auburn hair pulled back into a pony tail. Chris remembers the picture from Holly's print-outs of Madeline in a green dress. This is her, born into another life. "She's brought Rachel. She looks like Madeline."

Yet, as Penelope shuts the car door and the two of them began to walk toward the building, Rachel two steps behind and apart from Penelope, he realises that there are some differences. Rachel's face is squarer, her nose bigger and eyes wider. Her shoulders are round and set back and, as she reaches the doorway, Chris thinks he recognises a glimpse of James Tailor in her stance.

"Well, she's weak but awake, if you want to bring them in."

"Okay, we'll be there soon."

"Don't take too long. Her SATs have dropped considerably overnight."

Chris expected that, so it isn't a surprise. "I'd better go and welcome them." He puts the telephone down and passes it back to the receptionist who barely looks up at him. When he turns back to the door, Penelope and Rachel are inside. Cecelia in front of them.

"You shouldn't have come," Cecelia says.

Penelope makes eye contact with Chris and he moves forward to grasp Cecelia by the arm. "I don't think that's for you to judge."

She pulls against him and his grasp on her slips. "Do you really want to know the woman who tossed you to one side once she'd been paid?"

Rachel glances between Penelope and Cecelia with a panicked expression. Chris can see she doesn't know Cecelia, and she has no idea who this raving woman is at the entrance to the hospice.

Chris steps in front of Cecelia. "I'm Doctor Wright, I've been caring for your biological mother."

Rachel offers him a small, limp hand. She leans away from him toward the door as if she wants to escape.

"She's a liar," Cecelia hisses from behind Chris. "She'll do nothing but disappoint you."

Chris spins on his heels to face Cecelia. "Miss Hartland, I don't think we need to hear this. If you want to stay, then fine. But wait over there." He points back to the chairs where her over-sized handbag with that bizarre collection of rubbish rests. She squares up to him, shoulders back and chin raised.

"I'm only telling her what she ought to know."

"She's aware," Penelope inserts herself into the conversation. "I've told her how we arranged the adoption. Cecelia is right," Penelope glances over to Rachel, still hovering in the doorway. "Madeline Tailor does lie."

Chris can understand why Rachel had been two steps behind Penelope.

"Of course, Rachel has a right to find that out for herself." He smiles reassuringly at Rachel. "Are you ready?"

Rachel nods and steps forward.

"She'll ruin your life," Cecelia whispers.

Rachel glances at Cecelia as she passes. It is a wary look that suggests more curiosity than dismay to Chris.

"I've changed my mind." Cecelia grabs her bag and starts walking with them.

"About what?"

"I do want to see her again, say my goodbyes."

Penelope shoots him a questioning glance and Chris shakes his head. "I'm sorry Cecelia, that won't be possible."

"A few minutes ago you were telling me it was."

He quickens his pace but Cecelia keeps up, right on his heels, voice in his ear. "You said I needed to. And you owe me the chance, after I helped you out yesterday."

Chris pictures the small, moleskin notebook with Doctor Gregory's notes scribbled inside. "Well, I can only permit two visitors at once."

"Do you know what she did?" Cecelia calls out to Rachel and then to Penelope. "Have you told her about the last time they met?"

Rachel stops. Penelope whirls around to face Cecelia and glares at her. "You would do well to remember who you are talking to."

Chris puts a hand on Cecelia's arm and starts to gently try and guide her away. "I think it's time you left." Cecelia succumbs, for a second, then when Chris relaxes - thinking she is giving way -

she manoeuvres herself away and holds out a piece of paper right under Rachel's nose. They don't have time for this.

"No, let her stay." Rachel speaks for the first time. Her voice is stronger than she looks, it rings out with a clarity that Chris isn't expecting. He recognises the print out. It is the one he rescued from the floor when he and Holly were talking, the same image of Madeline Chris thought of when he saw Rachel. Cecelia must have retrieved from the chair they left it on.

"What's she talking about Mum?" Rachel's blue eyes turn to Penelope. She has the same way of holding people captive, drawing them in while remaining expectant and shrewd.

Penelope lifts a hand to cover her eyes. "You met her as a child. When you were seven. Briefly. We didn't know who she was."

Cecelia grins. Rachel takes possession of the page and Cecelia crosses her arms triumphantly. "That's right around the time you fled the country, wasn't it?"

Rachel's mouth shapes into a small 'o', as if she is realising something for the first time. "You took me away from my biological mother?"

Penelope snatches the page out of Rachel's hand. "No, we didn't…I—" She turns her glare on Chris. This is exactly what she didn't want to happen. But, within a second she draws herself up and composes herself. "There were lots of reasons we moved to France, Rachel. It had already been planned when you met Madeline. We didn't realise until after who she was, and by then it was too late."

Chris recognises this for a lie, but says nothing.

"So she wasn't the reason we left?" Rachel asks.

"No, I promise you."

"Rachel, I know you have a lot of questions," Chris interjects. "But I'm afraid Madeline doesn't have very much time. If you want to see her, we have to go now."

She stands taller, despite the uncertainties Cecelia has forced between her and her mother. She looks ready now, more so than when she arrived. He hopes that Madeline won't drive a wedge between Rachel and Penelope, although Cecelia seems to be intent on doing this already.

They continue down the corridor with Cecelia trailing behind. Chris ignores her. In some ways he still feels sorry for her, her whole life turned upside down by a woman she cannot break free from. As an outsider looking in he now recognises how embedding one person, one experience, one memory, can control who you are as a person. He did it with his father but now he knows it is time to let that go. He supposes Cecelia is simply trying to rob Madeline of the chance that she herself had missed with her own father. But that isn't fair on Rachel.

"This way," Chris herds them toward Madeline's room, stopping as they reach the door.

"You have to wait here," he tells Cecelia. "I'll come and let you know when."

She rolls her eyes and leans against the wall and gives him a petulant closed mouth smile.

Chris opens the door and steps in. Rachel hesitates with Penelope behind her.

"It's okay if you don't want to go in," Penelope tells her. "After all this time, I'm sure she'd understand."

Rachel fiddles with her necklace and stares at Madeline's door. Chris wonders if it is the same necklace Penelope mentioned; the one Madeline gave her that she often wore. But Rachel's hand obscures it.

"I think I need to do it," Rachel says after a pause. "If I don't, I know I'll regret being here but not going in." She takes a tentative step forward but Penelope clings on to her.

"Prepare yourself," she whispers. "She's very sick." Rachel sets her mouth, a slight quiver to her bottom lip betraying her, and nods. She lifts her chin a fraction and then takes a deep breath in.

Betsy is sat in the chair but stands to leave as soon as they enter. "I'll give you some privacy."

Madeline's body is a sheeted mole-hill in the expanse of the hospice bed. Betsy has sat her up slightly, not enough for the fluid to fully settle in her lungs but enough to allow her to see across the room when she wakes. The oxygen mask covers the bottom half of her face which is a sickly yellow. Her organs are shutting down one by one. For a moment Chris is worried they are too late but stepping closer he can hear the slight, shallow breaths she is taking.

Rachel stumbles back.

"It's okay." Chris encourages her forward. Madeline opens her eyes and focuses on Rachel almost immediately. She tries to sit further up in bed and Chris goes to steady her. She fights against his hand on her arm, pushing against him so that he feels obliged to help rather than hinder her, lest she lose too much energy trying to defy him. She pulls the mask down.

"Rachel."

Her daughter stands at the bottom of the bed transfixed by her mother's stare.

Madeline's lips have lost their colour and are cracked and dry from dehydration. Chris tries to reach for the glass of water on the side but he is at an odd angle, struggling to support Madeline in an upright position. Penelope steps around Rachel, takes the glass and holds the straw to Madeline's lips. After barely a sip, Madeline nods and Penelope moves away. Chris takes a moment settling Madeline as best he can and as soon as he releases her she motions for Rachel to come closer.

Slowly, Rachel comes to stand beside Madeline with one hand still at her throat, fiddling with the necklace and the other wrapped around her own waist.

"Hi," Rachel whispers.

Madeline smiles. It is not as full of a grin as Chris has seen on her face since they met, but in her current state a smile is the best description for it. He looks between the two of them and can see the resemblance more clearly than in the corridor outside, although Rachel is taller and her hair is lighter. She carries herself differently – more akin to Penelope than Madeline – but there is no doubt she is Madeline's daughter. As if acknowledging this Penelope makes a laboured sigh with a hand over her mouth. Neither Madeline or Rachel seem to notice as their eyes are locked on one another but Chris sees the tears in Penelope's eyes as Rachel takes Madeline's hand in her own.

"Can you tell me why?" Rachel asks. Her voice is soft, as if she is talking to a child.

"Oh," Madeline sighs. "I, could, never...Penny, gave you, a much, better life. I, was, so, young." Her words are stilted because of the ragged breaths she takes between them. It gives the impression she is panting. Chris restrains himself from retrieving the mask she has hung around her neck.

"But you came back to see me?"

"I did. But, it was, selfish." Madeline shifts her attention from Rachel to Penelope. "I hope, you can, forgive me."

It isn't a question. The moment she has finished her sentence her gaze flickers back to Rachel without waiting for a response. Penelope wipes away her tears and remains silent. Having heard Penelope's story he is certain she will not forgive Madeline's intervention in her life, no matter what the circumstances.

"You, kept, it?" Madeline asks, raising her free hand to her own throat.

"You gave me this? I wear it a lot. I always thought it was special. Now I know why."

Madeline pulls her hand away from Rachel and holds it out toward Chris. "Fetch, me, that, would, you?"

He collects the box that she's gestured to – the small wooden chest with an intricate pattern carved into its lid – and places it on the bed. It isn't heavy, but Chris can tell it's full. Just as he shuffles it across to sit between Madeline and Rachel, Cecelia slips into the room. Chris opens his mouth to protest but Madeline lays a cold hand on him and shakes her head.

"Want, you, to, have, this," Madeline says. She is beginning to sink back down into the bed again as her limbs give way to gravity. Her eyelids droop too.

Rachel tries to open the box but the lid won't open. She furrows her brow and rattles it but to no avail.

"Here," Madeline pats her neck again, her movements slow and heavy.

All eyes rest on Rachel's sternum where an ornate key is hanging from her necklace. Rachel's face mirrors Chris' shock, her mouth slightly agape as she reaches up to remove the key. Chris is impressed by the significance of the gift Madeline is making and how long ago she planted the seed of it. For some reason Rachel's gaze locks on Chris' face as she places the key in the lock and turns. They are all amazed when the mechanism clicks. Rachel's eyes widen and her shoulders drop, like she was holding her breath until she was sure the key would fit. She shifts her gaze down to the box and tries the lid once more.

Collectively, the rest of them move as one, taking a small step forward in order to get a glimpse of what is inside. Chris' suspicions are confirmed when he recognises the notebooks he's caught Madeline writing in so often during her stay. However, there are far more than he has seen. They range from flimsy school-book type notepads to velvet covered books and are lined up neatly in the box in some kind of order.

"I—" Rachel doesn't know what to say until she picks out one of the books and flicks though it. "Thank you."

"What is it?" Penelope asks from over Rachel's shoulder, peering down at the box with narrowed eyes.

"Diaries," Rachel answers, her gaze on Madeline. "I wish this wasn't the only way for me to learn about you."

Madeline gives a little shrug but her reply is cut short when Cecelia pushes her way forward with outstretched arms and her hands grabbing for the box.

"Are my answers in there too?"

Chris places his body between Cecelia and the bed, shaking his head. "This is hardly the time."

He grabs her elbow and herds her toward the door intending to escort her out. But, as he reaches it there is a knock from the other side.

Chris halts. He isn't expecting anyone else. Looking through the window he can see the broad shoulders of someone in a blue shirt and the greying edge of a beard on a chin. He leans forward to open the door and Cecelia slips from his grasp and out of his reach.

"James?" Chris mumbles. "I didn't think you were coming."

"I didn't feel I had much of a choice." James shrugs. Beneath his beard his face is ashen. He looks shattered.

"Well, isn't this the family reunion?" Cecelia comments.

For a moment, the whole room is chaotic with their reaction. Penelope gasps and reaches for the wall for support and Cecelia pushes James into place opposite Rachel with a half-grin on her face.

"Is it true?" James stammers. He stares down at Rachel and she looks up at him.

"Is what true?" Rachel asks without taking her eyes from him.

"Of course it is," Cecelia announces. "I should know. I was the one who organised the whole thing after Maddy ran away."

Chris notices Cecelia is working her way closer and closer to Madeline, with furtive glances from Rachel to the box on the bed.

Penelope leans forward and snaps the lid shut. "Just because you've contacted her birth father doesn't mean you can take what rightfully belongs to Rachel."

"Actually, that was me." Chris holds a hand up on contrition. "I thought it only fair to Rachel."

Cecelia butts in. "All I want are some answers. If those really are her diaries surely I can find out why she lied?"

"Why didn't you tell me?" James asks, ignoring Cecelia. "When you came to see me? Why didn't you say that my baby was alive?"

"I didn't know," Chris answers. He puts a hand on James' shoulder to try and steady him. James holds out his hand to Rachel.

"I'm James." He says it with an awkward shrug, as though he is apologising. "I didn't even know you existed until today."

Rachel goes straight in for a hug. It takes James by surprise and he stumbles back and needs to be bolstered upright again by Chris.

"Why didn't you tell me?" Penelope's question is accusatory in tone. She keeps her hand firmly on top of the box.

"She deserves to know her father. Just like I deserve to know what's in those diaries." Cecelia makes an attempt to swipe at the box but Penelope bats her away with a graceful move.

"That should have been my decision." Penelope gives Chris a levelled gaze. Cecelia screws up her eyes and pouts as she stalks to the far side of the room.

"Actually, it should be my decision," Rachel cuts in. She stands next to James with their shoulders touching. She smiles wistfully at Chris. "Thank you for inviting him."

Penelope sighs and leans over to introduce herself to James. James takes her hand with a confused look.

"Doctor Wright." Cecelia's high-pitched voice rings out as Chris tries to explain the situation to James.

"Madeline gave your daughter up for adoption, to Penelope, as soon as she was born."

"Why?" James asks.

Cecelia moves to a position beside Chris and prods him with a finger. "Doctor."

Just as Chris turns to look at Cecelia, whose eyes are fixed on Madeline, Penelope, Rachel and James all look down at his patient for an answer. A heavy silence blankets the room and it is only when Chris follows their gazes that he understands why.

At first glance she appears to be sleeping, as she had been when he brought Rachel in. But, he can no longer hear the stilted gasps for breath in the stillness, and he realises Madeline is resting of a different kind.

Chris clears his throat. "I'm afraid Madeline appears to have left us."

There is a sob from Rachel, who immediately moves back toward Madeline's side and takes up her hand again. "I'm so sorry," she whispers, leaning in close enough to touch their foreheads together.

But Cecelia takes up the grief for all of them by falling to her knees in sobs. "After everything she did, I still care. How is that right?" Her voice is muffled from pressing her face into her hands.

"No matter how people might hurt us we can still love them in the end," Chris says. And this time he believes it for himself too.

Penelope comforts Rachel, who sits on the edge of the bed caressing the box with one hand and still gripping onto Madeline with the other.

"I think it would be best if I waited outside." And James is out of the door before anyone can stop him.

"Perhaps we should all give Rachel some time," Chris suggests.

Penelope stares coldly at Chris and he simply puts a hand up to demonstrate he doesn't expect her to leave too. Her glare recedes and she folds Rachel into her arms. Chris leans down to place an arm around Cecelia to help her up from the floor and they shuffle out of out the room together.

Chris deposits Cecelia on one of the chairs in the corridor. A few seats down James is sitting with his elbows on his knees and a hand running through his beard. Chris suspects his life might never be quite the same. Betsy is at the Nurses' Station, leaning against the desk, waiting for him. He gives a solemn nod.

"She's left a box for Penelope and James, you know," she says in response to the news.

"She has?"

Betsy nods. "She told me last night. Asked me to make sure they got them."

"And Cecelia?"

"She thought the truth was enough for her."

They watch Cecelia for a moment as she sobs. After a minute, when the crying is not as violent, James moves closer and puts a hand on Cecelia's back. He whispers something to her. Cecelia shakes her head and places a hand over James' and starts talking. James listens intently. Chris thinks it might be the story of how Madeline lied to him and how Rachel was adopted.

Betsy grazes Chris' shoulder and then sits down on one of the chairs at the desk, beckoning him with a sympathetic smile.

"Fascinating woman." Chris shakes his head as he sits across from her. "For all that trouble she caused she still managed to gather them all here to be with her for her final moment."

"That's wasn't her. That was you. You're a good man Christopher Wright."

He is taken aback by her compliment. He expected her still to be angry with him.

"It's almost like she knew," Betsy continues. "Like she planned it this way all along."

Chris nods and furrows his brow. Betsy doesn't know about Madeline's admission to him. She was so adamant in the beginning that she deserved to die alone. Yet, she called Cecelia, who led him to James and in the end gave him permission to contact Penelope and then meet Rachel. He knows she intentionally chose a place that was close to all of the people most important to her. He would like to believe that this was her way to make up for all her past regrets, to reunite them all.

"I don't suppose we'll ever know if that's what she really intended," Chris replies as he fiddles with a loose thread from his shirt tickling his wrist. He counts to ten and then asks; "Have you had chance to think about...?" But he hasn't planned how to phrase it so he trails off, hoping Betsy understands.

"I have." She grazes his knee with her fingertips so that he looks up at her. She is smiling. "I think it could work. I can't imagine a better father for our child Chris." She pauses and then sighs. "Madeline told me a little about Holly, from when she knew her. Providing she was honest I think Holly would make a great mum."

Chris raises his eyebrows in surprise. He can't imagine what Madeline might have said, but if it has helped convince Betsy they will make good parents he isn't going to delve any further. "She will, I promise."

Chris feels the old familiar ache in the core of his chest at the disappointments he and Holly have lived through. He would never have thought a solution such as this would have come along. Yet, the idea he and Holly might soon have a child of their own – that would be his own – forces the feeling up and the sting of tears itch his eyes. He pulls the back of his hand across his face.

"I'm going to go back to Northern Ireland once I've had the baby. I think I need to go back and start again. There are people there who I need to make my peace with."

Chris glances at Cecelia and James and then, over his shoulder where he can just see Penelope and Rachel through the door. Madeline changed them in unimaginable ways, not necessarily for the better, and yet here they all are. He doubts they will remember her any more fondly than they did before. Cecelia, especially, has discovered a much worse secret than the truth she believed. But they will remember her; Chris, Holly and Betsy too. That's all Madeline said she wanted.

The ring of the telephone makes him jump and he grabs at it before it has chance to disturb the peace.

"Oh, Chris, it's you," Holly's voice sounds tired. "I just wanted to know if I could come and see Madeline, I mean if, that's okay?"

"She's gone Holly, I'm sorry."

"Did she get to see her daughter?"

"Just," Chris replies. He is distracted by Betsy mouthing something at him. He asks Holly to wait and then covers the mouthpiece.

"Tell her we need to get together to talk things over," Betsy says.

Chris' breath catches in his throat. Even though he asked he didn't expect a decision this rapidly.

"Are you sure?" Has one exchange from Madeline turned his life around? Betsy nods as she fights against a yawn. "Okay, then. But maybe once we've had some sleep?"

Betsy beams at him and agrees. Chris goes back to Holly.

"Are you okay?" he asks.

"Yes," Holly replies. "Shocked, I guess. I know I shouldn't be, but it feels so strange to think I only saw her yesterday." She pauses. "Have you seen her yet?" Chris knows immediately who she means.

"She's here with me now. She wants us to get together and talk through the possibility of us adopting the baby, Holly." He maintains eye contact with Betsy as he tells his wife. She keeps her gaze on him and he realises she will be giving up this baby to save his marriage.

"Really? When?"

"Tomorrow, maybe. When we've all had some rest."

Chris looks away from Betsy. He takes a breath and then goes with what his gut is telling him. "Why don't we have dinner tonight Holly? We can talk about Madeline and honour her memory as your friend."

Holly 'hmm's down the telephone before speaking. "Could you tell me some more about her? I didn't quite understand what was going on when I was there. I was a little…distracted."

Chris wonders how Holly will react to the secrets Madeline managed to keep throughout her life, and how she will feel knowing that her old friend convinced Betsy to trust her with her child. As he agrees, Penelope and Rachel step out of Madeline's room, a gap between them that could represent a gulf.

"I have to go Holly. I'll pick you up at seven?"

"Don't be late." It almost feels like she is teasing him and they are back to where they started, though Chris knows that isn't true. They will have to start over again. They have a lot to talk about before Holly might move back in. He puts the phone down with a weary sigh and stands up just as Penelope reaches the counter.

"Were any arrangements made when she checked in?" Penelope asks. Her voice is low and husky, full of emotion not quite surfaced. Rachel hangs back, her gaze on Cecelia and James who are still talking together down the corridor.

"She provided a funeral home and place of burial on her records." Chris says. "I believe they have some instruction from Madeline herself."

"Would it be possible for me to oversee the funeral? Make sure things are carried out as per her wishes?"

Chris is taken aback by Penelope's sudden interest and they fall into an awkward silence. Eventually Penelope elaborates.

"I feel it would give Rachel some closure if we were able to help organise things provide a connection to Madeline, albeit a difficult one."

"Well, I suspect it will fall to the funeral home to make the decision, but I'll let them know you've expressed an interest in assisting."

"I'll pay any additional costs."

Chris nods, though Penelope's gaze has already drifted back to her daughter. Rachel's eyes are now fixed on the ground with one arm by her side and the other across her body as she fiddles with her necklace. Chris can't imagine what might be going through her mind. In a few hours she has gone from finding her biological mother to losing her again. He wonders how long it will take for her to read through all those diaries she has been left.

"Does she want to take the box?" Chris asks. "We can pack up the rest of her things and send them on."

"I'll ask."

Penelope goes back and a moment later Rachel ducks into the room and returns with the box. Betsy stands a few steps away, waiting for the opportunity to tidy Madeline's things away. She holds Madeline's file, clasped to her chest just as she had on the morning of Madeline's arrival.

"I think James would like to speak with you," Chris calls out to Rachel, pointing to where James is sitting with Cecelia.

"Rachel, shall we ask James for his contact details, then you can speak with him later? You look like you need some time to adjust right now." Penelope leads Rachel to James. Chris hopes that, somehow, being brought together by Madeline they will be able to make the best of their complicated relationships.

Cecelia slips away from the group and Chris cuts her off before she can enter Madeline's room.

"She can't tell you anything anymore."

"But now what do I do?" Cecelia collapses in his arms and he squeezes her shoulder in sympathy.

"Go home, get some rest. Move on with your life. You deserve at least that." He tries to make it sound soothing, and he thinks Cecelia takes it as it is meant. But still, it sounds harsh. Cecelia peels herself away from him and walks away without looking back. Chris can't help wondering if she will move on, or if she will be haunted by Madeline's lie for the rest of her life.

There is a short burst of activity as Rachel, Penelope and James leave. Betsy momentarily stops them to hand Penelope and James small boxes that Chris assumes must be the gifts Madeline had left for them. James receives his with a timid 'thank you'. Penelope rolls her eyes and drops it into her leather handbag. Once they have gone the hospice returns to normal, as if nothing has changed. But Chris knows that it has; not just for the people he found from Madeline's life, but for him too.

He sighs. He can't remember the last time he was truly happy. Perhaps that will come in time, with all the things he has to look forward to. He joins Betsy in room four to prepare Madeline for the funeral home. They work in silence, a glance every now and then tempered with a sad smile. It is some time later that Chris discovers the box with his name on it hidden in the bedside cabinet.

He opens it to reveal a piece of Madeline's artwork. It is a small canvas about the same size as a hardback book covered in newspaper articles. The ones in the centre are about Madeline, and Chris half-recognises the article about Harry Watt's suicide covered by a more positive announcement of her success in a gallery show. There is the notification of James and Madeline's wedding, and half-hidden in a corner, that photograph of Madeline and Penelope Chris has already seen: with Madeline in her green dress. Framed around these are newspaper articles about him. Two seem to be from the reported incident with the Porters and another documents his start at the hospice. A picture of him and Holly on their wedding day from the society pages – done at Holly's parent's insistence – show them both looking so young. She even managed to find the advertisement for the class she taught that Holly had taken. He wonders, absent-mindedly, if this is the type of thing she left for Penelope and James too.

"Everything okay?"

Chris looks up to see Betsy standing over him and then around the room. It has only taken them half an hour to pack up Madeline's possessions but the repercussions of Madeline's life will last so much longer than the time taken to tidy up at the end of it. She was so much more than he had anticipated, more than anyone had really expected it seemed despite the trouble she caused.

He tucks the canvas into the large pocket at the front of his doctor's coat, next to the resignation letter he plans to hand to Doctor Gregory. Betsy isn't the only one who needs a new start.

"Yes," Chris answers. "I think it will be."

ACKNOWLEDGEMENTS

Thank you.

Thank you for taking a chance and reading this book. I am grateful to all my readers – friend or stranger – for allowing me to distract you from your busy lives and take a ride with me in my imagination. If you enjoyed this story, come and find me on social media and let me know – I love hearing from readers!

I wouldn't be able to do what I do without the support of my annoyingly lovable partner, Luke, who feeds me, keeps me in tea and snacks, and constantly makes me laugh with teasing and silliness. Oh, and his hard work in building me the Plotting Shed – cheers babe!

Thanks also goes to my family for never doubting that I could makes these dreams of mine come true, and encouraging me forward even when it seemed challenging.

And, of course, I'm forever grateful to my wonderful friends and worldwide comrades who believe in me when I need reminding what I'm capable of, and never let me settle for anything less. Especially those I've met on writing retreats and courses such as Arvon, Mslexicon, and at Garsdale – one in particular turned out to be my writing guardian angel: thank you Kathryn!

Not forgetting Mac, to whom this book is dedicated; my furry friend who helped heal me from chronic illness and who sat at my feet as I wrote these words. He is missed, even though my new companion, Hugo, has taken his spot and now keeps me in my place.

Mac would be proud.

ABOUT THE AUTHOR

Cat Lumb is a Yorkshire Writer and Writing Coach who lives on the wrong side of t'hill in Stalybridge, Manchester, with her wedding-phobic fiancé (engaged 14yrs and counting!) and a particularly stubborn Westie, named Hugo The Destroyer.

She released her debut novel – In Lies We Trust – in March 2021 less than a year after leaving her Museum Educator role during the pandemic to live the dream of being a writer and coach. Her first publication was a short story collection in 2018 – The Memorial Tree. In the same year another story was published in a Comma Press anthology; Short Stories by New Manchester Writers (Book 9).

She returned to writing seriously when diagnosed with Myalgic Encephalitis (M.E) in 2009, and Fibromyalgia in 2011; the only thing that kept her sane was her rescue Westie (Mac) and the stories she could make up in her head.

She's an active committee member for the Huddersfield Literature Festival (her Yorkshire hometown), and is a keen champion for the Partition Education Group – which supports the campaign for including South Asian History in schools. She can also read ancient Egyptian hieroglyphs.

She now supports aspiring authors as The Write Catalyst, and coaches them into finishing their manuscripts with gentle guidance and encouragement.

If you've ever thought about writing your own book, find her online here: www.catlumb.com/the-write-catalyst

IN LIES WE TRUST

Catherine Lumb

"A gripping spy thriller packed with twists and deception."

Liz Abbott used to be a spy, now she's PA to an interior designer and favourite Aunt to her 5-year-old niece. Dismissed by The Agency for getting a bit too close to arms dealer Armand Bishop in her four years undercover, she was the one who finally lured him into their trap.

In the five years since, Liz has settled into ordinary life but a mysterious envelope soon changes that: her spy alter is being reactivated, but by who and for what purpose?

When Liz's sister and niece are taken, and Liz is framed as Armand's accomplice, she's no longer sure who she can trust. With her family still in danger, the only way out is to escape with the criminal she once loved and lead him straight to them.

Can Liz trust him, or is someone else using her family as pawns in a much more dangerous game?

"Moves at a blistering pace, and kept me hooked with its tightly woven plot."

"Captured my interest from the first page."

Printed in Great Britain
by Amazon

81825191R00185